More praise for M. W. Craven

'**Gleefully gory** and witty, with
a terrific sense of place'
Sunday Mirror

'So dark and **twisty!**'
Elly Griffiths

'Compelling'
Heat

'Thrilling'
Mick Herron

'Brutal and **thrilling**'
Sun

'The **writing is silky smooth** and
the plotting is ingenious'
Deadly Pleasures Mystery Magazine

'Britain's answer to Harry Bosch'
Matt Hilton

'**Twisted and dark** and I loved it'
Simon Toyne

'Craven has created one of the **most
charismatic crime fighting
duos** of recent years'
Vaseem Khan

Also by M.W. Craven

Washington Poe series
The Puppet Show
Black Summer
The Curator
Cut Short (short story collection)

Avison Fluke series
Born in a Burial Gown
Body Breaker

DEAD GROUND

—

M.W. CRAVEN

CONSTABLE

CONSTABLE

First published in Great Britain in 2021 by Constable
This paperback edition published in Great Britain in 2021 by Constable

A CIP catalogue record for this book is available from the British Library.

ISBN: 978-1-47213-200-0

Typeset in Adobe Caslon Pro by Initial Typesetting Services, Edinburgh
Printed and bound in Great Britain by Clays Ltd, Elcograf S.p.A.

Papers used by Constable are from well-managed forests
and other responsible sources.

Constable
An imprint of
Little, Brown Book Group
Carmelite House
50 Victoria Embankment
London EC4Y 0DZ

An Hachette UK Company
www.hachette.co.uk

www.littlebrown.co.uk

To Joanne – my 'lockdown' buddy, my best friend, my wife.
You type too loudly and had me doing early-morning Pilates,
but you're OK really . . .

The mongoose I want under the stairs when the snakes slither by

Attributed to Hannibal

Chapter 1

The man wearing a Sean Connery mask said to the man wearing a Daniel Craig mask, 'Bertrand the monkey and Raton the cat are sitting by the fire, watching chestnuts roast in the hearth.'

Which was as good a way as any of getting someone's attention.

'OK,' Daniel Craig said.

The men wearing George Lazenby and Timothy Dalton masks stopped what they were doing to listen. Pierce Brosnan, with his headphones on and his laptop spitting out complex instructions, was oblivious to everything but the vault door and the Diebold three-keyed timer and combination lock in front of him. Roger Moore was outside in the van.

'Bertrand tries brushing the coals aside but he's scared of burning his hand,' Sean Connery continued. 'But he wants those chestnuts and he doesn't want to wait for the fire to cool. Instead, he persuades Raton to scoop them out, promising him an equal share.'

'And the cat does?'

'He does, yes. Raton moves the red-hot coals and picks out the chestnuts one by one. And each time he does, Bertrand gobbles them up. Eventually a maid disturbs them and they have to flee. Raton gets nothing for his pains.'

Timothy Dalton was Sean Connery's man, but the rest were Daniel Craig's. George Lazenby was *his* muscle, Pierce Brosnan was *his* technical guy and Roger Moore was *his* wheelman. As

1

crew leader, Daniel Craig felt he should be the one to ask the obvious question.

'Why are you telling us this?' he said.

'No reason,' Sean Connery said. 'It's a fable adapted by the French poet Jean de La Fontaine. It's called "Le Singe et le Chat" and it's about people sacrificing others for their own ends. The saying "cat's paw" comes from it.'

'It's an idiom, actually,' Timothy Dalton said, 'not a saying.'

Sean Connery turned and glared at Dalton. The mood in the vault's anteroom changed. It had been tense; now there was an undercurrent of menace.

'What part of "You do not speak, ever" didn't you understand?' he said, his voice low.

Under his mask they sensed Timothy Dalton blanche. Daniel Craig glanced at the Bonds in his crew and shrugged. Sean Connery was paying and he paid well. If he wanted to talk about monkeys and cats and chestnuts and humiliate his own man then who were they to stop him?

The anteroom descended into silence.

Pierce Brosnan broke it.

'We're in,' he said.

Few banks offer a safety deposit box service these days. The vault that the Bonds had broken into was one of several purpose-built facilities belonging to a specialist provider. It had cutting-edge security, but a combination of offsite hacks and Pierce Brosnan's onsite safecracking skills had rendered them redundant.

At least until the backup systems kicked in.

'How long?' Sean Connery said.

'We've had eighteen minutes, twenty seconds,' Daniel Craig replied.

He glanced at the watch on the inside of his wrist. They still had plenty of time.

2

The vault was rectangular, fifteen feet by thirty, and had a low ceiling. It was lit by neon lights. A steel table was fixed to the wall opposite the door. Safety deposit boxes stretched from floor to ceiling on the two longer walls. The boxes were suitcase-sized at the bottom and got progressively smaller as they reached eye level and above.

The CCTV cameras were working but had been fixed so they were on a sixty-minute delay. The staff monitoring the vault would see what they were doing, but not for another hour.

'We'll start here,' Timothy Dalton said.

Sean Connery had hired him to evaluate the boxes' contents and he was keen to contribute. So far he'd been a passenger. He made a move to one of the larger boxes.

'Not that one,' Sean Connery said, removing a piece of paper from his pocket. He read out a serial number: 9-206.

The Bonds spread out and searched for the box. George Lazenby found it. It was at head height and was one of the smaller boxes.

'Mr Brosnan, if you will?' Daniel Craig said.

Pierce Brosnan studied the lock. The vault's door had been a challenge but, as no one should be in the vault unsupervised, the security on the boxes was perfunctory, little more than cylinder locks. He pulled a snapper bar from his bag: a locksmith tool specially designed to break and open cylinder locks. It took less than a minute. He put the snapper bar back in his bag and stepped away.

Sean Connery opened the small door. The safety deposit box was empty, as he'd been told it would be. Under his mask, he smiled.

'Never mind,' Dalton said. 'We have hundreds more to check.'

'Actually,' Sean Connery said, 'we're not here to make a withdrawal.'

'We're not? Well, what *are* we doing?'

'Making a deposit.'

Sean Connery pulled a snub-nosed revolver from his waist-band, pressed it against the back of Timothy Dalton's head and pulled the trigger.

He was dead before he hit the polished floor. A cloud of pink mist hung in the air where his head had just been. The vault smelled of cordite and blood.

And fear.

'What the hell!' Daniel Craig snapped. 'No guns, I said! We don't carry guns on jobs.'

'You know what's always bothered me about that fable?' Sean Connery said. He held the gun by his side but it was clear he'd use it again if he had to.

'Enlighten me,' Daniel Craig said, tearing his eyes from the twitching corpse.

'There was no mention of what happened next. No mention of what Raton the cat did to Bertrand the monkey *after* his betrayal.'

Daniel Craig looked at the corpse again. It had stopped moving. 'This man betrayed someone?' Betrayal was a legitimate motive in the circles he moved in.

Sean Connery said nothing.

'Dalton was a shit Bond anyway,' Daniel Craig said, looking at his watch. 'We done?'

'Almost,' Sean Connery said. He removed something from his pocket and placed it on the lip of the empty safety deposit box. He spent some time making sure it was in the right position.

'Now we're done,' he said.

And with that, the Bonds left.

Thirty minutes later, alerted to a robbery in progress by the security company monitoring the vault's CCTV, the first police officers arrived.

But all they found was a corpse cooling on the floor and a ceramic rat looking over it . . .

4

Chapter 2

Detective Sergeant Washington Poe usually hated attending court. He found the bureaucracy and the subservience to idiots in wigs archaic. He hated being at the beck and call of barristers and he hated the way cops were universally viewed with suspicion when they gave evidence. He hated that so-called experts were allowed to pull apart decisions made in a fraction of a second.

But most of all he hated that when he attended court it meant someone had been failed. A family would never see a loved one again. A woman would never trust a man again. An old man would never leave his house again.

There were many reasons to hate being in court.

But not this time.

This time he was attending as the defendant.

And he planned to enjoy it.

His case was being heard at the Carlisle Combined Court, a modern building in the centre of the city. Its only nod to the past was the Grade II-listed statue of the nineteenth-century Member of Parliament who'd dropped dead outside. Poe approved of statues like that. He wished there were more of them.

The district judge, who had lost patience with him a while ago, tried again.

'I must impress upon you, Mr Poe,' he said, 'I know this is only a civil matter but I strongly advise you to get *legal* representation. I'm sure your friend is' – he checked his notes – '"as clever as Stephen Hawking's wheelchair", but what happens here today cannot easily be undone.'

'Consider me advised, your honour.'

'And it's been explained that refusing legal representation is not grounds for a later appeal?'

'It has.'

The district judge had jowls like a bulldog and an unsettling resemblance to Rumpole of the Bailey. Tufts of hair sticking out from his ears made it look as though furry animals were burrowing in them. He peered at Poe over his half-moon spectacles. Poe stared back.

'Very well,' he sighed. 'Mr Chadwick, you may proceed.'

The council solicitor got to his feet. Small and moustached, he was an officious-looking man, the type who would take the minutes at Neighbourhood Watch meetings.

'Thank you, your honour.' He opened a thick manila file and picked up a summary sheet. 'The facts in this case are not in dispute. Almost five years ago Mr Poe legally bought land on Shap Fell from a Mr Thomas Hume. This land—'

'Mr Hume is now deceased, I understand?'

'Regrettably that is the case, your honour. Mr Hume was the legal owner of the land and he was well within his rights to sell it to Mr Poe. This land included an abandoned shepherd's croft.'

'The building in question?'

'Yes, your honour. We understand that Herdwick Croft has been there since the early 1800s. It has recently come into the catchment area of the Lake District National Park. The position of the local planning authority is that the croft has been a designated heritage asset since 2005, and therefore cannot be modified without the express permission of our office. Herdwick Croft's original owner was informed of this designation.'

'Mr Poe, would you like to interject?' the judge said.

Poe looked at the person beside him. She shook her head.

'No, your honour,' he said.

'You're aware that challenging the heritage-asset status of the croft is one of the few legal avenues you have left at this point?'

'I am, your honour. Although to be fair, I was unaware of Herdwick Croft's status when I bought it. Thomas Hume must have . . . forgotten to tell me.'

Poe felt, rather than saw, someone stiffen in the public gallery. He knew that Victoria Hume, Thomas's daughter, was there to support him. She felt responsible for her father's duplicity despite Poe reassuring her she wasn't. Poe hadn't completed the usual legal checks prior to handing over his cash and he was now paying the price.

'As a serving police officer, I'm sure Mr Poe will be aware that ignorance of the law is not a legal excuse,' Chadwick said.

Poe smiled. He had hoped he'd say that.

Chadwick spent ten minutes detailing the modifications Poe had completed at Herdwick Croft: the roof he'd fixed; the borehole and pump he'd installed to provide fresh running water; the septic tank he'd buried; the generator and how it supplied power. In short, everything he'd done to make the croft modern and comfortable. Even his beloved wood-burning stove got a mention.

When Chadwick had finished the judge said, 'And how was it you came to be aware of Mr Poe's modifications?'

'Your honour?'

'Who told you, Mr Chadwick?'

'A concerned citizen, your honour.'

'That wouldn't be the member for Oxenholme, would it?'

Chadwick didn't rise to the judge's bait. 'How we came to find out about the modifications is not the business of this court, your honour.'

Poe knew the judge had got it spot on, though. The man who'd informed the council about his unauthorised restoration project was a former police officer, a direct-entrant detective chief inspector called Wardle. They'd butted heads during the Jared Keaton case. Wardle had double-downed on the wrong line of enquiry and it had cost him his career. He had since left the police and was now pursuing his new calling: local politics. Poe turned in his seat, half-expecting to see him sitting in the public gallery but, other than Victoria Hume, the benches were empty. It didn't matter; if it hadn't been Wardle it would have been someone else. Poe collected enemies the same way the middle class collected Nectar points.

'Get on with it then, Mr Chadwick,' the judge said.

The local authority solicitor spent another ten minutes detailing the planning regulations Poe had fallen foul of. After two minutes Poe had drifted off.

He'd had an extended stay at Herdwick Croft recently. The Serious Crime Analysis Section, shortened by everyone to SCAS, hadn't had a major case since the Curator and, given how that had ended, no one was looking for a new investigation. The director of intelligence, Edward van Zyl, had given everyone involved a month off.

The break had done Poe good. The Curator case had almost broken him, physically and mentally, and he'd got off lightly compared to some. He'd enjoyed spending time at home. Most days he'd packed some food in a rucksack and headed on to Shap Fell. Just him and Edgar, his springer spaniel, and thousands of sheep.

'How's DI Flynn?' he whispered to the woman beside him. Stephanie Flynn, SCAS's detective inspector, had given birth during the case and it hadn't been straightforward. She was still off sick and he wasn't sure she'd be coming back.

'Shush, Poe!' the woman whispered back. 'I need to hear this.'

Poe returned to his thoughts. Even when it concerned his own future he didn't have the type of brain that could listen to legal arguments for more than a minute. He made a mental note to call

Flynn later. He'd avoided speaking to her recently – it brought back bad memories, for both of them he suspected.

'Are you ready to respond, Mr Poe?'

Poe blinked. Chadwick was back in his seat and everyone was looking at him.

Poe stood up.

'Am I right in understanding that the local authority is seeking a court order to compel me to return Herdwick Croft to the condition it was in when I bought it, your honour?' Poe said.

'That's correct. Are you ready to respond?'

Poe looked at the person on his right. She nodded.

'I am, your honour.'

'And despite her not having a legal background, you're confident your colleague is up to representing you, Mr Poe?'

'She is, your honour. You may trust me on this.'

He sat down. When he'd lived in Hampshire he'd had an address. Now, he had a home. To protect it, he was willing to fight dirty.

And what he was about to do was as dirty as it was possible to get.

'Over to you, Tilly,' he said.

Chapter 3

Matilda 'Tilly' Bradshaw was an oddity, but in a good way. She had two DPhils from Oxford University, their equivalent of PhDs, but probably didn't know who the Prime Minister was. She could quote pi to a thousand decimal places, and would if you let her, but wouldn't be able to tell you who the Sex Pistols were. She'd started higher education at thirteen, an Oxford admissions professor having persuaded her parents that her 'once in a generation mind' needed more stimulation than the state was capable of providing.

Pure mathematics was her speciality, but she excelled at most scientific disciplines. With governments and private companies all over the world throwing research grants at her, she'd been expected to stay at Oxford her entire working life. And for a while that had been enough for her.

Until it wasn't.

Because what the admissions professor had failed to understand – or perhaps had deliberately overlooked – was that curtailing a childhood on the cusp of adolescence had consequences. Not being around people her own age, and not being exposed to anyone who didn't operate at her intellectual level, meant she'd never needed to develop the skills to talk and think in a socially conventional way. The result was an innocent, guileless woman who verbalised every thought she had and believed everything she was told.

Poe had never got to the bottom of why she had chosen to leave the world of academia and join the National Crime Agency's Serious Crime Analysis Section. He suspected she'd inherited a wilful streak from her father. In her early thirties she'd left Oxford and taken a job as a SCAS analyst. She told Poe she wanted to implement real-world applications to her theoretical models of mathematics. Poe didn't know what that meant but he knew a diamond when he saw one. He'd taken her under his wing and helped her navigate the new and exciting world she was being exposed to for the first time. In return, as best she could, she softened his sharp edges and helped him manage his demons.

And, to the surprise of everyone, they'd become friends. Not mates, *friends*. The type of friend that might come along once or twice in a lifetime.

Which was why, when she'd found out about Poe's housing problems, she'd taken a week's leave and become an expert in planning law.

Chadwick didn't know what was about to hit him.

If Bradshaw was nervous, it wasn't showing. She didn't have any legal training, but Chadwick, with his four-year degree, his year-long Legal Practice Course and his back-office support, was no match for Bradshaw and a day on the internet.

'Hello,' she said.

She gave the judge a small wave. Bemused, the judge waved back.

'My name is Matilda Bradshaw, your honour. I am very pleased to meet you.'

'It's very nice to meet you too, Matilda.'

'What is this?' Chadwick said.

'Nothing wrong with exchanging pleasantries, Mr Chadwick,' the judge said.

Poe smiled. Bradshaw had already won over the judge.

'Nothing at all wrong with being civil, your honour,' Chadwick said. 'I was referring to how someone should dress if they wish to be heard by this court. By dressing like this, she not only disrespects you, she disrespects centuries of tradition.'

Bradshaw was wearing a T-shirt and cargo pants with large side pockets. Pretty much the same thing she wore every day. Her T-shirt was black with 'You Matter' in large white letters. Underneath, in much smaller writing, were the words, 'Unless you multiply yourself by the speed of light squared . . . then you energy.'

Poe stood. 'That's your favourite T-shirt, isn't it, Tilly?'

'It is, Poe. It's a Neil deGrasse Tyson quote. It's a limited edition.'

'Yeah, she *has* dressed for the occasion, your honour.'

Chadwick stood.

'But—'

'Mr Chadwick, in this court *I'll* be the one who decides if I'm being disrespected, not you,' the judge said. 'I *will* hear from Miss Bradshaw. If you want to hear from her as well, I suggest you sit down.'

Chadwick sat.

'Please continue, Miss Bradshaw.'

As they'd rehearsed, Bradshaw removed two documents from her rucksack. 'May I approach the bench, your honour?' she asked.

'You may.'

Bradshaw walked up to the judge and passed him one of the documents. On her way back she handed the other to the sulking Chadwick.

'Our position is simple, your honour,' she said. 'We believe it will be illegal for the county court to rule against Poe.'

'What!' Chadwick yelled.

The judge frowned at him then said, 'I think you'd better explain, Miss Bradshaw.'

'It is really quite simple, your honour. In 1901 the municipal borough of Kendal proposed Byelaw 254, later confirmed into law by the Secretary of State. It is for the protection of Shap Fell and Mardale Common. As you can see from the enclosed map, Poe's home falls within these boundaries. I understand that Byelaw 254 was to stop the unlawful expansion of the quarry. You both have a photocopy of the original document. When the borough of Kendal became part of South Lakeland in 1974, all its byelaws were adopted and subsumed into the current portfolio of planning laws. It was then ratified by Cumbria County Council. It has never been repealed.'

Chadwick had put on a pair of thick reading glasses and was frantically turning the pages of the document he'd been handed.

The district judge appeared relaxed. 'And what does this byelaw prohibit, Miss Bradshaw?'

'Section 2, Subsection F, explicitly prohibits the wilful removal, rearrangement or defacing of any rock within the specified boundaries.' Bradshaw turned to Poe. 'Poe, how did you fix up Herdwick Croft?'

'I used whatever rocks were lying around,' he said.

'Your honour, if you turn to Section 3, Subsection E, you'll see the cutting or damaging of any plant or vegetation is also explicitly prohibited. Poe, how did you install your septic tank and borehole?'

'I had to dig them in.'

'And did you damage the surrounding plants and vegetation?'

'I'm afraid I did.'

'And what penalty is attached to these two crimes, Miss Bradshaw?' the judge said.

'The schedule at the back states that any person who offends against any of these byelaws shall be liable to a fine not exceeding fifty pounds in today's money.'

Poe stood. 'It would be my intention to plead guilty to such offences if charges are brought against me, your honour.'

'Oh, this is ridiculous,' Chadwick snapped. 'How can the local authority possibly be expected to know the ins and outs of a century-old byelaw it was forced to adopt in the seventies? Your honour, this is clearly a desperate attempt to—'

The judge smiled. 'But Mr Chadwick, as you said earlier, ignorance of the law is no excuse.'

Chadwick flushed.

The judge continued. 'I've only had a quick look but it appears to be a legal document. And this court certainly doesn't have the authority to disregard a law ratified by the Secretary of State.' He looked over his half-moon glasses. 'And neither does the local authority.'

Bradshaw stood again.

'Your honour, if this court compels Poe to return Herdwick Croft to its original condition, they would also be compelling him to break the law again. He would have no choice but to rearrange the rocks he used to build up the walls, and the plants and vegetation would undoubtedly be damaged when he dug up his septic tank and borehole pump.'

'Mr Chadwick, would you like to explain how Mr Poe is to restore his home to its original condition without breaking the law?'

Chadwick stared at the document in front of him.

'I'd like a two-week adjournment, your honour,' he said.

'Denied. This is your petition and I expect you to be prepared. Now, unless you have anything else to add I'm going to retire. When I return I'll be in a position to make a judgment. Mr Chadwick, if I were you, I'd mentally prepare for my finding. And furthermore, this court will take a dim view of any local authority that changes the law just to pursue a grudge. Do I make myself clear?'

'Crystal, your honour,' Chadwick said.

Poe smiled at Bradshaw. They bumped fists.

It had gone exactly as they'd hoped.

Which was when two men entered the courtroom and everything turned to shit.

Chapter 4

The two men approached the bench. One had ginger hair, the other's was long and grey. Poe silently nicknamed them Ginge and Gandalf. Ginge whispered something to the judge. To Poe's surprise, instead of telling them to get out of his courtroom, the judge whispered back. More than once he glanced in Poe's direction.

Eventually he nodded.

He cleared his throat and said, 'It seems you're going to get your adjournment after all, Mr Chadwick – Mr Poe is urgently needed elsewhere.'

Two minutes later the courtroom was empty. The judge had retired to his chambers and Mr Chadwick had sloped off to lick his wounds.

'Washington Poe?' Ginge said. Gandalf had yet to speak.

Poe nodded.

'Can you come with us, please, sir?'

'And you are?'

'My name's Jonathan.'

'You have a surname, Jonathan?'

'Could you come with us, sir?'

'Where?'

'It'll take a couple of hours to get there.'

'I see,' Poe said. 'I don't suppose you could show me some ID?'

'Sorry, sir. I don't carry any.'

'I'm going nowhere then,' Poe said. 'My dad told me never to get in cars with strange men.'

Jonathan looked at Gandalf. He nodded.

'There's been a murder,' Jonathan said.

Victoria Hume and Bradshaw were waiting outside. Poe explained the little he knew.

'I'll go and get Edgar,' Victoria said. 'You can collect him later.'

'Thank you,' he said. 'Tilly, would you be able to take my car back to my place? Yours is parked there anyway.'

'Actually, sir, we'd like Miss Bradshaw to come with us as well,' Gandalf said, the first time he'd spoken.

'You would?' Bradshaw said.

Gandalf gestured towards his colleague. 'Jonathan will be driving your car home for you. It's why he's here.'

'Is he now?' Poe said. 'And do you have a name?'

'That isn't important, sir. What *is* important is getting you to where you need to be.' He glanced at his watch. 'And we're already running late.'

'You do realise that the judge was about to rule in my favour? Who knows what the council will come up with in the extra time you two clowns have just given them.'

'I'm sorry, sir,' he said, 'but this is time sensitive. People are waiting for you.'

'It's OK, Poe,' Bradshaw said. 'Legally, there's nothing they *can* do.'

Poe wasn't convinced. The Lake District National Park was obsessed with the past. Everything had to be as it was during Beatrix Potter's time, and anything that wasn't was discouraged and legislated against. Two weeks was a long time for people searching for a loophole.

'Sir?'

17

Poe looked at Bradshaw. If Gandalf and Jonathan were from the agency he thought they were, then Gandalf probably wasn't exaggerating about it being time sensitive.

'You up for this, Tilly?'

'Let's do it, Poe.'

'Lead the way then, Gandalf.'

'Excuse me?'

'Nothing.'

Chapter 5

Gandalf turned his nondescript but powerful Audi south on to the M6 and put his foot down. He didn't say where they were going but Poe had a fair idea.

They hadn't offered surnames and they hadn't shown any ID. The journey would take 'a couple of hours' and they were heading south. That would put them near Manchester and, because of an astonishing blunder when the builders who were contracted to put up their northern operations centre had put pictures of it in their corporate brochure, Poe even knew to what postcode they were heading.

He didn't say anything, though. Better to keep his suspicions to himself for now.

Gandalf took them to an industrial estate on the outskirts of Manchester. Poe was sure he was taking a circuitous route so they wouldn't be able to remember the way.

'You should have made us wear hoods,' Poe said.

Gandalf ignored him.

When they arrived at their destination – a low, flat building that looked like an Amazon distribution centre – Gandalf turned towards an underground car park, slowing as he approached a checkpoint. He rolled to a stop in front of a black and yellow wedge-shaped anti-ram barrier. The man behind the glass was armed and wearing a bulletproof vest.

'Gosh,' Bradshaw said.

Poe, who had seen fortified police stations when he'd toured Belfast with the Black Watch, said nothing.

Gandalf lowered his window and flashed the ID he'd earlier denied having.

'Not alone today, sir?' the man behind the glass said.

'Got two for the briefing.'

The man bent down to check who was in the back of the car before picking up his phone. After a short conversation the anti-ram barrier lowered.

After they'd parked, Gandalf escorted them to a lift. Like some inner-city hotels, it had a card reader to activate it. Unlike inner-city hotels, none of the floor buttons were marked. Cameras in all four corners of the ceiling ensured there was nowhere to hide.

Gandalf touched the card reader with his ID card. The floor buttons lit up. He shielded them with his torso before pressing one.

'Seriously, mate, you should have made us wear hoods,' Poe said. The more they tried to conceal procedures, the clearer everything became.

The lift moved. Down, not up. Made sense, he supposed. The building was only high enough for a couple of floors, but there was no limit to how deep it was.

The doors opened and Gandalf gestured for them to step out. They were led through a succession of security checks. They had their fingerprints taken and their retinas scanned.

Poe's mood worsened.

Eventually they were shown into an enclosed reception area. It was clean and functional. Moulded plastic seats, a water dispenser and harsh lighting. Clocks showing the time in major cities across the world were the only items on the wall.

Gandalf took them to the reception window. The woman behind the glass looked capable and organised. The kind of person who knew the right bus to catch.

'Washington Poe and Matilda Bradshaw from the National Crime Agency,' Gandalf said, his voice amplified electronically through a metal grille. 'They're here for the three p.m. briefing.'

'ID cards, please,' the woman said.

A flap opened underneath the window and a tray slid through a slot. Gandalf picked it up and put it on the counter.

Poe looked at Bradshaw and shrugged. They put their ID cards in the tray. Gandalf pushed it back through the slot. The flap closed. The woman took their IDs and entered their details into her computer. She put two credit card-sized passes in plastic wallets, attached them to lanyards and sent them back in the tray.

Poe looked at his. It had his name, VISITOR in large red letters and an access area code that presumably allowed him into certain parts of the building but not others.

'Wear these at all times,' the woman said. 'Failure to do so is a criminal offence. When you leave here you'll hand them back. Your ID cards will then be returned to you.'

Gandalf pulled out his own ID and slung it round his neck. His didn't have VISITOR on – or his name – Poe noticed, and his access area code was different to theirs.

'Now, if you'll pass me your mobile phones and any other electronic devices we can get you to where you need to be.'

Bradshaw removed her work mobile, her tablet, her personal mobile and two different laptops from her bag. It took three goes of the sliding drawer to get them all through.

The woman slipped them into a black case and wrote Bradshaw's name on it.

'Wow, is that a Faraday sleeve?' Bradshaw said. 'That's a Faraday sleeve, Poe.'

He shrugged.

'It's designed to shield what's inside from wi-fi, Bluetooth, mobile signals, GPS and radio signals,' she continued. 'It means that if I attempted to send or receive messages I wouldn't be able to, not while my gear's in there.'

'And are you?' the woman said. She narrowed her eyes and looked at Bradshaw.

'Golly, no. I don't even know where I am.'

'Sergeant Poe, your mobile phone, please.'

She slid the drawer open.

'No,' Poe said.

'No? What do you mean, "no"?'

'Easy enough to understand, surely. Extremely common word. Used to express an answer in the negative.'

'No one gets in here with a mobile phone, Poe,' Gandalf said.

Poe said nothing.

Gandalf said nothing.

The woman behind the window said nothing.

Bradshaw's eyes flitted between the three of them, probably wondering how much self-inflicted trouble Poe was about to get himself into.

Poe knew where he was and what agency he was dealing with. He also knew that if he didn't put a marker down early on, one that said he wasn't their lapdog, then he'd never be allowed to work independently. And something told him that working independently was going to be important over the next few days.

Gandalf blinked first.

'Fine,' he said. 'You can't come in then. I'll ring downstairs and let them know you're on your way back out. Noreen, can you arrange transport to take Mr Poe and Miss Bradshaw home, please?'

He made no move to do anything. Neither did Noreen.

'Take Tilly's stuff out of your faraway sleeve then,' Poe said.

'*Faraday* sleeve, Poe,' Bradshaw said.

'What did I say?'

'Faraway.'

22

'Did I? Where did I get that from?'

'I don't know. Enid Blyton's *Magic Faraway Tree* perhaps?'

'Oh yeah. I'd forgotten about them. I was more into the Famous Fi—'

'Pack it in, Poe!' Gandalf snapped. 'You have two choices: either you give Noreen your phone or I'll have you arrested.'

'Poe, give them your phone,' Bradshaw said. 'Pleeeease.'

'No,' Poe said again.

'Noreen,' Gandalf said. 'Please call security. Tell them to place Sergeant Poe under arrest.'

Noreen picked up her phone. She dialled a three-digit number then whispered into the mouthpiece.

Bradshaw gasped.

'Don't worry, Tilly,' Poe said, keeping his gaze on the feckless Gandalf. 'We won't be getting arrested. We haven't done anything wrong and no one from this agency has the power of arrest anyway. That's why we're here, I suspect. And there's no need to arrange transport for us. I know exactly where we are.'

Poe told him.

'How the hell could you know that?' Gandalf demanded.

The woman behind the glass looked at him with suspicion.

'What?' he said. 'I didn't tell him!'

Poe sighed. 'I guess you MI5 clowns aren't as clever as you think you are.'

Chapter 6

'MI5?' Bradshaw said.

'The very same, Tilly,' Poe said. 'Or the Security Service, or Five, or whatever name they think's cool this week.'

'So, shouldn't we do what we're told?'

'Yes, Sergeant Poe, shouldn't you?' someone behind them said.

They all turned. A man had entered the reception area. Poe didn't know where he'd come from. He had neither seen nor heard him approach – one minute he wasn't there, the next minute he was.

He was in his fifties and had a stiff, jerky gait. Tall and slim, he had neatly parted salt-and-pepper hair, and an air of authority that only those used to serious command radiated. His suit was the colour of shadows. Poe was sure it had been fashionable once, and probably would be again. But not right now. Completing the illusion of someone born a century too late was the pocket watch secured to his waistcoat by a gold chain. All he was missing was a top hat and a monocle. If Poe had been wearing a cap, he'd have doffed it.

The man's piercing grey eyes took in what was happening in a single swoop.

Gandalf paled. Noreen found something to do on her computer.

The man gave Poe a droll smile. 'This all looks rather exciting,' he said.

His voice was cultured. An Eton-educated patrician drawl that could spout obscure Latin phrases at will.

'Sergeant Poe won't hand over his mobile, sir,' Gandalf said.

'We were about to call security.'

'Why ever not?' the man replied. 'You have told him why he's been invited here?'

'Invited,' Poe said. 'That's what you call it?'

'Yes, sir. I told him there'd been a murder.'

'And?'

'Sir?'

'And what else did you tell him?'

Gandalf reddened. 'Nothing, sir.'

'Really? But I was at the same briefing as you this morning, the one where Sergeant Poe's involvement in this matter was discussed. I specifically remember you and Jonathan being told that he was to be fully briefed on what has happened and where he was being invited to attend. That he is doing us a favour, not the other way around. I also remember it being said that if Sergeant Poe wasn't fully briefed, or if you tried to strong arm him or got into some sort of pissing match, then . . . well, things like this were likely to happen. And I specifically remember this being said, Andrew, *because I was the one who said it.*'

'Yes, sir.'

'Very well. I'm sure you have things to be getting on with.'

Andrew scarpered. There was no other word for it.

'They sometimes take themselves a bit too seriously in here, Sergeant Poe.' The man thrust out his hand.

Poe shook it. It was firm and dry.

'Alastor Locke,' he said.

'That your real name?' Poe said.

'Good heavens, no.' He turned to Bradshaw. 'And you must be Matilda Bradshaw.'

'Yes, my lord.'

Poe snorted. He had almost said the same thing.

'Alastor's fine, Matilda. Didn't we try to recruit you when you were at Oxford?'

'Twice, Alastor. And you should call me Tilly.'

'I will. And should I call you Washington, Sergeant Poe?' Locke said. 'Or would you prefer it if we kept things formal?'

'He likes being called Poe,' Bradshaw said. 'Don't you, Poe?'

'Poe's fine,' he agreed.

'You are usually a coterie of three, I understand?' Locke said.

Poe looked at Bradshaw.

'It means a small, exclusive group, Poe.'

He sighed. It was going to be like that, was it?

'It's just the two of us now, Alastor,' he said.

'Oh?'

'And I'm sure you already knew that. Now, can you stop messing about and tell us why we're here?'

Locke said, 'Splendid. Now that we've all agreed you can't be intimidated, Poe, be a good chap will you and put your damn phone in the tray?'

Poe did.

'Right, let's go and see what all this fuss is about, shall we?' Locke said.

Chapter 7

Locke led them out of reception and into a long corridor. Cameras clung to the ceiling like geckos. At the end he opened a door for them.

They stepped into an air-conditioned, open-plan office. It was windowless and looked like a call centre. There was no Q blowing up walls with a ghetto blaster, no one was throwing bowler hats onto coat stands and there wasn't a single Aston Martin in sight. People were sipping coffees, not martinis.

It was most disappointing.

Instead, pasty-faced men and women worked at computers in little cubicles, all clacking keys and serious faces. Poe glanced at one as Locke led them to the back of the room. Her computer monitor was protected by a privacy filter – only the person sitting directly in front of it could see the image on the screen. As soon as Poe got close, her screen went blank. Some sort of kill switch.

She turned to see what had happened. When she saw Poe she tutted.

'It's your pass, Poe. They have RFID tags in them,' Locke said.

'Tilly?'

'Radio-frequency identification, Poe. They're using electromagnetic fields to automatically identify and track us. These ones must also be configured so we can't wander into unauthorised areas. If we do, computers will automatically turn off and someone will be alerted.'

'Blimey,' he said.

As they followed Locke down the central aisle the computers either side went blank, like someone had turned off the runway lights at an airport.

'I know, I know,' Locke said with a smile, 'we should have made you wear hoods.'

Which confirmed Poe's suspicions that Locke had been watching and listening from the moment they had arrived.

'This is all a bit dreary, isn't it?' Poe said.

'It's not all dead drops and park-bench meetings these days.'

'You sound disappointed.'

'We all have to adapt. Advances in the cyberworld have been a big leveller in the intelligence world.'

'How so?'

'I'm sure young Tilly would be able to explain it better, but nowadays anyone can threaten a country. *Anyone*. You wouldn't believe how vulnerable our infrastructure is. Crude acts of terror might steal the headlines but at least when they drive a lorry into a crowd in London, the lights don't go off in Birmingham.'

'That's a thinker,' Poe said.

'You have no idea what keeps me awake at night. Anyway, look sharp, we're here.'

What Poe had assumed to be a frosted-glass partition wall was in fact a self-contained conference room. Locke opened the door and they stepped inside. Poe immediately felt at home.

The conference room was undoubtedly used for a variety of meetings – you probably had to book it through something as mundane as an office manager – but right now Poe recognised it for what it was.

An incident room full of worried people.

Poe and Bradshaw took seats at the back. Locke made his way to the front and whispered into the ear of a woman with sandy-brown hair. She was wearing a no-nonsense suit and had a formidable face. She glanced in their direction. Locke sat at the front and the woman stood up.

The background noise stopped immediately. Obviously a big cheese.

'Good afternoon, ladies and gentlemen,' she said. 'For those of you who don't know me, I'm Mary Hope, and I'm leading on this incident. Now that our colleagues from the National Crime Agency are here, we can make a start.'

A few heads turned. Bradshaw smiled and waved. Poe didn't.

A screen came down from the ceiling. A photograph of a man appeared on it. The kind of photo found in the brochures of blue-chip companies. He was middle-aged and had good teeth. Carefully parted hair and a chiselled jaw.

'Christopher Bierman. British national but lives in America.'

Another picture. A graphic one this time.

Poe's spine stiffened. They were now in *his* area of expertise.

'Mr Bierman was found this morning in a residential property on the outskirts of Carlisle. It appears he's been beaten to death. A bloodied baseball bat was found in the same room as the body.'

'Motive?' someone at the front said.

'It's possible he might have been looking for love in the wrong places – early indications are that the house may have been used as a brothel. It was probably a shakedown gone wrong but, given what's just around the corner, we felt it prudent to exercise due diligence.'

Mary Hope spent the next few minutes telling them what they knew. Poe guessed she wasn't used to this type of briefing as there were things, obvious things, she failed to mention.

What had been achieved in the first hour? The 'golden hour' was important as forensic evidence was at its freshest. Blood might still be wet and therefore easier to see, witnesses hadn't drifted off, alibis hadn't yet been established. Was the scene undisturbed or had people been in it? If he was going to lead on the investigation, Poe hoped the person who had first responded was a cop, not a paramedic. Even when the body was green and gamey, with maggots crawling out of an open ribcage and a four-slice toaster where the head should have been, paramedics still tried to insert a drip. More than a few murderers had evaded justice because crucial evidence was lost to the paramedics and their size twelve, clue-stomping boots.

But if a cop had arrived first, as soon as they had established that the victim's injuries were incompatible with life, their next thoughts would have been about preserving the scene's integrity.

These were procedures that an experienced senior investigating officer – in fact, any decent SIO – would know to brief the troops on at the first opportunity. That Hope *didn't* know was indicative of why he was there.

'We've sought and received permission for the National Crime Agency to co-lead on the criminal investigation. For appearances' sake, Cumbria Constabulary will nominally be in charge, but all major decisions will go through Sergeant Poe.'

Poe made a mental note to call Detective Superintendent Jo Nightingale the moment he got his phone back. Nightingale was Cumbria's most senior detective and Poe knew she'd be fuming that the case had been taken from her. They had worked the Curator case earlier in the year and, although they'd had their disagreements, Poe liked to think there was a mutual respect between them. He'd need her onside when it came to ensuring resource-heavy tasks such as door-to-door enquiries and passive data searches weren't messed up.

Mary Hope struggled on with her briefing, looking relieved when she was finished. As the room emptied she beckoned them over.

'Sergeant Poe, I'm responsible for forming this executive

liaison group. I can formally include you in the ELG, and share sensitive information and raw intelligence, as you've both previously signed the Official Secrets Act.' Poe raised an eyebrow and looked at Tilly. 'Miss Bradshaw signed when she accepted a research grant from the MoD.'

'You never said you'd worked for the MoD, Tilly,' Poe said. He had signed his when he had served in the Black Watch.

'Duh, it was a secret.'

'You've met Alastor, of course, but I'd like to introduce you to the final member of the group: Hannah Finch.'

A young woman, casually dressed in jeans and a jacket, stepped forward. Her face was made up but not heavily. Her black hair was pulled into a no-nonsense ponytail. She looked brand new, as if she hadn't done anything yet. She scowled at Poe in the same way he scowled at the L and T in a BLT.

She didn't offer him her hand.

'Hannah's our liaison officer,' Hope said.

She scowled some more.

'I don't think she likes me, Tilly,' Poe said.

'You do take a bit of getting used to, Poe.'

'What, and you don't?'

Hope coughed. 'Hannah was the first of our people at the scene last night. She's been there coordinating our response. You'll have to forgive her, she's a bit tired.'

'Fair enough,' Poe said. He knew all about unexpected thirty-six-hour shifts and what they could do to your smile.

'You know about the upcoming summit?' Hope said.

'The one at Scarness Hall? Not much.'

He knew there was an impending summit, it had something to do with trade and it was taking place in Cumbria. And there was a lot of local disruption. Other than that, he'd taken no notice. He was sure the local cops were heavily involved but he only lived there, he didn't work there any more.

'No reason you should,' Hope said. 'It's deliberately been kept low-key. It's why Cumbria was chosen. Decent transport links but not exactly a media hub. Unlikely to attract big crowds of protestors. And the lower the profile, the fewer grandstanding opportunities there are for the world's leaders.'

'World leaders?'

'At some point, possibly. If there's a breakthrough they'll fly in to sign treaties. Shake hands in front of the cameras, that type of thing. Maybe plant a tree.'

Poe put two and two together. Came up with four.

'And Christopher Bierman was involved somehow?'

Hope nodded. 'In a minor logistical way. His company, Bierman & McDaid, is providing executive helicopter travel to and from the airport. Scarness Hall was chosen as it has a helicopter landing pad and there's a fuel depot nearby.'

'And you've asked for the NCA to lead because you want to keep the investigation, and therefore the summit, low key.'

'And, because the NCA has a national remit, there are no cross-border implications.'

Poe understood that at least. Lines of responsibility weren't easy to establish when a murder investigation crossed force areas. And Carlisle was only nine miles from Scotland. By having the NCA lead, Hope was keeping the loop small and tight.

'OK, why don't you tell me the real reason I'm here?' Poe said.

Hope frowned. 'I've just explained—'

'No, you've given me a palatable reason why the National Crime Agency are here. You haven't told me why *I'm* here. Apart from the fact I don't always play well with others—'

'I can certainly confirm that,' Bradshaw said, nodding. 'DI Stephanie Flynn says that Poe is the throbbing pain in her . . . bottom.'

'Thank you, Tilly,' Poe said. 'Anyway, we both work for the Serious Crime Analysis Section. Our job is to catch serial killers and serial rapists. I'm not blowing our own trumpet here, and I'm very sorry for Mrs Bierman, if there is one, but a murder in a seedy Carlisle brothel is well below our pay grade. So, I'll ask you again, why am I here?'

'Why does it matter?'

'It matters.'

Hope said nothing.

Hannah Finch filled the silence. 'This is exactly what I was talking about, ma'am.' Her voice had an upward inflection, the kind that makes every sentence sound like a question. 'You've read the briefing paper. Right at the top it says Sergeant Poe doesn't obey orders: he either chooses to cooperate or he doesn't. And while that might be an asset in his world, it isn't in ours. I implore you – please don't go outside with this.'

'We're not discussing this again, Hannah.'

'Perhaps we should. This has to be managed with discretion and tact – neither of which are qualities Sergeant Poe seems to possess.'

Poe looked at Bradshaw and shrugged.

'And she's only just met me,' he said.

'Can we please not do this in front of the children?' Locke said. He hadn't stopped smiling since the moment Poe had laid eyes on him. 'Hannah, you're well aware of the reasons Sergeant Poe is here. And Mary, I think you should tell Sergeant Poe why it's him and not someone from counter-terrorism.'

Mary Hope seemed to be in two minds.

'I'll make this easy for you, shall I?' Poe said. 'If you don't tell me why I'm here, I'm walking.'

Finch said, 'Let him go.'

'Hannah, you're not helping!' Hope snapped.

The room descended into an awkward silence, quiet enough for Poe to hear the low hum of fluorescent lighting.

'How y'all doing?' a voice said from behind him. 'Seems like things are getting a little heated in here. I think y'all need to take a few minutes. And you're here because I asked you to be here, Sergeant Poe.'

Poe frowned. He knew that voice . . .

Chapter 8

Poe turned. A woman he didn't recognise was leaning against the doorframe. She was tall and slender. Her brown skin was flawless and her hair was fashionably short. Her cheekbones were high and prominent, and her eyes looked as though they missed nothing.

She aimed a cynical smile at him. 'You're Poe,' she said.

She didn't phrase it as a question and Poe frowned in concentration. Where had he heard that voice before? Recently, he thought. It was American, one of the southern states. Louisiana or Mississippi. Possibly one of the Carolinas.

Bradshaw got there first.

'Hi, Special Agent Melody Lee. I'm Tilly Bradshaw. We spoke on the phone earlier this year. Do you want a cup of fruit tea?'

'Sure, sweetie.'

Now he remembered. She was the FBI agent who had first alerted them to the existence of the Curator. She had been in a minority of one then, and repeatedly voicing her theory meant she had been a year into a punishment posting in the South Dakota boondocks when she called him. When the case had been resolved, and she'd been vindicated, she had been posted back to Washington, DC. They kept in sporadic touch via email.

And now she was in an MI5 building on an industrial estate on the outskirts of Manchester.

Her presence didn't clear things up.

'What are you doing here, Special Agent Lee?' Poe said.

'I'm making sure it's safe for my guy to land in this country.'

'"My guy"?'

'Our Secretary of Commerce.'

'I thought it was the Secret Service who provided executive protection?'

'Sure they do. But that's reactive. Something goes down and their job is to run away. It's the FBI that's proactive.'

'OK, then what am I doing here?' Poe said. 'Miss Hope is curiously reluctant to tell me.'

'It's because they're embarrassed, Poe.'

'Embarrassed? Why?'

'Because the FBI rejected their first choice to lead on this investigation.'

'Who was it?'

'No one you know.'

'What was the problem?'

'It was no one *we* knew either.'

'I don't understand.'

'It's simple really, summit security has to be airtight . . .'

But Poe had stopped listening. Bradshaw had gone to get Melody Lee her fruit tea from the drinks station and for the past few seconds he'd been watching a small group of men who had popped back into the conference room to get a brew. One of them, a chubby-faced man with bug eyes and a Boris Johnson haircut, had just nudged one of the others. He pointed in Bradshaw's direction and winked. He walked over to her and poured himself a drink, stirred it, but left the teaspoon in the cup. Poe tuned out Special Agent Melody Lee and focused on what was happening at the drinks station.

'Have you met Bernie Spoon, Tilly?' Boris Johnson's Haircut said.

'I haven't. Is he here?'

'Kind of,' he sniggered. He took the teaspoon out of his mug.

'Oi, you!' Poe shouted.

Everyone in the room jumped. Boris Johnson's Haircut turned.

'Me?' he said.

'Yes, you, you tubby little prick,' Poe said. 'Touch the back of Tilly's hand with that hot spoon and I'll kick the fucking shit out of you then arrest you for assault.'

The silence was sudden and absolute. Boris Johnson's Haircut went purple.

'Who the hell do you think you are!' he blustered. 'You come into our house and—'

'You know exactly who he is, Graham,' Locke cut in. 'Did you read anything in Sergeant Poe's file to make you think he won't do exactly what he's just said? Now, please go and wait in my office.'

'But, sir, he can't speak to us like—'

'Perhaps I wasn't making myself clear,' Locke said. 'You must have mistakenly thought I was making a suggestion.'

Graham left the room, shooting Poe daggers as he shut the door behind him.

Bradshaw rejoined Poe.

'Who's Bernie Spoon, Poe?' she said. 'And why did you shout at that man?'

'He was going to burn you with the teaspoon, Tilly. Bernie Spoon means a spoon that will burn you.'

She looked at the closed door.

'What a numbskull,' she said.

Poe turned to Melody Lee. 'I'm sorry, you were saying something about summit security.'

'Sergeant Poe, if there's a hint of a risk to our guy, the Secret Service won't let him come,' she said, a smile dancing across her lips. 'And if our guy doesn't come then neither will the others.

Three years of planning goes down the toilet. That's why you're here: the FBI has asked for an independent investigator – a real murder po-leece. Someone who won't simply rubberstamp what the Brits want. You came highly recommended.'

'I was? By who?'

'By me. The FBI wanted someone who'll investigate without giving a rat's ass about the politics or who he upsets.'

Alastor Locke smiled. 'A task for which Sergeant Poe has just demonstrated he's singularly suited,' he said.

Chapter 9

Hannah Finch gave up trying to get Poe excluded from the investigation. She tried a different tack instead.

'OK, Sergeant Poe stays,' she said. 'But I insist that he runs all decisions through me.'

'That doesn't seem so unreasonable,' Mary Hope said. 'Poe?'

'Not a chance.'

'I concur,' Melody Lee said. 'Sergeant Poe needs to investigate this like he would any other murder. And that means without excessive oversight.'

Mary Hope shrugged.

'Fine,' Finch said, 'but I'm coming with him.'

'Excellent,' Alastor Locke said. 'It sounds like everyone's going to get on famously. Where do you want to start, Sergeant Poe?'

'Where else?' he said. 'The crime scene.'

Finch drove. Bradshaw and Poe sat in the back. Melody Lee sat in the passenger seat but twisted herself round for most of the journey up to Carlisle.

She was eager to know what had happened to the Curator. Poe suspected she knew and it was a way to express gratitude. It wasn't just her career that had been saved when Poe dragged the Curator out of the shadows; it had got an innocent kid out of prison.

'Pleaded guilty to everything a couple of months ago,' Poe said. 'Judge gave him a whole-life tariff. He'll die in prison.'

She grunted in satisfaction.

'What an asshole,' she said.

'You going to tell me why the FBI are so interested in this? Bierman's a Brit. It's likely a Brit killed him. Other than he flew helicopters, I'm not getting the link.'

'He was in the Secret Service's security bubble. They're jittery.'

'But Bierman was killed in a Carlisle brothel. He wasn't *in* the Secret Service bubble. Why do they think there's a risk to the Secretary?'

'Not saying they do.'

'What's the problem then?'

'Secret Service have lost people before. They're risk averse. They want an investigation before they'll sign off on the Secretary attending.'

'So we're here to dot the i's and cross the t's?' Poe said. 'Nothing more than a comfort blanket.'

Melody Lee grinned. 'Welcome to my world.'

Chapter 10

They dropped Bradshaw off at Durranhill, Carlisle's newest police station, where they'd been promised a room they could use. They then made the short journey to the crime scene.

Christopher Bierman had been found in a semi-detached house in a tired cul-de-sac called Cranley Gardens. One of the houses the council built, rented out, sold, then forgot about. Poe took stock of his surroundings. No CCTV. Plenty of on-street parking for the punters. Nice and quiet. Ideal for a brothel.

Detective Superintendent Jo Nightingale, the head of Cumbria's CID, met them at the outer cordon. She was a tough, no-nonsense cop. A good detective and a good manager. Poe had called ahead and warned her they were coming. As he'd expected, being told she was working under the NCA hadn't made her happy. Poe wasn't concerned; she was a professional and he knew she'd offer him the support he needed.

'Well, this is awkward,' she said.

'Wasn't my idea, ma'am.'

'Oh, I know this wasn't your idea, Poe. The instruction to put the investigation on hold came from the very top.'

'I'm here to start it again. And I'd like it if you'd work this as you would any other murder. Just loop me in on any major operational decisions and lend me some resources if I need them?'

'Sounds like a plan,' she said. 'This summit has us pretty stretched, though. Uniform are providing some of the security and they're being run ragged. All leave's been cancelled and we've had to borrow firearms units from neighbouring forces.'

'Whatever you can spare, ma'am.'

She nodded in appreciation. 'How's DI Flynn?'

'She'll get there.'

'And her son?'

'Doing great. Healthy. Got a right pair of lungs on him.'

'And Tilly? Still keeping you safe?'

'Always. She's at Durranhill now, hogging your wi-fi in all likelihood. Pop in when you get back. I know she'd like to see you.'

'I will.' She nodded at Finch and Melody Lee. 'And I see you have an entourage?'

'Special Agent Melody Lee, ma'am.'

She offered Nightingale her hand and the two women shook.

'And I'm Hannah.'

'Do you have a surname, Hannah . . .?'

'Finch,' Poe said. 'Her full name is Hannah Finch. Well, her pretend name is anyway. She's with MI5 so she likes to keep secrets.'

Finch glared at him.

'We met yesterday,' Nightingale said.

'So I heard,' Poe said.

'I was making sure Bierman had nothing compromising on him,' Finch said.

'And did he?'

'He didn't.'

'You heading up international task forces now, Poe?' Nightingale said.

'Ma'am, I'm here purely as an observer,' Melody Lee said.

'Fair enough.'

'What's it like in there?' Poe said, pointing at the house.

'Messy,' Nightingale said. 'CSI are still working it but their

42

preliminary view is that it's not the deposition site, it's the murder site.'

'And it was definitely a brothel?'

'Yep. A pop-up.'

'Who found the body?'

'The maid.'

'The jizz mopper?' Melody Lee said.

'If that's what they're called,' Nightingale frowned. 'She went in every morning when it was empty. Changed the sheets and towels, made sure there were enough condoms and lube for the dayshift, that type of thing. She's at Durranhill but it's obvious she doesn't know anything. She doesn't even know who pays her. There's an envelope left on the hall table every morning with fifty quid inside.'

'Can we speak to her?'

'I'll arrange it. Your old mate DS Rigg was taking her statement when we were told to stop. We put her in a cell because we didn't know what else to do.'

'Rigg's a detective sergeant now, is he?' Poe said. He'd been Detective Constable Rigg last year.

'He'd already passed the sergeant's exam. I imagine what you did together didn't harm his chances at the promotion board.'

'Good for him.' Poe had a lot of time for Rigg. He'd put his career on the line for Poe during the Jared Keaton case. 'Can you ask him to take the rest of her statement? Was anyone else in the house?'

'We don't think so. The jizz . . . maid said it was empty when she arrived.'

'Early thoughts?'

'What you've been told, I suspect. The victim was in an unregulated brothel and these transactions sometimes end violently. Either someone tried to rob him or there was an argument about the fee. The beating went too far and everyone ran. CSI are

43

lifting forensic transfer as we speak. Someone's prints or DNA will be on file. Bound to be.'

'Why was he here, though?'

'I'm not following,' Nightingale said. 'You know as well as I do that there's no limit to the stupid things men will do for sex.'

'No, I meant why was he at *this* brothel?' Poe said. 'He's lived in the States for years so how did he even know about this place? If the local police didn't know it existed, how did an out-of-towner?'

'I haven't really thought about it. Perhaps he liked seedy sex and had a natural talent for seeking it out.'

'Maybe. You like anyone for it?'

'We don't know who's running the girls in Carlisle,' Nightingale said. 'It used to be someone called Nathaniel Diamond but I'm fairly sure a cop called Avison Fluke found a way to take him down last year. Certainly no one's seen him around since then.'

'*Fairly* sure?'

'Wasn't anything official.'

'Fluke?' he said. 'I recognise the name. Wasn't he in prison?'

'He was.'

She didn't embellish and he didn't push it.

'And no one's filled the power vacuum?' he said.

'There's no intelligence to suggest that.'

'But?'

'But there's been none of the chaos a power vacuum usually leaves.'

'Curious.' He made a mental note to revisit his old snouts. He'd not spoken to some of them for ten years but they might remember him. 'How long has this place been a brothel?'

'According to the neighbours, not long. It's a legitimately privately rented property but it's between tenants. The last one left two weeks ago so that's the maximum window.'

That made sense. A lot of organised crime gangs were going for the 'pop-up' variety of brothel these days. A week, ten days.

Long enough to pocket a five-figure profit, not long enough for local intelligence to build up. He thumbed a text to Bradshaw asking her to put together a briefing on Carlisle's sex market.

'Eyewitnesses?'

Nightingale shook her head.

'So we don't know what time Bierman arrived.'

'No,' she said. 'And so far we can't find him on CCTV, which is unusual.'

That *was* unusual. Carlisle had one of the most sophisticated CCTV operations in the country.

'Do we know his last movements?'

'He left Scarness Hall at eight p.m. and was found dead twelve hours later.'

Poe looked at the house. 'Well, we're not going to find out what happened standing here clucking like hens,' he said. 'Let's suit up and get inside.'

Chapter 11

The entrance to the house was protected by a forensic tent. Poe, Melody Lee and Hannah Finch signed in to the inner cordon and stepped through the slit. Nightingale stayed outside.

The door led into a hallway with peeling woodchip wallpaper. Cheap prints hung askew. The fleur-de-lis patterned carpet was worn and frayed.

A woman in a forensic suit met them on the stairs. 'Julia Carver,' she said. 'I'm the crime scene manager.'

They introduced themselves. To avoid any cross-contamination they didn't shake hands.

'We're processing the whole house but preliminary findings indicate that all bloodstaining is restricted to the bedroom the victim was found in.'

'I want to see it,' Poe said.

'Follow me.'

'Hannah,' Poe said as he climbed the stairs, 'I'm going to tell you something a pathologist once told me: if it's wet and it's not yours, don't touch it.'

'Yeah, yeah,' she muttered. 'And if anything's marked "clue" I'll be sure to point it out.'

Poe smiled under his face mask.

Carver led them into the bedroom Christopher Bierman had died in. It was small, but not box-room small.

Certainly enough room to swing a bat . . .

Unsurprisingly for a brothel, the bed dominated the room.

Two small bedside tables, each with a bowl of condoms and lubricants, were set against the wall either side of the headboard. A mantelpiece with some cheap ornaments and a three-bar electric fire were the only other things in the room.

Despite the body being in the mortuary, Poe could smell death. He suspected it was partly psychological.

Blood had pooled on the sheets and the pillows. It was the colour of dried coffee. Poe could see more on the bedside table and on the headboard. Arrow stickers indicated where bloodstaining too small to see without scientific assistance had been found. More stickers were on the floor. The arrows also acted as gravitational markers to demonstrate the direction, speed and force of the blood spatter. The bigger stains on the carpet were teardrop-shaped and well-spaced. It meant the blood had been moving fast.

'The body was found on the bed,' Carver said. 'His hands had been secured behind his back, and his feet had been bound together. Both with dressing-gown cords, almost certainly from the ones we found hanging on the back of the door. They've been sent to the lab in case there was forensic transfer.'

Poe grunted in satisfaction. If the killer had been improvising, he might have made a mistake.

'Anything out of place?' he said.

'Nothing. Looks like what it was. A beating that went wrong.'

'Or right,' Melody Lee said.

'Exactly,' Poe said. 'We don't know what this is yet.'

Finch scowled but said nothing.

'You got a video walkthrough we can watch?' Poe said.

Carver nodded. She left the room, returning a minute later with a laptop and a digital camera. She connected them, then pressed play. She angled the screen so they could all see it.

Poe had seen hundreds of video walkthroughs. They were taken before anything, including the body, was removed. It was the closest thing to seeing a fresh scene.

The CSI camera operator had approached the task methodically. Commentary was offered but no opinions. Everything was covered, nothing was missed. Carver paused the screen on the body.

Even via the medium of video, Poe could see that Christopher Bierman had not died well. It had been a frenzied murder. His head was matted with blood and the left side of his skull was horribly misshapen, presumably from repeated blows with the murder weapon. His left eye socket was so badly fractured that bloodied bone fragments had pierced the surrounding skin. Blood and saliva drooled from his open mouth. His teeth had been smashed to jagged stumps.

Carver pressed play and the camera continued down the body.

'Stop,' Poe said. He pointed at Bierman's feet. He was wearing tan, lace-up brogues. 'His right shoe is tied with a double knot but the left is tied in a single. Why would that be?'

'No idea,' Carver said.

'You think it's important, Poe?' Melody Lee said.

'No, just odd.'

'It's not odd, Poe,' Finch said. 'Laces become untied.'

'Oh good, you've solved it.' He turned to Carver. 'Was there blood on either of the shoes, Julia?'

'Both. Spatters, though, not contact stains.'

'Can I see the photographs?'

Carver stopped the video and found the close-up photographs of Bierman's shoes. He studied them but nothing stood out. It was probably irrelevant, time to move on.

'OK, can we see the murder weapon now?'

The baseball bat was wooden. The end was stained with blood. The manufacturer's stickers had been removed. Poe could see the faint outline of where they'd been. One on the handle and another on the meat of the bat. He knew Nightingale was trying to identify the make but he doubted she'd have much luck. And

48

even if she did, the Americanisation of British culture meant that baseball equipment was available pretty much everywhere. They were no longer exotic weapons.

'A weapon of convenience?' Melody Lee said.

'Possibly,' Poe said. 'I suppose any onsite muscle might have carried one. Certainly worth looking into. What about cast-off bloodstaining?'

If you knew what you were looking for, blood could tell a story, and Poe had been taught by the best there was: the forensic pathologist Estelle Doyle. Cast-off staining didn't come from the body; it came from the weapon. When the bat smashed into Bierman's face, his blood would have been transferred on to the wood. When the bat was swung next, gravity would shed some of that blood in a pattern that could be read and understood. Each swing of the baseball bat would have left a separate arc of bloodstaining, and each arc would be different. A straight arc on the floor that travelled up to the ceiling indicated an up-and-down chopping-type blow, whereas a curved arc indicated more of a roundhouse swipe.

'We counted seven distinct cast-off stains, all originating from his head wounds.' Carver pointed them out. 'We have no idea if the victim took any to the torso. There was no obvious blood.'

The cast-off stains were marked on the carpet and on the photographs. They were on the right side of the bed, the mantelpiece and the wall behind the headboard.

Poe asked Carver to go back to a photo of the corpse. He fixed where Bierman was positioned in his mind and walked over to the right side of the bed. Holding an imaginary bat he tried a few swings. The up-and-over swing, like he was chopping firewood at Herdwick Croft, wouldn't have produced these bloodstains. He tried a roundhouse and was equally unhappy. The bloodstaining didn't match his swing. He went back to the laptop and studied Bierman's injuries. Although his nose was broken and off to one side, Poe suspected that was from a punch, not from one of the seven blows from the bat he'd taken to his head. The main area of impact was around his left temple.

Poe returned to the side of the bed. He stood where he imagined Bierman's feet would have been. This time he raised his imaginary bat over his right shoulder and swung it down on the same trajectory as if he were beach casting for sea bass. He looked round and nodded.

'That's how it happened. Seven targeted blows to the left side of his head.'

'What's that mean?' Finch said.

'It means that, despite what it looks like, this was clinical. This wasn't a beating-gone-wrong, this was stone-cold murder.'

Chapter 12

'We don't know that, Poe,' Finch snapped. 'We have no idea what happened and, until you do, I can't have you spouting off wild conspiracy theories.'

'Poe's right, Hannah,' Melody Lee said. 'Y'all's crazy if you think this ain't a murder one. You think it was premeditated?'

Poe shrugged. He didn't know what to think yet. Outwardly, at least, it was a chaotic crime scene. There had been no attempt to clean it and the murder weapon had been left with the body. Blood was everywhere. In theory, there should be enough forensic material for CSI to compile a complete profile of their assailant but Poe had an uneasy feeling about this. The seven blows to the head were brutal but clinical. There hadn't been any hesitation. The killer hadn't built up to a lethal blow with a series of punishing but less violent ones. He'd acted with conviction – any one of the seven blows could have been fatal.

'Can we see the rest of the video?' he said.

Carver pressed play. There was more of the body on the bed, more of the baseball bat, more of the bedroom.

'Again, please.'

Something wasn't right but he couldn't put his finger on it.

They watched it again in silence. At the end they all looked at Poe.

'One more time.'

'Oh, come on, Poe!' Finch said. 'We can watch this any time.'

'Not while we're standing in the same room we can't,' he said, his eyes glued to the laptop.

The video started again. The camera operator walked into the house, up the stairs and into the bedroom. The entire room was covered methodically. The primary focus was on the obvious evidence: Bierman's corpse, the bloodied baseball bat, the pools of blood on the bed, the larger bloodstains . . .

They had then moved on to making sure everything else was filmed. The bedside tables. The bowls of condoms and lubricants. The dressing gowns on the back of the door that were missing their cords. The three-bar electric fire and the small drops of cast-off bloodstaining. The mantelpiece and ornaments.

'Again,' Poe said.

Finch swore in frustration. Even Melody Lee sighed.

He watched it again.

And again nothing stood out.

Until it did.

'There,' Poe said, jabbing his finger at the paused screen.

'The ornaments?' Carver said. 'There was nothing unusual about them, Poe. Just some cheap tat: a woman, a man, a boy and a bird. They're at the lab but I don't think we'll get anything from them.'

'Not the ornaments,' Poe said. 'The mantelpiece.'

Melody Lee and Carver crowded in. Finch was sulking.

'Tell me what you see,' he said.

For a few moments no one spoke.

'Nothing,' Melody Lee said eventually.

'Exactly,' Poe said. 'There's nothing there.'

He walked over to the mantelpiece and checked. It was bare now but he knew what he was looking for. He made his way back to the group.

'There's no blood. There's not even any dust.' He pointed at the ornaments on the screen. 'But look, the ornaments *do* have blood on them. And that's because they were in the path of the baseball bat's cast-off. All seven blows would have sent droplets flying over the mantelpiece.'

'So why's it clean?' Melody Lee finished for him.

'I don't know,' Poe said, 'but it shouldn't be. The wall behind it isn't. It's covered in bloodstaining.'

Carver shouted out, 'Mark, can you pop in for a moment, please?'

A small, wiry man carrying a plastic box entered the room. 'We missed something?' he said.

She shook her head. 'We haven't luminoled the mantelpiece, have we?'

'Not yet, Julia. Davy Fennell and I will do the whole house after the sheets and mattress are recovered.'

In the past luminol had been blamed for the degradation of DNA samples, so Poe knew it was used at the end of a crime scene investigation rather than at the beginning. All available trace evidence was recovered first.

'What's luminol?' Finch said.

'It's a chemical that reacts with the iron in haemoglobin,' Mark said. 'It picks up the tiniest amount, so if someone has tried to clean the mantelpiece, unless they've used bleach, we should see something.'

'And it's basic knowledge, Hannah,' Poe said. 'The fact you had to ask is why you had no business asking to lead this murder investigation.'

Finch scowled.

'Can we do it now?' Carver said. 'We've already swabbed it, I assume?'

'We have.'

The effects of luminol can only be seen in the dark so Mark closed the door and drew the curtains. He kept the main light on for now so he could see what he was doing. He removed a bottle the same shape and size as an indoor plant sprayer.

'Can I ask you to document it, Julia?' he said.

She nodded. Mark removed the camera from around his neck and passed it across to her.

'And can I ask you to turn off the light when I give you the say-so, ma'am?' he said to Finch.

'This is a waste of time,' she muttered, but moved over to the light switch anyway.

Poe knew the effects of luminol only lasted about thirty seconds, which was why Mark needed Finch on the lights and Carver ready to record anything. Poe removed his mobile, opened the video function and started filming.

When he was ready, Mark said, 'Can you turn off the light, please?'

Finch flicked the switch and the room went dark. Mark sprayed the mantelpiece.

The results were immediate.

'Gotcha,' Poe said.

The mantelpiece glowed blue, as bright as a fibre-optic Christmas tree. Carver began taking photographs and Poe scanned his phone all the way along, making sure he'd filmed everything.

After a while the blue dulled and eventually faded to nothing.

'You can put the light back on now, ma'am,' Mark said.

Finch did so while Mark opened the curtains.

'I don't know about you guys,' Melody Lee said, 'but it looks to me like that mantelpiece has been wiped down.'

Chapter 13

'No doubt about it,' Poe said. 'The mantelpiece *has* been wiped down.'

'And clumsily, judging by the smudge patterns and how much was missed,' Melody Lee added. 'Theories?'

'Two spring to mind,' he said. 'The maid's money could have been left on the mantelpiece and she decided to take it before dialling nine-nine-nine. Cleaned it so there was no envelope-shaped gap in the blood to make us curious.'

'Or?'

'Or, for some reason, the killer was trying to hide the blood.'

Which didn't make sense. He hadn't attempted to clean anywhere else. Not even a token effort. He'd even left the murder weapon. What was so special about the mantelpiece? Poe looked round the room, tried to see if anything else was dust and blood free. Anything that might indicate the mantelpiece wasn't the only area that had been wiped.

There was nothing. The whole room was dusty. The woman who looked after the brothel obviously wasn't paid to clean. Restock the condom bowl and change the sheets. Probably did it a few times a day.

He asked Carver if he could have a look at the photograph of the mantelpiece taken before the ornaments had been removed.

There were four of them. Cheap things. Looked as though they were part of a set. They were equally spaced, about a foot between each one.

'Maybe something was taken from the mantelpiece,' Poe said. 'And removing it left an obvious bare patch in the dust. The killer could have been wiping dust away, not blood. Maybe he's taken something, wiped the mantelpiece down, then rearranged the remaining four ornaments so there was no obvious gap for us to see. Hoped we'd miss that he'd cleaned.'

After a while Melody Lee said, 'You see, Miss Finch, this is why we wanted Poe involved.'

'I need to speak to the maid,' he said.

Durranhill, in Carlisle, was the Northern Area Command's headquarters building. It was built to replace the station that was lost to the 2005 floods. It looked like a cross between a multi-storey car park and the back of a football stand. Its sloping roof gave the impression it was sinking.

Hannah Finch said she had to make a phone call in private. She was probably the type of person who imagined all her phone calls were important enough to be made in private.

DS Rigg was still taking the maid's statement so Poe and Melody Lee went off to find Bradshaw. Nightingale had come through for them. Instead of the dark and dingy rooms they were usually allocated when they worked in Cumbria, they were in a bright and airy room with views over the rooftop garden. Well, it would have been bright and airy with views over the rooftop garden if Bradshaw hadn't shut all the blinds and windows.

'Can we get some light in here?' Poe said.

'I couldn't see my screens properly,' Bradshaw said.

'If Tilly is exposed to sunlight she needs immediate medical attention,' he said to Melody Lee as he raised the blinds. 'And while we're on the subject, a bit of fresh air won't kill you either. It's roasting in here.'

'What about my hay fever? And I get plenty of fresh air.'

Poe looked at her. 'When do you ever get fresh air?'

'Duh, I play Muggle Quidditch every Tuesday.'

He looked at her blankly.

'Jeez, Poe, try cracking open a book once in a while.'

'I read plenty of books. What's Muggle Quidditch?'

'It's a sport. We're in a league and everything. We play at the hockey stadium. I'm a beater but I want to be the seeker.'

A thought dawned on him. 'It's not that thing you're always trying to get me to come and watch you play?'

'It is. And you always say you're too busy.'

'I *am* always too busy. But I thought that was all about wizards or something?'

'And witches. It's from *Harry Potter*.'

'But the hockey stadium's not covered. What if your laptops get wet?'

'It's not played on computers, Poe. Quidditch is a proper sport – it's played on broomsticks.'

'Excuse me?'

'Each team has seven players and we're all mounted on broomsticks. The beaters have to try and knock them off with bludgers while we try and catch the quaffle—'

'You know something, Tilly,' Poe cut in. 'I think I will come and see you next time you play. I think I'd enjoy that.'

'As long as you're not coming just so you can laugh at me and my friends.'

'I wouldn't do that.'

'Puh-lease . . . What about that time you walked in on us when we were playing *Warlocks & Witches*? You laughed then.'

'You were wearing a pair of wings, Tilly.'

'Of course I was wearing wings – I'm a level twenty Avariel.'

'A what?'

'An elf of the sky, Poe. We have hollow bones and—'

Melody Lee cleared her throat.

'You guys do this often?'

'What?' Poe said.

'Disappear down the crazy rabbit hole.'

Poe considered this for a moment. 'It's pretty much all we do,' he said.

Bradshaw nodded in agreement.

'But point taken,' Poe said. 'What you got for us, Tilly?'

'I've put together a ten-page briefing on the sex markets in Carlisle, Poe.'

She handed them both a slim file. Poe skimmed Bradshaw's summary. From *Harry Potter* to prostitutes in three easy moves – that was quite the turnaround.

'I found an independent study that was written in 2012. I correlated that with local intelligence then cross-referenced it with the national picture. There are four kinds of female sex workers in Carlisle.'

'We sure Bierman was seeing a *female* prostitute?' Poe said.

'I spoke to Detective Sergeant Rigg while you were out. Paulina says that—'

'Paulina?'

'Paulina Tuchlin. She's the woman who found the body. She's from Poland.'

'OK.'

'Paulina says her houses only ever have female sex workers.'

'Fair enough.'

'Anyway, of the four categories of sex workers, I think we can discount those working for north-west escort agencies.'

'I agree,' Poe said. 'The escort agencies working up here are all fairly legit businesses; they wouldn't put their girls into pop-up brothels.'

'The next category are women who live in Cumbria and offer incalls and outcalls. They'll visit their client or receive them in their own home. I think we can discount them as well.'

'Yep. Women like that aren't interested in the type of bottom-feeder who visits somewhere like Cranley Gardens.'

'You think Bierman was a bottom-feeder, Poe?' Melody Lee said. 'That's not what our profile says.'

'No, but I do think Cranley Gardens is the type of brothel that caters for the bargain end of the market. Another thing that doesn't add up. What are the other two categories, Tilly?'

'The final two are the ones we're probably going to be interested in, Poe. The first is women who work in brothels and the second is survival sex workers.'

'Survival sex workers are usually streetwalkers, aren't they? Trading sex for what they consider are essential resources.'

'Yes, Poe. Usually drugs or alcohol but sometimes it's accommodation.'

'OK, we'll keep survival sex workers in. If Superintendent Nightingale says they don't know who's running the girls it could be that no one is. Maybe a group of survival workers got together and formed some sort of cooperative.'

The phone rang. Bradshaw picked it up. 'Matilda Bradshaw, Serious Crime Analysis Section, National Crime Agency . . . Oh, hello Detective Sergeant Rigg, do you want to speak to Poe? We've been talking about Harry Potter and Muggle Quidd— OK, I'll tell him.'

She put the phone down.

'Detective Sergeant Rigg has finished taking Paulina Tuchlin's statement, Poe. She's ready to see you now.'

Chapter 14

Paulina Tuchlin was Polish, but legally living in the UK. It was the first thing she said when they entered the clean, modern interview room.

'We're not from . . . whoever deals with that sort of thing,' Poe said. 'And you're not in trouble. I know you've just given a statement but we have a few questions.'

She eyed them suspiciously but nodded. Her hair was brown and thick and long. It was held back from her face with a purple hairband. Her hands were calloused and raw, the hands of someone who had been doing rough, manual labour from an early age. Paulina noticed Poe looking and put them on her lap, under the table. She stared at him defiantly. She wore baggy jeans and an oversized, unbranded jumper. He figured her to be in her early twenties. He wondered how someone so young had ended up on the facilities management side of the sex trade. He doubted it would be a nice story. He'd ask Rigg to do a welfare check later in the week. Make sure she was safe.

'May I call you Paulina or would you prefer Miss Tuchlin?' Poe said.

'It is *Mrs* Tuchlin. I am married, but you should call me Paulina.'

'OK, Paulina, you told the other police officer that the house is empty when you clean it. Is that *always* empty or just most-of-the-time empty.'

'Sometime there are girls sleeping. No men, though. This

morning there was no girls. No girls night before too. I was there to take all things away. House being rented soon and the landlord need it clean.'

'The brothel was—'

She clipped his sentence with, 'It is not brothel, it is massage parlour.'

Poe didn't want to waste time arguing semantics. 'OK, so the massage parlour was closing down? It was about to be rented out again?'

Paulina nodded.

'And no one had been working the night before?'

She shifted uneasily in her seat. Poe thought he knew why.

'They're working in a new broth . . . massage parlour, aren't they?' he said. 'This one closed and another one opened?'

Paulina nodded again, unhappily.

'When did this new one open?'

'Two days ago. I clean this too.'

'So the house had been empty for the two nights before you found the body?'

'Yes.'

'And no one would have taken some private . . . massage clients there? Took advantage of an empty house with bowls full of . . . massage accessories?'

'Not allowed,' she said, shaking her head vehemently.

She seemed adamant, which was interesting. If it had been a collective of likeminded survival sex workers, he doubted they'd have been so strict with each other. Far more likely this was an organised brothel, and that meant someone was running girls in Carlisle again.

Poe knew that at some point he was going to have to get out onto the street, speak to people who lived in the shadows. If he could find out who was running the girls, he might find out who knew the house had been standing empty.

He reached into his file and removed a photograph of the mantelpiece. 'Do you recognise this, Paulina?'

She stared at the photograph.

'It is the fireplace from bedroom two.'

'It is. Can you tell me if there's anything wrong with the picture?'

She leaned in. Poe got the impression that, despite her questionable employment, Paulina had a decent brain.

'I see nothing,' she said eventually.

Poe put four more photographs in front of her. One of each ornament: the woman, the man, the boy and the bird.

Paulina gave him a puzzled look.

'We think there might have been something on the mantelpiece that the killer took with him. We were hoping you might know what that was.'

She studied the photographs again.

'No,' she said. 'They all there.'

'You're sure?'

'Of course. They are of famous Polish fairy tale, *The Glass Mountain*.'

Poe frowned. 'I've not heard of it.'

'May I touch?' she said, gesturing towards the photographs.

'Be my guest.'

She picked up the photograph of the woman.

'On Glass Mountain there is apple tree with golden apples. Anyone who pick one can get into a golden castle where this beautiful princess live.' She pointed at the ornament. 'This is the beautiful princess.'

She picked up the photograph of the man.

'Many brave knights try to climb Glass Mountain so they can get into the castle. This one knight he try but an eagle' – she picked up the bird photograph – 'attack him and he die.'

She picked up the last photograph, the one of the small boy.

62

'This one schoolboy, he kill a mountain lion. He chop off its claws and tie them to his feet so he can climb Glass Mountain better. He get halfway up when the eagle attack again but this boy is clever. Instead of falling he grab hold of the eagle who tries to fly away. When he is at top of mountain he cut off the eagle's feet and he fall onto the apple tree. He take an apple and he marry the beautiful princess.'

She put down the photographs and looked at him.

Poe wasn't surprised it was so macabre. From Hansel and Gretel, with its themes of child abuse and cannibalism, to the Brothers Grimm version of *Cinderella*, where the ugly sisters' punishment for being mean to 'Cinders' was to have their eyes pecked out by doves, there was nothing more disturbing than a children's fairy tale.

'*The Glass Mountain*,' she said, 'these are the four people in it.'

Poe wasn't convinced. Not yet.

'And it's not possible that there were five ornaments in the set?' he said. 'Maybe there was another knight. Or the mountain even?'

She shook her head. 'Is not possible.'

'You seem pretty sure.'

'I am sure. I buy from a Polish shop when I go to Manchester one day. My son, he was born in United Kingdom. He has never been to Poland. I bought so he could learn . . . how you say, our ways?'

'Your culture?' Poe said.

'Yes, our culture. I buy so he could learn the culture of Poland. I want him to hear the same stories I hear when I was little girl.'

'So how did they end up at Cranley Gardens?'

'My husband, he says Glass Mountain story scare our son. It gives him nightmares. I take them out of house and make bedroom number two look nice. They my ornaments in your photograph.'

Poe sighed. He had only been working the murder for a few

hours and it already felt like he was trying to unmake soup. He had a victim who'd visited a brothel he shouldn't have known existed; a pair of shoes with inconsistently tied laces; and a crime scene where the only thing the killer had tried to clean was a mantelpiece displaying nothing but ornaments from a Polish fairy tale.

He felt a headache coming on.

Chapter 15

'What's next, Poe?' Melody Lee said.

They were in the room Nightingale had requisitioned for them. Bradshaw had four different computers running. There was a Post-it note on one of them. It said she was out on an errand and would be back soon. He had no idea where Hannah Finch was. Probably off redoubling her efforts to get him removed from the case.

Bradshaw had been out and bought a cheap filter-coffee machine. She didn't drink caffeine but knew Poe mainlined it during active investigations. He helped himself to a mug and filled one for Melody Lee.

'No cream?' she said.

'This is England. Cops don't put cream in their coffee here. We use milk.' He thought about the almond milk Bradshaw sometimes had on her muesli. 'And if that milk comes from a cow then all the better. There'll be some UHT knocking around somewhere.'

'What the hell's that?'

'No idea. All I know is that it comes in little pots and lasts forever.'

'It stands for ultra-high-temperature milk, Special Agent Melody Lee,' Bradshaw said as she entered the room. 'I don't drink it as I'm vegan and Poe doesn't drink it because he says it tastes like wee.'

Melody Lee grimaced. 'Black's good.'

'Good call,' Poe said. 'And I don't know about you but I'm shattered. How about we call it a day after this? Meet back here first thing tomorrow?'

'You guys get some rest if you want but I'm still on DC time – I'm five hours behind y'all. Still the middle of the afternoon as far as this gal's concerned.'

There was a knock on the door. Detective Sergeant Rigg entered. He was tall and thin. He used to have buck teeth but he must have had some work done in the last year, as they weren't quite as pronounced.

'Good to see you, Andrew,' Poe said, filling him a mug of coffee.

'You too, Poe.'

'Congratulations on the promotion. Thoroughly well deserved. This is Special Agent Melody Lee. She's here to observe and make sure any American interests are protected.'

Rigg frowned.

'Don't ask,' Poe said. 'And I mean that literally. You'll probably do ten years in the slammer if you do.'

'One of those cases, is it?'

'Yep. I was at their northern headquarters this morning. You've never met a more arrogant bunch of arseholes in your life. Anyway, we've just finished with Paulina Tuchlin.'

'I don't think she's involved.'

'We don't either. She did clear up something, though. Actually, she made things more confusing but at least we know where we are.'

He brought Rigg up to speed on the wiped-down mantelpiece and the ornaments from the Polish fairy tale.

'Were you the first CID officer on scene?' Poe said when he'd finished.

'I was. Superintendent Nightingale was there within the hour and took charge. I've been on house-to-house and chasing up the passive data since then.'

'Anything on the passive?'

'Nah. The brothel was in a carefully chosen location. The city centre CCTV doesn't reach that far and there are none of the bigger shops. Not even a cash machine camera to check. The house-to-house found one private camera but that was aimed at the bloke's motorbike and wasn't street-facing.'

'Shit,' Poe said. 'Uniform were there first, I take it?'

'Yep. A PC Nathan Wilkes. Been with us a few years. I took his statement if you want to read it, but he didn't mess it up. Went in, confirmed the victim was dead, then secured the scene. Stood his post until the circus arrived.'

'Jo Nightingale said Hannah Finch turned up fairly quick.'

'Within half an hour of him being ID'd through his wallet,' Rigg confirmed. 'I think she was already at Scarness Hall. Something to do with that conference they're having in a few weeks.'

'Who called her?'

'I don't know. I assume his name was flagged so when it went into our system it triggered something at her end.'

'She saw the scene?' Poe said.

'She did. Said she needed to make a positive ID. She got suited and booted and went up there. Didn't stay long.'

'Good,' Poe said. 'If she gives you any shit, tell me straight away.'

Rigg nodded.

'Any chance we can speak to this PC Wilkes?' Poe said. 'Sometimes the first person at the scene sees things that get lost when the cavalry gets there. Smells, room temperature, that type of thing.'

Poe didn't have to elaborate. Rigg was a good cop and he knew the value of getting first-hand accounts.

Rigg checked his watch. 'You can probably speak to him now. I'm sure I saw him in the locker room earlier. Must still be on nights.'

PC Nathan Wilkes hadn't yet started his shift so was in a T-shirt, jeans and trainers. He was in his mid-twenties and had elaborate tribal tattoos on both biceps. Rigg introduced Poe as an NCA officer. Wilkes wasn't fazed, just curious.

They were using an interview room, although nothing was being recorded. It was an unofficial chat.

Poe asked him to talk them through what had happened, from getting the call to being relieved. Wilkes did. He'd been at the bottom end of Botchergate, the cultural drip tray of Carlisle, when control had dispatched him to Cranley Gardens. A hysterical Paulina Tuchlin had met him at the door. He'd calmed her down, and checked the perimeter and the rest of the house to ensure the killer wasn't still on the premises. He'd then entered the bedroom and checked Bierman for signs of life. With half his head caved in it hadn't taken long to confirm he was dead and it was CID rather than the paramedics that needed to be called. He left the room, went downstairs and began controlling access to the crime scene. Rigg, as duty sergeant, was the first CID officer to arrive. Jo Nightingale arrived soon after. Hannah Finch arrived half an hour after the victim had been identified. She'd been allowed upstairs to make a positive ID.

'You notice anything untoward?' Poe said.

Wilkes frowned. 'Like what, sir?'

'I don't know.'

He'd obviously anticipated why Rigg had asked to see him as he had his pocket notebook with him. Poe knew he would have meticulously recorded all the actions he'd taken. Not only did it protect him, it was also admissible in court. Accurate notebook entries stopped slippery defence solicitors from saying protocols hadn't been followed. He read through his notes.

'No. I think I've covered everything.'

'Can I have a look at your notebook?' Poe said.

'Of course.' Wilkes handed it across. Poe didn't know what he was looking for and it was obvious Wilkes had done everything by the book. As soon as he'd confirmed life was extinct he had made sure as much evidence as possible had been preserved.

'What's that stand for?' Poe said, pointing to an acronym he didn't recognise: PTBE. The time beside it showed it had been entered early on in his callout. He flicked back through the notebook and saw Wilkes had entered it on different callouts as well.

Wilkes leaned over.

'Photo Taken Before Entering,' he said.

'You took a photo before you checked for signs of life?'

'I did. On my mobile.'

'Why?'

'I always do, sir. In case the victim is still alive and I have to go balls out to save him until the paramedics come. You'll know as well as I do that they wreck crime scenes. I take it so there's at least one photograph of everything before it gets trashed.'

Poe nodded in appreciation. It was a good idea. 'Was it logged?'

'No need, sir. The victim was dead and no one entered the bedroom until CSI recorded everything professionally.'

'Apart from DC Rigg and Superintendent Nightingale, you mean,' Poe said.

'And that lassie that turned up later. Hannah someone or other.'

'She's called Hannah Finch.' For some reason Poe was taking a perverse delight in telling everyone her full name. 'But other than those three, no one else entered the scene until CSI photographed and videoed everything?'

Wilkes checked his notes and nodded. 'That's correct, sir.'

'Do you still have the photograph?'

Wilkes removed his mobile. It was an iPhone. A large one

like Bradshaw's. He opened the photo app then scrolled down until he found the right one. He passed over the phone.

It was high-def and had been taken from the doorway, the same doorway Poe had just been standing in. Wilkes's focus had been on the victim but almost two-thirds of the room was in the frame.

'What happened there?' Poe said.

'Where?'

'The photo, it moved.'

'It's a live photo, sir,' Wilkes said.

Poe looked at him blankly.

'It means that the photograph is wrapped by animation before and after the shot is taken.'

'So it's a short video?'

'Not exactly, sir. The animation doesn't start when I press the button; it starts a second and a half before. The photograph is the mid-point of the animation, not the end.'

'So there's another second and a half I haven't seen?' Poe said.

'Yes, sir. If I hold it down it will play the whole three seconds.'

Wilkes touched the photograph and it did exactly that. The second and a half recorded before the shutter had been pressed must have been shot while Wilkes was still positioning his camera – it briefly showed the mantelpiece.

It was only a flash but Poe saw the anomaly immediately.

He breathed out slowly. He had a problem. A big problem.

'Can you send this to me, please?'

'What's up, Poe?' Rigg asked.

'The video clearly shows five ornaments on the mantelpiece.'

'So?'

'There are only *four* ornaments on the CSI photographs. We'd assumed the killer had wiped down the mantelpiece to hide the fact he'd taken something, but we've got it the wrong way round – he didn't take something, he *left* something.'

Rigg considered what Poe had just said.

'Shit.'

'Exactly,' Poe said. 'The killer left us something and someone on the investigation team stole it.'

Chapter 16

'I've broken down the live photograph into frames, Poe,' Bradshaw said, 'but as the camera was moving before PC Nathan Wilkes pressed the shutter, the resolution isn't brilliant. The first few are a bit blurry. I've enlarged the best one.'

Poe had just come back from an urgent meeting with Jo Nightingale. Together they had compiled a list of people who'd had access to the fifth ornament before CSI had arrived and logged everything.

There were three names but only one that mattered.

He had left a voicemail for her. Melody Lee and Bradshaw had tried to talk him out of it. Rigg was in two minds.

'This is a terrible idea, Poe,' Melody Lee said.

'We won't know how terrible until we've done it.'

He took his mind off how bad it might get by trying to work out what the fifth ornament was.

'Is it a rabbit?' Rigg said.

'It looks more like a squirrel, DS Rigg,' Bradshaw said. 'I think a rabbit would have bigger ears.'

'But a squirrel would have a bushier tail,' Melody Lee said. 'Could be a mouse.'

'Some sort of rodent anyway,' Poe said.

Whatever it was, it was in the middle of the mantelpiece, flanked by the ornaments from Paulina's Glass Mountain fairy tale. Poe compared Wilkes's photograph with the more professionally shot CSI ones. In Wilkes's, the four Glass Mountain ornaments looked as though they'd been pushed out to the left and right to make room in the middle. Whoever had removed the fifth ornament had rearranged the remaining four so there was no obvious gap. They'd probably had to wipe down the mantelpiece to hide the gaps in blood spatters. If they hadn't, it would have been obvious that the ornaments had been moved.

'Can you make this sharper, Tilly?' Poe said.

They never found out if she could or couldn't, as at that moment the door opened and the person who had removed the fifth ornament stepped into the room.

'Can you do the honours, Sergeant Rigg?'

'You sure?'

'I am.'

'Very well.' He stepped forward. 'Hannah Finch, you are under arrest on suspicion of perverting the course of justice. You do not have to say anything, but it may harm your defence if you do not mention when questioned something that you later rely on in court. Anything you do say may be given in evidence. Do you understand?'

Chapter 17

'What the hell do you think you're doing, Poe?' Hannah Finch hissed.

'My job.'

'Yeah? Well, if that fool is stupid enough to try and handcuff me, your career's over.'

'What career?' he said. 'And, Hannah, if you keep struggling, uniform will be called and you *will* be squirted in the eyes with pepper spray.'

'Fuck you, Poe!' she said as Rigg cuffed her.

He was escorting her from the room when Poe said, 'Just one moment, Andrew.'

Rigg stopped. Poe pointed his phone at her. Finch struggled, but it's hard to cover your face when you're handcuffed to the rear.

'Don't you dare!'

She was becoming foam flecked and hysterical.

'Never dare an idiot, Hannah,' Poe said. 'Is "say cheese" still a thing?' The phone's artificial shutter noise told Finch everything she needed to know. She'd been snapped in handcuffs and she had no control over what happened to the photograph.

Her bluster disappeared so quickly it looked like she was having a stroke. It was replaced by fear. If the photograph got into the public domain it was her career that was over, not Poe's. Even her agency director having to speak to his agency director to get her un-arrested would be a career-defining moment.

She set her expression to grim and glowered.

'OK. Now what, Poe?' Melody Lee said after Rigg had taken Finch down to the cells.

Poe shrugged.

'You don't have a "now what", do you?'

'She'll be processed,' he said. 'And because we've been working late, we'd be on legally dodgy ground if we interviewed her now. She's entitled to uninterrupted rest.'

'Really?'

Poe shrugged again. 'I don't know. Probably. I do know I'm going home.'

Melody Lee looked at him shrewdly. 'You want the boss man here tomorrow, don't you?' she said.

'Absolutely. We need the evidence Finch removed and that means we need someone who can put the sort of pressure on her that we can't.'

'And if they won't play ball?'

'Then I get Tilly to show me how to put that photograph on Twitter.'

'Ha!' Bradshaw snorted. 'Poe on Twitter, I'd like to see that. Here's a photograph of my tea, oh look, it's a big sausage. Here's a photograph of my breakfast, what a surprise, it's another big sausage. And here's a picture of a boring hill I've been looking at for six hours.'

Poe stared in astonishment.

'Tilly,' he said, 'it's going to be fine.'

He didn't mention that he had in fact had a big sausage for breakfast.

'Hashtag MI5 agent tampers with crime scene?' Melody Lee said. 'Ballsy strategy, Poe. You think they'll go for it?'

'Find out soon, I suppose,' he said. 'In the meantime Tilly can draw up a profile on Christopher Bierman. There's something going on here that we're not being told.'

'I've already started, Poe.'

He nodded his thanks. 'And I'll pick you up at your hotel first thing, Special Agent Lee. We'll go to Scarness Hall and see where Christopher Bierman was staying. Maybe speak to some of his colleagues. Have a poke around.'

'Security will be tight. You won't get in without prior authorisation and I doubt Miss Finch will be in the mood to put your name on the guest list.'

'I'm sure you have contacts there.'

She sighed. 'I'll see what I can do.'

'Outstanding.'

'And if they ask why Hannah Finch isn't authorising you?'

'You're a resourceful woman,' Poe grinned. 'I'm sure you'll think of something.'

Chapter 18

Poe didn't sleep well. A combination of the evening coffees with Melody Lee, the nagging suspicion he'd overreached by arresting a member of MI5, and the muggy heat had him tossing and turning, searching for that sweet cool spot on the pillow. If Edgar had been there he'd have taken him for a midnight walk across Shap Fell. The fresh air would have helped clear his mind. But Edgar was still with his neighbour, Victoria.

When it got to 5 a.m. and the croft started to heat up, he abandoned sleep and decided on a carb-free breakfast instead. He put a whole ring of Cumberland sausage, three eggs and some butcher's black pudding into his skillet and fried it up.

'Hashtag this,' he muttered as he piled it on a tin plate.

He ate his breakfast outside, washing it down with cups of thick black coffee.

The air was shimmering by the time he had drained his third cup. He checked his watch. It wasn't yet 6 a.m. and he was already too hot.

Herdwick Croft was two miles from the nearest road. He usually took his quad bike to Shap Wells Hotel, where he had an arrangement to leave his car, but that morning he decided to walk. He needed to think. He stopped after a mile and sent Rigg a text asking if he knew how Hannah Finch was. The detective sergeant replied immediately and confirmed that she was still in custody and that no overtures had been made to have her released.

He covered the last mile in fifteen minutes. The grass was pale and stunted, the heather brittle and colourless. The sheep droppings were so dry they were rolling in the light breeze. The cowpats had a speckled white crust and were curled at the edges. He arrived at Shap Wells panting and with a sweat moustache.

He climbed into his BMW, cranked up the air conditioning and drove out of the hotel car park.

Next stop, Scarness Hall.

A sleepy country house in a sleepy village and the location of an upcoming international trade summit.

Melody Lee had taken a room at the Crown Hotel in Wetheral. Poe had been to a probation officer's wedding reception there once. He pulled into the car park at seven-thirty. She was outside waiting. She climbed in the passenger side but before he could set off his text alert sounded.

'Tilly's at Durranhill already,' he said. 'Wants to know when we'll get there.'

'What will you tell her?'

'Depends how this goes.'

Scarness Hall was near the village of Hallbankgate. It was twelve miles from Carlisle, close enough to have a CA8 postcode. Poe guessed it would take fifteen minutes to get there, but he hadn't counted on the security arrangements.

Tilly had downloaded and printed a copy of the leaflet that had been sent to residents in the immediate vicinity of the summit. It started with, 'The eyes of the world will soon be on Cumbria and during this time we will be the centre of attention for the world's media' and got increasingly hyperbolic from there. The world's leaders weren't due to arrive for a fortnight but the leaflet warned of disruption for weeks before as various security protocols were put into place.

Residents were told that as the summit approached, parking would become difficult and more roads would be closed until eventually there would be one route in and out. They were advised to use public transport, car share or walk whenever possible to avoid the inevitable delays. The Foreign and Commonwealth Office had already issued permits to everyone living in the catchment area to speed things up, although Poe got the impression that was just to make them feel better – in the run up to the summit, residents were going to be inconvenienced and a natty FCO permit wasn't going to change that.

The houses on the outskirts of Hallbankgate were detached with large gardens but as they neared the heart of the village they began to bunch up. There was a school and a few local shops but not much else. Nice and quiet, a place to raise a family.

The first sign they were nearing the summit area was when they passed a small group of protesters. Six of them. They were drinking from Styrofoam cups and were being watched by a bored-looking uniformed cop. One of them held up a homemade sign as they passed.

A few hundred yards later two cops waved him down. One of them was armed. Poe didn't know if this was part of the planned arrangements or whether security had been tightened because of Bierman's murder. The unarmed cop was red-faced and beefy. He approached the driver's side and Poe lowered his window.

The armed cop moved so his colleague wasn't in his line of fire. He held his weapon casually but confidently.

'Maybe now's not the time to mouth off, Poe,' Melody Lee said.

He turned off the engine.

'Do you have a resident's permit or legitimate business in this area, sir?' His breath smelled of bacon.

Poe showed him his ID. 'I'm investigating Christopher

79

Bierman's murder. This is Special Agent Melody Lee from the FBI. She's here in a liaison capacity.'

'May I reach into my purse?' she said.

The cop frowned. 'Of course you can.'

Carefully, she found her ID and handed it to Poe. He passed it through the window.

'We should be preapproved for entry, officer,' she said.

'I'll check, ma'am.'

'Are there checks like this on all access roads to Scarness Hall?' Poe said.

'We're in the last two weeks now, sir. Things are being ramped up.'

He moved to the front of the car, made a note of the registration number then called it in.

In less than a minute they were on their way.

And a minute after that, Scarness Hall came into view.

Chapter 19

As well as the residents' leaflet, Bradshaw had sent Poe a report on the summit and on Scarness Hall itself. Poe hadn't been there before but knew of it. It had a good reputation for food, particularly afternoon tea.

The main building was an elegant, ivy-clad, two-storey mansion straight from a storybook. The sun had long ago washed away the vibrancy from the red sandstone but, unlike anything on Shap Fell, the ivy remained green and glossy.

Cottages, guesthouses, a jumble of converted stables, outhouses and staff quarters sat within the hall's extensive and impeccably landscaped grounds. A stream languidly ran in front of the house, ending in a large duck pond. The grass was cut short and still had its green tinge. He suspected the summit had made them exempt from the countywide hosepipe ban.

Poe stopped at the checkpoint at the bottom of the drive. Unlike the one they had just passed, it was static, not mobile. It had a purpose-built guardhouse, a heavy automatic barrier and looked like it had been there for a few weeks.

He parked in the designated bay. They were asked to leave the vehicle and follow a suited man into the guardhouse. Their ID cards were checked again and their names were entered into a database.

'Look at the camera please, sir,' the man said, pointing to a small device hooked up to a laptop.

Poe did as he was asked. Melody Lee did the same. Two

cardboard name badges shunted their way out of a loaf-sized printer. The man slipped them into plastic wallets and attached a lanyard to each one.

'Please wear these at all times,' he said. 'They'll stop you from getting shot. Now, if you follow the drive all the way to the hall someone will meet you and show you where to park.'

Poe would have expected additional perimeter security between the gate and the hall but he saw it wasn't needed. The drive had high banks on either side and was naturally chicaned. Even the most determined terrorist would struggle to get above ten miles an hour.

On the way up the leafy drive Poe saw armed men patrolling the grounds. He assumed there would be more that he couldn't see. There would also be hidden observation posts around Scarness Hall's border. The security looked light but Poe knew that was an illusion – he could feel many pairs of eyes on him. It didn't feel nice.

As they neared the hall, and as the road turned to the right, something on the left caught his eye. It was the helicopter landing area. It wasn't a concrete pad with a big 'H', just a field protected on three sides by a ten-foot-high red brick wall. The grass had purposefully been kept long so the helicopters didn't kick up dust when they landed and took off. The fourth side was open. Wide stone steps led up to a large guesthouse as well as a pathway that ran parallel to the road they were on. A white-jacketed chef carrying a box of brightly coloured vegetables walked down it.

Three helicopters were parked in a triangle formation. They were the same make and model and had the same red, white and blue livery on the tail section. Poe presumed they all belonged to Bierman and his partner. He didn't know a lot about civilian helicopters, but these were only a bit smaller than the Lynxes he'd occasionally flown in during his time with the Black Watch, and they had been able to transport ten fully armed soldiers. Poe reckoned these would comfortably seat six. The rotors on one were turning slowly as the engine cooled.

Someone's just arrived, he thought.

As they approached the main hall a man in a navy-blue jacket and tan trousers stepped out to meet them. He had a forehead like a walnut and looked like the type of man who would brag about being an advanced driver. He waved them into an empty parking space. It was beside a small patio area set up with ornate metal garden furniture. A natural suntrap. Fig trees were trained in fan shapes against the high wall at the back. Butterflies moved from flower to flower. Poe could hear the buzzing of bees but couldn't see any. Did they produce their own honey? It was the type of place that might. Intricate animals had been carved into the stumps of felled trees. Poe saw an owl, and what looked like a squirrel but could have been a stoat.

He got out of the car, stretched and nodded to some people taking tea. They nodded back but said nothing. He wondered who they were.

'My name's Talbot,' the man in the jacket said. 'I'm the summit coordinator. I work for the Foreign and Commonwealth Office and for the next two weeks all hotel operations are under my purview.'

Poe and Melody Lee introduced themselves. Talbot gestured for them to move away from the patio area, all but confirming that the people taking tea were more important than he was.

'May I?' Talbot said, gesturing towards their name badges with a handheld bit of electronic bullshit.

Poe nodded and Talbot scanned the barcode. The machine beeped and Talbot read the screen. He repeated the procedure with Melody Lee.

'Excellent,' he said. 'You're now in a secure bubble. You've been authorised to speak to any staff member and any of the ancillary people brought in to support the summit. Don't worry about going somewhere you shouldn't – someone will stop you.'

'I want to see where Mr Bierman was staying,' Poe said.

'He was in the Old Laundry Room.'

For a moment no one spoke as the familiar whump-whump of a helicopter taking off beat all other noise into submission. Poe watched as it appeared over the roof of Scarness Hall, dipped its nose then sped off. The one with the slowly turning rotors hadn't been cooling down, it had been warming up.

'I'd like to speak to Mr McDaid, Bierman's business partner, as well please,' Poe said. He knew that Nightingale had sent detectives to interview him before they had been told to down tools, and he knew the American hadn't been able to tell them anything helpful. To the best of his knowledge Bierman had never visited prostitutes. He was happily married and had two cute kids. McDaid didn't have the first clue as to why his business partner of fifteen years had been found in a backstreet Carlisle brothel.

No one did.

Christopher Bierman had left Scarness Hall through the designated checkpoint in the evening. He hadn't told anyone where he was going and he was on foot. He hadn't used public transport, he hadn't called a taxi and none of the villagers had seen him walking. He hadn't been seen again until Paulina discovered his battered corpse the following morning.

Poe had asked Nightingale to work on identifying Bierman's movements but he didn't expect to gain anything. Between Scarness Hall and Cranley Gardens there wasn't much CCTV. There wasn't much of anything.

'I'm afraid that won't be possible, sir,' Talbot said. 'Mr McDaid's just left. He's flying to Newcastle Airport to pick up Mr Bierman's wife and children. He's then got an interview with a replacement pilot.'

'Already?'

'The summit's in two weeks, sir, and Bierman & McDaid are contracted to provide the executive transport. It's too late to vet another company now. If he pulls out he'll face stiff penalties.'

'Where are Mr Bierman's wife and children staying?'

'I don't know, sir, but it won't be inside the perimeter. They haven't been vetted.'

Poe suspected Talbot didn't give a shit where they were staying. He suspected he didn't give a shit about anything that happened outside the perimeter, not even when it involved grieving widows and fatherless children.

'Do you have access to the vetting files, Mr Talbot?' Poe said.

'I do.'

'I need you to send them to my colleague.' Poe scribbled Bradshaw's secure email address into his notebook, tore off the page then handed it to Talbot. He slipped it in his top pocket.

'I'll get that done today, sir. Now, if that's all, I'll find someone to take you to the Old Laundry Room.'

'Thank you.'

'I'll lend you Lewis. He's been here a while and gets on with everyone. Picks up more gratuities than anyone else and I doubt he's skimmed a penny.'

He turned and waved. A man in his forties bounded over. He had shoulders like a piano remover and the face of a rugby player. Everyone but Bradshaw – who used so much sunblock she may as well wear a wetsuit and a diver's helmet – had been affected by the extended heatwave, and most were permanently in the red, dry and peeling phase. Not Lewis. He was nut-brown. Clearly a man who worked outside and in the sun. He had friendly blue eyes that shone when he smiled.

'This is Lewis Barnes,' Talbot said. 'He's the porter at Scarness Hall. He'll take you across. He can also show you around the rest of the hall and introduce you to any staff member you might want to talk to.'

'You're the man in the know, are you, Lewis?' Poe said. Porters, drivers and pot washers were founts of knowledge in places such as this. Because of their perceived lowly status people talked in front of them as if they weren't there.

'I'm your man, sir!' Barnes said, his face split by a goofy grin. His eyes drifted over to Poe's car. 'Nice car, sir! BMW X1. Turbocharged, two-litre diesel xDrive. Eight-speed automatic. Has a longer wheelbase than the first-generation models.'

'It does?' Cars were tools to Poe, nothing else. When they were working he didn't notice them, when they weren't he got rid of them.

'Yes, sir.'

'Lewis knows a lot about cars,' Talbot said. 'Don't you, Lewis?'

Barnes nodded enthusiastically.

'You can take it for a spin later if Mr Talbot agrees.'

'Can I?' he said excitedly. 'Just round the grounds?'

'Lewis has a notifiable medical condition,' Talbot said. 'He's not allowed to drive on the roads.'

Barnes frowned in concentration as his lips struggled to form the words. 'I have special educational needs, sir.'

Poe paused, but not for long. 'Not from where I'm standing.'

Barnes smiled happily.

'Can you take me to where Christopher Bierman was staying, Lewis?'

'This way, sir.'

And then Poe's phone rang.

Chapter 20

Poe stepped away from Talbot, Lewis Barnes and Melody Lee to answer his mobile. He thought he knew who was on the other end of the unlisted number.

'Ah, Poe,' Alastor Locke said.

'Mr Locke. What can I do for you?'

'You can tell me where my agent is for a start.'

Poe said nothing.

'Poe . . .'

'You know exactly where she is, Mr Locke.'

'I do. I'm not sure why you took it upon yourself to arrest a member of the Security Service, though. That bit remains hidden, even from me.'

Poe doubted that. Alastor Locke was like a great detective – he would never ask a question to which he didn't already know the answer.

'Meet me at Durranhill at four o'clock,' Poe said. 'If you're one minute late I'm charging her with perverting the course of justice.'

The Old Laundry Room was fifty yards from the main hall. According to Barnes, it had been renovated recently. He wasn't sure of the date but it had been while he was working there.

'And how long have you worked here, Lewis?' Melody Lee said.

Poe frowned. She wasn't supposed to ask questions, not even

inconsequential ones. He liked Melody Lee but letting her ask small questions opened the door to bigger ones. Poe wasn't being a protectionist – a slimy defence barrister would make a big deal out of British witnesses being questioned by unauthorised foreign agents.

'I think it's three years,' Barnes said. 'When it's my birthday Cookie bakes me a cake. The first time it was chocolate, the second time it was chocolate and fudge but last year it was a fruitcake. I remember because it had sultanas in and I don't like sultanas.'

'Yeah, sultanas suck,' Poe said. 'Three cakes, three years then?' It was as good a way as any to remember the passing of time.

'Yes, sir. Three cakes long I've been here.'

'And do you live on site, Lewis?'

'No, sir. I used to but then Cookie started working here. He's full-time and I'm part-time. I live in the village now.'

'That's a shame,' Poe said.

'Cookie's a very experienced chef, sir. We're lucky to have him.'

Those sounded like someone else's words, not his. Poe would have dug into that a bit more but they had arrived at the Old Laundry Room.

On the outside it had the same rustic charm as the rest of the estate; on the inside it was like a Barker & Stonehouse showroom. Lewis Barnes had said it was self-contained, usually rented as a self-catered apartment to guests of a wedding or other big event. Like all ancillary buildings at Scarness Hall it was being used as quarters for summit staff.

Bierman's room was medium-sized. A roughly made double bed centred the room. He'd used a wooden-framed chair as a suitcase stand. Poe opened it and rooted through his dirty laundry. Underneath the underwear and crumpled shirts were some glossy corporate brochures. He flicked through one but it was just the paper version of the PDF Tilly had downloaded from the Bierman & McDaid website.

He opened the wardrobe. Hanging inside were olive flight suits with the Bierman & McDaid logo on the right breast, and five dark jackets. Day attire and night attire presumably. Other than the clothes he'd been found in, he didn't seem to have brought anything casual with him. In his bedside cabinet was an iPad.

'No one's been in here?' Poe said.

'Other than a cursory look, no,' Melody Lee said.

'The investigation was stopped before the Cumbrian cops could recover his possessions?'

'That's my understanding.'

Poe walked back outside. 'Lewis,' he said, throwing him his car keys, 'in the boot of my car are some brown-paper evidence bags. You couldn't bring me half a dozen, could you?'

'I'm your man, sir!'

He went back inside and said to Melody Lee, 'Can you do a quick examination of his iPad? See if there's anything obvious we need to know. I'll get Tilly to have a proper look later.'

'Sure.'

Poe threw her some forensic gloves.

'Wear two pairs, please.'

An hour later and Christopher Bierman's possessions were in six evidence bags in the boot of Poe's car. He'd personally examined everything and there was nothing that raised his pulse. He'd get CSI to go through it but he doubted they'd have any more joy than he'd had – the answer to why Bierman had been in a Carlisle brothel wasn't going to be found in his room.

Melody Lee powered down the iPad.

'Anything?' he said.

'If there is, it's well hidden. The only thing he's done recently is email his wife and go on a couple of antique sites.'

'Antiques?'

'I guess you guys have more of that old shit over here.'

'Our IKEA bookcases are older than your antiques,' he agreed. 'Right, let's finish up and get back to Durranhill.'

'Where do you want to go now, sir?' Lewis Barnes said when they stepped outside.

'Who's in charge, Lewis?'

'Mr Talbot, sir.'

'I thought Mr Talbot was part of the summit staff?'

'Yes, sir.'

'So, who's normally in charge?'

'Oh, that'll be the hotel manager, sir. He's called Mr Anderson.'

'Is he here?'

'He was talking to Cookie – am I to fetch him?'

'That's OK, Lewis. We'll go to him – I want a look round the main hall anyway.'

Much to Talbot's annoyance, Barnes led Poe and Melody Lee through the large, ivy-clad front door and into a spacious lounge. It was as grand as Poe had expected, *Downton Abbey* stuff. High ceilings and velvet curtains. Sofas and chaises longues scattered everywhere. Busts of figures from history and ornate lamps on incidental tables. A place to take tea and listen to sheet music, whatever that was. Poe checked his shoes for mud.

Barnes asked them to wait in the lounge area while he disappeared into the bowels of the building to get Mr Anderson.

'Nice place,' Melody Lee said. 'Old. Classy.'

'There are loads of these estates in Cumbria. Living museums most of them. This is actually small compared to some.'

'We ain't got none of this shit back home.'

'I'm Mr Anderson. Can I help you?' a brittle voice said.

A small man had appeared at their side, the carpets muffling his approach. His expression was thin, sour and officious. Definitely a man on his second or third career, and probably not one he was proud of. He was sweating so much his skin had the texture of wet bread.

Poe showed him his ID card. Anderson paled. Melody Lee showed him her FBI ID card and he almost passed out.

'Haven't you got work to do, Lewis?' he said.

'Yes, Mr Anderson.'

Barnes gave Poe and Melody Lee a wide grin and went back outside.

'Nice man,' Poe said.

'He is,' Anderson agreed. 'He's not one of our great thinkers but he always has a smile for the guests and he works harder than anyone here.'

'What does he do?'

'Pretty much helps out anyone who needs it. He can lift heavy things and he doesn't mind doing repetitive tasks. Loves working in the garden, as you can see by his tan. Does a lot of caddying for the guests.'

'He's a golfer?' Poe said, surprised. He'd have pegged Lewis as a rugby league player if anything.

'No, he doesn't play.'

Barnes went up in Poe's estimation; golf was an absurd game. Any sport that required middle-aged men to wear tailored shorts with knee-length socks needed chucking in the sea as far as he was concerned.

'I thought caddies had to help the player read the greens, club selection, that type of thing?'

Anderson shrugged. 'All I know is that Lewis loves driving and golf buggies are one of the few vehicles he's allowed to get behind the wheel of.'

'If a guest wanted some female company, who would be the best person to arrange it?' Poe said, changing tack suddenly.

'I'm sure I wouldn't know, sir.'

'Who would?'

'I don't know what you've heard but Scarness Hall is not that type of establishment.'

'You're saying a guest would have to go into Carlisle to pay for sex?'

'A guest's business is their business, sir. But I can tell you that no one on my staff facilitates such a thing.'

'What about out-of-area call girls? A guest who checks in alone but goes upstairs with a lady he's just met?'

Anderson wasn't as quick with the bluster this time.

'Occasionally,' he said carefully, 'a guest might have a "niece" visit. But that's very rare and we would never accept a booking from them again. This is a family business and we don't want that sort of person staying in Scarness Hall.'

'Any chance one of your staff is running something you don't know about?'

'Absolutely not.'

'You seem certain.'

'I am. We're a small team and I'd notice if one of them was up to something like that.'

'Anyone new here?'

Anderson shook his head. 'We were discouraged from hiring staff after the host shortlist was announced. If we absolutely have to, there is a rigorous vetting process to go through. Luckily we have a loyal bunch here and staff turnover is very low.'

'Everyone working here now was working here before the shortlist was announced?'

'Yes.'

'And no one's grown facial hair recently?' Melody Lee said. 'Or shaved off a beard?'

Anderson looked confused.

'My colleague is asking if someone could be impersonating a member of staff,' Poe said, shooting her a look.

'Other than the additional staff that Mr Talbot, the summit coordinator, has brought in, there has been no one new here for almost two years. I know them all like my own family and I can assure you: no one is impersonating anyone.'

Which effectively ruled out someone getting a job here to settle a grudge. Another potential line of enquiry ticked off.

'You've heard what happened to Mr Bierman?' Poe said.

'I have. Dreadful business.'

'Any insight?'

'I've already been asked this by someone called Detective Sergeant Rigg. I barely spoke to Mr Bierman. He was out flying most days, collecting guests from Newcastle and Manchester. I think he and Mr McDaid only used the Old Laundry Room to sleep.'

'When they weren't asleep or flying, where were they?'

'In here,' Anderson said, gesturing to the lounge. 'They couldn't drink and they couldn't go far as they were on call. They sometimes ate in the restaurant – ancillaries are allowed to before the summit starts – but mostly they had their meals in the lounge.'

'Did he or Mr McDaid argue with anyone?'

'There's always tension with these executive travel companies. They're dealing with clients who aren't used to waiting, always expect the best and if they think someone else is getting a better service they can get . . . upset.'

'The millionaires are jealous of the billionaires and the billionaires won't talk to the millionaires?'

'That type of thing, yes.'

'Did you see anything like that?'

'I didn't, although I'm not here all the time, obviously.'

'I want a list of staff members and a list of all the guests that were here at the same time as Mr Bierman.' He handed Anderson his business card.

'I'll see to it.'

***

93

'Well, that was a bunch of wasted time,' Melody Lee said as they made their way out of the building. She put on her sunglasses but immediately took them off and looked up.

While they had been inside the clouds had gathered and darkened. It wasn't hot and airless any more; it was now hot and humid. If his old neighbour, Victoria's father, Thomas, had still been alive he'd have said something like, 'There's weather coming' and his farmer pals would all have nodded and said, 'Aye.'

Melody Lee folded her sunglasses and put them in her top pocket. She frowned and said, 'What the hell's he doing?'

Lewis Barnes was on his hands and knees cleaning the alloys on Poe's car.

'What's up, Lewis?' Poe said.

'Just cleaned your windscreen, sir. There was a load of bug splats on it. They'd all dried so your wipers won't be able to clean them off. I've done your wheels as well.'

'Did Mr Talbot tell you to do that?'

'No, sir. I do it for all cars. If I had a car I wouldn't want bugs on the windscreen and you're important people, you probably don't have the time to clean them yourself.'

'That's very kind of you, Lewis.' Poe dug into his wallet and pulled out a twenty-pound note. 'For your trouble.'

'Thank you, sir!'

'And here's my card. It has my telephone number on it. If you think of anything we might be interested in, or see something you think is wrong, I want you to call me. It doesn't matter what time it is. Call me.'

'I will, sir! Thank you, sir.'

As they pulled out of the hall and prepared to go through the same security system, Melody Lee said, 'That was about twenty-five bucks you gave him.'

Poe grunted. 'You want to know what's really happening in a place like this, you don't talk to people like Talbot or Anderson, walking round like their arses have been superglued shut, you talk to people like Lewis. He'll see everything, he'll *hear* everything. That twenty quid was an investment.'

'And you also want your car cleaned again.'

Poe smiled.

'You ever tried scraping dry bugs off a windscreen?' he said. 'They go harder than summer snot.'

Chapter 21

Getting out was almost as bad as getting in, but they were soon heading towards the village of Hallbankgate.

'So, we still don't know if he walked, got in a car or called a cab?' Melody Lee said. 'I'm not sure we gained anything there, Poe.'

'We don't know what we've gained yet. All we're doing right now is building up intel.'

'Fair point.'

'But we don't think he called a cab, and it's a hell of a walk. My bet is he either hitched or was picked up by arrangement.'

'And he didn't tell anyone where he was going?'

'Nope.'

'Not even McDaid?'

'We'll speak to him when he gets back, but apparently not. It seems McDaid's just as confused as everyone else.'

Poe turned on to the A689 and into Hallbankgate. He slowed down to twenty – it was the middle of the day and kids were out playing.

'That Cumbrian cop, Jo someone-or-other, the one you were talking to. Did she have these houses canvassed?' Melody Lee said.

'Yep. And on every other route he might have taken. No one saw Bierman after he signed out.'

Poe eased up to sixty as the village disappeared in his rear-view mirror.

'But did she ask these beatnik assholes?'

She pointed at the group of protestors they had passed on the way in. Their numbers had swelled to about a dozen. The uniformed cop keeping watch was now a sweaty-looking female. Probably a probationer. As the summit approached, making sure this lot didn't become a nuisance would become a more pressing matter, but at the moment the only people passing were support staff and villagers; exactly the type of job a newbie could handle without much oversight.

'Let's go and see, shall we?' Poe said, pulling into the layby opposite.

The cop tensed when they approached but relaxed when they showed their IDs.

'Just wanting a quick word with them, if that's OK?' Poe said.

'Be my guest,' she said. 'You don't mind if I nip off for a quick smoke, do you? I'm getting sick of these twats. Every time I light up they start filming me.'

Poe checked his watch. 'Fifteen minutes?'

'Perfect.'

As she disappeared behind some trees and into the shade, Poe turned to the protestors. There was something fundamentally British about them. For all their puffed-up self-importance, and for all the energy they wasted arguing about whose cause was more worthy, they could be surprisingly effective. Cynics like him might think it was only because the people in charge were eventually worn down by their sheer bloody-mindedness but, whatever it was, one WI woman with a bee in her bonnet about the new bypass had more chance of stopping it than a bunch of weirdoes chaining themselves to trees.

Poe introduced himself and Melody Lee. The group were predictably impressed with her FBI credentials and predictably unimpressed with his. The NCA still didn't have the aura of their US counterparts. He blamed shit TV.

'We're investigating a murder,' he said.

'Around here?' the self-appointed spokesperson said. She was a ruddy-faced woman. Slightly overweight, but judging by the scone in her hand she didn't give a shit. Despite the blazing heat and her tweed jacket, she was barely sweating. 'My name's Irene, by the way.'

'In Carlisle,' Poe said. He'd already authorised Nightingale to make a press statement so they would know soon enough anyway. 'But he was staying at Scarness Hall. We're trying to find out how he got from there to the city.'

'Is he a politician?' she said. 'I'm not saying that's a deal breaker.'

'He was a helicopter pilot. Little more than hired help.'

'Oh, they've got helicopters? Drat, we didn't think of that. Oh well, never mind. How can we help?'

'We're trying to retrace his movements. We know he left Scarness Hall on Tuesday evening but he seems to have disappeared. Were any of you protesting—'

'We're campaigners, not protestors, Sergeant Poe.'

'There's a difference?'

'We want something to happen, protestors want something to stop.'

'My mistake then. Were any of you *campaigning* here on Tuesday? Around eight p.m.?'

'We will have been,' Irene said. 'Our permit says that if it isn't permanently staffed our designated site can be shut down. This close to the summit, we'll never get another one.'

'Who was here?'

'I'd have to see the rota.'

Of course there was a rota, Poe thought. There's always a rota.

'Jeffrey!' Irene yelled. 'Do you have the rota on that iPad thingy of yours?'

A small man broke away from the group that had been

watching them. Unlike Irene, he was sweating. Profusely. His hair was stuck to his forehead and his face was beetroot-red.

'Jeffrey's my husband. He doesn't do well in the heat.'

'Yes, my dear?'

Poe could see a flesh-coloured hearing aid in Jeffrey's ear. He was probably glad he had the option of turning her down.

'Who was here on Tuesday?'

'What time?'

'Say between six and ten p.m.,' Poe said.

'That'll have been Max and Margaret's lot.'

'Oh. Were they filming?' Irene said. She faced Poe. 'Max is doing a mixed media course at the university so he has all the gear. He's going to film during the summit and he's been rehearsing at different times so he gets used to the light.'

'Why is he filming?'

'We want a visual record of everyone who attends the summit. If it doesn't go well some of these men and women will deny they were even here. That's why I was annoyed they have helicopters.'

'I think that's why Scarness Hall was chosen. It has its own landing pad.'

'Fuck-a-doodle-do,' Irene said.

Poe laughed. He loved it when posh people swore.

'Jeffrey will ring Max tonight to see if he was filming. I'll get him to email you what he has.'

Poe jotted down Bradshaw's email address in his notebook and ripped out the page. 'Can you send it here?'

'Consider it done.' She tucked it into her hip pocket and patted it.

The grumpy probationer cop wandered back across. The cigarette hadn't improved her mood.

Poe said, 'You ever thought about just . . .'

'Just what?'

'You know, not bothering.'

Irene smiled. 'Never doubt that a small group of thoughtful, committed citizens can change the world, Sergeant Poe. Indeed—'

'Indeed, it's the only thing that ever has,' Poe said, finishing the Margaret Mead quote.

She smiled again. 'I'll get that video to you as soon as I can.'

Chapter 22

'What next, Poe?'

He glanced at the clock on his dashboard. It was coming up to 1 p.m. and they hadn't yet eaten. He also wanted a crack at Hannah Finch before Alastor Locke arrived.

'Head back to Durranhill, I suppose.'

Melody Lee nodded.

Poe's phone rang through the car's speakers. A picture of Tilly appeared on the central display unit. He pressed the telephone button on the steering wheel.

'Tilly, you're on speakerphone.' He always warned her when she was talking to an audience. To date, it hadn't made a shred of difference.

'Oh, hi, Special Agent Melody Lee.'

'Hi, Tilly.'

'How are you?'

'I'm good.'

'What did you have for breakfast?'

'What the . . .' Melody Lee muttered.

Poe muted Bradshaw for a moment.

'She's trying to improve her small talk. Just go with it. Doesn't last long as she finds it boring.' He unmuted her.

'I had the full English breakfast experience,' Melody Lee said. 'And some spotty asshole tried serving me a local delicacy on the side. Unless I heard wrong, he said it was fried blood clots.'

'It's called black pudding and it's my third-favourite thing to eat,' Poe said. 'Couple of slices sets you up for the day.'

'You eat that shit?'

'Poe buys it by the catering pack, Special Agent Melody Lee,' Bradshaw said.

'Economy of scale,' Poe said. 'What you got, Tilly?'

'I've emailed you Christopher Bierman's profile. It's a bit odd.'

'Odd, how?'

'Bierman & McDaid's company brochure states that Christopher Bierman attended the Royal Military Academy Sandhurst, where, after passing the required aptitude, medical and flying grade tests, his application to become a commissioned helicopter pilot was approved. He became an officer in 1999.'

'Go on.'

'The Sovereign's Parades at the Royal Military Academy Sandhurst are in the public domain so I was able to check the three parades that occurred in 1999.'

RMA Sandhurst was where the British Army trained its officers. The Sovereign's Parade marked each intake's 'passing out'. Poe knew they were high-profile – certainly higher than when he'd passed out of the Black Watch – usually with a member of the royal family inspecting them.

'And?' he said.

'No Christopher Bierman attended a Sovereign's Parade in 1999, Poe.'

'Ah.' He knew she'd have checked but he asked anyway. 'Is it possible the brochure has the wrong dates?'

'No one called Christopher Bierman has *ever* attended Sandhurst.'

Poe thought about what that meant. In the circles in which they did their business, a company founded by an ex-officer would have more kudos than a company founded by someone from the rank and file.

'Perhaps he never actually attended Sandhurst,' he said. 'Non-commissioned officers also fly helicopters in the army. Maybe they pimped up the company's CV?'

'I can't find any public record of him ever having served in the army, Poe.'

'Well, that is odd, Tilly.'

'And no one called Christopher Bierman is registered with the Civil Aviation Authority either.'

'That's even odder.'

'Unless he never bothered to register here,' Melody Lee said. 'While they're serving, military pilots don't need to register with a civilian authority. Maybe he went straight from the army to the States and registered there instead. I think our countries consider it a transferable qualification.'

'Only Tilly says he was never in the army.' He twisted to face Melody Lee. 'These companies have to be vetted thoroughly. You know anything about this?' The special agent would undoubtedly have access to information he didn't.

She shook her head. 'All on-site support is vetted locally.'

'But they're a US company. I know Bierman's British but his company's registered in the States. That's right, isn't it, Tilly?'

'It is, Poe. Bierman & McDaid was registered in Washington, DC.'

'Don't matter; they were hired by the Brits. And, as we're both a Five Eyes country, intelligence, which includes high-level vetting, from one of us is accepted as accurate by the other four anyway.'

Five Eyes was the intelligence collaboration entered into by the UK, US, Canada, Australia and New Zealand. Its original remit, signals intelligence, had grown and it now included anti-terror information sharing. Poe only knew about it because a fictionalised version had been mentioned in the Bond film, *Spectre*. Poe liked Bond films. Liked the escapism.

'What does this mean, Poe?' Bradshaw said.

'It means that me and Alastor Locke have more than just Hannah Finch's fate to discuss.'

'Are you coming back here to see him?'

'We're on the city outskirts now. We'll be back soon.'

He was about to end the call when Bradshaw said, 'I have more.'

'What is it, Tilly?'

'I got bored last night so I ran some data though a predictive mapping program.'

'Okaaay. Why?'

'I wanted to see if I could generate some new insight from the existing data. See if there *is* organised crime in Carlisle. I thought it might help if you knew.'

'It absolutely would help, Tilly.' If someone was running girls, someone would have also known when the pop-up brothel was likely to be empty.

'Which predictive mapping program did you use, Tilly?' Melody Lee said. 'IntuitPol? Hunch.com?'

Bradshaw blew a raspberry.

'As if I'd use something that basic, Special Agent Melody Lee.'

'You used one of your own?'

'I did.'

'Wow. Impressive. Talk me through it.'

'Don't!' Poe yelled.

But it was too late.

For ten minutes Bradshaw told Melody Lee about her program. It was all spatiotemporal analysis modelling and regression, classification and clustering techniques. Poe didn't understand a word of it.

'What data caches did you use, Tilly?' Melody Lee asked.

'You understood that?' Poe said.

'You *didn't* understand that?'

'The usual, Special Agent Melody Lee,' Bradshaw said. 'Crime recording, incident logs, custody records, crime intelligence and PNC records.'

'You use data from non-law enforcement agencies?'

'Adult social care, children's services, NHS and A & E, school disciplinary and attendance records. Plus a few other smaller ones.'

'Seems thorough. I'm surprised you were given access so quickly. You guys obviously aren't as concerned with privacy as we are over there.'

Bradshaw said nothing.

'And what do you reckon, Tilly?' Poe said before she told the FBI which databases she'd been creeping round.

'There *is* an organised crime group operating in the city, Poe. The data is all too random to be random, if you know what I mean.'

'I do not know what you mean,' Poe said, 'but that's OK. If you say there's organised crime in the city again, then there's organised crime in the city again.'

'Thing is, Poe, it's a bit too organised. It's a pattern I haven't seen before. It's multi-layered but none of the levels bleed into each other. I'd go as far to say it isn't so much organised as *disciplined*.'

'That's weird,' he said. Even the best crime gangs became frayed at the edges. The people who sold their drugs, ran their women and did their enforcement were never reliable. They messed up eventually. It was how the police took them down. Start at the bottom and offer incentives so they could work their way up to the upper echelons. Tried and tested. He could do without an anomaly right now.

'And that's not all, Poe,' Bradshaw said. 'The city's drug pattern has changed. Arrests for possession-with-intent-to-supply are down. The drugs team's major busts are down. And for over a year there hasn't been a single arrest for drug supply anywhere near a school.'

'OK, that's even weirder. Unless there's no longer a reliable source of drugs.'

'That's not it, Poe,' Bradshaw said. 'The number of people being arrested for simple possession remains constant, as does the type of acquisitive crime associated with drug addiction. A & E admissions for overdoses haven't changed over the last year either. Drug consumption hasn't changed, Poe, just the way they're being distributed.'

Drug dealers with discipline and principles. That didn't make sense. He checked the clock on his dashboard again. Looked up at the ever-darkening sky. They had three hours before Alastor Locke was due and he suspected the weather would break before then. Poe had planned to sweat Hannah Finch for a while – more to annoy her rather than any real expectation that he'd get his stolen evidence back.

'Change of plan, Tilly,' he said. 'I'm popping into town for a while. If Alastor Locke arrives before I get back, stall him, can you?'

'How?'

'Tell him about your predictive mapping program. That should buy us a week.'

'Ha-de-ha-ha, Poe.'

'Tell him I have a doctor's appointment then.'

'OK,' she said. 'I'll say you have a spastic colon.'

He glanced across at Melody Lee. Her shoulders were shaking with silent laughter. And Poe knew that if he protested, Bradshaw would only come up with something worse. It was how she discouraged him from asking her to lie.

'Fine,' he said. 'It sounds awful but tell him that.'

He ended the call.

'Outstanding,' Melody Lee said. 'Where we going anyway?'

'Into the city,' Poe said. 'We need to find a lunatic called Bugger Rumble.'

106

Chapter 23

Bugger Rumble, low-grade mutterer, occasional barker, had been 'intentionally homeless' – the legal term the council used to absolve themselves of all responsibility – for as long as Poe had known him. He had no idea where Bugger had come from. One day he landed in Carlisle and he'd never left.

He was a street entertainer, but only if you used the very loosest of definitions. He basically did stupid things then stared at people until they gave him money to stop. As soon as he had enough, he dived into the nearest pub and drank it. It was then wash, rinse and repeat until closing time or until he was too drunk to get served. He was as mad as a soup sandwich.

He was also the most reliable snout Poe had ever had.

Like bellboys and porters at hotels, Bugger Rumble went where he chose without anyone paying him the slightest bit of attention. People either pointed at him or ignored him, never suspecting that beneath the grime and skin diseases there was a sporadically bright and engaged mind. When he'd been a Cumbrian cop, Poe had bunged him the occasional tenner – Bugger Rumble could drift in and out of the criminal fraternity at will. Sometimes he'd help; sometimes he'd piss on your shoes and run off cackling.

Poe parked on Fisher Street. Bugger's preference was to work in front of the Town Hall and drink his profits in the Kings Head. It was as good a place as any to start looking for a man who essentially trolled the public.

Or it would have been a good place to look if the gathering clouds hadn't decided it was the right time to make good on their threats.

There was no warning. The day moved from overcast to a wall of water in a matter of seconds. The rain was monsoon-like in its ferocity.

Poe and Melody Lee dived back into the car and watched everyone else try to find shelter. The Kings Head and Cranstons the butcher suddenly became very popular. People crowded under the awnings of any shop that had one. Water ran down the cobbled street in fast-moving rivulets, carrying a month's worth of dust with it.

'Close one,' Poe shouted. The rain was hitting the BMW's roof so hard it was like being inside a snare drum.

For five minutes they sat and watched the extraordinary amount of water falling from the sky. It was breathtaking. Really quite magnificent. He said as much to Melody Lee.

'It's like a cow pissing on a flat rock,' she said.

The rain stopped as suddenly as it had started, as if someone had closed off a valve.

They made their way past the Kings Head and on to the pedestrianised Greenmarket area of the city. Farmers' markets and the occasional funfair were held there, but today it was empty. Even the lunch-going crowd was thinner than normal. Still inside drying off, Poe suspected. He studied the paved area in front of the Town Hall, grunting in satisfaction when he saw what he was looking for.

'He's here.'

'How do you know?'

He pointed at a washed-out line of chalk on the ground. 'That's how he earns his money,' he said. 'But he won't be back until the pavement's dry. We may as well go and get something to eat.'

Cakes & Ale was a coffee shop on Castle Street, the street parallel to where they were parked. It was attached to Bookcase, Carlisle's only independent bookshop, a building with almost forty different rooms to get lost in. Apart from his local butcher's, it was Poe's favourite shop in Cumbria. The café sold homemade cakes and served their tea in china cups.

It also had a record player and a load of old vinyl LPs that customers could put on. Poe had been there last year when someone had brought in a copy of *Inflammable Material* by Stiff Little Fingers. He'd stayed while the old punk had played both sides, lost in the music of his youth. Today, someone had a jazz record on, all trumpets and saxophones and improvisation. Poe liked jazz, but not as much as he liked punk.

The café had its own doorway but they entered via the bookshop, as Poe needed to buy something. After he'd made his purchase they worked their way through a succession of different rooms until they found the café.

Poe ordered the sandwich of the day; Melody Lee got a salad. They both asked for coffee.

'This is nice,' Melody Lee said.

'It's not all Costas yet. There are lots of independent coffee houses popping up.'

When their food came Poe took a bite of his sandwich, then said, 'What's really going on, Special Agent Lee? You think Bierman's murder is related to the summit?'

She stabbed a cherry tomato with her fork, popped it in her mouth and chewed thoughtfully.

'My gut says no,' she said eventually. 'Christopher Bierman was a glorified chauffeur, there to ferry the smallwigs around. The bigwigs have their own transport. It's hard to see how he could have had any usable intel on anyone worth making a violent statement against.'

Poe nodded and took another bite. Decided he agreed with her. There was something strange about Bierman's murder, but he didn't think it was summit-related.

'Saying that,' Melody Lee said, reading from her phone, 'I've just been told that we have five days. If a satisfactory explanation isn't forthcoming by then, the Secret Service are cancelling my guy's visit.'

'And the summit will be cancelled?'

'Not necessarily. Other countries aren't so risk averse.'

'But it'll be less effective?'

'Undoubtedly. The US has deep pockets.'

'Eat up then,' he said. 'It's time I introduced you to the world's only low-rise tightrope walker.'

Chapter 24

'Well, this is different,' Melody Lee said.

'Just a tad,' Poe agreed.

'Dude needs dewormed.'

Bugger Rumble looked like Worzel Gummidge's scruffier cousin. He was wearing a top hat and tails. The jacket and trousers were stained, shiny with grease and frayed at the knees and elbows. The hair that peeked out from under his hat reminded Poe of straw bursting from a slashed mattress. His beard looked as though it had been brushed with a toffee apple.

They had arrived as he was about to start his 'act'. He'd redrawn his chalk line and was standing at one end. A small crowd had gathered. He looked nervous. With outstretched arms, he took a tentative step on to the line and almost lost his balance. He bent backwards and forwards, side to side, before he recovered. He breathed out in mock relief.

A man in the crowd muttered, 'Wanker.'

Bugger Rumble ignored him and focused on the next few steps. He managed another ten or twelve before he started teetering again, met with the same attempts at regaining his balance, this time padded out with some windmilling arms.

When he got to the end he removed his hat, bowed and shouted, 'Ta-dah!'

'Wanker,' the man said again.

The tinkle of coins hitting the pavement was not deafening.

Nonetheless, Bugger Rumble got on his hands and knees and gathered them up. Poe doubted there was enough for a pint.

'It's quite possible I'll never forget this,' Melody Lee said, as people began drifting off.

'It's the crowd's reaction I love,' Poe said. 'They don't know whether they've witnessed urban street art or just had the piss taken out of them.'

Poe wandered over and waited for Bugger Rumble to look up.

'Hello, Bugger,' he said.

Bugger Rumble squinted in the sun. A flash of recognition was quickly replaced by a scowl. 'That you, DC Poe?' He had the scratchy voice of a heavy smoker. 'I haven't seen you in years. Someone told Bugger Rumble you lived in Southampton now.'

'Been back a couple of years, Bugger.'

'You still wearing the blue? 'Cos I don't do that any more.'

'Do what?'

'Give up the scuttlebutt.'

'Relax,' Poe said. 'I'm not with Cumbria.'

'Who's the coloured lassie?'

'And exactly what colour am I?' Melody Lee said.

Bugger leaned forwards and studied her. 'Kobicha,' he cackled.

'This is Melody Lee. She's a friend of mine, Bugger.'

He eyed her with suspicion. 'She's not Polish, is she?'

'No, I'm from Louisiana.'

'What you got against the Poles?' Poe said. When you spoke to Bugger Rumble you had to be prepared to have five or six mini conversations.

'They're bastards,' he growled. 'Coming over here with their fancy sand sculptures. Taking food out of the mouths of honest people like Bugger Rumble they are.'

Poe grinned. He'd seen the sand sculptors. They worked higher up the pedestrianised area. Started with a lump of wet sand and by mid-morning had fashioned a sleeping Labrador out of it. He wasn't surprised Bugger felt threatened. They had genuine skill, Bugger basically arsed about.

'What you harassing Bugger Rumble for anyway? I have a permit from the council.'

'No, you don't, Bugger,' Poe said.

'I've applied for one.'

'No, you haven't.'

Bugger Rumble scowled again.

Poe handed him a small book. 'I found this in Bookcase earlier. Thought you might like it.'

Bugger studied it. '*The Poetical Works of John Milton*,' he said, running his finger down the spine. He opened it and read the copyright page. 'Miniature edition. Printed in 1904. Good condition. I'll bet old Steve made you haggle for this beauty.'

Poe shrugged.

'Did you know there's an 1852 edition somewhere that's bound in human skin?' Bugger continued. 'A rat catcher called George Cudmore went to the gallows for poisoning his wife. Ended up as a book cover. Those were the days, eh Mr Poe?'

Bugger Rumble's knowledge of poetry was encyclopaedic. No one knew why. Poe suspected there was a classical education and a sad story in his past. But the fifty quid he'd spent on the book had served its purpose. Bugger was suitably distracted.

'Buy you a pint?' Poe said.

The Kings Head was the nearest pub. Poe ordered himself and Bugger a pint of Spun Gold. The landlord served them without comment. For all his eccentricities, Bugger always behaved when he was in a pub.

'What you drinking?' Poe said to Melody Lee.

She checked her watch.

'It's two in the afternoon.'

'So?'

'Jack and Coke then.'

They took their drinks to the back and found a corner table. Poe believed Bugger when he said he no longer snitched, but it made sense to stay away from the window anyway.

'Bugger Rumble's not a stupid man, Mr Poe. He knows you don't just *happen* upon a Milton book and then *happen* upon the only man in Carlisle who can appreciate it. You may not be with Cumbria any more but you're with someone.'

Poe nodded. Bugger's mind was as razor sharp as ever.

'I'm with a national unit, Bugger. My friend's a special agent with the FBI. I want to know who's running things in Carlisle now' – Poe checked his phone – 'that Nathaniel Diamond's no longer in the picture.'

Bugger drained a third of his pint and wiped his beard. He looked cagey. 'Buy me another?'

'Afterwards.'

'Nasty lad, that Diamond fella. Glad to see the back of him. You know he used to tax us? Said that these were his streets and we had to pay for the privilege of using them.'

'Who replaced him?' Poe urged.

Bugger shrugged. 'Don't know.'

'Don't know or won't say?'

'Don't know. No one does. Or if they do, they're keeping it to themselves.'

'That bad?'

'Just low profile.'

Poe supposed it was progress. Bugger Rumble had at least confirmed what Bradshaw had told them. There *was* organised crime in the city again.

'Anyway, I'm sick of you now. Interrupting old Bugger's afternoon. You should go and find somewhere else to drink. Buy me a pint then piss off – I want to read *Paradise Lost*.'

Melody Lee's nostrils flared. Poe shook his head slightly. In all the time he'd known Bugger he'd not easily given up his information. It always came in hints and suggestions, nudges and nurdles.

'And where do you suggest we go next?'

Bugger Rumble finished his pint. He sucked noisily at the foam clinging to the side of the glass. When it was as beer-free as it was going to get he put it back on the table.

'If you're feeling brave, you might want to go and have a drink in the Dog.'

Which was the worst thing Bugger Rumble could have said.

Chapter 25

The Dog.

If Botchergate was the cultural drip tray of Carlisle, the Dog was the thing that floated in it. The thing that no one wanted to touch. It was the grubbiest pub in the grubbiest part of the city. It was a rare month when it didn't have at least three windows boarded up.

People drank in the Dog because they weren't allowed to drink anywhere else, and no one who was allowed to drink anywhere else drank in the Dog. It was a self-contained bubble of shit.

Poe wasn't sure if he was up to going inside. The last time he had, it had got a bit . . . lively, and he was too old to be rolling on the floor trying to arrest someone off their tits on wobbly eggs.

Outside, a discarded chip leached oil into the pristine rain-water in the gutter. It was large, one of those unpeeled hipster chips that came in a small tin bucket. Served with organic rock salt and a side order of pretentiousness. They hadn't even bothered cutting out the eyes on the skin. Just left them on, all black and warty and inedible.

As unpleasant as the eyes looked, at least the chip had two of them. Which was twice as many as the one-eyed idiot standing in front of Poe.

Every copper knew him. Everyone in Carlisle knew him. He was as strong as a bear and had a head like a badly shaved testicle. He was called Steeleye Stan and he was the closest thing Cumbria had to a professional thug.

A violent child and a more violent teen, by the time he'd reached adulthood he had spent more time in secure institutions than he'd spent outside. When he was eighteen, he'd formed a consortium of like-minded knuckleheads and together they had cornered the doors of Carlisle's pubs and clubs, and, as whoever controlled the doors controlled the drug dealers, he'd done quite well.

Until one night when he'd turned up at A & E with a shard of glass in his eye. The on-call surgeon hadn't bothered trying to save it – he'd cut out what was left and sent him to recovery. Two days later he was discharged from the Cumberland Infirmary with painkillers, some anti-bugs and a prosthetic eye.

He was back on the doors that night.

And he was angry.

If it were possible, Stan got into more fights than he had previously. He lost so many prosthetic eyes during this new period of savagery that he took to jamming a steel ball bearing into his empty socket. It made him look so menacing that the pubs stopped using him – if Steeleye was on the door, the pub didn't make money – and he drifted into what had been his destiny ever since he'd stabbed his primary-school teacher with a compass: hired muscle.

Poe was unimpressed. 'Stand aside, Stan,' he said.

'Can't come in. Private club,' Steeleye said.

The bottom half of his jaw didn't line up with the top half, and when he spoke it clicked. It looked like he was rolling seeds between his teeth. Poe reckoned he'd taken a bad punch recently.

He was tempted to call it a day. Alastor Locke was going to be at Durranhill soon and he could come back later with some uniformed cops. Preferably ones that looked like PC Wilkes.

'You need backup?' Melody Lee said.

Which was as good as a dare to Poe.

'If you don't step aside, Stan, I'm punching you right in the balls,' he said.

'Private members' club,' Steeleye said again.

Poe frowned. Provocation like that would have ordinarily turned Steeleye into the modern-day equivalent of a berserker. He'd never seen him this restrained. Something was staying his hand.

'Piss off, Stan, the Dog's a fucking toilet,' Poe said.

Steeleye leaned forward. 'Watch my lips, dickhead. This is a private members' club, and you aren't a member.'

He jabbed a meaty finger into Poe's chest. The force made him stagger back two steps.

Melody Lee moved faster than he'd have thought possible. One minute she was hovering behind him, the next she was beside Steeleye, her hand jammed into his armpit. She was holding something Poe couldn't see.

Whatever it was, Steeleye Stan didn't like it. He disliked it so much he was on his tiptoes, trying to levitate. He let out a high-pitched mewl. His eye began watering.

A patrol car screeched to a halt beside them, no doubt alerted by the CCTV operators who kept the Dog under constant surveillance. Two cops jumped out, batons at the ready. Looked eager for a punch-up.

'You OK, Sergeant Poe?' one of them said.

'We're good. I'll need you to arrest this moron and take him back to Durranhill, though.'

'Fine with us. On what charge?'

'I'd say making Special Agent Lee put her hand in his sweaty pits is enough but assaulting a police officer will do.'

'I'm going to take you to your knees, big guy,' Melody Lee said. 'You come down with me, OK? Nice and easy.'

She kept one hand jammed in Steeleye's armpit, the other on his shoulder, as she controlled his descent. He was soon in handcuffs and in the back of the patrol car. Melody Lee slipped what she'd been holding into her inside pocket.

'Let him cool off until tomorrow,' Poe said to the cops. 'If he says he's sorry in the morning, let him go.'

After Steeleye had been taken away, Melody Lee said, 'I dated a linebacker like that in high school.'

'What the hell was that thing you used?'

'A pen,' she said.

'A pen?'

'A Smith & Wesson Military and Police Tactical Pen to be precise.'

She handed it across to Poe. It was sleek, black and made of steel. The writing end came to a vicious point.

'These are legal?'

'It's a pen,' she said.

'It's a weapon.'

'Anything's a weapon if you're prepared to improvise.'

Poe grunted his agreement. During the recent Curator case he'd been forced to fashion a cosh out of a sock and a large stone.

'Yeah, but this thing really is a weapon.'

She shrugged. 'Secret Service may get to keep their firearms over here but we sure as hell don't. Anyway, it's yours if you want it – the manufacturers send us a bunch of these things to try out.'

Poe was about to refuse. Other than his time in the Black Watch he'd never carried a weapon. He didn't want to start now. But . . . it was just a pen.

'Thanks, I will. Walk tall and carry a pointy metal pen, I always say.' He clipped it to his inside pocket. 'Anyway, that was the easy part. You ready?'

'Sure.'

Poe opened the door and stepped inside.

And immediately knew something was wrong.

Chapter 26

The last time Poe was in the Dog it had been full of meth drinkers and 'don't-catch-my-eye' headcases. The décor – worn carpets, peeling wallpaper and cheap lager served in dirty glasses – had all the charm of a 1980s social club. The TV screen had been permanently tuned in to an illegal football channel.

This time it looked different. It was clean. The carpet had been vacuumed. The stench of sweat, piss, shit and vomit didn't materialise. The air was fresh. No one was smoking cannabis and the carpet by the entrance wasn't sticky.

The glasses were sparkling, the bar polished. The ice buckets held ice instead of cigarette ends. There was a touchscreen till to take orders. The fridges were stocked with craft beers and imported lagers. The tatty, mismatched furniture had been replaced by comfortable leather seats and solid wooden tables. And, unlike last time, there were no obvious crimes being committed.

Instead of the inbred mutants who normally drank in the Dog, lean and muscled men sat in groups. They were drinking tea and quietly chatting. They had short hair and were wearing jeans and regimental T-shirts. Their tattoos were all 'Death From Above', 'These Colours Don't Run' and 'Death Before Dishonour'. Poe could see men with Royal Marines Commando dagger tattoos chatting to men with Parachute Regiment wings inked on their shoulders.

Poe knew a squaddie bar when he was in one.

They usually sprang up in garrison towns. Nothing official,

it was just where squaddies started to hang out when they were off duty. And eventually the locals stopped going. The landlord didn't care – squaddie bars made a lot of money and the clientele policed themselves.

The last time he'd been in the Dog, he was meeting an ex-paratrooper called Jefferson Black – and whether he liked it or not, by putting his girlfriend's killer behind bars, Poe had changed Black's life. Now the pub was full of ex-paras and ex-marines and a whole bunch of ex-infantry soldiers, if he were any judge of things.

Bradshaw had said there was *disciplined* organised crime in Carlisle.

Poe didn't believe in coincidences.

The noise level dropped when they entered but that always happened in the Dog. If you weren't a regular you were probably a cop. They made their way to the bar, more to get their bearings than anything else.

'You want a drink?' Poe asked Melody Lee.

'Soft drink, I guess.'

He ordered two Cokes and surveyed the bar in the mirror. The squaddies were watching them, the same way lions might watch a couple of gazelles that had wandered into the middle of their pride. Curious, but not wary. There was no hostility.

'That'll be three quid, mate,' the barman said, putting two frosty glasses on the beermat in front of them. Poe reached for his wallet.

And then someone walked into the Dog, someone Poe had never expected to see again.

As one, the squaddies stood.

'These are on the house, Wayne,' Jefferson Black said.

Black had obviously decided to live. And he'd also decided that he and his friends were ideally placed to take over the vacuum

121

left by Nathaniel Diamond's disappearance. Bradshaw had said the crime in Carlisle was disciplined, and that's because it was. Elite soldiers, well trained and at the peak of physical fitness. Used to obeying orders and squaring up to the enemy. If someone could harness that firepower, that person would be formidable.

'You're looking well, Jefferson,' Poe said.

Black tilted his head and appraised him. 'What can I do for you, Sergeant Poe?'

'Somewhere we can talk?'

'Over here. We won't be disturbed.'

Black led them to an empty table. The men near it moved to give them space. Someone brought over a teapot and three mugs. Black filled them with dark, stewed tea. Poe noticed all three mugs had the Parachute Regiment's wings insignia on the side.

'Now, how about you tell me why you've assaulted my doorman and forced your way into my social club?'

'Social club?'

'Yes, social club.'

'Fine,' Poe said. This wasn't his argument. 'And I suspect you already know why we're here, Jefferson.'

Black took a drink from his mug.

'This is about Cranley Gardens, isn't it?'

Chapter 27

'I owe you a favour, Sergeant Poe,' Jefferson Black said, 'but I'm no Whitey Bulger.'

'Who?'

'Irish mob boss in Massachusetts,' Melody Lee said. 'He was an FBI informant. Died a couple of years ago.'

'I'm not looking for a snitch, Jefferson,' Poe said, 'but if I don't find out what you know, I'm going to assume that your social club is involved.' He wrapped 'social club' with a pair of air quotes. 'I don't give a shit what you've got going on here – it's a local matter, but, given that the National Crime Agency, the FBI and another agency you really don't want in your life are all involved, it's very much in your interest to make me go away as quickly as possible.'

Black studied his face. 'The music's about to stop and I don't have a chair yet. Is that what you're saying, Sergeant Poe?'

'Something like that.' He sighed. 'Look, I don't expect you to drop a mate in the shit, but the killer used that house because he knew it was empty. We need to know how.'

'Off the record?'

'Do you see a pen?'

Black said nothing.

'If you're not involved then, yes, it's off the record,' Poe said.

'OK, that property does belong to my . . . club. Every now and then, in between rentals, we use it as a massage parlour.'

'Go on.'

'One of my associates was approached by a man who said he needed the property for a one-off event. Entertainment for an important client.'

'And this man wasn't one of yours?'

Black shook his head.

'And your associate believed him?'

'He did. Said he didn't recognise him but he spoke like one of us. He assumed he was new and they hadn't yet been introduced. There are a few of us now.'

Poe thought about what Black had just said.

'What do you mean, "he spoke like one of us"? You mean like a para?'

'Possibly a hat,' Black said. 'Definitely infantry.'

'A hat?' Melody Lee said.

'Crap hat,' Poe said. 'It's what the Parachute Regiment calls anyone who doesn't wear a maroon beret.'

'So . . . they're kind of assholes?'

Poe smiled. Black didn't.

'What made him think he was infantry?' Poe said.

'He got my associate to approach by putting his hand flat on his head.'

'What the hell's that mean?' Melody Lee said.

Poe explained. 'It's the infantry field signal for close in on me.'

Black nodded. 'As good as an ID card.'

'So this man was either ex-forces or he'd been on the internet.'

'Don't be facetious, Sergeant Poe. You can't pretend to be ex-army and expect to get away with it. Not to other ex-army anyway. You'll be spotted straight away. You know that.'

He did. Being in the military gave you an attitude, a certain bearing that never left you. Poe could spot an ex-squaddie across a crowded room.

'So he did or said something else that convinced him?'

Black nodded. 'He asked my man how his bum was for spots.'

'That'd do it,' Poe admitted. 'How's your bum for spots?' was a uniquely British squaddie way of asking after someone's health. He had no idea where it came from or who started it. It was just something they all said.

'OK, so this man, who for now we'll agree is ex-military, told your associate he needed Cranley Gardens. And that was it? No ringing in with the boss to check it was OK?'

'He knew some of our . . . procedures,' Black said. 'My associate had no reason to disbelieve him.'

'Procedures?'

Black said nothing.

Poe filled the silence. 'If I were running some disciplined men I might be tempted to have a daily password. Maybe not refer to anything directly. Use words like "associates" and "social club".'

'And "massage parlours",' Melody Lee added.

'Exactly.'

Black nodded. 'And this man still passed for a member of our club. What's that tell you, Sergeant Poe?'

'That he *was* one of you?'

'But I can assure you he wasn't. We have made . . . enquiries and we are certain.'

This time it was Poe's turn to say nothing.

Black prompted him. 'What is time spent on never wasted?'

'Reconnaissance,' Poe said automatically. 'You think, whoever this man is, he'd watched you for long enough he could pass for one of you?'

Black nodded. 'Scary, isn't it?'

'Then what?' Poe said.

'Excuse me?'

'I'm assuming at some point the woman who cleans your properties called in to say she'd found a body?' Poe checked his notebook. 'A Mrs Paulina Tuchlin.'

'She rang for advice, yes.'

'And?'

'My associate phoned for instructions and, after we'd got the facts together, I told her she should touch nothing and call 999 immediately.'

'That's all? You didn't fancy a drive up to have a look?'

'It wasn't one of my girls and it wasn't one of my men. Other than happening to own the property, my social club wasn't involved. Why wouldn't we call the police?'

Poe finished both his tea and his Coke. Wiped his lips and stood up. Melody Lee did the same.

He passed Black his card. 'We'll need to speak to your associate, the one this man approached.'

'I'll see to it,' Black said. 'It won't help you. The person you're looking for was wearing a hat and wraparound shades.'

'The kind mountaineers wear?' Poe said. 'The ones that cover half your face?'

Black nodded.

'I'll need to speak to him anyway.'

'Like I said, I'll see to it.'

Poe started to leave but stopped. He turned back.

'What are you doing, Jefferson? You were a chef, one of the best in the country.'

'Just trying to bring order to chaos, Sergeant Poe. Some like-minded friends are helping me.'

'Be careful, Jefferson. Please don't do anything that brings you to my attention.'

'Not our style,' Black said. 'Anyway, I've told you: we're a social club, why would that be brought to your attention?'

Chapter 28

'If you were sensible, Poe—'

'I'm not. Ask anyone.'

'*If* you were sensible, Poe,' Alastor Locke repeated, 'you would let Hannah go and put this favour in your back pocket.'

Poe was back at Durranhill. He and Locke had started their dance. As soon as he'd arrived, Poe had taken him into an interview room. Predictably, Locke had asked him to release Finch without charge. 'Put it down to an administrative error, old chap,' he'd said, which showed he didn't know Poe at all.

'Let me tell you what's going to happen, Alastor,' Poe said. 'In about four hours I will be charging Miss Finch with perverting the course of justice, and, as she's been unwilling to provide an address, we will have no choice but to remand her in custody.'

'You wouldn't dare.'

'I won't have a choice, Alastor. I'm not dropping this and pre-charge custody limits are pretty clear. Hannah has rights, although she might be wishing she didn't. I can only hold her for twenty-four hours.'

'I could have you replaced,' Locke said. 'Find someone less discommodious.'

'You could, but you won't.'

'And why not?'

'Because I have a photograph of her in handcuffs and you know I won't have a problem with sharing it.'

Locke picked an imaginary piece of lint from his lapel. 'Have you heard of the phrase, "*Quis custodiet ipsos custodes*", Poe?'

'I have.'

It meant 'Who guards the guards?'

'And you do not think it applies here? That you might be over-stepping your bailiwick?'

Poe folded his arms and said nothing.

'You really are the rock of Prometheus, Poe,' Locke said. 'All right, what do you want?'

'I want the evidence she took.'

'She doesn't report to me.'

'You're an important man, Alastor; I'm sure you have influence.'

'You flatter me, Poe.'

'I did? Then I must have said it wrong.'

'And if this evidence no longer exists?'

'Then there's nothing you or I can do.'

'May I see her?'

'Take as long as you want, but' – Poe checked his watch – 'in three hours fifty-three minutes I'm charging her.'

'That's not helpful, Poe.'

'I'm not trying to be.'

'Be reasonable,' Locke said. 'I've only just found out about this. Four hours is nowhere near long enough for me to do what you ask.'

Poe was silent.

'I understand you have the option of asking for an additional twelve hours before you have to make a charging decision?'

'The duty superintendent can authorise an extension to her custody,' Poe confirmed.

'I think we may be able to come to some sort of understanding by then.'

Poe was torn. With twelve additional hours Locke might be able to get his missing evidence, but it was also enough time to go above his head and get Finch released without charge. He made the pragmatic decision. Charging her had never been the goal and it gained him nothing. Poe was only interested in the leverage.

'I'll get you the extra twelve hours,' he said. 'That's sixteen in total. But I want that evidence.'

Locke stood. 'I'll see her now. A chat without coffee seems to be in order.'

'Sit down, Alastor. There's something else I need.'

'What is it now, Poe?'

'Why can't Tilly find any record of Christopher Bierman at Sandhurst? And why isn't he on the Civil Aviation Authority's database?'

Locke sighed. 'That didn't take you long.'

'What didn't?'

'Tilly's quite correct, Poe. No Christopher Bierman has ever passed out of Sandhurst, nor will he be on the Aviation Authority's database. But Christopher Bierman passed the vetting with flying colours nonetheless. What does that tell you?'

'That he used to go by a different name.'

'Exactly.'

'Which was?'

'Jack Duncan.'

Poe shrugged. The name meant nothing to him.

'You might not know that name but you'll recognise the nick-name the press gave him.'

'I will?'

'It's Captain Jack, Poe.'

And everything became that little bit clearer.

Chapter 29

Poe knew about Captain Jack. Not a huge amount, just what had been on the front pages. Uplifting tales of heroism are newsworthy at the best of times but, when they're followed so closely by tragedy, they become the type of stories that dominate the tabloids and the broadsheets.

Captain Jack was a helicopter pilot, missing in action, believed *killed* in action. He'd been shot down during Operation Herrick, the name for all British operations in Afghanistan, by a shoulder-launched surface-to-air missile. He had crashed in an inhospitable, barely accessible valley. His navigator's mangled corpse had been recovered near the crash site. The prevailing theory was that Captain Jack had been thrown clear and eaten by scavengers, or dragged off by the same men who had shot down his helicopter.

Two months later, an FV432 armoured personnel carrier transporting call sign Tango Two-Four, an infantry section from the 1st Battalion, King's Royal Rifles, stumbled upon an isolated pocket of al-Qaeda. After a brief one-sided firefight – one that would later earn them all the Military Cross – the British troops cleared the compound and found Captain Jack chained to a bedstead. He was suffering from appalling injuries and, due to witnessing barbaric executions, including beheadings and immolations, had untold psychological damage. Scarecrow thin, he had survived by eating things even the starving insurgents wouldn't.

According to documents found by Tango Two-Four, arrangements had been made to transport him to an even more fanatical al-Qaeda group the following week, where his beheading was to be livestreamed.

He was flown to the hospital at Camp Bastion. He'd lost a third of his bodyweight and one of his kidneys had to be removed, but he'd been stabilised and declared out of immediate danger.

The nation rejoiced. A legitimate hero, sharply juxtaposed against the vapid wannabe celebrities the media usually bickered over. It was also a rare good-news story out of that deeply troubled country.

Then, just as quickly, the nation despaired.

Two days after their rescue of Captain Jack, Tango Two-Four got lost and wandered into a 'hot' area, an area yet to be cleared. Whether it was targeted revenge for their fallen comrades or bad luck, a VBIED, a vehicle-borne improvised explosive device, in this case an ambulance packed with Semtex, drove into the section's vehicle. Al-Qaeda successes had been reducing year-on-year but on this occasion they got it right. Tango Two-Four's FV432 was outdated and rarely used in Afghanistan but, even if they had been operating in the newer, more heavily armoured Warrior Infantry Section Vehicle, they wouldn't have survived. The ten-man section, the driver and the gunner, twelve men in total, were killed immediately.

'Jack Duncan couldn't handle the guilt or the fame,' Locke said. 'When he had recovered he left the army. He moved to America and started an executive travel business with a US pilot he had met at Camp Bastion. Changed his name and applied for dual citizenship.'

'Why wasn't I told this?'

'Try not to take it personally,' Locke said.

'I take *everything* personally.'

'Telling you Bierman's previous name was seen as over-egging the pudding.'

'You mean you didn't want to besmirch a national hero. Survived al-Qaeda, beaten to death in a seedy Carlisle brothel.'

'Quite,' Locke said. 'It was felt that a good man's name could be sullied before we even knew what had happened. The press hadn't picked up on it, and it has no bearing on his murder.'

'You don't know that. You can't possibly know what might or might not have a bearing on the case. That's why we investigate. It's why we interrogate the evidence, why we look at it from every conceivable angle. We do *not* assess relevance on how embarrassing it might be!'

Locke raised his eyebrows.

'At least I don't,' Poe added quietly.

'Where are you in your investigation?'

'Not far.'

'You think it might be what it seems? That Christopher Bierman had appetites of which his wife, the vetting team, even his business partner were unaware?'

'It's the post-mortem tomorrow. I'm hoping I'll know more then,' Poe said.

'But you've been doing this for a long time. What is your instinct telling you?'

'I'm nowhere near ready to answer that question, Alastor.'

After Locke had left, Poe rubbed his eyes and rolled his shoulders. Did knowing Bierman's old name change things? It raised the stakes, certainly. He'd keep it between him, Melody Lee and Bradshaw for now. If word got out, the press would be all over it like white on rice. Poe didn't think he needed to change strategy though. He had a man in a brothel he had no right knowing about, and he had a killer who'd gone to extreme lengths to find out when it would be empty.

Everything else was case-tinsel and the trick was to avoid the sparkles becoming a distraction. He picked up his phone and sent

Bradshaw a text asking if she was still in the building and if she wanted to meet for tea.

She was and she did.

Good. He'd ask her to work up a full profile on Christopher Bierman/Captain Jack Duncan while he attended the post-mortem. She could talk him through it when he got back.

Tomorrow was moving day, he reckoned. Estelle Doyle had never let him down. The pathologist always found something he could use. And if he was lucky, Alastor Locke might have located the evidence Hannah Finch stole.

Tomorrow was going to be a good day.

Chapter 30

The argument that morning had gone like this:

'Tilly, you stay and finish the profile on Christopher Bierman and Melody Lee and I will go to the PM.'

'No, Poe.'

'What do you mean "No, Poe"?'

'I mean I'm coming with you.'

'It's only the post-mortem, Tilly, and we need that profile.'

'I finished the profile last night. I can brief you on the way.'

'But it's a waste of your . . .' He paused. Remembered every other disagreement they'd had. 'There's no point arguing with you, is there?'

'No point at all, Poe.'

'Fine, you can come.'

'Good. Estelle Doyle and I have a lot of catching up to do.'

'Catching up? You've only met her the once.'

'We have regular correspondence.'

'What the hell do you two have to correspond about?'

'You.'

'Me?'

'Yes, Poe. She likes to know how you're keeping,' Bradshaw said. 'She thinks you're interesting.'

'Interesting? What does she mean by that?'

'It means "to hold the attention", Poe.'

'I know what the word interesting means, Tilly. I meant what does she find interesting about me?'

'I don't know, Poe.'

'I bet she wants me to sign over my body when I die. She's always said I'll make a noteworthy corpse.'

'I'm sure that's it, Poe.'

'That's *not* it, is it, Tilly?'

'You've cleaned your windscreen. About time, I was sick of looking at all those gross bugs.'

'Nicely dodged,' he said. 'And it wasn't me. A man at Scarness Hall called Lewis Barnes did it. He's daft about cars but isn't allowed to hold a driving licence. Think he has a mild learning disability. He even cleaned the alloys. Nice bloke.'

'You don't think anyone there killed Christopher Bierman?'

'No. I don't know why he was killed, but I do know it wasn't random. And everyone at Scarness Hall was already working there before the summit was announced.'

Thirty minutes later Poe was on the A69, on his way to see the oddest forensic pathologist in the country, accompanied by probably the brainiest person in the country and an FBI agent who took down Steeleye Stan with nothing more than a pen.

He smiled.

Today wasn't going to be boring.

Chapter 31

At Estelle Doyle's insistence, the Royal Victoria Infirmary in Newcastle now boasted a state-of-the-art post-mortem suite. They had been led straight into the observation area. It was chilly. All mortuaries were chilly, but this one had been designed so the cold air flowed from the designated clean area they were in, into designated dirty areas like the body store and the PM rooms.

The air pressure on the back of Poe's neck changed. Someone had opened a door somewhere. Three seconds later, Estelle Doyle entered the post-mortem room. Her team – the men and women who would photograph and record the procedure, who would weigh and measure the organs, who would turn the body and take samples – trooped in behind her.

'Ah, Poe,' she said. 'You've finally made it.'

'It's only half past eight. We're not supposed to start until nine. We're thirty minutes early.'

'I'm not a farmer; I don't believe in BST, you should know that by now, Poe.'

Poe winced. He did know that. For some reason, when the clocks went forward in March, Estelle Doyle continued working to Greenwich Mean Time. He'd asked her about it once but all she had said was, 'You're the detective, Poe, work it out.'

'You've started without us?' Poe said.

'Does it look like I've started without you?'

To be fair, it didn't. She was still in her civvies: an edgy outfit of figure-hugging jeans, a burgundy leather jacket and heels that, if he hadn't been standing in the raised viewing area of the mortuary, would have made her tower over him. Her jet-black hair had been cut a little shorter since the last time he'd seen her. It was now spiky on top, stylish but still funky enough to suit her. Her neck was pale and long, her dark blue eyes pools of ink, her mouth a slash of crimson. Poe felt his face heating up. Estelle Doyle did that to him, always had. She affected him on a primal level – he had no control over it.

'Cat got your tongue, Poe?' she said.

Her mouth twitched. He was sure she was fighting a smile.

'Well, maybe you can think of something clever to say while I'm cutting into your victim.'

Poe forgot about Estelle Doyle the person and focused on Estelle Doyle the scientist the moment the first incision into Bierman was made. Doyle spoke to the room's digital recorder but used plain English. Bradshaw had her laptop open although he wasn't sure if she was making notes or playing a game – the last time she had been there she'd been close to vomiting. Melody Lee was having a cup of coffee and checking her phone. Poe wondered how many post-mortems she'd been to.

Doyle started with Christopher Bierman's clothes. She cut them off with shears rather than slipping them off. Less chance of evidence being lost. A man with a pronounced Adam's apple completed the menial tasks, but not until he was told to do so. The PM was Estelle Doyle's responsibility and hers alone. Poe had considered asking her to focus on the feet – he wanted to know why one shoe had been tied with a double knot while the other hadn't – but he resisted.

'It's an observation area, Poe, not an audience participation area,' she'd told him once.

He needn't have worried. She noticed the anomaly, had close-up photographs taken, then removed the shoes. She left both knots intact. She offered no opinion. Doyle dealt with facts, not suppositions – that the shoes had been tied differently was a fact, the *reason* they'd been tied differently was Poe's area, not hers. She'd supply him with as much hard evidence as she could but she wouldn't guess for him.

With Bierman naked, the picture of what had happened at Cranley Gardens became a little less foggy. The catastrophic injuries to his skull may have been what had killed him but, before the baseball bat had rained down the deathblows, he'd been tortured.

'Sweet baby Jesus,' Melody Lee said.

'This man was badly beaten,' Doyle said.

'That much I can see,' Poe said.

'No, Poe, you misunderstand. I'm not talking about the new injuries.'

'I know you're not. What happened in Carlisle wasn't the first ordeal he'd been through. Talk me through the old injuries first.'

Doyle raised her eyebrows but didn't ask what he knew. She turned on a monitor in the observation area and, using a hand-held camera, showed them what she was looking at.

'On the screen you can see evidence of healed compression fractures, cuts and broken bones. The external scars are consistently silver and smooth. Judging by the callus around the broken bones this happened a few years ago. Does that fit with what you can't tell me, Poe?'

'It does. When you cut him open you'll find evidence of malnutrition and a missing kidney as well. Tell me about the recent injuries. We've only seen the ones on his head.'

Doyle slowly panned her camera across the fresher wounds. They were horrific. Livid bruises covered Bierman's legs, arms and torso like a rash. Some were small and round, others were square and ridged. The round ones were primarily around the joints and shins, the square ones on the softer areas. The fleshy bit under the upper arm had come in for particular punishment. Poe winced – he knew how sensitive that area was.

'Pliers for the square bruises?' Poe said.

'The ridges would support a small gripping tool,' Estelle Doyle said.

'Ball-peen hammer for the round ones?'

'Possibly. Something round anyway. When the depth of the blow was limited by bone, like here on the shins,' – she moved the camera to Bierman's legs – 'the size of the injuries is consistent.'

'Meaning?'

'The same instrument was used.'

'And the round end would be less likely to tear the victim's clothes,' Poe said. 'If the killer needed to give himself a bit of time before the torture was discovered, keeping the evidence under Bierman's clothes was as good a way as any, I suppose.'

'There's something else, Poe,' Doyle said. She returned the camera to its fixed position above the body. 'If you look, he's smashed both of Mr Bierman's elbows and knees to a pulp.' She prodded them. 'They're almost jelly-like. He's also smashed the left ankle.'

'But not the right?' Poe said.

'No. As far as I can tell, it's not been touched.'

'It was the right ankle that had the shoe with the double knot.'

'I know,' she said. 'I wonder . . .?'

She walked to the computer and brought up a photograph of the right ankle. The same image appeared on the monitor in the observation area. Poe switched his attention from the live action to the screen. Doyle expanded the image then dismissed it. Brought up another one; this time a close up of his toes. Again, she expanded the image.

'Gotcha,' she said.

She walked back to the cadaver, collecting a magnifying glass on her way. She pulled apart the big and index toes.

'Please photograph here,' she said to the assistant with the Adam's apple.

Poe looked away to avoid getting flash-eye.

Doyle studied the image on the digital camera. 'Enlarge that and put it up so Poe can see, please.'

An image appeared on the monitor. Poe studied it. Melody Lee joined him.

'What the hell's that?' she said. 'A tiny mole?'

'It's a puncture wound,' Doyle said. 'I'll have to dig into it but I'd be amazed if it wasn't made by an IV needle.'

'What possible reason could there be for that?' Poe said. He usually tried to avoid asking questions he knew Doyle wouldn't answer.

To his surprise, she did.

'It actually ties in with something I found in his blood work. I found irregularities in two enzymes that suggest there was methylphenidate in his blood.'

'And what's that?'

'You'll know it under the trade name Ritalin.'

'Ritalin? Why would that be in his system?'

'No medical reason,' she said. 'Not unless he had ADHD.'

'He was a helicopter pilot.'

'No, then. But something has been injected directly into the muscle between his toes, and methylphenidate is the only anomaly on his blood work. I'll get a dome magnifier on the wound later but I estimate that a twenty-four-gauge IV needle made this puncture. That's very small, the kind only used in paediatrics.'

'A kid's needle? Why so small?'

'Not for me to say. But there's no medical reason to use one. Bierman was a healthy adult with healthy veins. He could have taken a larger needle.'

'There is a *criminal* reason to use one, though,' Melody Lee said. 'Heard about this once in DC. A mob victim had been

140

injected with adrenaline during an interrogation. They'd taken a blowtorch to his balls and used the adrenaline to keep him awake. Burnt those suckers to raisins. And they used a small-ass needle to hide the fact they had a doctor on the payroll.'

Poe winced.

'Which fits with the use of methylphenidate,' Doyle said. 'Neuroscientists are now advocating its use in helping to bring patients out of surgery. It reduces the grogginess by hours.'

'If it were injected into an unconscious person it would wake them?' Poe said.

'Or stop them falling unconscious in the first place.'

'It was an interrogation then, not torture. When the time came, Bierman was dispatched quickly. Causing pain wasn't the killer's primary motivation.'

'It was a means to an end,' Melody Lee said.

'Exactly.'

'And sticking the needle between his toes meant there would be a decent chance the pathologist would miss it.'

'Not this one,' Poe muttered.

'Thank you, Poe,' Doyle said softly.

She was looking at him strangely.

Poe shook it off. Now wasn't the time to find out what was up with the Pathologist Grim. He'd give her a call when he found some time but right now he had to regroup. The use of Ritalin changed things. It suggested Bierman had been privy to information someone wanted.

Find out what that was and they'd be a step closer to finding his killer.

'I'm finished here, Poe,' Estelle Doyle said, washing her hands in one of the large sluice sinks. 'I assume you want my report sooner rather than later?'

'Please.'

'I'll do it this evening then.'

'Thank you.' He turned to Bradshaw and Melody Lee. 'We ready?'

'Not so fast, Poe,' Doyle said. 'If I'm working tonight the least you can do is buy me lunch. I have a reservation at an Italian not far from here. They do a stunning *spaghetti alle vongole*.'

Poe looked at her blankly.

Her expression softened. 'Spaghetti and clams, Poe. It won't kill you.'

'Poe doesn't like pasta, Estelle Doyle,' Bradshaw said. 'He says it doesn't taste of anything and he can't go to the toilet properly the next day.'

Poe sighed. Every now and then Bradshaw passed for normal but it never lasted long.

'In *confidence* I told you that, Tilly,' he said.

'Oh. Sorry.'

'Perhaps his bowels will be able to cope with the soup?' Estelle Doyle said, smiling.

'He doesn't like soup either. He says soup is just a wet salad.'

Melody Lee guffawed. 'Awesome.'

Poe was about to say he didn't have time but he thought better of it. Doyle clearly had something on her mind and he may as well find out what. And if she wasn't yet ready to share, an hour discussing the case wasn't going to be wasted. She had a mind like Bradshaw's and right now he'd take any help he could get.

'I'll buy lunch on one condition, Estelle.'

'This should be good.'

'You don't tell me that dead bodies can fart, grow hair, get goosebumps or even have orgasms.'

'I prom—'

'And you don't explain why hearts shouldn't be used on Valentine's Day cards.'

'Why shouldn't hearts be used, Estelle Doyle?' Bradshaw asked before Poe could stop her.

'Pink is the universal colour of love, Tilly,' Doyle said. 'And, as hearts are covered in epicardial fat, they're yellow.'

'What do you think should be used on Valentine's Day cards instead?'

'The vulva.'

'Gosh,' Bradshaw said. She reddened.

Poe did too. He gave the pathologist a look.

Doyle's eyes twinkled. She sealed her lips with an imaginary zip.

'You two happy with Italian?' he said to Melody Lee and Bradshaw.

Melody Lee briefly looked up from her phone. 'I could eat a risotto.' She pronounced it riz-zo-toe.

'Special Agent Melody Lee wants to see the Black Gate and the Castle Keep,' Bradshaw said. 'Don't you, Special Agent Melody Lee?'

'What? Oh yeah, that thing we were . . . I mean, sure. The Keep. Don't have none of that old shit back in the States.'

'Really?' Poe said. '*You* want to see the castle?'

'Sure, why not?'

'Yet when we drove past Carlisle Castle the other day you barely glanced at it.'

She shrugged and went back to her iPhone.

'I said I would take her, Poe,' Bradshaw said.

'And when I suggested we visit Shap Abbey the other day, I distinctly remember you telling me to stop living in the past.'

'I've changed my mind. I like history now.'

She was staring at him. There was something going on here; something they all knew and he didn't.

His phone rang. The caller ID said it was DS Rigg. Alastor Locke must have arrived. He pressed the green phone icon.

'Bad news I'm afraid, Poe,' Rigg said.

He told him.

'She did fucking what?' Poe shouted. He looked at his watch. 'I'll be back in an hour.'

Estelle Doyle looked at Bradshaw and sighed.

'Maybe next time, Tilly.'

Chapter 32

'Tell me again,' Poe said. 'Don't leave anything out.'

They were racing back to Carlisle. Poe had called Rigg back and told him he was on the BMW's speakerphone.

'I don't know anything more than I told you ten minutes ago,' Rigg said. 'Hannah Finch has been bailed. Orders of the chief constable.'

'Why the hell would she do that?'

'She didn't say, Poe. Shocking really – it was almost as if she didn't have the urge to take me through her thinking. And you did run out of time.'

'Finch should have been charged and remanded or some-one should have gone to Carlisle Magistrates and requested an extension.'

'I agree,' Rigg said. 'But I spoke to Superintendent Nightingale and she thinks the chief was leaned on. I got the impression nei-ther of them was happy about it. And it's not as if it's been swept under the carpet – she's been bailed to reappear.'

'Yeah, but it's the last we'll ever see of her. And we don't even know her real name. How the hell are we supposed to swear out a warrant when she doesn't come back?'

'You could always release the photograph you took of her in handcuffs,' Rigg said.

'I'm not doing that. We've been outflanked; releasing the photo would be spiteful.'

'What's next then?'

Poe had thought about nothing else since Rigg had called. The next steps weren't easy to see. He slowed down for a horse and rider, grunting in annoyance as he did – any animal that could be spooked by an empty crisp packet had no business being on the road, in his opinion – then sped up again.

'I need time to think,' he said eventually. 'I'll see you soon.'

'You reckon Locke's behind this, Poe?' Melody Lee said.

'Him or someone like him. Funny, I actually thought he was telling the truth. That finding out what happened was more important than protecting his own.'

'He's a spy, Poe. I doubt he's told the truth since he was fourteen.'

Poe nodded. She was probably right. 'Here's what we're going to do,' he said. 'There's no point going back to Durranhill now. Alastor Locke isn't going to be there with our missing evidence and I don't want to bump into the chief constable while I'm in a bad mood. We'll go to mine and look at everything together. Have a bit of food and see if we can come up with a new angle.'

Chapter 33

Herdwick Croft clung to Shap Fell like someone was trying to steal it. Abandoned for two hundred years before Poe had bought and restored it, it was an ugly, squat building of jagged, weather-beaten grey stone and moss-stained slate. It was root-cellar cold in winter, greenhouse hot in summer and the smell of sheep had soaked into everything. Perfumed echoes of the days when the flock had taken shelter on the ground floor while the shepherd slept upstairs.

Poe loved it. It felt like his whole life had been leading up to discovering and learning to love Shap Fell and Herdwick Croft. And now someone was trying to take it from him. He sighed. It was out of his hands. The judge would either agree with Bradshaw or he wouldn't.

The boiling pan of water snapped him out of what was, for him, a rare moment of introspection. He selected three mugs from his collection, all chipped and stained with tannin. He'd once told Bradshaw they had been carefully curated over the years, that they were eclectic. They weren't, they were just mugs he'd accumulated. As a metaphor for his life it was depressingly close. He never really planned anything. Everything he had – Herdwick Croft, his friendship with Bradshaw, even Edgar – had just happened. Nothing was by his design.

He popped a foul-smelling teabag into one of the mugs and poured coffee into the other two. Melody Lee joined him.

'You like the simple life, huh?' she said.

Poe paused before answering.

'I like the *quiet* life,' he said.

'Been reading your file. Ain't nothing quiet about your life, Poe. That's some crazy shit you've been involved with.'

'The last few years have been complicated.'

'Speaking of which, I have something for you. A list of names.'

Poe's mouth went dry. When he'd resolved the Curator case he had also vindicated Melody Lee and her long-held theory that the killer even existed at all. Out of the career-doghouse, she'd said if he ever needed a favour . . .

A couple of years ago Poe had discovered that the man who'd raised him wasn't his biological father. That honour went to the man who'd raped his mother at a party at the British Embassy in Washington, DC. His mother had left Poe and his father long before the face of her rapist appeared on the face of her son – she'd even named him after the city he was conceived in as a reminder she had to leave. By the time Poe had found out, she'd been killed in a hit and run. Poe had asked Melody Lee to get him the Washington party's guest list. It seemed she wasn't all talk.

'I could only get the Americans,' she said. 'The Brits might have the full list somewhere but we ain't got access to it.'

Poe nodded his appreciation. 'It's more than I had this morning,' he said. 'Can you send it to my private email address?'

'Sure.'

Poe glanced at the door. Bradshaw was still outside.

'Don't tell Tilly,' he said. 'She doesn't know yet.'

They settled into an easy silence. Poe liked Melody Lee. She was the FBI equivalent of him. An outcast, but too useful to get rid of. He wasn't surprised she was given the liaison officer gig. He suspected her superiors were glad to be rid of her for a while.

Chapter 34

After sandwiches and hot drinks, they stayed outside and opened their files.

'Let's recap,' Poe said. 'See what we do know before we get into what we don't know.'

'I'll take notes, Poe,' Bradshaw said. 'I can cross-reference with my data to make sure we cover everything.'

'Good.' He removed a photograph of the victim and put it on the table. 'Christopher Bierman, aka Captain Jack Duncan. He signs out of Scarness Hall's security bubble one evening and twelve hours later is found dead. The house he was in had been used as a pop-up brothel, because that's a thing now apparently, but it was temporarily vacant. The murder is called in by Paulina Tuchlin. Paulina works as a . . . is a . . .'

'Jizz mopper.'

'Yes, thank you Special Agent Lee. Paulina services the brothels and makes them ready for tenants when they aren't being used. The brothel is owned by a new, highly organised criminal gang that exploited the vacuum left by the demise of the previous crime boss. Jefferson Black, an ex-paratrooper, is the man in charge and most members of this gang are ex-military. Judging by the tattoos we could see, they all come from the teeth arms.'

'What's "teeth arms", Poe?'

'Infantry and tanks, Tilly. The units that close in and kill the enemy.'

Bradshaw made a note.

'After talking to Jefferson Black we believe the murderer briefly infiltrated the gang to gain access to the empty Cranley Gardens property. Somehow he gets Bierman to Cranley Gardens where he interrogates him, almost certainly using Ritalin to keep him conscious while he does. He then kills him.'

Bradshaw put her hand up.

'Tilly?'

'Has Detective Sergeant Rigg interviewed the man who handed over the keys to Cranley Gardens?'

'He has. And he was no help whatsoever, I'm afraid. He confirms that the man was wearing a hat and wraparound sunglasses and, because of the nature of their business, it was conducted away from any CCTV as a matter of routine. The only thing of note is that Jefferson Black thinks the killer is ex-British Army. Says his associate is an ex-para and he'd have spotted a fake.'

Poe picked up another document – a screenshot of the live photo PC Nathan Wilkes had taken before he'd entered the bedroom at Cranley Gardens. Bradshaw had tidied it up as much as she could but it was still blurry.

'There are five things on the mantelpiece in this photograph. Paulina swears there should only be four.'

Opening his mobile, Poe found the photograph he'd taken of Hannah Finch in handcuffs.

'Hannah Finch, MI5 and all-round berk, is given permission to enter the crime scene before CSI have mapped it. She claims it was to ensure there was nothing compromising on Christopher Bierman. For reasons unknown she removes the fifth item on the mantelpiece. We can surmise that removing it left a gap in the blood, so she wiped down the mantelpiece. I have Hannah Finch arrested and think I've secured the return of said item by putting pressure on her boss, Alastor Locke.'

'And then the chief constable has her released,' Melody Lee said. 'What an ass-hat.'

'Which she isn't, usually, so she's undoubtedly had pressure put on her,' Poe said. He checked his notes. 'Have I missed anything, Tilly?'

She looked at Poe. She looked at Melody Lee.

'What's jizz?' she said.

Chapter 35

After Poe had refreshed everyone's drinks, he said, 'OK, we've been through what we know. How about we go through what we don't know. Specifically, what don't we know that we could?'

'I've been making a list, Poe,' Bradshaw said.

'Go for it, Tilly.'

'Why was Christopher Bierman killed? Was he selected at random or was he chosen?'

'Perp's crazier than an outhouse rat if it was random,' Melody Lee said.

'My thoughts exactly,' Poe agreed. 'Bierman's murder was extremely violent but, now we've had the PM, we know it wasn't chaotic. There were two distinct phases to it: the application of pain then the murder. We assume he'd been interrogated before he was killed.'

'Why interrogated?' Bradshaw said. 'Why do you think it's not the work of a sadist?'

'Because the blows to the head were methodical, systematic and un-survivable,' Poe said. 'If the perp was a sadist I doubt he'd have killed him so quickly.'

Bradshaw made a note.

'He went to extraordinary lengths to secure an empty property where the neighbours were used to not looking, and he administered an IV line to keep Bierman awake. That tells us the killer was in complete control at all times. I'm not overreaching, am I?'

'You're saying what I'm thinking, Poe,' Melody Lee said.

'The Americans are confident that neither Bierman nor his business partner, Patrick McDaid, knew anything that could compromise safety at the summit,' Poe continued. 'So, if the information the killer was trying to extract from Bierman wasn't about the summit, what was it about?'

'I'll start a new list,' Bradshaw said. 'What information could Christopher Bierman have had access to that was worth his life?'

'Whatever it was, judging by his injuries, he didn't give it up willingly. And even then there's something not quite right with this scenario.'

'What's that, Poe?' Bradshaw said.

'The killer applies pain to get what he wants. We don't know what that is but we have to assume it was important to him.'

'So?' Melody Lee said.

'So, why the baseball bat to the head afterwards?'

'He couldn't let him live to identify him?'

'That's not what I'm getting at,' Poe said. 'We already know he had an IV line in Bierman. Why not give him a lethal dose of something? There was bleach in the house; he could have just used that. Cleaner, less chance of forensic transfer.'

'Yuk,' Bradshaw said.

'Horrible, isn't it?' Poe said.

'No, not that.' She pointed over his shoulder.

Poe turned to see what it was.

'Yuk,' he said.

Chapter 36

Poe's neighbour, Victoria Hume, had appeared over the crest of the hill. Edgar bounded ahead of her. He had a fish carcass in his mouth. Unless one of Bassenthwaite Lake's resident ospreys had taken a massive wrong turn, Poe couldn't begin to imagine how it had ended up on Shap Fell.

'I was inspecting my sheep and saw you were in,' she said. 'Thought I'd see if you wanted Edgar back yet.'

'He been fishing?' Poe said, pulling up a chair for her.

'I'm sorry. I couldn't get it off him.'

Poe reached down to take the stinking carcass from him but Edgar bared his teeth and growled. He really was disgusting sometimes.

'How's your flock, shepherd?' he said.

'Healthy.'

'You're a shepherd?' Melody Lee said.

'A sheep farmer, so yes, technically I suppose I am.'

'We're not big on sheep in the States. Don't know a whole lot about them.'

For the next few minutes Victoria told Melody Lee all about her Herdwicks. How they were a hardy mountain breed, originally brought over by the Vikings. That although their lambing yield was low compared to other sheep, they were prized for their ability to survive on foraged food alone.

'Even up here they do well,' Victoria said. 'I've had them trapped in snow drifts for three days and they've eaten their own wool to survive.'

By the time she'd finished extolling the virtues of her prized sheep, some had joined them, braving Edgar's presence, no doubt tempted by the fresh shoots of grass the recent rainstorm had encouraged. Life on Shap Fell didn't need much encouragement to flourish.

'What's that red shit on their backs?' Melody Lee said.

'Wax,' Victoria said. 'It's tupping season.'

Melody Lee looked at her blankly.

'In nine months I want to be selling spring lambs, and that means the tups, rams to everyone else, have to be on the fell now. They're fitted with a harness called a raddle. The raddle holds a coloured wax block that marks the ewe, so I know if she's been mounted.'

'Clever.'

Bradshaw scowled.

Poe laughed. 'Tilly doesn't like tupping season,' he said. 'She says it's rude.'

'I just don't see why they have to have sexual intercourse right in front of me,' she said. 'Why can't they go behind a wall or wait until it's dark?'

Melody Lee and Victoria laughed too.

'What?' Bradshaw said.

'How's your case coming along?' Victoria said.

'We could do with a break,' Poe said. 'Something to make sense of it all. That happens and I'm convinced we can get to the bottom of this.'

Which was when Edgar cocked his head, twitched his ears and started to bark . . .

Chapter 37

Poe knew Edgar's barks. The annoyed 'woof' when sheep strayed too close to his 'turf', the excited bark as he fruitlessly chased game birds, the 'reminder' bark when he was hungry and Poe's mind was elsewhere.

But this was a warning bark. It was followed by a continuous low growl, raised heckles and a rigid tail. Someone was coming and the spaniel didn't know them.

Poe retrieved his binoculars from his quad bike and looked in the direction Edgar was staring. A tiny figure came into view. A man, judging by his stride. He was heading towards Herdwick Croft.

'I don't believe it,' he said eventually.

'Who is it, Poe?' Bradshaw said.

'Alastor Locke.'

'You don't make things easy, do you, Sergeant Poe?' Locke said when he eventually got to them. He was wearing another three-piece suit, light cotton this time, and carrying a small bag.

Poe said nothing.

'Miss Bradshaw, Special Agent Lee, good to see you again.' He looked in Victoria's direction. 'But I don't believe I've had the pleasure, Miss . . .?'

She stepped forward and offered her hand.

'I'm—'

'He knows who you are, Victoria,' Poe cut in. 'Don't let the ridiculous suit fool you, he's not an idiot.'

Locke smiled.

'Quite,' he said. 'Victoria Hume. Eldest daughter to the recently deceased Thomas, my condolences by the way, and Sergeant Poe's nearest neighbour. One of the few people he trusts enough to call his friend.'

'How the hell could you—'

'He's a spy, Victoria,' Poe said. 'Don't worry about it, he's just showing off.'

'Old habits, I'm afraid,' he said, dipping his head in apology. 'May we speak, Sergeant Poe?'

'Unless you have Hannah Finch in that little bag of yours, I doubt you've got anything I want to hear.'

'No?'

'No.'

'Not even if I come bearing gifts?' He put the bag on the table. 'Your missing evidence. Miss Finch wanted to hand it to you in person but I convinced her that might not be politic.'

'We had an agreement,' Poe said. 'Return it this morning or she would be charged.'

'I couldn't get to the damned thing, Poe. Miss Finch made a mistake in removing it from your crime scene but she wasn't reckless. She kept it in her safe at home. She didn't have her keys with her so I had to convince her neighbour to let me in. I then had to get one of our . . . specialists to open her safe. And yes, in the meantime I made sure she was released and her career wasn't ruined before it had begun, but I got back to Carlisle as soon as I could. It took me another three hours to find this place. People round here don't like talking about you, do they?'

Poe didn't respond. Finch's release still rankled.

'Recognise when you're winning, Poe,' Melody Lee said.

'Fine,' he said, reaching for the bag. It was thick and black, not unlike the Faraday pouch they'd had to put their phones in when they had been in Manchester. He unzipped it.

The item Finch had removed from Cranley Gardens was still in a brown evidence bag. Poe arranged it so it could be seen through the clear window. They stared in confusion.

'Is that it?' Poe said. 'This is what Hannah Finch risked her career for?'

'Indeed,' Locke said.

'I mean, why even bother?'

Locke shrugged.

Poe picked it up. Held it up to the afternoon light. It was definitely the item in PC Wilkes's live photograph.

But it wasn't a squirrel.

And it wasn't a rabbit.

It was a rat.

A ceramic rat.

Chapter 38

'I have upheld my end of our arrangement, Sergeant Poe,' Locke said. 'Perhaps you might see your way to grant me a small favour?'

Victoria had gone back to checking on her sheep. Edgar had followed her. Bradshaw had disappeared inside. She'd said she needed to check something, although Poe suspected she hadn't wanted to be there if he and Locke started arguing again.

'Tell me what happened first,' Poe said. 'Why did Hannah Finch take it? How did she even *know* to take it?'

'You might not believe me, Poe, but Miss Finch is a good agent who made a bad decision. She was doing her job when she checked the crime scene. She needed to check that Bierman's ID card wasn't missing and that there was no sensitive information on his person.'

'I thought he didn't have access to sensitive information?'

'He didn't. Not really. But he was privy to the travel itinerary of some of the minor players. A bright young thing might be able to work out when the big names were due by studying the arrival times of others.'

'Fair enough,' Poe conceded.

'And what you don't know is that Hannah is in overall charge of security for the summit. It's the first time she has led on something this big and she's understandably a little jittery. Her immediate impression was what was said at the Manchester briefing: that Bierman had been ill advised in where he went

159

looking for love. She could have lived with that. The *summit* could have lived with that.'

'So what happened?'

'Like I said – she's a good agent. Observant. And she noticed that, while the other ornaments on the mantelpiece were covered in blood, the rat was clean. The other ornaments had been moved to make room for it. Conclusion: it had been put there after Mr Bierman had been killed, presumably by the killer.'

'Which doesn't explain why she took it.'

'She panicked, Poe. Simple as that, I'm afraid. Bierman being beaten to death in a brothel was scandalous, but only for his family and his clients. The rat being put there after he died made it weird. Certainly weird enough to sow doubts about the motive for his murder.'

'And sowed doubts threatened the summit.'

Locke nodded.

'So she stole it.'

'She made an error in judgement.'

'But now there's a gap on the mantelpiece,' Poe said. 'And, because the rat had been placed on *top* of the blood spatters, there would have been an obvious mark.'

'Word for word, that is almost exactly what she said. So, instead of replacing it and letting the police decide on its relevance, she made what she thought was the pragmatic choice – she wiped down the mantelpiece and repositioned the remaining ornaments.'

'And hoped we wouldn't notice?'

'Folly of my profession, Poe. We have higher entry standards and younger agents wrongly assume that those not working for us must therefore be stupider than us. It's a lesson Miss Finch has just learned the hard way, unfortunately.'

'She hasn't interfered with it?'

Locke shook his head. 'She was wearing a forensic suit and

160

had evidence bags in case there were things she needed to take away.' He pointed at the rat. 'She sealed it in this bag and hasn't touched it since.'

Poe grunted. He didn't think a killer this meticulous would have left trace evidence behind, but stranger things had happened. It was something for Nightingale's team to check.

'She didn't just forget about it, though,' Locke said. 'She checked all available law enforcement databases for ceramic rats being left at crime scenes.'

'And?'

'And it's not the calling card of anyone and it doesn't represent any organisation.'

Poe put the rat back on the table. 'You said you wanted a favour?' he said.

'I'd like you to consider taking Miss Finch back.'

'Not a bloody chance.'

Locke sighed. 'Poe, whether you like it or not, we need people such as Hannah. She's a talented agent, but if she can learn from you she has the potential to become an *exceptional* agent. Teach her how to investigate. At the minute, she's too concerned with threat assessments. There's no subtlety, no linear thinking. Help her channel her natural instincts. If you do, I think you might start to see her as I do.'

'And what's that?'

'An asset. Someone who will serve this country selflessly and well.' He held Poe's gaze. 'What do you think, old bean?'

'Like you've just put red wax all over my back.'

'I beg your pardon?'

Poe sighed. Some battles really weren't worth fighting. 'OK, but she does what she's told this time.'

'Excellent decision and one you won't regret.'

'I think we both know that's a lie. But tell her to be at Durranhill at eight o'clock tomorrow morning.'

'She'll be there.'

Locke refused his offer of a drink and said he needed to get back to Manchester. He didn't say it, but Poe got the impression he resented having to waste so much time on Hannah Finch and the missing evidence.

Melody Lee picked up the evidence bag and stared at the rat. It was about four inches tall and brightly coloured. Not exactly anthropomorphic, but closer to the cartoon rat from *Ratatouille* than the ones that got into the pub cellar, pissed on the beer bottles and gave everyone Weil's disease.

It was glazed and hand painted. Poe had never seen a vaguer piece of evidence.

'What do you think?' she said.

'If it was a ceramic fish I'd say it was a literal red herring,' Poe said. 'Put there with the sole purpose of introducing tangents into the investigation. A way to divert our resources. I suspect it's absolutely meaningless.'

Bradshaw peeped out of the door. 'Has Alastor Locke gone, Poe?'

'He has.'

He waited for her to take a seat at the table.

'Why didn't you join us earlier?' he said. 'I could have done with your input on whether we should have taken Hannah Finch back.'

'I had something to check.'

'And it just happened to finish at the exact time Alastor Locke left?'

'No. I was waiting for him to go.'

'You were? Why?'

'Because, Poe, as you've said many, many times, I'm rubbish at telling fibs and I'm rubbish at hiding what I'm thinking.'

'It's true you're no poker player, Tilly. What was it you didn't want him to know?'

'The ceramic rat, Poe,' she said, her eyes shining with excitement, 'we've seen it before.'

Chapter 39

Poe had a good memory. It was nothing like Bradshaw's, which was extraordinary, but it was good enough to know he'd never been involved with a case that had featured a ceramic rat. He said as much.

'Not "we" as in me and you, Poe,' Bradshaw explained. 'We as in SCAS.'

'We have?'

Bradshaw nodded. 'It was while you were suspended for gross misconduct. Do you remember that, Poe?'

'No, Tilly, I'd completely forgotten about being suspended for eighteen months.'

'Really?' she said. 'It was when that man died after you'd—'

'Just tell us about the rat.'

'It was on a referral SCAS received almost three years ago. It was from Hampshire Constabulary.'

'And it was left with a murder victim?'

'Sort of.'

'What do you mean "sort of"?'

'You'll need to read the referral document, obviously, and I don't see how their case can possibly be linked to ours, but it was left at the scene of a bungled robbery. Their words, not mine.'

'Whose words?'

'Detective Constable Ben Slater. He was with the Major Crimes team at Southampton Central Police Station.'

Poe frowned. 'Hannah Finch claimed to have checked all

available databases. I assumed that meant ours as well as hers. Why didn't she find it?'

'Because it's not online, Poe.'

'Why not? I thought we were supposed to be paperless these days.'

'We are.' She looked at him accusingly. 'Well, most of us are anyway.'

'Hey, my files never get hacked.'

For at least the hundredth time, Bradshaw shook her head at the absurdity of someone still having a filing cabinet.

'Anyway,' she said, 'it wasn't entered on our system as the referral was withdrawn the same day. Instead, it went straight to archives. And there was no mention of the rat in the press coverage.'

'The senior investigating officer will have withheld it to filter out the loonies.'

'That's what the form said.'

'What about PND? Finch should have been able to find it on there.' The Police National Database captured intelligence from over two hundred different systems and had three and a half billion searchable records. Withholding information from the press was a legitimate tactic, leaving it off PND wasn't.

'It wasn't down as a rat, Poe.'

'What's it down as?'

'A mouse.'

'But it's a rat.'

'I agree, but it's an easy mistake to make. Other than size, there's not much obvious difference between the two. But whether it's a rat or a mouse is immaterial; the fact is, Hannah Finch thought it was a rat and there wasn't one on PND. Detective Constable Ben Slater thought it was a rat too, but Hannah Finch didn't have access to our paper-based archives.'

'If it's not discoverable online, how on earth did you find it?'

'I read all the archived files when I started with SCAS.'

'Why?'

'Our job is to look for patterns. Just because information is no longer relevant to a referring police force doesn't mean we don't need to know about it.'

It was a valid point. SCAS's main function was to spot emerging serial murderers and rapists. They did this by stringing together the smallest of clues, and there was always a bit of 'one man's trash is another man's treasure' when it came to the national intelligence picture. One force assessing something as having no value didn't mean it wouldn't end up being the cornerstone of another force's investigation.

'Did you tell DI Flynn there were referral forms that hadn't been scanned?'

'I did, Poe.'

'And what did she say?'

'She said I was to go and boil my head. I think she was in a bad mood.'

She must have been; Flynn was ordinarily incredibly courteous. Poe missed her. Knew that he worked better when she was there to help him focus. He wasn't convinced she would come back, though. In his experience nothing changed a person's priorities like a new family.

In her absence he'd make sure all archived files were entered on their system. Intelligence was like bacon: you could never have too much.

'You didn't scan it by any chance, did you, Tilly?' he said. 'Maybe kept it on your laptop?'

'I most certainly did not, Poe! That would have been an egregious breach of data security.'

'OK, calm down. We'll get hold of it later. Just tell us what you remember.'

Which of course turned out to be everything.

Chapter 40

'It was a safety deposit box robbery,' Bradshaw said. 'Men wearing James Bond masks somehow breached the security and opened the vault door.'

'You said it was a murder?'

'They were only interested in one box apparently, and when they found it was empty the man wearing the Sean Connery mask shot the man wearing the Timothy Dalton mask in the back of the head.'

'Damn,' Melody Lee said. 'Dalton was my favourite Bond.'

Poe glanced at her. 'Weirdo,' he said.

He turned to Bradshaw. 'So it was a falling out among thieves?'

'Apparently.'

'I agree then. I can't see how it can be connected to our murder.'

'Apart from the rat.'

'Yes. Tell me about it.'

'It was in the safety deposit box, Poe. Angled down to look at the murder victim.'

'Is it the same rat?'

'No way of telling until we've had a look at it.'

'So it might not be?'

She shrugged.

'Was it already there or did they take it in with them?'

'The referral form said Sean Connery placed it in the safety deposit box after he'd killed Timothy Dalton.'

'How can they be sure? Maybe whoever they were robbing knew they were coming and left it as a warning. It might even explain the significance of the rat. It's always been used with informers.'

Bradshaw shook her head. 'No. The whole thing was caught on video. Sean Connery definitely brought the rat with him.'

That changed things. The murders were three years apart and at opposite ends of the country but the rat link was curious.

'OK, I'm officially interested,' he said. 'What else do we know?'

'That's it, Poe.'

'That's it?'

'The referral was withdrawn, remember?'

'Do we know why?'

'Detective Constable Ben Slater had overreached his authority. Detective Inspector Flynn must have followed it up as she'd written "Spoke to the SIO, Superintendent Elspeth Yarrow, who confirmed it was a straightforward robbery gone wrong. Request for SCAS involvement rescinded. Referral closed." DI Flynn's comment was dated the same day the referral was received.'

Poe frowned. Some SIOs didn't like calling in SCAS as they saw it as a sign they were out of their depth. He wondered if that had been the case here.

'So it was shut down before it even started?'

'Yes, Poe.'

'Do we know if Hampshire got anyone for the murder?' he said.

'It's open. That's what I was checking when I went inside. I read their cold-case summaries but I got the impression they're paying lip service.'

'In other words, they think they know who did it but they also know it isn't going to be solved.'

He considered his options. Speaking to the SIO was the obvious choice but he was reluctant to do that. As the person who'd withdrawn the SCAS referral, she was unlikely to welcome the news that she might have got it wrong.

Far better they went to the source.

'We need to speak to the cop who made the referral,' he said.

Fifteen minutes later it was all sorted. Ben Slater would meet them first thing in the morning at his house. He'd retired from Hampshire Constabulary a year earlier but had kept hold of his private file.

'Where the hell's Southampton?' Melody Lee said.

'Bottom of the country,' Poe said.

'And we're at the top, right?'

'Less than fifty miles from the Scottish border.'

'You want me to book us on the next red-eye? Uncle Sam's dime.'

Poe laughed. 'We'll drive, Special Agent Lee.'

'Drive? How long will that take?'

'About five hours. Six if we hit traffic. If we leave now we'll be far too early.'

'You live in a small-ass country, you know that, don't you?'

'We're supposed to be meeting with Hannah Finch tomorrow, Poe,' Bradshaw said, opening her laptop. 'Do you want me to email her and tell her our plans have changed?'

'I don't think so.'

'But you said Alastor Locke wants her to learn from you.'

'All Alastor Locke wants is a spy in the camp, Tilly.'

Bradshaw closed her laptop. 'OK, Poe.'

'If we're lucky, we'll be in Hampshire long before she realises we've ditched her.'

Chapter 41

They left at midnight and took turns driving. It was over three hundred miles to Southampton but most of the route was covered by motorway. They arrived physically tired but mentally refreshed.

They were a couple of hours early so they found a greasy spoon close to where Slater lived. Much to Bradshaw's disgust, Poe ordered the full English. Melody Lee settled for black coffee and Bradshaw had bottled water.

'Neither of you hungry?' he said.

'I'm not eating anything in here, Poe,' Bradshaw said.

'And this coffee tastes like it came out of an asshole,' Melody Lee added.

'Lovely,' Poe said through a mouthful of beans and hash brown. 'Are you sure I can't tempt you with—' His phone rang. An unknown number.

'Poe,' he said.

'Where are you?'

It was Hannah Finch.

'Change of plan,' he said. 'We had to come down to Southampton late last night. That rat has featured in a crime before.'

'It has not. I searched every database you have access to and a few you don't.'

'Yet here I am.'

Finch paused. 'What did I miss?'

Poe was close to saying 'the point' but relented. As the fat congealed on his plate he told her about the withdrawn referral to SCAS.

'And Tilly was able to recall this?' she said.

'When you get to know her you'll realise that's not actually too extraordinary.'

'No wonder Alastor is keen to recruit her.'

After he'd hung up Poe looked at his plate. The bacon fat had turned white and hard.

'Marvellous,' he said.

Ben Slater lived in a detached house in the market town of Romsey, seven miles from Southampton. The front garden was hemmed in by a neat hedge. The lawn was green and freshly mown. Poe could see a sprinkler, although it wasn't turned on. The borders were a riot of colour, fragrant and crawling with bees.

Poe parked behind a rust-pitted Volvo with an 'I'D RATHER HAVE A BAD DAY FISHING THAN A GOOD DAY AT WORK' bumper sticker.

Slater had obviously been waiting for them; his front door opened as soon as they got out of the car.

He was a serious-looking man. Grizzled and in his early fifties, his grey hair was buzzcut short. He was wearing a tatty pair of olive corduroys and a light linen shirt. A stye in his left eye was causing it to run and he dabbed it with a chequered hankie. Otherwise he looked as fit as a weasel and twice as mean.

'Mr Slater?' Poe said.

'Ben,' he said. 'You must be Detective Sergeant Washington Poe?'

'Call me Poe. Call me Washington and no one will know who you're talking to.'

They shook hands. Slater's grip was firm and leathery. His calluses pressed into Poe's palm. A man who liked working outdoors.

'This is Tilly Bradshaw, also NCA, and Special Agent Melody Lee from the FBI.'

If Slater was surprised he didn't show it.

'Come in, come in. The kettle's just boiled and I've stocked up on coffee, tea and biscuits.'

They followed him into the kitchen. Children's drawings and doctor's appointments covered the fridge door. A schoolbag hung off the back of one of the stools around the central island. Despite the accoutrements of a noisy domestic life, the house was quiet.

'Asked Mrs Slater to take the kids out for the day,' Slater explained. 'Thought it best.'

'Appreciate it, Ben,' Poe said. 'We're sorry for the intrusion. We'll try and get you back to your fishing soon.'

'I have all day, Poe.'

'Hopefully it won't take that long – we just need a bit of background on the heist you were involved in and why you made the referral to SCAS.'

'What do you know?'

'Just what was on the referral form. The odd bits and bobs from PND. A few press clippings we could find.'

Slater flashed them a weary smile. 'Have I got a story to tell you then,' he said. 'You'd best sit down; this is going to take a while.'

Poe sat then leaned forwards. 'What don't we know, Ben?'

'There was a ceramic rat left at the scene, right?'

He nodded.

'Well, what you don't know is the rat was only the start of it. In my thirty years on the force I was never involved in a case as strange as this one.'

Chapter 42

'You see what I mean?' Slater said. 'The "falling out among thieves" narrative the SIO was pushing never sat right with me. It didn't seem to match what was on the CCTV.'

They had just watched the video of the heist and the subsequent murder of the man wearing the Timothy Dalton mask. His name was Terry Holmes. Slater had left Hampshire Constabulary the previous year but had made copies of the heist file, including a digital copy of the vault's video. Bradshaw had uploaded it to one of her laptops.

'Play it again, please,' Poe said.

There was no audio so they watched in silence. It lasted twenty-two minutes. Five men wearing James Bond masks entered the vault foyer. The man in the Pierce Brosnan mask started working on the vault door. For something so shiny and modern it took him a surprisingly short time to open.

The camera then switched to the internal vault. The men either didn't know they were being filmed or they didn't care. Timothy Dalton moved towards one of the larger safety deposit boxes but stopped when Sean Connery said something. Connery then removed a scrap of paper from his pocket and presumably read out the number of a specific box because they all spread out and started looking for it. George Lazenby found it. Pierce Brosnan, the Bond who'd cracked the vault door, was called over. He gave the box a cursory examination, then used a snapper bar to break the lock. He didn't look inside, just stepped back and allowed Sean Connery to open the door and inspect the box's contents.

After seeing it was empty, Sean Connery stepped back to let Timothy Dalton have a look.

Which was when he shot him in the back of the head.

Other than a passing glance at the summary sheet, Poe had purposefully left the official file alone. First, he wanted to hear from the one cop who hadn't followed the company line.

'Tell me about Hampshire's response,' Poe said.

'There were three major lines of enquiry,' Slater said. He held up a finger. 'One: what were they after? We know the safety deposit box was empty but what was supposed to be in it?'

'And how did that go?'

'Not well. The box was *always* going to be empty. The owner had hired it over the phone and paid for it via bank transfer. For the entire period of the lease it had never been accessed. The person who leased it had never even stepped in the building.'

'The Bonds had been given duff information?'

Slater shrugged. 'That was certainly the prevailing thought. And it fitted with the SIO's theory that someone had ratted out the gang. The box's leaseholder had been told his safety deposit box was going to be hit, which was why it hadn't been used.'

'The murder was the punishment and the ceramic rat was the warning to anyone else thinking of doing something similar.'

'The SIO said it fitted the facts.'

'It does,' Poe said. 'Just not with ours.'

'What did the person who'd leased the box have to say?' Melody Lee said.

'This is when it gets even weirder,' Slater said. 'The woman was called Sarah McIntyre and she didn't know anything about it. The deposit box fee had come out of her account but she had no knowledge of it.'

'She legit?' Poe said.

'She's in her seventies and lives in the Shetlands. Didn't know what a safety deposit box was. The money that left her account had been replaced at the same time. Came from an untraceable account.'

'OK, that is odd. What was the second line of enquiry?'

'Who the rest of the gang actually were,' Slater said. 'The dead man, Terry Holmes, was a well-known fence but he wasn't affiliated.'

'A literal dead end then?'

Slater shook his head. 'The man in the Pierce Brosnan mask made a mistake,' he said. 'Only for a second, and it was negligible. When he reached down to get the snapper bar from his tool bag, his sleeve rode up over his wrist. For the briefest of seconds you can see a sticking plaster.'

'I noticed that,' Poe said. 'I take it you didn't think it was a pimple?'

'We checked with your organised crime lot, and they confirmed what we already knew: there were only five crews operating in Europe with the technological expertise to get into that building and open the vault.'

'And someone on one of those crews had a distinguishing mark on his wrist?'

'Bryce Dickinson. Part of a four-man London team. He had a stethoscope tattoo on the inside of his wrist.'

'And stethoscopes were tools of the trade for men like him back in the day,' Poe said. 'You bring him in?'

'We did. Rock solid alibi.'

'Standard operating procedures on jobs like that, though. They won't do anything unless they can demonstrably prove they were doing something else fifty miles away at the exact same time.'

'That's how they work.'

'And the rest of the crew?'

'Same. Each of them had thirty people who swore blind they were with them.'

Poe knew that decent, legally tight alibis cost money. A professional alibi could be broken but it took time and a lot of resources. Even then, in the absence of direct evidence, they usually held up. Juries liked alibis. Always had, always would. Something Slater had said pushed its way to the front of his mind.

'You said Bryce Dickinson "had" a stethoscope tattoo? He doesn't any more?'

'He does not. Two months after he was released he was using stolen gelignite to prepare a shaped charge when he made a mistake.'

'A bad one?'

'Bad enough to blow his own head off.'

'Ouch,' Poe said.

'And without their technical guy, the other three had to slum it,' Slater continued. 'They were caught red-handed on what we assume was their first job without him. Broke into the basement vault of a fine art museum and managed to lock themselves in. They had to ring nine-nine-nine to get someone to let them out. They're all serving fifteen years.'

'Why so harsh?'

'One of them, we think the new safecracker, had clubbed the custodian over the head with an adjustable spanner. He had a heart condition and he died a few days later.'

'They were done under joint enterprise?'

'Yep.'

'Still leaves one man unaccounted for,' Poe said. 'Probably Sean Connery.'

'Good, you noticed the weird hierarchy that was going on in the vault room too.'

Poe had. It had sometimes appeared as though there were two crews in the vault, not one.

'The man in the Timothy Dalton mask looked as though he was deferring to Sean Connery, but the rest were taking their instructions from Daniel Craig,' he said.

'I agree,' Slater said. 'But before he does anything, Daniel Craig checks with Sean Connery first. We think Daniel Craig is a man called Keith Bloomfield. He's known to design bespoke robberies for his clients. Sometimes his crew carries it out on his client's behalf, other times he just takes a cut.'

Poe considered what that meant.

'So Sean Connery hired Daniel Craig's crew,' he said. 'And he brings Timothy Dalton, this Terry Holmes, with him. Maybe with the express purpose of killing him.'

'That's what I think.'

'So, Timothy Dalton was killed by Sean Connery, Pierce Brosnan blew his own head off a few weeks later and Daniel Craig and George Lazenby botched their next robbery.'

'Don't forget Roger Moore,' Slater said. 'He was the wheelman on this robbery, but he locked himself in the museum vault with the others.'

'Just Sean Connery left then,' Poe said.

'The missing link. And we didn't get close to identifying him. Not even a sniff.'

Poe took a sip of his coffee. It was cold but that was OK, he was hot. He swigged it down in one gulp. Slater refilled his mug.

'We need to speak to the remaining crew members,' Poe said.

'The three that are in prison?'

'If they were hired by Sean Connery, they'll know who he was. Gangs like that don't accept blind jobs.'

'Their names are in the file,' Slater said, 'but it won't do any good. They didn't say a word when we brought them in and they have less motivation to talk now. They'll be out in twelve years or so. If they get charged with a cold-blooded murder like this, they'll die inside.'

Poe knew Slater was right: speaking to the remaining gang members was the definition of a waste of time.

'Anything on the bullet?' he said.

Despite what the press would have the public believe, criminals in the UK didn't routinely use firearms.

'It was a thirty-eight,' Slater said.

'What did NBIS say?'

The National Ballistics Intelligence Service, the agency charged with maintaining the database of recovered firearms and ammunition used in the UK, and providing a ballistics comparison to any force that needed it, was a partner agency of the NCA. If the gun had a history, the bullet removed from the skull of the man wearing the Timothy Dalton mask would have linked them to it. Identify the weapon and you had a lead on who had bought it.

'Virgin,' Slater said.

A virgin gun was one that wasn't on any database to which NBIS had access. It meant that in all likelihood, the gun had never been fired during the commission of a crime.

'The expert we got to look at the CCTV footage says the gun was probably a Colt Detective Special,' Slater continued. 'Mainly used as a concealed weapon in the US. Rare here but not unheard of. We didn't get anywhere with it.'

Poe checked the time. They'd already been there two hours; he needed to move on.

'You said there were three lines of enquiry,' Poe said.

'The third line of enquiry was *how* they did it,' Slater said with a grin, 'and that was when things got really weird.'

Chapter 43

'Do you know much about safety deposit boxes, Sergeant Poe?' Slater said.

'Only that they're not as common as they used to be.'

'That's not quite right,' Slater said. 'While it's true that high-street banks no longer offer them, all that did was leave a gap in the market, a gap the private sector was happy to fill. Over the last decade or so, a large number of safety deposit box companies have popped up.'

'And they're dodgy?'

'Actually, they're not. They're highly regulated. Most have unparalleled security, security surpassing that of most major banks. We're talking cutting edge. Facial recognition, biometric software, digital photo recognition, offsite twenty-four-hour monitoring.'

'And this company had all of that?'

'And more. The vault walls were explosive and diamond crown drill-bit resistant. The vault door was made by Diebold. Five thousand pounds of solid steel protected by a three-keyed timer, two different combination locks and a master key. The combination lock numbers were held by two members of staff, the key by the vault manager.'

'So how did they . . .?'

'How did they circumnavigate combination locks, the timer override key and the master key? How did they manage to stop the offsite monitoring team calling it in? How did they fool the biometrics, the photo IDs, the facial recognition?'

'Yeah, all that,' Poe nodded. 'I'm assuming that . . . what,' – he did some mental arithmetic – 'seven or eight unrelated individuals didn't suddenly decide to club together and help someone steal from their employer.'

Slater held Poe's gaze. He had a twinkle in his eye.

'Oh, you've got to be joking,' Poe said.

Slater laughed. 'Nothing quite as grand, Sergeant Poe,' he said. 'But you saying seven or eight people all clubbed together to steal from their employer in a massive conspiracy isn't as far off as you might think.'

Poe considered what he knew about similar robberies. Most involved either weeks of backbreaking effort with tunnels and mechanical tools or a few minutes of breath-taking violence. Storm in during the day with guns and lots of noise, frighten the shit out of the staff, and get out before the cops can respond. The rest seemed to be a combination of technical expertise and coercion. Take the bank manager's kids hostage and half your problems were solved.

'They broke it down into five main areas,' Slater continued. 'The first was getting hold of the key. The lock on that vault door couldn't be fooled and forcing their way past it would have taken more time than they had. The second was getting the current numbers to the combination locks. They were changed weekly and the person who set one lock didn't know the combination to the other. The third was the timer. We think this is the one they did onsite. Bryce Dickinson, the man wearing Pierce Brosnan, had travelled abroad to train on this type of safe, and the equipment we can see on the CCTV footage lends itself more to the timer override than the other locks.'

He paused to take a drink of coffee. It was his third cup. Poe was on his fifth and starting to feel jittery.

'The fourth issue was all the security they had to overcome before they could even get to the vault's anteroom. The biometrics, the facial recognition, all that nonsense.'

'And the fifth?'

'The fifth, for a long time, was the one we just couldn't get our heads around: how the offsite monitoring team had missed what was happening right in front of them. If it was just one person watching the cameras then, fair enough, you'd say he'd been paid to look the other way. But this company doesn't have just one vault; it has several, and their CCTV is monitored centrally. At any one time there are at least half a dozen people in their control room.'

Melody Lee said, 'I've worked robbery and you can't buy off that many people. One of them would have gotten cold feet and gone to the cops. And judging by the video we've just watched, those men knew they weren't walking into an ambush.'

Poe agreed. Not only was the FBI's experience in armed robbery second-to-none, surely no professional crew would have relied on so many people doing what they had been paid to do.

'There must have been a single coercive factor,' she continued. 'Possibly something illegal they'd all been involved in. If the gang had found out about it then they could have used it as leverage.'

'Is she right?' Poe said.

'Nope,' Slater said. 'They got around the security by doing something we've never seen before. And I've checked.'

'You'd better explain.'

'I will, but first I need a prop.' Slater reached into the table drawer and pulled out a small plastic bag. He passed it to Poe.

It contained a mobile-phone charging cable.

Poe looked at Slater, confused. 'I'm not following.'

'You will,' Slater said. He reached into his file and pulled out a photo. 'The first domino to fall: Diane Story. Worked in the CCTV monitoring control room.'

'She admitted getting a bung?' Melody Lee said.

'Not even close. She did, however, admit to getting one of these charging cables through her door. It was professionally packaged and the accompanying letter said she'd been selected to trial a new, robust cable. Faster charging, faster uploads and faster downloads when it was connected to your laptop.'

Bradshaw blew a raspberry.

'What a dunce,' she said.

'I think Tilly may have skipped to the end,' Slater said.

Chapter 44

'And for the dunces who haven't skipped to the end?' Poe said. 'And go easy on me if it's going to get technical.'

'I'll use the language the jury heard,' Slater said. 'Diane Story thought nothing of trying what she thought was a brand-new charging cable.'

'She used it?' Poe said.

'What would you have done?'

'I dunno,' he admitted. 'Probably kept it as a spare. These things are always fraying.'

'You're an idiot, Poe,' Bradshaw said.

'Diane used it as her travel cable,' Slater said. 'Connected it to her laptop when she was away for the weekend. Uploaded a family video to clear space on her phone. And the cable did everything it was supposed to do.'

Bradshaw exhaled. Loudly. 'Why would someone trust anything other than an OEM cable?' she said.

'OEM?' Slater said.

'Original Equipment Manufacturer. Anything that's purchased direct from Apple or Samsung or Google, in other words.'

'I assume it wasn't an ordinary cable?' Poe said.

'The street name is a JANUS cable,' Slater said. 'It's basically a highly covert malicious USB cable.'

'Bloody hell,' Poe said. 'Is nothing safe any more?'

'Hidden inside the shell of the USB connector was a tiny hardware bug that ran code on her computer. I don't understand the tech but the moment Diane Story plugged it in, it started an application that connected her to a cloud server. Malicious software was then wirelessly transmitted to her laptop. A keystroke logging program that covertly logged what she typed on her keyboard and—'

'What would someone gain from that?' Poe said.

'Duh,' Bradshaw said. 'Passwords. Bank details. Everything is vulnerable.'

'Exactly,' Slater said. 'The other program was malware that gave them remote access to her computer.'

'What program did they use, Mr Slater?' Bradshaw asked. 'Poison Ivy? Dark Comet? Blackshades?'

'None of the above. Our forensic IT department head claimed he hadn't come across it before. Probably new or bespoke.'

'Writing malware isn't easy,' Bradshaw said. 'If it wasn't bought then whoever is behind this has serious skills.'

'Could you write them, Tilly?' Slater said.

'Pur-lease. I was writing them when I was still at school.'

'But Tilly is the exception rather than the rule,' Poe explained. 'If she says it takes skill, we have a lead. It's tenuous, but it's more than we had yesterday. I assume Diane Story had something on her computer she didn't want the world to know?'

'She was in an abusive marriage and was planning to leave her husband. Had a house purchase lined up. New name, the works. Was getting support from a local domestic abuse charity. Rather than telling him she was leaving him – which statistically is the most dangerous thing a woman can ever do – she planned to disappear then tell him through her solicitor.'

'And they threatened to out her?'

'They did.'

'But she was only one of . . . how many did you say were in the CCTV control room at any one time, six? Surely they didn't all get a snide cable? I'm not buying that everyone on that shift had something on their computer they needed to hide, and I'm not buying that the crew were confident the shift schedule would remain the same. That no one would call in sick. That a supervisor wouldn't pop in for a surprise visit.'

'Far subtler than that, Poe,' Slater said. 'The same day she was contacted, a memory stick was posted through her door. Her instructions were to insert it into the CCTV mainframe and leave it there for ten seconds.'

'That was it?'

Slater nodded.

'And what did that do?'

'It took us a while to figure it out, but the software she uploaded did something to the British Summertime configurations. On the day of the robbery, everything in the control room was on a one-hour delay. It was still recording and none of the footage was hidden. But what they were seeing had happened an hour earlier.'

'Clever,' Poe admitted.

'Very.'

'Although . . . and, Tilly, feel free to jump in here, wouldn't it have been easier to just shut it down for the time they were there?'

'The security company had a protocol for that. If a camera went down, a live body had to be on site within fifteen minutes.'

'But,' Bradshaw said, 'for someone with this level of technical proficiency it would have been easier to simply play back a previous night's footage. It's actually more complex to put in an hour delay.'

'Which begs the question: why?' Poe said.

They descended into silence. The washing machine burped.

'I'll put the kettle on again, shall I?' Slater said.

'Not for me,' Poe said, covering his cup. 'I have any more coffee and I'll be awake until next year.'

'I'll have some cold water please, Mr Slater,' Bradshaw said.

'It'll take a while for the tap to get cold but I have some ice in the freezer.'

'No thank you, Mr Slater; I don't have ice in my drinks.'

'Oh.'

'Coliform, the bacteria found in human faeces, has been shown to be present in a significant percentage of ice cubes.'

Poe shook his head. 'Every. Single. Time,' he said.

'Really?' Slater said. 'How extraordinary. I wish I'd known that twenty years ago. I'd have made sure every drink I made for my ex-wife had shit in it.'

Melody Lee snorted. 'You Brits,' she said. 'But can we get back to the question of the day? Why would they go to all that trouble of finding a way to disable the CCTV, to not bother? From what Ben said, that almost cost them – if they hadn't been caught on tape you wouldn't have been able to see that Band-Aid.'

After a short pause, Slater said, 'There *isn't* a reason. Why would they risk it? It doesn't make sense.'

And just like that, Poe understood.

'It doesn't if you only look at the heist as a singular, isolated event,' he said. 'But it absolutely does make sense if you put it next to our murder.'

Slater looked at him blankly.

Bradshaw frowned.

Melody Lee nodded. 'You're saying—'

'Someone's sending us a message,' Poe said. 'The rats, the theatre of it, deliberately capturing everything on tape, they're all chapters in a story we're being told.'

'But what story can possibly join my murder to yours?' Slater said.

'And more importantly, how does it end?' Poe added.

186

Chapter 45

Slater smiled.

'What?' Poe said.

'Nothing. It's just nice to think about the things we should have been thinking about back then.'

'They cover the CCTV because Diane Story was vulnerable to coercion,' Poe said. 'Most people won't be, though. How did they circumnavigate the rest of the security?'

Melody Lee cleared her throat.

'What?' Poe said again.

'I think you'd be surprised just how vulnerable we all are to this kind of shit, Poe,' she said. 'You telling me you don't have a single secret you don't want kept hidden?'

That made him pause. If you opened Poe's closet it would look like the entire cast of Walt Disney's *The Skeleton Dance* were hiding in there. Over the last few years he had accumulated at least three secrets he'd have to take to the grave. If two of them got out he'd probably do time. He supposed the odds weren't so outlandish that other people might feel the same about the darkest corners of their own lives.

'Still . . .' he said.

'The man who helped them bypass all the digital security was shagging his wife's sister,' Slater said. 'He shared a cloud folder with her and the pictures they kept there were graphic. One of the combination lock keyholders was hiding assets from his wife so he could cheat her during the divorce

187

she didn't know was coming. The other was part of a swingers' club.'

'Money and sex. It's always money and sex.' Poe paused, then added, 'That's why I'm glad I don't have either.'

Slater laughed.

'What about the keyholder?' Melody Lee said. 'The dude with the safe key, the one you said couldn't be cheated. What surreptitious bullshit was he keeping hidden?'

'Mr O'Sullivan?' Slater said. 'He did the same as everyone else. Got a JANUS cable through his door. Unwittingly uploaded the malware, but it seemed he was the one person who didn't have a secret worth breaking the law for.'

'So how did they . . .?'

'How did they get their key?'

Slater turned to Bradshaw. 'What would you have done if you couldn't find a secret to exploit, Tilly?'

'And the keystroke logging and the malware were running, Mr Slater?'

He nodded.

'Well, if I were a nasty pasty I'd probably *give* him a secret.'

Poe said, 'So, instead of threatening to expose something that was actually happening, they uploaded a . . . a what? What did they upload?'

'They created a cloud account and filled it with extreme porn. Water sports mainly.'

Poe put his head in his hands. *Please don't ask . . . Please don't ask . . . Please don't ask . . .*

'What are water sports?' Bradshaw said.

He groaned. 'I don't suppose you'll believe me if I say windsurfing?'

'No, Poe,' she said. 'Windsurfing, while undoubtedly a stupid pastime, is hardly a shameful one.'

He paused. If he didn't tell her she'd only google it, then ask her mum why people did that type of thing. He could do without another of those phone calls.

'It's when people wee on each other, Tilly,' he said eventually.

She reddened and said, 'I suppose that's on me for asking.'

'That was enough to get the key?' Poe said, anxious to move on. Bradshaw filled pauses in the conversation with questions you didn't want to answer.

Slater nodded. 'They kept it overnight and had a copy made. If you know the right people in London it's not that difficult a thing to do, apparently.'

'And the night of the heist everyone did what they were supposed to do?'

'They did,' Slater said. 'You have to admire their ingenuity.'

Poe said nothing. Ingenuity and ruthlessness weren't good combinations as far as he was concerned. He didn't admire anything about them.

Chapter 46

'I assume this was your hobby case,' Poe said, 'the one you couldn't walk away from? That's why you kept a copy of the file and the video?'

Slater nodded.

'Maybe take it out with you in case the fish aren't biting.'

'We all have one,' Slater admitted.

'Every case is a hobby case for Poe,' Bradshaw said. 'That's why his hair is falling out.'

'My hair is not falling out, Tilly,' Poe said. 'It's receding gracefully.'

'I don't know if it was because the more we knew the less we understood,' Slater said, 'or because I was the one who had to go and keep Susan Holmes up to date with the murder investigation, but I couldn't let this one go.'

'Susan Holmes?' Poe said.

'Terry Holmes's daughter. When it became apparent he was just a low-level crook, no one really gave a shit about his family. I thought someone should.'

'She in the family business?'

'If by "family business" you mean the pawnshop her father used as a front, yes. If you mean was she involved in fencing stolen goods, I really have no idea. I suspect not.'

'How'd she take it?'

'Badly. She knew her dad was a crook but he'd done OK by her. Sent her to a fancy school. Didn't skimp on the alimony payments after his divorce. Doted on her, from what I could gather.'

'Was she able to shed any light on anything?'

'Not a thing. She told me that when uniform had turned up to do the death knock she assumed they'd made a mistake. Said her dad didn't get involved with people like that. Certainly wouldn't have been involved in robbing a bank.'

'How old is she?'

'She'll be mid-twenties now.'

'And she hadn't seen the ceramic rat before?'

'Nope.'

Poe picked up Slater's file and removed a photograph of the rat that had been left in the vault. It was grainless and highly detailed. Every fleck of paint was visible. Bradshaw picked up the rest and began flicking through them. On his phone, Poe brought up an image of the rat found in the Carlisle brothel. They looked identical. And they looked rough and ready. Not valuable but not mass-produced either. Bradshaw had looked online but hadn't been able to find them.

Poe sighed and threw the photograph on the kitchen table. All they'd done was add confusion to an already confusing case. It was time to let Slater go fishing and for them to get back up north. The obsessed cop hadn't found anything in three years; Poe wasn't going to in a single morning.

'We've taken up too much of your time today, Ben,' he said. He passed the ex-cop his last business card. 'Call me if you think of anything. Day or night, I'm always available.'

Slater glanced at it and said, 'Every case is a hobby case. I like that, Poe.'

'Come on, Tilly,' Poe said. 'Let's leave Mr Slater to his fishing.'

Bradshaw didn't move.

'If we stay much longer, Tilly, we're going to have to buy a house down here.'

But she wasn't listening. She was staring rigidly at a photograph of the rat.

Poe recognised that look.

She'd found something . . .

Chapter 47

Bradshaw held up a photograph of Slater's rat and another of the rat Hannah Finch had stolen.

'Look at the photographs, Poe. Really look at them.'

Poe did. Didn't see anything. He looked at her quizzically.

'Tell me what you see,' she said.

'Four inches tall,' he said. 'Glazed. If they weren't hand-painted, they're meant to look as though they are.'

'They *are* hand-painted, Poe,' Bradshaw said. 'If you look at the blown-up photographs you can see some small imperfections. I think the manufacturer probably had a template they stuck to for the paint scheme. I imagine every rat had the same coat of grey ceramic glaze fired in the kiln then, after they'd cooled, the overglaze – the paints used to add decoration and detail – was added. They would have then been baked again, but at a lower temperature.'

'You know a lot about ceramics, Tilly,' Poe said.

She shrugged. 'I research anything I think might be relevant.'

'OK, I agree: it's hand-painted. I'm not seeing what you see yet though, Tilly.'

'What I'm seeing, Poe, is a lengthy process for something with no long-term commercial value. I mean, it's a yukky rat. Who wants one of those as an ornament?'

'So?'

'I'm guessing now, but I think the potter who made it probably did it as a bespoke commission. And as the size of the thing being fired dictates how long and how hot the kiln is fired for, it makes sense that he'd have done a few together. One for the person who commissioned it, a few in case he messed up the painting or dropped it or something. The rest he kept to sell to whoever wanted one.'

'What's your point?' Poe said.

'My point is that handcrafted ceramic pieces like these are made with care and attention. Anything with an error would be destroyed. He'd have only sold the perfect ones. And look, these aren't perfect. They both have flaws. The same flaw – a small red splodge of paint on the left forelimb that's on top of the overglaze, not under it. It's matt, not gloss, which is why it doesn't catch the light the same way.'

Poe studied the photographs. Compared them against each other. She was right. Both rats had a small smudge of red paint in the same place. He'd noticed it on his rat, but had dismissed it as an imperfection in the painting process. But, put next to the Southampton rat, it looked anything but a mistake – it looked deliberate.

'They were added afterwards,' he said.

'That's the only conclusion, Poe.'

'Why, though?'

'I don't know,' she said, 'but I'm starting to think you're right: everything that's happened in this case has been deliberate and meaningful. You said earlier that it was all chapters in a story we're being told.'

'I did.'

'I think these rats are what's on the next page.'

'So the cases are linked?' Slater said.

'They have to be,' Bradshaw said. 'The chances of two uncon-nected ceramic rats having the same *unintentional* flaw are astronomical.'

'But there's nothing in Christopher Bierman's profile to

suggest he moved in the same circles as Terry Holmes,' Melody Lee said. 'Either when he was Jack Duncan the war hero, or Christopher Bierman the successful businessman.'

'We need to tug on the Terry Holmes thread first,' Poe said. 'His murder was three years before Bierman's. If we're going to understand the story we need to start at the beginning.'

'You think there's something else?' Slater said. 'Something we didn't uncover during our investigation?'

Poe shrugged. 'I think it's where we need to start. We know more now.'

'Terry Holmes's daughter still manages his shop. I think she'll take my call. I can make an introduction.'

'That would be helpful.' But not as helpful as going to see her with someone familiar with the area, he thought. Although SCAS were Hampshire-based, their remit was national and Poe had never investigated a case in the county before. He wondered if Slater fancied keeping his fishing lines dry for a few more hours.

'You fancy a trip around your old haunts, Ben?'

Slater's grin was ear to ear. 'Thought you'd never ask,' he said.

Chapter 48

Susan Holmes wasn't due back in Southampton until the following day. Poe was disappointed but soon realised it was a blessing in disguise. They were exhausted and, if Susan had been in, they'd have had another five-hour drive north immediately afterwards. No, better they booked into a hotel, had a nice meal and a decent night's sleep. Start tomorrow like a squirrel – bright-eyed and bushy-tailed.

After the SCAS office manager had made their reservations, they said goodbye to Slater and made their way to their hotel. It was before the official check-in time but the receptionist took one look at their bloodshot eyes and washed-out faces and moved things around so they could have their rooms early.

The plan was to have a light lunch followed by an afternoon power nap. They would then meet in the hotel lobby around five and find somewhere to eat. After that, Bradshaw had arranged with Zoe, DI Stephanie Flynn's partner, for them to pop in to see the boss and her baby.

Poe doubted that Zoe had been happy about it. He'd wanted to visit Flynn the previous month but Zoe had insisted her best chance of recovery was to avoid having contact with anyone who might remind her of her last case. Poe wasn't convinced; Flynn was a scrapper, easily the toughest woman he knew, and he thought she needed to get back in the game. He could count the number of friends he had on one hand (and he wouldn't need to use all his fingers) and he wanted to help. And he thought he could. Zoe had her wrapped in cotton wool but you didn't fix Stephanie Flynn that way. She needed something to fight. Always had. Ten minutes of listening to how he was bolloxing up her unit, and she'd be back in her power suit, yelling instructions and keeping him in line.

Before he'd left Slater's house he'd sent Hannah Finch a text telling her they wouldn't be back in Cumbria until tomorrow. She hadn't responded.

The office manager hadn't exactly booked them into a spa hotel, but the rooms were airy and the sheets were white and starched. Poe didn't bother showering. He removed his shoes, closed the curtains and lay on top of the bed.

He was asleep in seconds.

Poe was having an incoherent dream. There was a rat in it, a giant one with a ceramic body but a real tail. There were bank robbers too and they seemed to be friends with the rat. Until they weren't. And when they weren't, it didn't go well for the robbers. The dream was on the cusp of becoming a nightmare when something made the rat and the robbers freeze. An incessant ringing noise.

He opened his eyes. It was his room phone. It was bound to be Bradshaw. The cheap digital clock next to the phone told him he'd been asleep less than twenty minutes. He didn't need much, usually managed to get by on six hours a night, but Bradshaw needed even less. She'd be in her room working, no doubt. Probably found something.

'Tilly, unless it's urgent, I need to get a couple of hours in,' he said. 'If you want, we can meet before we eat.'

But it wasn't Bradshaw, it was the receptionist.

'You have a visitor, sir,' she said. 'Wants to know your room number. Are you OK if I let her have it?'

'What's her name?'

'Hannah Finch, sir.'

Poe groaned.

'Sir?'

'Let her up,' he said. 'And it's OK, she'll already know which room I'm in.'

The moment Poe opened his door for Hannah Finch, Bradshaw opened hers. He was right, she hadn't been sleeping. She didn't even have the grace to look tired.

'Do you need something, Poe?' she said.

'Hannah Finch is on her way up, Tilly. I'll deal with her, you go back to . . . whatever it is you were doing in there.'

'I was cross-referencing Mr Slater's file with our own.'

'Anything?'

'Nothing yet.'

The door to Melody Lee's room opened. She stuck her head out.

'What have you assholes got against sleep?' She was bleary-eyed and had a serious case of bedhead. Her hair was sticking up on one side, flat on the other. She still had pillow marks on her face.

'You off out?' Poe said.

'Oh, ha ha,' she said. 'And seriously, what the hell's wrong with you two?'

'Hannah Finch is on her way up, Special Agent Lee,' Bradshaw said.

'I'll get dressed,' she said, and shut the door.

'Fucking marvellous,' Poe muttered.

'Listen, I know not telling me where you were was punishment for taking that rat,' Finch said. 'I get that. I shouldn't have done what I did. But you have to believe me when I say I just want to know what's happening.'

Poe didn't respond.

They were crammed into his hotel room. Bradshaw and Melody Lee were perched on the bed, Finch had taken the chair in front of the mirror and Poe was on the armchair. He could have insisted on meeting in the bar or somewhere quiet, but if he had, that would be him up. Better to listen to what she had to say, then tell her to piss off so he could get some sleep.

'So, by all means, keep me in the dark if you want. I won't complain and I'll do everything you tell me to. I'll share anything I get and I'll take all the shit you throw at me. I'm just here to learn, Sergeant Poe.'

He turned to Bradshaw. 'That was a good speech, wasn't it, Tilly?'

'Very good, Poe.'

He turned back to Finch. 'How long did it take you to get the tone right?'

'About three hours,' she smiled. 'Practised it all the way here.'

Chapter 49

Poe had only seen pawnshops on television; he'd never been inside one. Holmes's shop was in Southampton, not quite the city centre but not quite the suburbs. He'd assumed it would be in among bookmakers, discount shops and takeaways but he was wrong. It was in a quiet, leafy street with pavement cafés, artisan bakers and microbreweries. They had been there less than five minutes when Slater parked behind Poe's BMW.

'Find it OK?' he said.

'Satnav,' Poe said.

'What did you do last night?'

Poe said, 'Visited a friend,' but didn't elaborate.

He and Bradshaw had gone to see Flynn. As expected, Zoe had received them frostily. Bradshaw hadn't noticed but he had. Zoe blamed Flynn's job for what had happened, but, as she could hardly take it out on her recuperating partner, and because Bradshaw seemed to be off limits for everyone, when they were out of earshot he got both barrels. Poe took it without saying a word. It was the price he had to pay for what had happened earlier in the year. Flynn had given birth to her son in the most appalling of circumstances. It was a minor miracle either of them had survived. She had been on maternity leave followed by long-term sick leave ever since.

Poe had stood his ground. Flynn was his friend and he wanted to see her. Eventually Zoe relented and let him in. He was shocked by her appearance.

She was whip thin, almost bony, and her lank hair stuck together in clumps. Her skin was sallow and clammy. She'd flashed him an anxious smile then went back to watching Bradshaw hold the baby.

'How are you, Poe?' she'd asked.

'Missing your common sense, Steph,' he'd said. 'Tilly's getting out of control.'

'I most certainly am not!' Bradshaw had said. 'It wasn't me who arrested a member of MI5.'

'He did not!'

'Yes, he did, DI Flynn. And then Hannah Finch started shouting at Poe and then Poe took her photograph when she was in handcuffs and said if she didn't calm down he'd post it on Twitter then have her squirted in the eyes with pepper spray. And then *I* said that Poe probably wouldn't even know how to upload a photograph to Twitter.'

'Just another day at the office then,' Flynn had said.

He'd shrugged. 'We're a bit short on adult supervision at the minute.'

Zoe glared at him and Poe knew why. In all the times he'd visited Flynn he hadn't yet broached her returning to work. And now he had. He'd said it jokingly, but everyone in the room – Bradshaw excepted – had known it was the opening thrust in a difficult conversation.

Before Flynn could answer, Zoe had parried it.

'I think Stephanie is getting tired, Mr Poe,' she'd said, her lips flat, her eyes cold.

'Aww,' Bradshaw had said. 'Can we not stay for a bit longer?'

'We'd best be getting back, Tilly,' he'd said, matching Zoe's glare. 'We're meeting Special Agent Lee for dinner, remember?'

'Yes, but that's not for another two hours, we can easily stay—'

'Come on, Tilly, let DI Flynn rest. We can come back another time.'

'I'm not ready yet, Poe,' Flynn had said.

Poe had looked at her. She was right; she wasn't ready. She'd looked weak and vulnerable and nothing like the woman he knew. But there was something else there if you looked carefully. A spark of defiance. A sign that the old Flynn was in there somewhere. That she'd allow Zoe to make her decisions for now, but at some point she wouldn't. Flynn stared at him, then almost imperceptibly she winked, watched to make sure he'd seen it. He nodded. Message received.

Zoe might have known Flynn longer, but he knew her better. It was the curse of the single-minded cop. The people you worked with became your surrogate family, your real family became strangers. And Poe reckoned Flynn was sick of playing the victim. She'd be back soon; he'd bet Herdwick Croft on it.

He had left in a surprisingly upbeat mood.

Poe eyed the business Susan Holmes had inherited from her father.

From the outside it looked more like an antique shop than a business that offered loans secured against items of personal property. The only nod to the pawn trade was the traditional sign hanging above the door: three golden balls suspended from a bar. Bradshaw, answering a question no one had asked, told them the symbol dated back to medieval times and the powerful Medici family, well-known bankers whose family crest was gold circles.

Shading his eyes, Poe peered in through the window. He couldn't see anyone inside but the 'Open' sign was showing and it was past nine o'clock.

He opened the door.

A quaint jangler announced their presence.

A woman called from the back, 'Can you flip the sign to Closed? May as well have some peace while we talk. I'm brewing some coffee. If you take a seat I'll be out in a tick.'

Susan Holmes had set up one of the tables for sale with cups and saucers and biscuits. Poe took one, saw Bradshaw stare, and put it back. He examined his surroundings. His initial assessment – that the shop was more antique than pawn – seemed to be holding up.

Instead of glass-topped counters displaying costume jewellery, mobile phones and cameras, and shelves stacked high with laptops, microwave ovens and musical instruments, there were oil paintings in elaborately carved frames, gilded mirrors and vintage, paint-distressed advertising signs. Poe saw the Coca-Cola girl, the Marlboro man and the Bisto kids. There were china dolls and silver candlesticks, dainty figurines and grandfather clocks. Crystal chandeliers and ornate lamps dangled from the ceiling, handmade rugs covered the floor. The shop smelled of wood and leather, of paper and polish.

He wondered if it had always been this way or whether Terry Holmes's daughter had moved the business in a new direction. A pawnshop seemed out of place in an area like this, an antique shop not so much. Poe had always liked antique shops; like him, they had a built-in resistance to change.

Bradshaw jumped to her feet and marched towards a box on the next table. 'Oh, wow,' she said. 'Have you seen this, Poe?'

'What is it?' he said, getting to his feet. 'You found something?'

'Only a complete set of *Spider-Man* comic books in superb condition. And look, these are the ones where he has a black costume instead of the red and blue. It caused a massive controversy at the time but the creators eventually revealed that the black costume was actually an alien symbiote. It was where the villain Venom came from.'

Poe sat down.

'I wonder how much they are,' she said. 'I bet I can't afford them.'

'If you find the man who killed my father,' a woman behind them said, 'you can have them as a gift.'

They turned.

Susan Holmes wasn't at all like Poe had expected.

Chapter 50

Poe had assumed Susan Holmes would be the stereotypical daughter of a known criminal – foul mouthed and defiant. Demanding justice while spitting invective at the people charged with delivering it. If he'd been given a pound for every time the family of a murder victim had snarled that they didn't speak to the 'filth' or the 'bacon', he'd be able to afford more bacon.

So, when he turned and saw the young woman, he was momentarily taken aback. Susan Holmes was tall and willowy and tastefully dressed in jeans, a cream blouse and knee-length brown boots. Her long hair was almost white. She wore it loose rather than tied back. It framed her face and made it look as though she were peering through a pair of curtains. Poe wondered why someone so attractive was doing her best to hide it.

'Hello again, DC Slater,' she said.

'Just Ben these days, Susan.'

'Oh, I didn't know you'd left the police.'

'A year now. These are the people I told you about. This is Sergeant Washington Poe and Tilly Bradshaw from the National Crime Agency, Special Agent Melody Lee from the FBI and Hannah Finch who works for the . . . government.'

Susan put the coffee pot on the table and shook hands with everyone. As she did, her hair fell away and Poe understood why she wore her hair like she did: a scar divided the left side of her face. It stretched from her cheekbone to her chin and was long and pale and as thin as a crack in ice. It looked like there was a fishbone embedded in her alabaster skin.

She saw him looking. With a practised flick her hair hid the left side of her face again.

'Sorry,' Poe said.

She shrugged. 'I've had it since I was child. I'm used to it.'

Poe held her gaze. Saw someone who'd been forced out of the shadows by her father's death. Probably had to overcome a natural shyness at the same time.

Before he could ask, she said, 'It was a car accident. My father hit black ice on the way back from school one day. A shard of windscreen glass did this. I didn't think it at the time but I was lucky really. An inch to the right and it'd have taken my eye.'

She reached down and filled everyone's cup. Bradshaw was about to say she didn't drink coffee but Poe shook his head.

'My father blamed himself, of course. I did too for a bit. He ended up sacrificing a great deal to make up for it. Private schools. Music lessons. Horses. It cost him his marriage, his integrity.'

Which was as good a place as any to start.

Chapter 51

Susan Holmes had moved her father's business out of fencing and into antiques, a natural jump for someone with a fine arts degree who specialised in vases and bowls by the designer Clarice Cliff.

'Did you know what your father did, Susan?' Poe said. They had agreed that he'd lead and bring others in as he needed. He only planned to talk about the Southampton murder. 'His non-pawnshop side of things?'

Susan nodded. 'I did.'

Poe didn't respond.

'You want to know how complicit I was?' she added. She turned to Slater. 'I thought you said they wanted to find the truth? If all they're here for is to dig up more dirt you can leave now.'

'Hear Sergeant Poe out, Susan,' Slater said. 'He's made more progress on your father's murder in one afternoon than we did in years.'

She settled down.

'Unless you're hiding things we need to know about, I'm not interested in how complicit you were,' Poe said. 'But I do want to know what else he was up to.'

She frowned.

'One moment, please.' She got up and went into the back room again, returning seconds later with a large cardboard box. 'I knew my father handled stolen goods, but if he had other irons in the fire I didn't know about them. In here is everything I've gathered on what happened. As long as I get it back you're welcome to take it away with you.'

'Do you still have the computer he used?' Poe said. 'Tilly wants to examine it.'

'A laptop,' Susan said. 'The police have already searched it, though.'

'Ah, but we have Tilly; they didn't.'

She went into the back again, returning with a dusty laptop. She handed it to Bradshaw. 'Sorry,' she said. 'I don't have the power cable.'

Bradshaw turned the laptop on its side and examined the power port. She opened her satchel, pulled out a lead from a jumble of them and plugged it in. A blue light began to flash at the front. She connected it to one of her own laptops.

'I can't remember the password,' Susan added. 'I'm sorry, I'm not being very helpful, am I?'

'Tilly won't need the password,' Poe said.

'I'll see if Hampshire Constabulary missed anything,' Bradshaw said. 'I'll be a few minutes.' She stood and carried both laptops to another table. Before long she was typing faster than the eye could see.

Poe left her to it. If there was something in there, they would know shortly.

'I understand you used to live in London, Susan?' he said.

'We did. My father moved here after the divorce. I was at boarding school so split my holidays between him and my mother.'

'Why did he move here, though? Southampton couldn't have been as lucrative as London.'

'He never said. Just bought the shop and continued doing what he'd always done.'

'Tilly, can you see if his finances make sense?'

'I will, Poe.'

He turned back to Susan. 'He didn't mention working with

this crew before, the ones in the Bond masks?'

'As far as I knew he never did things like that. I really don't know what he was thinking of. He was a gentle man. Certainly not cut out for armed robberies.'

'Was anything worrying him? Had someone threatened him? Had a deal he was involved in not gone to plan? Had he, heaven forbid, stolen something or informed on someone?'

'You mean can I think of anything to link that rat with him being shot in the back of the head?'

'Yes.'

'No. And if you think I haven't been thinking about this ever since it happened then you're not the detective Mr Slater made you out to be.'

'I had to ask,' Poe said.

'Sergeant Poe, my father was a good man, but he'd be the first to admit he wasn't an *honest* man. But, in his defence, he did it for what he considered the right reasons – giving me the life he'd never had.'

'You think he became a fence because of guilt? For what happened to your face?'

'I do. And the reason I do is that my mum told me. When she met him he was an honest man – or as honest as pawnshop owners can be. It wasn't until the accident that he decided he wasn't making enough money.'

Poe had heard of flimsier reasons to break the law and, although fences had always had a symbiotic relationship with acquisitive crime and the misery it caused, he had a certain amount of sympathy for Terry Holmes. Poe knew he'd never have children, but he knew if he had there wouldn't be much he wouldn't do for them.

'What do you think happened, Sergeant Poe?' Susan said.

'I don't know,' he said, 'but we're not leaving here until we do.'

Which was when Bradshaw said, 'I've found something.'

Chapter 52

'I checked Mr Holmes's finances, Poe, and there's a discrepancy,' Bradshaw said. 'He was making more money here than he was in London.'

'Probably rates and overheads differentials,' Poe said. 'He'd have made more money in London but his outgoings would have been higher too. More money but less profit.'

'I'm not talking about profit, Poe, I'm talking about income. Mr Holmes had more money coming in here than he did in London.'

'OK. That's actually good. It fits the theory that he had more going on than fencing. A side business to his side business. Anything on his laptop to indicate what that might be, Tilly?'

'No, but there's something else. Another discrepancy: the hard drive has less space than it should. It's only a couple of megabytes out, but I can't account for them.'

'Meaning?'

'I can only think of one reason: there's another operating system on here somewhere.'

'In the hidden volume?' Melody Lee said. 'That's where I'd have it.'

'That's where I'd put it too, Special Agent Lee,' Bradshaw said.

'Me too,' Finch said.

Everyone looked at Poe.

'Me too,' he said.

'Yeah, right,' Bradshaw snorted. 'Volume, sometimes called

outer volume, is the space on the disc that is filled with random values. Hidden volume resides within that space and has its own file system, password and encryption. It's almost impossible to detect as the content resides in the free space of the outer volume, space that would otherwise be filled with random values if the hidden volume didn't exist.'

Poe looked at her blankly; a look she recognised well.

'Imagine you have a jar and you add some water,' she said. 'The jar was full of air but the water replaces it. But, any space left in the jar is still filled with air. With a computer's RAM, any space that doesn't have data is filled with random values instead of air. The hidden volume is hidden in those random values.'

'Gotcha,' Poe said.

Bradshaw sighed. 'It means there's enough spare RAM on this computer to operate a completely new operating system.'

'So when you bypassed my dad's password you got the main system,' Susan said. 'The one with his pawnbroker files, his accounts, that type of thing.'

'And some encrypted files about his handling stolen goods business.'

'But if he knew how to encrypt files, why bother with a different operating system?' Poe said.

'It is very difficult to detect an operating system in the hidden volume, Poe. The only way to confirm there is one is to calculate how much hidden volume there should be, then compare it against what you actually have.'

'But you think you've found one, Tilly?' Finch said. 'How? Even we can't be sure when we seize computers.'

'I wrote a program that differentiates between random and non-random values,' she said. 'It is calibrated to measure the size differently to conventional programs.'

'Can you get into this hidden operating system thing, Tilly?' Poe said.

'I'll have to reverse engineer the specialist software Mr Holmes used, and then I'll need the password, but I think so.'

'Crack on then.'

'I don't understand this, Sergeant Poe,' Susan said. 'My dad wouldn't have known how to do any of this. I did all his accounting and software updates. He could upload stock pictures and post items on the website, but that was all he could do. I couldn't do what Tilly has just described and a large part of my degree was spent on computers.'

Poe didn't doubt she was right. If Terry Holmes had been able to do what Bradshaw was suggesting, he probably had the skills to do something more lucrative for a living. Crooks with computer skills were in high demand.

'And I don't know where this laptop came from,' Susan said. 'I wouldn't have bought this brand.'

Poe felt a tingle in his spine.

'It sounds like your father and I were alike in this area, and I wouldn't go out and buy any old computer. I'd ask someone who knew about them. In other words, I'd ask Tilly to come with me.'

'Like we did with your digital radio, Poe?' Bradshaw said.

'Exactly. So if he wouldn't have known how to put this hidden operating thingy on his computer, and you weren't there when he bought it, what does that suggest?'

Slater, the only other proper cop in the room as far as Poe was concerned, got there first. 'He was given it,' he said.

'With the program already installed,' Poe added. 'Which means—'

'He'd have been given the hidden system's password as well,' Finch said.

'And if it was me I wouldn't change it,' Poe said. 'Probably wouldn't know how to anyway.'

'It won't be a word,' Bradshaw said. 'It'll be a stream of randomly generated letters, numbers and symbols.'

'Not one he could remember?'

'Doubtful. It'll be at least twenty characters long.'

'It's got to be here somewhere then. Hidden but easily accessible.'

They all stood.

Everyone except Susan.

'I think I know what the password is,' she said. She opened her purse and extracted a piece of folded paper. She passed it to Bradshaw. 'I gave this to the police officer who examined the computer but he said it didn't open anything.'

Bradshaw rolled her eyes.

'When he gave it back to me I never got around to throwing it out,' Susan continued. 'It's been in my purse for years.'

Bradshaw unfolded the paper. It was as she'd said – a random set of numbers and letters. She entered them into Terry Holmes's laptop.

The screen changed.

'I'm in,' she said.

It wasn't like any home screen Poe had seen before. There were no icons to click on and no background photograph. All there was were rows and rows of text, like an Excel spreadsheet.

'Right, Mr Holmes,' Bradshaw said, 'let's see what you've been hiding.'

She didn't usually like people standing behind her while she worked, but on this occasion Poe doubted she even knew she had an audience. No one spoke as they watched her rattle through screen after screen, pausing sometimes to read something, dismissing others the second they opened.

'I was right,' she said. 'It is a hidden operating system. It seems to be linked with hidden operating systems on other computers.'

'What's on it, Tilly?' Poe said.

'Bear with me, Poe,' Bradshaw said, moving to her own laptop. 'My decryption program will take about five minutes to run. We should know then.'

Four minutes, as it happened.

It took four minutes to understand why Terry Holmes had moved the family business from London to Southampton.

'Bloody hell,' Poe said.

Chapter 53

'What's the one thing Southampton has that London doesn't?' Poe said.

'A decent football team,' Slater said.

'A port,' Finch said. 'I mean, yes, London does have docks, but nothing like the deep seaport here.'

'Exactly,' Poe said. 'This is why Terry Holmes moved here. The container terminal for freight and cargo is the second-largest deep seaport in the country.'

'Damn,' Slater said. 'While we were looking in, we should have been looking out.'

'I think the fencing business was just a cover for his real illegal business.'

'Smuggling?'

Poe nodded. 'It ticks every box.'

'And don't forget the cruise companies have four terminals here,' Slater said. 'They go all over the world and there's little to nothing in the way of customs checks for passengers when they return. Even less for crew members.'

'And every commercial port has smuggling problems,' Melody Lee said. 'The dope run by mules who tunnel under the US/Mexico border is insignificant compared to the dope that comes into the country via cargo containers with a whole bunch of correctly filled in paperwork. One of the drawbacks of free trade agreements is that nothing really gets checked any more.'

'Freight for the larger items and individuals for the smaller stuff,' Poe said. 'As a way of getting things in and out, ports are ideal.'

'But you don't think Mr Holmes was smuggling things for himself,' Finch said. 'You think he was the point man for the Port of Southampton?'

'If Susan's right, her father didn't have the technical skill to set up his computer like this, and if Tilly's right, and she always is, then Terry Holmes was making more money from handling stolen goods here than he was in one of the world's richest cities.'

'So he was a link in a chain?'

'That's my guess. The people behind this will be a transnational organised crime group. Probably have offices in London, New York, even Beijing. They'll have recruited him and asked him to relocate to receive and broker their goods. They'll have a Terry Holmes strategically placed in all major sea- and airports.'

The pawnshop went quiet as they all considered what they had learned.

'What *had* my dad got himself into?' Susan said eventually.

Chapter 54

Antiquities.

That was what Bradshaw had found on Terry Holmes's hidden operating system. Lots of antiquities.

Or, to use the correct term, *looted* antiquities.

Holmes's computer had a record of stock he'd moved, stock he was holding and stock he was expecting. Mosaics from Syria and statues from Cambodia; tablets from Iraq and chessboards from China; gazelle-skin books from Jordan and golden cylinder seals from Egypt. Enough history to fill a small museum had passed through Terry Holmes's hands.

Poe doubted he'd physically touched anything. He probably just arranged safe storage and transport for the organisation's product. He'd be told when something was coming and when it was due back out. Greased a few palms, hired storage if it wasn't being moved immediately. Made sure the looted items reached the dealers and auction houses with all the correct documents and permits. Probably took a cut of the gross price. Not much, but enough to make it worth his while.

The National Crime Agency had whole units dedicated to fighting the trade in looted antiquities. It was worth millions, possibly billions, of pounds and that meant it was enforced with violence, it was a breeding ground for corruption and the people at the user end were the most exploited. Profits were often funnelled into terrorism. You didn't need to have the brains of Bradshaw to see the evolutionary line between an IED in Afghanistan and an ancient mask stolen from a burial cave near Cairo. It just depended on how hard the museums and collectors wanted to look. Diligently checking an object's provenance often came second to having something no one else had.

And the smugglers went to extraordinary lengths to give their objects a more palatable history. Poe knew of a statue stolen in India being smuggled to Hong Kong, on to London then New York, before finally being sold to a museum in Australia. A convoluted route but, due to the differing import and export regulations in each country, it was a route that all but guaranteed a seamless transition from the black market to the open market.

Complicating the matter further were the organised crime bosses. They had started to buy rare art and antiquities in bulk, not as an investment, but in case they ever needed leverage: 'Prosecute me to the full extent of the law and these irreplaceable antiquities are lost forever.' The charges are reduced and a country gets its cultural heritage back.

'The trade in stolen antiquities has huge parallels with the US dope trade,' Melody Lee said. 'It's not the looters that are the problem, it's the collectors. Just like cocaine, demand causes supply. And in Colombia, illegal crops like the coca leaf are actually the rational response to the artificially low prices of the West's heavily subsidised legal crops.'

'Exactly,' Finch said. 'Try telling a starving man in Syria that his country's heritage is more important than feeding his children. And ISIS and all these other organisations are surprisingly pragmatic. They issue permits and take a percentage of anything found, more if you used their equipment to dig it up.'

'All very interesting,' Poe said, 'and what's on this computer is going straight to our transnational organised crime unit, but it doesn't help us link Terry Holmes's involvement with the trade in stolen antiquities to the murder of Christopher Bierman. Unless I'm missing something?'

Silence.

'You are,' Bradshaw said eventually.

Because by then she'd discovered the other thing secreted in Terry Holmes's hidden operating system.

Chapter 55

'What the hell?' Poe muttered, his eyes glued to the laptop.

The still image of Christopher Bierman looked back at him. It wasn't crisp, but it was definitely him. His hair was a little shorter and he had a tan he hadn't got in the UK. He was thin and showed faint traces of a beating. A cut on his lips that hadn't quite healed, an eye socket stained yellow with an old bruise. He was wearing a short-sleeved shirt and a pair of chinos.

'I'll get a date stamp and find out when this was taken,' Bradshaw said. 'It shouldn't take long.'

'Don't bother, Tilly,' Poe said. 'I know when this was taken.'

'You do?' Finch said. 'How?'

'That's a soldier's tan. Comes from wearing open-collar shirts with the sleeves rolled up. Regulations state the top button has to be unfastened and the sleeves have to be two fingers above the elbows. If you look carefully, you can see his tan doesn't extend much past the forearms and the V between his collarbone.'

He pointed at the cuts and bruises.

'Add in his injuries and the timeline is obvious. This was taken shortly after he was medevacked to the UK after his rescue. Judging by how much the cuts and bruises have faded, I'd say this was two or three weeks after he got back. Maybe a month.'

Melody Lee leaned in beside him. Their shoulders touched.

'Hard to argue with that,' she said. 'So what the hell was he doing here?'

'It looks like Terry Holmes had a hidden webcam,' Bradshaw

said. 'Perhaps he used it to catch the faces of people who came into his shop?'

Poe shook his head. 'If that were the case there would be thousands of photographs. There are only six in that folder.'

Finch frowned. 'Maybe he only turned it on when he was dealing with someone he didn't know?'

'Go on.'

'Organisations like this have complicated smuggling routes to make sure as much of their stuff gets to where it needs to be. And keeping these routes viable costs serious money. They can't have their employees putting them at risk with freelance smuggling jobs. Special Agent Lee will tell you, the easiest person to flip is the person who's been dealing on the side.'

'Because they know if they don't make a deal they're dead,' Melody Lee said.

'And what if Bierman found something when he was in Afghanistan?' Finch said. 'It's always been a melting pot of cultures. Civilisations from China, Central and South Asia have been mingling, trading and fighting there for millennia. The whole area's basically a giant trove of prehistoric, Indo-Greek, Buddhist and Islamic treasures.'

Poe nodded.

'That works,' he said. 'And he'd certainly have had the opportunity. Officers get more freedom on ops like that and controlled socialising with the local population is actively encouraged. If these objects are as abundant as you seem to think, it wouldn't have been hard for him to get hold of some. And the military's kit doesn't get searched as rigorously as civilians'. Anything you put in your MFO box is pretty much guaranteed to get back to the UK unchecked.'

'MFO box?' Melody Lee said.

'Stands for Movements Forwarding Office. Basically a packing crate soldiers use to transport their personal belongings to and from postings. Once that lid's screwed on, it would be a tenacious military policeman who bothers his arse opening it to see what's inside. And even if it was opened, all Bierman would have had to say was that they were souvenirs. An MP isn't going to know the difference between a four-thousand-year-old relic and a bit of tat from the bazaar.'

'So,' Finch said, 'Christopher Bierman stumbles upon something valuable. He gets it back to the UK and goes searching for someone who can offload it for him.'

'Someone like my dad,' Susan said.

'Who'd have been careful dealing with someone outside the smuggling ring,' Finch said. 'Careful enough to photograph him so he could do some digging before he committed to anything.'

'Would your dad have risked doing some freelance work?' Poe said to Susan.

'I know he wouldn't have liked having a job, Sergeant Poe. And working for this smuggling ring sounds exactly like having a job. I don't care what he was being paid; if someone offered him the chance to do a bit of business for himself he'd have jumped at it.'

'That's good enough for me,' Poe said. 'Before he's kidnapped, Christopher Bierman finds, buys or steals something valuable. He hides it among his personal effects, which are shipped back to the UK while he recuperates. As soon as he's well enough, he retrieves it and looks for someone who can move it. Somehow he finds Terry Holmes who, being a careful old so-and-so, takes a photo in case it goes tits up.'

A thought occurred to him. 'And while Holmes is checking up on him, maybe Bierman kept his antiquity in a safety deposit box.'

He turned to Slater. 'How far back did you look regarding ownership of the box Terry Holmes was killed in front of?'

'Just the owner at the time. We didn't see any reason to go back further.'

'I'll check that for you,' Finch said. 'No point having Terrorism Act powers if you can't abuse them.' She went outside to make the phone call.

'OK,' Poe said, 'we now have a working theory. Christopher Bierman brought something back from Afghanistan and asked Terry Holmes to sell it. Terry's employers find out he's risked their supply chain by selling something on the side and they take robust action. Not only do they kill the two men involved, they do it publicly as a warning to anyone else who might be thinking of doing something similar. Anyone think that doesn't work all the way to the end?'

No one did, apparently. The pawnshop stayed silent. The explanation worked.

Which was all well and good, Poe thought, it *did* explain everything. But he'd left one suspicion unvoiced. Because he didn't think it did work all the way to the end.

He didn't think it explained the ceramic rats.

That question remained unanswered.

Chapter 56

Hannah Finch needed to get back to the summit and Bradshaw could work anywhere, so Poe made the decision to take the investigation north again. With a confirmed link between the Southampton case and the Cumbrian case, he felt it sensible to base himself at the killer's last known location. He wasn't leaving Hampshire without assets in play, though. Ben Slater and Susan Holmes had promised to work together and keep digging into the events surrounding the death of Terry Holmes. Melody Lee had raised an eyebrow but Poe ignored her. In his opinion, a terrier-like ex-cop with new leads on a hobby case, and a daughter determined to find out who killed her father, would be worth far more than a cold-case team with a limited overtime budget.

'Any problems?' Poe said to Finch. He hadn't wanted to ask her about the effectiveness of MI5's Terrorism Act powers in front of Slater and Susan. It had been interesting listening to her work. The way she cut through layers of bureaucratic bullshit.

'I'll have an answer by this evening. I've asked for the records of everyone who rented that safety deposit box going back to when the branch opened in 2001.'

'Good. If Bierman did rent that box I doubt he'd have done it under an assumed name. He'd have had no reason to.'

'Won't matter if he did,' she said, shrugging. 'Our people know what they're doing. It doesn't matter what name he used, there will be a trail.'

'What do you want me to do, Poe?' Bradshaw said.

'I need an Unexplained Wealth Order on Bierman, Tilly. Army pilots aren't well paid and I want to know how he funded his share in the executive travel company. If he used money he got from smuggling antiquities, I need to know about it.'

'I'll get the Mole People on it, Poe.'

The Mole People was the nickname for Bradshaw's small team of analysts. Poe allowed the pejorative nickname for two reasons: one, an office that was able to tease each other was a healthy office; and two, he'd come up with the name in the first place. It had been after a long day and it had been better than calling them 'bloody nerds'. Bradshaw had initially been resistant – she preferred 'Scooby Gang' – but given what they'd achieved over the last couple of years, it was now a nickname they wore with pride. They even had T-shirts with 'I Am A Mole' on the front and '6.022 x 10^{23}' on the back. Bradshaw had explained the number was the base unit of the amount of substance in the International System of Units, otherwise known as a mole. Poe had said, 'OK'.

'What else do you need?' she said.

'We need to go deep into Christopher Bierman. We profiled him as a victim before, now I need him profiled as a criminal. The full works: immediate and extended family, psychological, financial, social media, service history—'

'I'll get you access to his service record, Tilly,' Finch cut in.

'Thank you, Hannah Finch,' Bradshaw said.

'Word of warning, Poe,' Finch said. 'Putting Bierman under the microscope is the same as putting his heroism under the microscope. A lot of people won't like that. You may find some pushback.'

'What's new?' he muttered. 'But point taken. We'll tread carefully. Last thing I want to do is besmirch a war hero, even if he was a bit of a crook.'

Finch nodded. Poe was warming to her. Now her summit wasn't being threatened, he was starting to see what Alastor

Locke meant when he'd said she was a good agent. She was perceptive and didn't suffer from rigid thinking. She was probably reporting everything they did back to Locke, but he had to admit it was useful having MI5's additional powers to call on occasionally.

'And do the same for Terry Holmes, Tilly,' he said. 'Turn over every rock you can, see what doesn't want to be found. Bierman didn't turn up at his pawnshop by accident; he knew to go there. If we can find that link, we'll be closer to finding the killer.'

'OK, Poe.'

'And where are we going?' Melody Lee said.

'Us? We're going back to Scarness Hall,' he said. 'I think it's high time we spoke to Christopher Bierman's business partner, don't you?'

'Patrick McDaid?'

'The very same.'

Chapter 57

'You think Patrick McDaid's involved?' Melody Lee said.

'I don't see how he can be,' Poe said. 'The seeds of these murders germinated way before he went into business with Bierman. But, they'll have spent a lot of time together over the years, probably been drunk together. It's possible Bierman let something slip. A secret can only be kept for so long, I've found. Sooner or later the urge to tell someone is overpowering.'

'You sound like you know what you're talking about.'

Poe said nothing.

Melody Lee didn't push it and they were soon hitting the outskirts of Hallbankgate, the nearest village to Scarness Hall. The protestors were there, still holding their handmade signs and still melting in the late afternoon sun. Irene, their self-appointed spokesperson, was sitting on a brightly coloured deckchair. She raised a mug of something to him as they drove past.

Poe waved, braked, and reversed back. Another bored-looking cop was watching over Irene's motley crew. He left the tree he'd been sheltering under and ambled towards them. Poe lowered his window and showed his ID.

'I'm still waiting for that video, Irene,' he called out when the cop had gone back to being bored in the shade.

Irene turned to Jeffrey, her beleaguered husband. 'Max hasn't sent that video to Sergeant Poe yet, Jeffrey. You did call him, didn't you?'

It was clear that Jeffrey had not. It was also clear that Jeffrey wouldn't be getting any pudding that night, if the look Irene gave him was anything to go by.

'Honestly,' she said. 'If you want something done, give it to a busy woman. I'll call him now, Sergeant Poe, and I can only apologise for my husband's wool-gathering.'

'No harm done,' Poe said.

'I think he was dropped on the head when he was a baby,' Irene added.

The summit was now ten days away and security around Scarness Hall's perimeter had visibly tightened. The outer cordon had three armed cops instead of one, and a mobile command trailer was parked alongside the police vehicles. After their names had been checked against the list of preauthorised personnel they were waved through.

The static guardhouse hadn't changed but the people staffing it now had a vibe. There was no smiling, no laughing. Just a curt 'Good afternoon, sir. Good afternoon, ma'am. Are you authorised to be here?'

When Poe handed his ID to a uniformed inspector, he could see at least two weapons being trained on him. He suspected there were more he couldn't see. An English springer spaniel was brought over. He looked similar to Edgar, although he had black and white markings instead of the more traditional liver and white. There to sniff out explosives and guns. If someone were hoping to smuggle in something nasty to use later, now would be the time to do it, he supposed. Poe was asked to open the doors and the boot of his car. The spaniel jumped in, sniffed around and jumped back out again without barking.

'Thank you,' the inspector said. He handed back their ID cards. 'If you proceed up to the same car park as last time someone will meet you.'

***

228

And that someone was Lewis Barnes. As soon as Poe drove into the car park, the man with the puppy-dog smile bounded over. 'Do you want me to clean your windscreen, sir? It's all covered in bugs again!'

'I've been down south, Lewis,' Poe said. 'A lot of motorway driving.'

'Do you know the first thing to go through a bug's brains when it hits a car windscreen, sir?'

Poe did. The joke was old. He let Lewis have his moment, though. Ruining punchlines was only fun when the person telling the joke was a dick.

'I don't know, Lewis.'

'Its bum, sir!'

Poe smiled. Melody Lee actually laughed. Obviously not a schoolyard joke in Louisiana.

'That's kinda funny,' she said.

'I'll fetch my bucket and scraper, sir,' Lewis said.

'You couldn't tell me where I might find Mr McDaid?'

'I'm your man, sir! And he's in the dining room talking to Cookie about something. I'll take you there if you like?'

'Thank you, Lewis,' Poe said. 'That's very kind.'

Lewis took them to the dining room and pointed out McDaid. Poe knew what he looked like from the corporate brochures he'd found in Bierman's room. Typical Yank, he'd thought. A climate-change denying, big-game hunting, concealed-carry nutjob. Bleached teeth and hair that looked as though it had been styled with spit and ironed flat. Would chant 'USA! USA! USA!' whenever anything remotely interesting happened.

The real Patrick McDaid was far less plastic. He was wearing a light jacket with the Bierman & McDaid logo on the breast, tan chinos and a white shirt. He was as tanned as he had looked in the brochure, but up close Poe could see it was an outdoor tan,

229

not an artificial one. He was deep in conversation with a man in chef whites. Cookie, Poe assumed. Whatever they were talking about, it was getting heated. McDaid was jabbing his finger at Cookie and the chef was glowering back.

They approached the table, the luxurious carpet masking their steps.

'Just think about it,' the chef snapped.

McDaid was about to respond when he saw Poe. Both men stood as he and Melody Lee approached their table.

'Mr McDaid?' Poe said.

'Yes?'

The chef said, 'I'd best be getting back to the mess, Patrick. We'll pick this up later.'

Before McDaid could respond, Poe said, 'Two secs.' He showed the chef his ID card. 'Can I ask who you are, sir?'

The chef leaned in and studied Poe's credentials. 'Sergeant Poe?' he said. '*The* Sergeant Poe?'

Poe didn't reply.

'Name's Nick Anstey, shipmate. Chef to most, Cookie to some. I'm Scarness Hall's pastry chef.'

Anstey was a big man, easily as tall as Lewis. And he was surprisingly burly for someone who spent his days baking. Muscles knotted his neck, his hands were like bunches of bananas and his knuckles were like walnuts. Poe put him around forty. As well as chef's whites he wore the traditional blue checked trousers. His sleeves were rolled up and he wore his watch on the inside of his wrist.

Dots of sweat beaded his forehead, which was interesting. Poe had been around fine-dining restaurants during a previous investigation and knew that dripping with sweat was a professional chef's default position. The lounge was air-conditioned, though, and, judging by the dregs in his mug, Anstey had been there at least twenty minutes.

'Can I ask what you were talking about?'

'Packed lunches, shipmate. Mr McDaid is taking some of our VIPs on a tour of the Lake District.' Anstey smirked before adding, 'Maybe take in some of those stone circles you've made us famous for.'

Poe winced. Cumbria's myriad stone circles, once sleepy and mysterious prehistoric monuments attracting a handful of visitors a year, had taken on an element of the macabre since the Immolation Man case. The circles where the bodies had been burnt were now objects of morbid curiosity and unscrupulous entrepreneurs had started running tours to them. Helicopter flights over the Immolation Man's stone circles were now a thing in Cumbria. There had even been talk of a TV series.

'Don't let me detain you then,' Poe said. He loved the implicit threat of that phrase. It was the kind of thing that only police officers and dictators could get away with.

As soon as he'd gone, Poe said to McDaid, 'What was that really about?'

'Just a misunderstanding.'

Poe was too experienced a cop to jump in. He waited for the silence to become uncomfortable. McDaid didn't bite, though. Remained quiet and waited for the next question.

'Do you have a few minutes to talk about Mr Bierman?' Poe said.

'About goddamned time,' he said.

Chapter 58

'Christopher Bierman was the finest man I've ever known,' McDaid said. 'A hero in an age when that word don't mean shit any more. Went through hell and came out the other side unbroken.'

'Tell me about him,' Poe said.

'What do you want to know?'

'Did it surprise you that he'd been found in a brothel?'

'You're goddamned right it did. Been all over the world with that man and not once did he do something like this.'

'How was his marriage?'

'Rock-freaking-solid. He adored his wife and kids. Absolutely adored them. If he was in a brothel it was because he'd been dragged there kicking and screaming.'

'It's possible his murder is connected to his time in Afghanistan. I gather you were there at the same time?'

Finch would have received Bierman's service records by now. Bradshaw would go through them with the finest of toothcombs, but hearing a first-hand account would be invaluable.

McDaid said, 'I was.'

'What was it like? Scary, I imagine.'

'Chris flew a Lynx,' McDaid said. 'Mainly reconnaissance and troop transport. And let me tell you, that was not a job for the fainthearted. When we were there al-Qaeda had just started having success with shoulder-launched surface-to-air missiles.'

'Were you friends out there?'

'All the flyboys were.'

'Why's that?'

'Because the Brit pilots were under US command, they were quartered at Camp Leatherneck, rather than Bastion.'

'Leatherneck? Where was that?'

'Conjoined to Bastion. US engineers sited it there to take advantage of the Brit airfield.'

'Your company brochure says you flew in the Marines and Mr Bierman attended Sandhurst. It doesn't mention any service in Afghanistan. Why is that?'

'Tactical business decision. We decided early on that we wanted contracts with *Fortune* 500 companies and, as most of them have a global reach, it made sense to downplay our role in the Middle East. One man's terrorist is another man's freedom fighter and all that. And to be honest, some of these companies resent it when the hired help has a higher profile than they do. It's one of the reasons Chris changed his name.'

'Did you see him in Camp Bastion's field hospital after he was rescued?'

'I did. He was heavily sedated but we had a few hours together.'

'Must have been hard to see?'

'You have no idea. Poor man looked like a goddamned concentration camp survivor. He'd been beaten daily for two months and had eaten things that would have made a wolverine puke.'

'That bad?'

'You not seen the pictures?'

'I haven't got his military file yet.'

'Well, when you do get it, ignore the ones they released to the press – they were taken after he'd been in hospital for a fortnight. Have a look at the ones taken right after he was rescued. Goddamned shocking. I'm telling you, Chris was a tough bastard, but if those boys hadn't showed up when they did al-Qaeda would have livestreamed his beheading. I spoke to one of his

233

surgeons and she reckoned he wouldn't have lasted more than another day or two.'

'Did you meet Tango Two-Four, the section of King's Royal Rifles?'

'The soldiers who rescued him?'

Poe nodded.

'I didn't. Never had the chance. When I heard Chris was back I rushed over to the field hospital. There was quite a crowd there, as you can imagine. I assumed, as did everyone else, that there'd be a chance to thank them properly at some point. Way I heard it, they were only back a short while before they went out again. I suppose it makes sense. It was a big deal for Chris, but for them it was just another task. Those guys were on a two-way range every day they drove out the gates.'

'I bet,' Poe said.

'And then an asshole suicide bomber drives an ambulance packed with TATP into them and nobody gets to thank them properly,' he growled. 'I've read my Bible from cover to cover, Sergeant Poe, and I won't often hear a word said against Our Lord, but sometimes, just sometimes, he can be a real sonofabitch.'

Poe didn't know how to respond to that. Instead he turned to Melody Lee and said, 'TATP?'

'Triacetone triperoxide. Bombmakers like it as it's one of the few explosives that doesn't contain nitrogen. Means it can pass through traditional scanners undetected. Easy to make but it's highly unstable. Terrorists call it the "Mother of Satan".'

Poe stared at her.

'I'm in the FBI,' she said. 'I know all kinds of shit like this.'

'And it ate Chris up,' McDaid said. 'We told him that he was being irrational, probably had survivor's guilt or some other psychobabble bullshit. Told him that soldiers like that put themselves in harm's way every day. That they knew and accepted the

234

risks. They'd died on a routine mission and it was nothing to do with him. Wouldn't accept it, though. I think if just one of those poor bastards had managed to crawl out of that burning vehicle he'd have been OK. If there'd been just one person to thank.'

'But there wasn't,' Poe said. It wasn't a question. No one in Tango Two-Four had survived.

'No. All twelve died instantly,' McDaid said. 'I was out on a mission of my own that day. And I can tell you we all converged on their position like we'd seen the bat signal. If there'd been anyone suspicious there, anyone at all, no one would have followed our fire and control orders.'

'Tensions were running high?'

'Very.'

Poe needed to move on. He wanted to know about Bierman's smuggling activities but suspected the interview would end abruptly when he asked McDaid. Better he dotted the remaining i's first.

'Talk me through your business,' Poe said.

McDaid shrugged. 'Chris and I kept in touch all through his recovery. I visited him in London a few times when I had leave. Wanted to make sure he was being looked after. Had everything he needed. Soon became clear that although Chris's body was healing, his mind wasn't. Guilt over what happened to the men who rescued him, guilt over surviving the crash when his navigator hadn't. It was eating him up inside. I have nothing to support this, but I don't think he'd gotten too far away from getting in a hot bath with a bottle of vodka and a razor blade.'

McDaid left that on the table for a few moments. Let it sink in.

'It was my idea for him to make a fresh start in the US,' he said. 'A new name and some new ideas on how to live his life. I'd left the Marines. Had a discharge grant and my family is not without money. Made sense to use our connections and experience to grab a slice of the executive-travel pie.'

'You know where his share of the start-up money came from?' Poe said. It would be a couple of days before the Unexplained Wealth Order started to bear fruit.

'I staked him.'

'You did?' Poe said. 'How much?'

'Fifty grand.'

Poe whistled, mainly to hide the fact that his Unexplained Wealth Order was down the toilet.

'That's a lot of money,' he said.

'I knew the man,' McDaid said. 'I *trusted* the man. And even though he didn't want to exploit his name, not after what happened to the boys who rescued him, having a genuine war hero as a partner was a USP our competitors didn't have. Even if we didn't put it front and centre. Chris agreed to take a reduced share of the dividends until the loan was paid back in full. Which it was within two years.'

Poe had read Bradshaw's summary of their company. Knew they were doing well. Lots of big contracts, lots of employees.

'Started out by renting a couple of Bell 429s,' McDaid continued. 'Picked up a couple of early contracts. Gained a decent rep among the ex-flyboys. The Pentagon and the defence industry are basically revolving doors, so when it came to hiring birds to take the CFO to Palm Springs there was always someone on the company board who knew of us, of what Chris went through. Pretty soon we had to hire more pilots, lease more birds. Rest is history. We ain't the biggest company but we are the best.'

Which sounded like a sales pitch to Poe. Too glib to have just tripped off the tongue like that.

'You're doing well then?'

'Put it this way; I don't need to work any more. Neither did Chris.'

'So . . .?'

'So why did we? Because we're pilots, Sergeant Poe. The

freedom you get when you leave terra ain't one you give up just because you can. No better feeling in the world.'

Which sounded like another sales pitch.

'How's his family taking it?' Poe said, immediately regretting it. 'I'm sorry. They must be devastated, of course. How are they holding up?'

'What do you think?' McDaid said. 'The world's just come crashing down on their heads. Melanie's devastation will turn to anger and a demand for answers before long. They breed 'em tough in Texas.'

'You know his wife well?'

'I've known Melanie longer than Chris. My wife introduced them. But they'll be all right. Chris's fifty per cent stake in the company will pass to her and she can be as involved as she wants. I'll make sure we stay afloat for her sake. It's why I've recruited a new pilot. Too big a contract to pay the penalty clause.'

Poe made a note to go and see the family liaison officer that Jo Nightingale had allocated to the Biermans. See if she'd picked up anything unusual. FLOs weren't just there to make cups of tea and open boxes of tissues; they had an investigative role too. He'd go and see Bierman's wife if the FLO thought it would bear fruit.

'Do you have any more questions, Sergeant Poe?' McDaid said. 'Only I'm flying to Manchester tonight and I have pre-flight checks.'

'Just one more, Mr McDaid.'

'Go for it.'

'How long had you known Mr Bierman was smuggling looted antiquities out of Afghanistan?'

No point leading with his chin. Get in there fast and hard, see what happened.

McDaid's face turned to granite. His muscles bunched up under his jacket. 'I beg your pardon?'

'You heard me.'

'I don't know what you're referring to, Sergeant Poe,' McDaid said, 'but I can assure you, if you repeat that in public my company's lawyers will own your house by the end of the week.'

Good luck with that, Poe thought.

'My business, the business that will now be making sure Chris's wife and children don't starve, is built on reputation,' he continued. 'You come after that reputation and I'll defend it robustly. Do we understand each other?'

'I think you're misjudging your audience, Mr McDaid,' Melody Lee said. 'This isn't someone who responds well to threats.'

Poe said nothing. That McDaid was protecting his own interests wasn't unusual. That he'd immediately gone on the offensive was.

'Plus, he ain't got a pot to piss in,' she added. 'Sue Poe for everything he's got and you won't have enough for the lunchtime special at Red Lobster. You can trust me on this; I've seen where he lives.'

'Hey,' Poe said.

McDaid sighed. 'Tell me what you know.'

'Not going to happen,' Poe said.

'Look, I'll assume you're not an incompetent asshole, and if you're throwing around accusations like this you must have cause. But if you're going to besmirch a dead hero, at least let me help you do it quietly.'

Poe completed a mental inventory of what he could safely share and what he'd go to prison for sharing.

He told McDaid about the link between Bierman and Terry Holmes. That Bierman was on camera, presumably selling something he'd brought back from Afghanistan.

'Only one problem, Sergeant Poe. Helmand was Chris's first foreign posting and his bird went down before he had a chance to take any R & R. The first time he left Afghanistan was in the back of an RAF C-17 Globemaster and he was unconscious at the time.'

'We think he'd already stashed it in his MFO box,' Poe said. 'When he got medevacked back to the UK, his possessions will have followed him. And no one was going to check the MFO box of a war hero.'

'Possibly,' McDaid nodded. 'Tootsie Roll proves that's a crock of shit, though.'

'Excuse me?'

'Something one of the guys organised. We knew he wasn't coming back so we all put a small gift in among his personal belongings so he'd have something nice to remember us by. I put in a bunch of Tootsie Rolls.'

'Which are?'

'Bars of candy,' McDaid said. 'I then personally checked his possessions to make sure there was nothing in there that would embarrass his family.'

'Like porn?'

'Like porn,' McDaid agreed. 'And I'm telling you, Sergeant Poe, the most antiquey thing in the personal possessions of Christopher Bierman was a Red Hot Chili Peppers T-shirt from their *Californication* tour in 1999.'

Chapter 59

Poe headed back to Carlisle. Bradshaw had emailed to say she'd finished her preliminary profile on Christopher Bierman. That was the good news. The bad news was that she didn't think there was anything helpful in it. He pulled into Durranhill and found her in the room they had been allocated when they first arrived. Finch was still off doing whatever it was that she did when she wasn't annoying him, and Melody Lee disappeared to put in a call to her Washington field office.

Bradshaw had set up the room how he liked it. A paper file for him and a murder wall for everyone to stalk up and down when they had the time. It was surprising how many times it had worked in the past. Photographs of key events and people were pinned to a huge corkboard. Terry Holmes lying in front of the open safety deposit box. The ceramic rats. Five photographs of Bierman – one from his service file, one from his company website and a tabloid front page showing him being helped from the back of the helicopter immediately after his rescue. Another one of him in his hospital bed, smiling for the camera, little more than a skin-covered skeleton. And finally, one of him spread-eagled on a bed in a Carlisle brothel, head crushed and bloodied.

Poe wandered up and down the wall. His mind processed visual images differently to text. With documents he had to make notes, put everything into an order he could understand and remember. With pictures they tended to burn themselves into his memory. He might not immediately take in all the salient details, but once they were in his mind, they were there for good, running in the background like an unwanted app.

Poe threw down the file in anger. Bradshaw was right; there was nothing in it that helped. For the first time since he'd worked for SCAS, an offender profile hadn't provided them with anything at all. Everything the Mole People had turned up, everything Bradshaw had turned up, supported what Patrick McDaid had told him: Christopher Bierman had been an upstanding citizen, a hero who'd survived a special kind of hell. Raised a family out of the limelight and ran a successful business. If he hadn't seen Bierman with his own eyes on Terry Holmes's hidden camera, he'd have assumed it was a case of mistaken identity. That there was actually another Christopher Bierman out there who'd dodged a baseball bat to the head.

But their Christopher Bierman *had* been photographed talking to a known smuggler of antiquities, he *had* been tortured and beaten to death, and an identical ceramic rat *had* been left next to his corpse.

'You need to find me something I can use, Tilly,' he said, unreasonably. 'If we don't keep moving forwards, the bad guy isn't going to be found. He's probably already out of the country as it is.'

'I'm sorry, Poe, but we've searched every available database – I don't think there is anything more to find,' she said.

But that was OK because that was the moment Hannah Finch chose to step into the room.

And she had found something.

Chapter 60

Hannah Finch had found gold. Pure gold.

The month before Christopher Bierman had entered Terry Holmes's pawnshop, he'd rented safety deposit box 9-206, the empty box that the James Bond gang had busted open. The box the rat had been left in. The box Terry Holmes had died in front of.

'I'm sold on this now, Poe,' she said. 'I wasn't before but I was willing to go along to get along. I don't know how Bierman got anything back from Afghanistan but I can't think of a plausible explanation for his murder that doesn't involve this smuggling network. I've passed it on to Alastor Locke.'

'I didn't authorise that,' Poe said, annoyed.

'I don't need your permission. Looted antiquities are a major income stream for terrorists so it's very much in our purview. My people will coordinate their response with the NCA's transnational organised crime unit.'

Poe grunted in annoyance. He knew she was right. This was bigger than two murdered men. The people who knew how to investigate global organised crime needed to get involved now.

'You and Tilly will be looped in on everything,' she continued. 'No filter, no redactions. Think of it like this, Poe: you've just got a whole army of resources. And this lot can go anywhere, speak to anyone. You won't believe the power the state has when terrorism is involved.'

It was as if a giant weight had been lifted from her shoulders.

Now the summit wasn't under threat, she could help the investigation without wondering whether she was a Nissan worker voting for Brexit.

The door opened again. It was Melody Lee. 'What have I missed?' she said.

'Hannah, do you want to do the honours?' Poe said.

After she'd been briefed, Melody Lee said, 'OK, so how does that help us?'

Which made Poe stop and think. How *did* it help them?

That Bierman had rented the same safety deposit box that Terry Holmes had died in front of only confirmed what they'd already thought. It didn't materially change anything. It didn't offer them a fresh line of enquiry. No one new had entered the Venn diagram of the two murders. There were still just two names where the circles intersected: Terry Holmes and Christopher Bierman.

'Bollocks,' he said. 'She's right. This vindicates our theory but it doesn't actually move us forward.'

'We have at least fifteen agents working the smuggling network now,' Finch said. 'Asking for bank records, tracking down shipment numbers, putting surveillance into place. Something will come up.'

'Maybe,' he said.

'You don't seem happy?'

'Oh, I'm sure this antiquities network is about to have a very bad year. But I wasn't brought in to catch smugglers, I was brought in to solve a murder. Now two murders.'

The room descended into a brooding silence.

Melody Lee got up and poured coffee for everyone, even Bradshaw. Poe took a sip of the stewed and bitter drink. It was awful, as bad as anything he'd tasted.

'Don't drink that, Tilly,' he said.

She looked at him gratefully. 'Thank you, Poe. I might go

down to the canteen to see if they have any nettle tea. Shall I fetch you one? Anyone?'

'I'll stick with this, thanks,' he said.

'I'm good, Tilly,' Finch said.

'Special Agent Lee?' Bradshaw said.

She didn't respond. Poe glanced at her.

She was standing in front of the murder wall, staring at the photographs.

'What's that red shit on his arm?' she said, pointing at one in particular.

It was the front page of the tabloid. Taken at Camp Bastion, it had been snapped by the *Daily Mirror*'s war correspondent. He had caught Bierman being supported out of the helicopter by two of the King's Royal Rifles who'd rescued him.

'HERO!' the headline screamed.

Poe had glanced at it earlier but the sensationalism had been a bit much. Long on flag waving, short on facts. Bradshaw had put copies of all media coverage of Bierman's rescue in his file, although the *Mirror* had been the only one to have a photo.

'Blood, presumably,' he said. 'He'd been held by a bunch of fundamentalists for two months; I doubt they offered a laundry service.'

'No, not on Bierman,' she said. 'What's the red shit on the arm of the guy holding him up?'

Poe stood and joined her at the murder wall. He put on his reading glasses and looked where Melody Lee's finger was.

And just like that, everything changed.

Chapter 61

'What is it, Poe?' Bradshaw said. 'What have we missed?'

'We didn't miss it, Tilly,' he said. He couldn't tear his eyes away from the photograph. '*I* missed it.'

He couldn't believe what he was seeing; the answer had been there all along. Bradshaw couldn't have known the significance. Neither could Melody Lee. And unless Finch was up on her military history, it was doubtful she'd have known either.

'Spill the beans, Poe,' Melody Lee said.

Poe jabbed the photograph. At a patch on the soldier's shoulder. It was small but, as the soldier had his arms around Bierman when the photo was taken, it was sharply in focus. It was square, about two inches by two inches, and split into three horizontal bars. The top bar was dark green, the middle was mustard yellow and the bottom was red.

'That "red shit on his arm" is a Tactical Recognition Flash,' he said. 'It's the coloured patch worn on the right arm that indicates the regiment or corps the soldier belongs to when berets and cap badges can't be worn. The King's Royal Rifles' TRF must be green, yellow and red.'

'And why's that significant?' Melody Lee said.

'It's not,' Finch frowned. 'There must be hundreds of combinations of colours for TRFs. Got to be dozens with red in them.'

'Hannah's right, it's not significant,' Poe said. 'But what's on his other shoulder is. You can't see it in this photograph as it's behind Bierman, but the left arm is where soldiers wear their brigade flash. This is the patch that indicates which formation the regiment belongs to.'

'And?'

'And I know that at the time this photograph was taken, the King's Royal Rifles were part of the 7th Armoured Brigade.'

'And the 7th Armoured Brigade's insignia is red?'

'Was. They were redesignated as the 7th Infantry Brigade in 2014. But yes, it was red.'

'I'll be damned,' Melody Lee said. 'So you think there's a link? That someone had daubed those ceramic rats with red paint to show there was a connection to these soldiers? These 7th Armoured Brigade guys?'

'I'm absolutely convinced of it.'

Melody Lee paused. Stared at him, *appraised* him.

'You seem surer than you have any right to be, Poe. What aren't you telling us?'

'What I haven't told you is that the 7th Armoured Brigade also went by another name. A nickname really, one that stretches back to the Second World War's North African campaign. It's a nickname known the world over.'

'And what is it?'

'The 7th Armoured Brigade, Special Agent Lee, were also known as the Desert Rats.'

Chapter 62

On the wall monitor, Bradshaw brought up an image of the 7th Armoured Brigade's flash. It was a simple design – a black square with a red rat in the middle.

'It's not actually a rat,' Poe said. 'It's a jerboa. You can tell by the long, thick tail. Apparently the first divisional commander adopted one, hence the picture on the patch.'

'Why were they not called the Desert Jerboas, Poe?' Bradshaw said.

Poe shrugged. 'I don't imagine the average British squaddie had seen a jerboa before, Tilly.'

'Probably a psychological element to it as well,' Melody Lee added. 'Who would you rather fight, the cute desert jerboas or the snarling desert rats?'

'Neither, Special Agent Lee,' Bradshaw said. 'But I take your point; statistically, rats are the most reviled animal in the United Kingdom.'

'Now,' Poe said, 'does anyone not think we've just taken a massive leap forward?'

Silence. Finch broke it.

'What does it mean, though, Poe?' she said. 'I get that Christopher Bierman was rescued by some soldiers from the King's Royal Rifles but I'm struggling to see how that can be connected to the looted antiquities network that he and Holmes were involved in.'

'I don't know. But both Holmes and Bierman had rats left at

247

their crime scenes, rats that have had red paint added to their left forelimbs, and the King's Royal Rifles wore Desert Rat flashes on their left shoulder. Someone associated with that regiment has to be behind all this.'

Melody Lee and Bradshaw both nodded.

Eventually Finch did too.

'Patrick McDaid said the American and British pilots shared a separate compound to any of the infantry regiments out there,' Poe said. 'The only time Bierman would have come into contact with the King's Royal Rifles was when Tango Two-Four rescued him. I think it's there we need to start.'

'I'll get the unredacted report into the vehicle-borne IED that killed Tango Two-Four,' Finch said. 'It'll have more detail than the one in the public domain. You and Tilly already have the right clearance level, but, Special Agent Lee, I'm sorry, you won't be able to see it.'

'Not a problem,' she said.

Poe heard an unsaid, *I'll get it from my own side.*

'Are we sure all twelve died in the attack?' he said. 'One of them hasn't survived and for reasons unknown holds Bierman accountable?'

Finch shook her head. 'They were badly burnt but the investigation was thorough and all bodies were positively ID'd.'

'How?' Poe said. He was always suspicious when bodies were burnt beyond recognition.

'Dog tags, initially,' Finch said, referring to the pair of metal ID tags worn by all military personnel on active service. In combat, one was gathered from the soldier's dead body, the other was left with it. 'They were then matched with dental records and DNA. If someone from the King's Royal Rifles is behind all this, they weren't on that 432.'

'432?' Bradshaw said.

'The armoured personnel carrier they were in, Tilly,' Poe said.

'It's a cross between a minibus and a tank. Gets the soldiers to within yards of the enemy then they all pile out and start fighting.'

'Oh my gosh, that sounds scary.'

'Can't imagine anything scarier,' Poe admitted.

'But even if someone did blame Bierman for their deaths, it doesn't explain why Terry Holmes was also murdered,' Melody Lee said.

'No, it doesn't.'

'What's your next move, Poe?' Finch said.

'You're not going to like it.'

He told her what he needed.

He was right. She didn't like it.

Chapter 63

'Are you insane, man?' Alastor Locke shouted.

'No, sir,' Poe said. 'I've been tested.'

'Well, it blasted well looks like it! There's not a thing you can say, not a clue you can uncover, that will make the MoD give you the details of dead soldiers' dependents. And if Miss Finch has told you otherwise she's an even bigger fool than you.'

To be fair, Finch had pretty much said the same thing Locke was saying now. Speaking to the families was out of the question. Poe had argued and in the end she'd agreed he could go over her head.

'If it's a matter of sensitivity, sir . . .'

'It's a matter of common bloody decency, Poe! Those families went through an unimaginable ordeal: their men were heroes one day, dead the next. Did you know they were not even allowed to see their bodies? They were too badly disfigured.'

'But—'

'And the last thing they need is someone making them relive it all,' he snapped. 'Now, I've given you a lot of leeway in this investigation, and you have done well, Poe, very well, but pay heed: the families of Tango Two-Four are absolutely off limits.'

Poe said nothing.

'I'm warning you, Poe. If you persist with this line of enquiry there will be repercussions. Serious repercussions. Do we understand each other?'

'We do.'

'Say it then.'

'I understand, sir.'

'What?'

'I understand that you don't want me speaking to the families of the dead soldiers.'

And with that the phone went dead.

'Fucking pinhead,' Poe said.

Hannah Finch had been as good as her word. She'd accessed the report on the suicide attack that had killed Tango Two-Four. She said it was the original, it was unredacted and it ran into hundreds of pages. She handed Poe and Bradshaw a tablet each. Poe didn't recognise the make; Bradshaw did.

Melody Lee, who still hadn't been given access, took the opportunity to go back to her hotel. It had been a long day and they had spent a large part of it in a hot and stuffy car.

'See you tomorrow, Special Agent Lee,' Poe said.

She waved but said nothing.

'This is a read-only tablet, the ones we use at Five,' Finch said. 'I apologise in advance for the headache you're going to get, but the brightness is set artificially high so you can't photograph what's on the screen. Both tablets are connected to this building's wi-fi. If they lose that signal they will automatically lock so they can't be taken off the premises. It needs a two-factor authentication to reopen them, neither of which you'll be given.'

'And when it self-destructs does it explode or only catch fire?' Poe said.

'Funny. If you try to disable any of the security functions, the contents will immediately self-delete and an alert will be sent to security and vetting. You *will* go to prison for breaching the Official Secrets Act.'

Poe frowned.

'I need to go back to Manchester,' Finch said. 'Read as much as you want tonight and when you're finished put them both in this lockbox. The lockbox is to go in the evidence room's safe. I'll be back first thing tomorrow to reconnect them for you.'

'Thank you, Hannah,' Poe said.

As soon as she'd left, he turned to Bradshaw and said, 'Can you get around this, Tilly? Without alerting anyone?'

'Of course, Poe.'

'Good. I'm taking mine home.'

'No, Poe.'

He looked at her in surprise. 'What do you mean "no"?'

'It means I most certainly will not disable the security functions for you.'

'Why ever not?'

'They're there for a reason, Poe. And because sometimes you break rules just because someone has told you not to.' She folded her arms and set her lips, a look he knew well. 'Sometimes you have to do what you're told.'

Poe scowled.

'Sulk all you want, mister; I'm not doing it. And anyway, how much would you get done tonight? We're all very tired. We should do what Hannah Finch suggested: read what we can now, then come back tomorrow refreshed.'

'Fine,' he sighed, knowing she was right, secretly glad he was being reined in. He thought he'd enjoy the freedom of being Flynn-free, but Bradshaw had reminded him exactly what the boss brought to the investigation. As well as being a brilliant detective, she kept him focused and on task. She made him rest and she protected him from his worst excesses. When this was all over, Zoe be damned, he was going to drag her back to work.

He decided to treat the report like a cold-case file. That meant ignoring the executive summary for now and going straight to the field report from the first person at the scene. Their thoughts were unfiltered and fresh. Later reports would be sanitised and more considered; with the first report you got a sense of what the person was feeling at the time. Bradshaw showed him how to navigate the tablet's menu and he found what he wanted in the appendices: a report from a warrant officer in the Royal Military Police's Special Investigation Branch, the RMP's equivalent of CID. He'd been the first person at the scene with a fact-finding remit.

It was seven pages long and Poe read it quickly the first time, then slowly the second. His forehead creased. He read it one more time, then passed it to Bradshaw.

'What do you make of that, Tilly?'

It took Bradshaw five minutes to read it. When she finished she looked up, confused.

'I'm not sure what you're getting at, Poe; it's a thorough and seemingly accurate report. Doesn't contradict anything I've read.'

'That's exactly it. It's too polished. When he was there, the bodies were still in the vehicle and the vehicle was still burning. It has none of the graphic descriptions I'd have expected. Helicopters were landing and taking off and the rest of the King's Royal Rifles had descended on his location en masse and were baying for blood. It was absolute carnage, yet this man, this WO2 Downing, was taking measurements, collecting samples of explosive and generally acting as if it were a sterile crime scene.'

'What are you saying, Poe?'

'I'm saying that WO2 Downing is either the most analytical, cold-hearted bastard alive or . . .'

'Or what, Poe?'

'Or he was never bloody there at all.'

Chapter 64

As keen as Poe was to test his theory, Bradshaw's eyes were starting to droop and she wouldn't leave until he did. He sent Finch a text and asked what time they could expect her the next day.

When she replied he said, 'We'll pick this up tomorrow, Tilly. Hannah's going to meet us here at half seven. Can you lock up these tablet things so we don't get into trouble?'

'I will, Poe.'

After Poe had collected a meal from his local Indian takeaway, he popped to Victoria's to collect Edgar. Half an hour later he was back at Herdwick Croft. After he'd eaten, he took the spaniel for a long walk. The silent vastness of Shap Fell, usually so good at facilitating uninterrupted thought, didn't help that night. He knew there was something off with the military policeman's account of the crime scene.

Knew it with the very fibre of his being. He was on to something, he was sure of it.

He just didn't know what yet.

Less than twelve hours later and Poe was back in the same room. He hadn't slept well, too many thoughts chasing each other for real sleep to take hold. By the looks of it, Bradshaw had managed even less than him. She looked exhausted. She'd even joined him for a coffee while they waited for Hannah Finch.

He ignored the tablet's glare and tried to get the sequence of events clear in his head.

On the day of the rescue, Tango Two-Four, Charlie Company, King's Royal Rifles, had been on a routine security patrol in one of the myriad valleys and ravines in Helmand Province.

They had arrived at a small compound and immediately come under small arms fire. The FV432 wasn't the British Army's best armoured personnel carrier, but its armour was thick enough to cope with 7.62-mm ball rounds. The section commander, Corporal Andrew 'Ev' Evans, decided to launch a counterattack rather than withdraw and wait for backup.

The way Evans described the events, it had been a classic section assault. With their pintle-mounted general-purpose machine gun laying down suppressing fire, Tango Two-Four disembarked and quickly overran the enemy. Evans called in a sitrep and the section started securing the immediate area. It was then they had found Captain Jack Duncan, the now murdered Christopher Bierman.

Two days later, Tango Two-Four were given the relatively safer task of a 'hearts and minds' mission – taking medicine and vaccines to villages known to be free of enemy combatants.

Things then became a little less clear. Because where they were killed wasn't where they were supposed to be. The report concluded that it was a map-reading error and they had driven too far into a valley that hadn't been declared safe. Whether it was bad luck or by design, they ended up on the same road as an ambulance packed with TATP, the unstable explosive McDaid had mentioned. The FV432's armour, effective against small arms fire, was opened up like a tin of sardines. The subsequent post-mortems revealed that every member of Tango Two-Four had suffered non-survivable shrapnel wounds, impact injuries and burns. Dog tags found at the scene, dental records and follow-up DNA checks confirmed that everything was as it had appeared. The dead men were Tango Two-Four.

None of the Desert Rats had survived.

Poe put down his tablet. Rubbed his eyes and reached for his mug. Took a swig and did what he did every time he read about a death in combat – reflected on the tragic loss of life. Thought about the war-mongering politicians, the ones who thought the lives of others were theirs to waste. Thought about the families who'd proudly attended the passing-out parades, who'd bought into the glamour of being a military family. The same families who were then encouraged not to go to the press when their loved ones came back in a bag or with missing limbs. Grieving families affected recruitment targets.

'Tilly,' he said softly, 'can I have a word?'

Because it was with the families that the answers would be found.

Alastor Locke had refused to let him speak to the dependents of Tango Two-Four but that didn't mean there was nothing they could do. For all her intelligence, for all her statistical brilliance, Bradshaw was employed as a profiler. He might not be able to speak to the families of the dead, but he could damn well find out everything there was to know about them.

'What is it, Poe?'

'I have a job for you. One you can't tell anyone about.'

Chapter 65

'I'll stay with this report, Tilly, but I need you to start digging into the families of the dead soldiers,' Poe said. 'Nothing that isn't in the public domain, nothing—'

'How public?'

'What do you mean?'

'I mean there's the public domain and there are people on the internet who think their settings are private when they're not. Technically that information is also in the public domain.'

'I was going to say, nothing that will get us into trouble. And don't tell Hannah what you're doing.'

'Why not, Poe?'

'Because she'll tell Alastor Locke and he'll use big words when he shouts at me.'

'I'll go back to the hotel and make a start,' Bradshaw said. 'I'll say I have a—'

'Spastic colon?'

'No, Poe; my bowel movements are extremely healthy. I was going to say a headache because of the bright screen.'

'That works. If you need information from the report then ring me.'

'I won't need to, Poe.'

'You might. We haven't read it all yet; there could be references to the family near the back.'

Bradshaw's cheeks flushed.

Poe stared at her for a few moments before he realised what he was seeing.

'You disabled the security function on your tablet last night, didn't you?' he said.

'I wanted to read it.'

'So did I!'

'Yes, but you'd have triggered something and gone to prison.'

'What if *you'd* triggered something?'

'Puh-lease. If they hadn't wanted me to disable the tablet's security they should have used something a bit more sophisticated than an EBS intrusion detection system.'

Poe shook his head.

'We need DI Flynn back,' he said.

With Bradshaw squirreled away in her hotel, Poe went looking for Finch. He found her in the incident room, discussing the summit's security arrangements with Jo Nightingale. Cumbria Constabulary was bearing the brunt of it, although all five forces in the north-west were chipping in.

'You after me, Poe?' Nightingale said.

'Hannah actually, ma'am.'

'She's all yours. We were just finishing up.' She turned back to Finch. 'Can we meet again this evening? The assistant chief will know what Home Office funding he can access by then. We can go through what we can and can't provide.'

'That's fine, ma'am,' Finch said.

Nightingale left the room, winking conspiratorially at Poe as she passed. He thought he knew why – she was a cop's cop at heart and an unsolved murder in her city was more important than some stupid trade summit.

Or it could have been she had some grit in her eye. Sometimes you could read too much into things.

'What's up, Poe?' Finch said.

'Can we go somewhere quiet?' He gestured at the cops and civilian staff going about their business.

'Where do you suggest?'

'Do you like dogs?'

Cumbria Constabulary's dog section was set in woods in the grounds of Carleton Hall, two hundred metres from the main building. Poe assumed it was because of the noise. Unlike most force's dog sections, Cumbrian police dogs lived with their handlers but, as they weren't required all the time, they still had to be kennelled when their handlers were on duty. The kennels were modern and the runs spacious.

Poe knew the staff and they were happy to let Edgar board there when he was stuck. The spaniel got to play with the drugs, explosives and cadaver dogs, although their common sense never seemed to rub off on him.

Although Edgar was back with Victoria, Poe had brought Hannah Finch to the dog section because he knew they could talk without being overheard. They walked to one of the training areas, leaned on the fence and watched an Alsatian being put through its paces.

'Where's Tilly?' she said.

'Back at the hotel.'

'Oh. Everything OK?'

'She has a spas . . . she has a headache.'

Finch nodded. 'Yep. The glare on those read-only tablets will do that to you, particularly if you've been reading them in a dark room. Tell her to put a damp cloth over her eyes for a while. I'm told that helps.'

'I will.'

A man in a padded suit started to run. A dog handler shouted instructions before slipping the Alsatian off its leash. They watched the dog chase him down.

'You didn't drag me here to watch a bloke getting bitten on his arse, Poe,' Finch said. 'What's on your mind?'

'That report, how much confidence do you have in it?'

'Complete confidence,' she said. 'Why?'

'Have you read it?'

'Poe, do you honestly think I'd let you read something like that if I hadn't read it?'

'I'll put it another way then. How much confidence do you have that the information in it is accurate?'

She didn't answer immediately.

'I can say with absolute certainty that the report is the original and it hasn't been altered in any way. As for the accuracy of its findings . . . well, there's always room for interpretation with these things. It was a horrific event in a hostile part of the world. I'm sure things were missed, but nothing that would have materially changed the conclusion.'

Poe frowned.

'You don't agree,' she said.

He told her about the sterile nature of WO2 Downing's report. That, as the first man on the scene, he'd have expected it to contain more . . . emotion.

'That's because you're thinking like a policeman,' she said. 'The reports you get from the first cops on the scene form part of an overarching investigative strategy, yes? And if a murder isn't solved it might be read by a murder review team, later by a cold-case unit.'

Poe nodded.

'Our reports go in front of the House Defence Select Committee. It may seem harsh to you, it may even seem bad practice, but there is no room for emotion at this level. The men and women these reports go to are elected officials and our job is to give them facts and conclusions based on those facts. We train our investigators to report *without* emotion.'

Which made a certain kind of sense. Despite this, he couldn't shake the feeling that something had been left out. Or if not left out, its importance had been purposefully downplayed.

His phone rang. It was Bradshaw.

'Poe, can you talk?' she said.

'Not really, Tilly.' He didn't think Finch was lying, but he didn't trust her either. No matter how helpful she'd been recently, she had still removed evidence from a crime scene.

'OK, I'll talk and you listen,' she said.

'This sounds important, Tilly.'

'I've completed my preliminary search of the available data.'

'And?'

'I've not found anything, Poe.'

'Oh, is that all?' he said, slightly disappointed. 'It's not been long; keep looking.'

'No, Poe, you don't understand. I haven't been able to find anything because there's nothing there *to* find. It's been removed . . .'

Chapter 66

'There's a lot of stuff in the public domain, Poe,' Bradshaw said, 'but some of what I was expecting to find just isn't there.'

They were back in their allocated room. The door was shut. Hannah Finch had walked in but he'd asked her to leave when she asked what they were talking about. This briefing was for his ears only.

'Like what?' he said.

'I found the surface stuff easily enough but when I went a little deeper someone had been there before me.'

'What do you mean?'

'I mean someone who thinks like me has been cleansing data. And I don't mean they've deleted it – all that does is remove the reference to the file; it's still intact until it's been written over. Someone has systematically and permanently removed data from all discoverable public sites.'

'They can't have removed everything about the families, surely – we'd be able to smell the stink that caused.'

'No, Poe, you misunderstand me. It hasn't been a wholesale deletion, it's been far more surgical than that. Just the odd thing. A photograph here, a bit of text there. I've been into the Facebook page set up for the families of Tango Two-Four and it's obvious some of it has been altered. And it's still happening.'

'How do you know?'

'Someone had commented on a photograph of the soldiers who rescued Christopher Bierman. It had been taken the day of the suicide bomb attack.'

'What was the comment?'

'Someone called Jambo134 had said, "Is that the oldest photograph there is?"'

'And it was deleted?'

'And Jambo134's account has now been deleted.'

'Someone's monitoring it then.'

'They are, Poe.'

'And were there older photographs?'

'A few, not many.'

'OK, what do you think it all means?'

'I have absolutely no idea. The data being deleted isn't coming from any sensitive sources. Most of it is social media. Someone is monitoring gossip surrounding Tango Two-Four and removing things they don't like.'

'You think it's the government? Remember who our partners are on this.'

Bradshaw shook her head. 'I don't think it's them, Poe. If this was the Security Service I doubt they'd have been that selective with what they removed. They'd have taken the sledgehammer approach and simply shut it all down.'

'Keep digging then,' he said. 'Whoever's doing this will have missed something and all we need is one thread to tug on. Get that and things will start to look a little rosier.'

Of course, a few hours later he really regretted saying that . . .

Chapter 67

The warning shot, when it came, wasn't from the scalpel-wielding data cleanser, it was from the sledgehammer-wielding state. And it came in the form of an expedited hearing on the fate of Herdwick Croft.

The listings officer at Carlisle Combined Court had called to say a gap had appeared in the judge's schedule and a ruling would be made that afternoon. And it would be made even if he didn't attend.

Poe had asked why it was being bumped up. The listings officer didn't know.

'Sorry for such short notice, Mr Poe,' the district judge said when he got there. 'I was advised of this hearing at the same time as you.'

It was the same courtroom and the same judge. Mr Chadwick, the council's solicitor, still represented bureaucracy.

'This is highly unusual,' the judge said, 'but I find myself bound by the very laws I have sworn to protect. I received a legally binding brief earlier today that concerns this case. Unfortunately it is not one I feel able to ignore. Mr Chadwick, this stinks of pettiness on behalf of your employer. Would you care to explain?'

Chadwick stood. 'I can't. We received the brief at the same time as you did, your honour. I can assure the court we didn't petition its contents. As far as I was concerned, this matter was closed. We fully expected the court to find in Mr Poe's favour and we did not intend to appeal.'

'Very well,' the judge said. 'But this is your name on the bottom of this application.'

'It is, your honour. I was instructed by the head of legal services. I got the impression she had been instructed to instruct me.'

'What's going on?' Poe murmured.

'I don't know,' Bradshaw whispered back.

'It seems we are all pawns in someone else's game of chess,' the judge said. 'This morning, Mr Poe, I received a notice signed by the Secretary of State for Housing, Communities and Local Government. It concerns Byelaw 254, which, as Miss Bradshaw so eloquently reminded us last week, was passed by the municipal borough of Kendal in 1901 and subsumed into South Lakeland Council in 1974. Section 2, Subsection F, prohibited the wilful removal, defacement or rearrangement of any rock found on Shap Fell and Mardale Common and Section 3, Subsection E, prohibited damaging plants and vegetation in the same area.'

Bradshaw stood. 'That's correct, your honour. It remains our position that compelling Poe to return Herdwick Croft to its original condition would be to compel him to break the law. The court cannot make that order.'

She sat back down.

'I'm afraid I can, Miss Bradshaw,' the judge said. 'In fact, I must.'

Bradshaw stood again. 'For what reason, your honour? I am certain our argument is legally sound.'

'It was, Miss Bradshaw. Twenty-three years I've sat on the bench. Never seen a defence like it. I've already written a paper on it.'

'But?' Poe said. He didn't bother to get up.

The judge ignored the breach of etiquette.

'But, Mr Poe, not four hours ago, the Secretary of State, in a staggering overreach of his authority, repealed Byelaw 254. An order to return Herdwick Croft to its original condition therefore no longer compels you to break the law. I have accordingly been instructed to find for the plaintiff.'

Poe did stand this time, more out of shock than respect. 'What's this mean?'

The judge removed his half-moon reading glasses and rubbed his eyes. 'I am truly sorry, Mr Poe, but I have no choice but to instruct you to return Herdwick Croft to the condition in which you found it. You have three months to do this and you may no longer use it as your primary dwelling.'

Chapter 68

'This is horrible, Poe! Just horrible!' Bradshaw cried when the courtroom had cleared. 'I've let you down – I'm so sorry.'

Her eyes were brimming and Poe didn't need that right now – he was too buzzed.

'Two things, Tilly,' he said. 'When do I ever do anything I'm told?'

'But—'

'But what? You think some pen-pushing council wanker's going to schlep across Shap Fell every night just to make sure I'm not there? I doubt they'd even be able to find it.'

'I suppose,' she sniffed. 'What's the other thing?'

'What happened in there wasn't random bureaucracy, Tilly.'

'What was it then?'

'A shot across the bows. We're being warned off and that means we're on to something.'

'But what, Poe?'

'When did the judge say he'd received the notification of the repealed byelaw?'

'He said the Secretary of State for Housing, Communities and Local Government had signed it four hours earlier.'

'We're being warned away from the soldiers' families.'

'But that doesn't make sense. Other than my theory someone has been censoring data in the public domain, we haven't found anything remotely suspicious.'

'Yet.'

'What do you mean?'

'Tilly, how long have you known me?'

'Almost three years, Poe.'

'And what happens when someone threatens me?'

'You usually do the exact opposite of what they want you to do.'

'Exactly,' he said. 'Someone—'

'Even when it's not in your best interests to do so,' she continued. 'In fact, it could be argued that sometimes you're a very stupid—'

'—*someone* hasn't read their briefing paper on me is the point I'm making,' he cut in. 'If they had, they'd know that threats only spur me on.'

'How did they find out, though, Poe? We only started looking this morning.' She looked thoughtful. 'I wonder if one of the Mole People triggered some drive-by malware.'

'Come again?'

'If someone is monitoring who's looking for specific kinds of information, they may have developed a website that would only be found if certain keywords or phrases were typed into our search engine.'

'Like Tango Two-Four *and* conspiracy?'

'Almost certainly something like that. As soon as the user visits this deception website, their computer automatically downloads spyware. Whoever installed it can then gather information on that person or organisation.'

'Sort of like a tripwire then?'

'Exactly like a tripwire.'

Poe thought about it. Although it was plausible, it seemed needlessly complex and labour intensive.

'There is another explanation, Tilly,' he said.

'There is?'

He nodded. 'Who walked in when we were discussing this very thing?'

Bradshaw grimaced. 'Hannah Finch.'

'Hannah Finch,' Poe agreed. 'All this "teach her how to investigate properly" bollocks that Alastor Locke spun was just a ruse so she could look over our shoulders.'

'What a . . . scoundrel! What should we do now?'

'First of all, I want deep searches on all the players involved in this. See what you can find on Hannah Finch and Alastor Locke.'

'What about the Secretary of State for Housing, Communities and Local Government, Poe?'

'Him as well.'

'Anything else?'

'It's time to stop pussyfooting about, Tilly,' he said. 'Tomorrow morning we're going to speak to Danny North's widow – the woman who set up the "Justice for Tango Two-Four" Facebook page.'

Chapter 69

Danny North's widow was called Lucy and she lived in a village in North Yorkshire called Tollerton. Poe called Melody Lee and told her they were following a lead but was unspecific. She didn't ask what it was and she didn't ask to come with them. With the summit close, her focus seemed to have shifted.

He didn't tell Hannah Finch anything at all.

The sun was out, the sky was azure blue and Poe had the windows open as the BMW ate up the miles on the A66. He wasn't a huge fan of summer but the Pennines were glorious that morning. Like a pimped-up version of Shap Fell. All crags and valleys and heather.

He said as much to Bradshaw. She complained about her hay fever.

'The air-conditioning's knackered, Tilly,' he said, 'and Edgar's in the back. There's nothing I can do, I'm afraid.'

'That's OK, Poe,' she sniffed. 'I went through the Justice for Tango Two-Four Facebook page last night.'

'And it was definitely Lucy North who set it up?'

'Yes, Poe.'

He didn't want to know how she could answer with so much certainty. Bradshaw dipped in and out of people's private social media accounts the same way he dipped sausages in and out of Tabasco sauce.

'The group has a life of its own now,' she continued. 'Mrs North barely contributes these days; leaves it to a few trusted page

270

administrators. The comments are moderated but it's hard to tell what criteria are being used to determine what's acceptable to post and what isn't.'

'Meaning?'

'It's a public group so anyone can comment, but a group admin has to approve it first.'

'They're approving everything?'

'It seems that way, Poe.'

'Anything useful?'

'There are some . . . strong views on what happened.'

'You mean some of them are from the tinfoil hat brigade?'

'I don't know,' she frowned. 'I don't think I saw any photos like that.'

Poe smiled. 'It's OK, Tilly. What's the dominant view on what happened?'

'There are two main ones. A: they don't believe that Tango Two-Four were lost; they think they were on some sort of secret mission.'

'And B?'

'They don't think they've been told everything about the suicide bomb.'

'That makes two of us,' he grunted.

'But I thought Hannah Finch said—'

'Look, I get that the MoD can't advertise the ingredients of a successful attack on their troops and equipment, and I'm not a bleeding-heart liberal who thinks he has a right to know everything about everything, but that bloody report just doesn't read right. I don't care what Hannah Finch says, the first investigator at the attack site may as well have been reading from a pre-prepared script for all the insight he had.'

'Do you think they were on a secret mission, though?'

'A bog-standard infantry section? Not a chance. Our special forces would have been out there from day one; if there was anything dodgy to do, they'd have been tasked with it, not Tango Two-Four.'

'So you do think they were lost?'

'I don't think that either. The British Army's a professional army, easily the best in the world. *Everyone* knows how to read a map. Even if the gizmos that connect to satellites had all failed, every person in that armoured personnel carrier could have pin-pointed where they were just by looking at the terrain. If they were where they weren't supposed to be, it was because they wanted to be there.'

'So what then?'

'I have no idea, Tilly.' Poe took the third exit at the Scotch Corner roundabout and hit the A1. 'But we'll be at Mrs North's in forty-five minutes – hopefully she'll be able to shed some light on it.'

Tollerton was a small, picturesque village, ten miles from the medieval city of York. It was a pleasant mix of new builds, older houses, pubs and amenities.

Lucy North lived in a house near the Black Horse pub, over-looking the triangular village green. According to Bradshaw, the Norths had bought it when the King's Royal Rifles had been posted to Catterick. They were trying for their first baby and hadn't wanted to raise their child in the largest army garrison in Europe.

Poe parked outside her house and turned off the engine. He purposefully hadn't told her they were coming. If their com-munications were being monitored, which he doubted, Alastor Locke would have to work that much harder to find out what they were up to. Bradshaw had suggested they power off their phones and remove the SIMs but he didn't want to advertise that they knew Finch was Alastor Locke's personal talebearer.

'Do you think she'll be in, Poe?'

'School holidays, Tilly. Could easily be out with her daughter somewhere. What's her name again?'

'Emily North. She's fifteen years old.'

'And Danny North never met her?'

'He didn't, Poe. Mrs North gave birth just after he died. It's very sad.'

Poe set his jaw. Wretched stories were a hallmark of every war, but Locke had made this one personal. If there was something hiding in the dark corners of Whitehall, he was going to grab it by the neck and drag it into the light. They'd brought him into this. Tried to keep him in their carefully contained box. Assumed they could point at what they wanted him to look at, shield him from what they didn't.

Which showed just how badly they'd misjudged him.

'Will we wait if she isn't in?' Bradshaw said.

'We don't need to.'

'Why's that, Poe?'

'Because she's looking right at us.'

Chapter 70

Lucy North was in her forties and in good shape. She'd just got back from her morning run and was still wearing Lycra jogging bottoms and a fluorescent green vest. She was sweating but only lightly. Her chestnut hair was cut short.

She'd heard their car pull up and had watched them through the kitchen window while she sipped a smoothie. When they saw her watching them, she opened the front door and waited. Poe had shown her his ID card and she'd invited them inside.

'The NCA, you're like a naffer version of the FBI, right?' Lucy said.

Bradshaw pouted. Poe laughed.

She had a strong Yorkshire accent. Poe approved. Even more so than Cumbrians, the men and women of Yorkshire had a deserved reputation for resilience, common sense and straight talking.

'Exactly right,' he said.

'You want a brew?'

He did.

'I hated Danny when it happened,' Lucy said.

They were seated around her kitchen table, mugs of strong tea in their hands. It was fifteen years since she was widowed but Poe offered his condolences anyway. She nodded and started telling them about her husband, and the impact his death had had on her and her daughter.

'Hated that he'd put me . . . no, *us* in this position. Hated that he'd permanently changed my life. Hated that because he insisted on following his dreams, all of mine were shattered.'

'A hollow kind of rage, though?' Poe said.

She nodded. 'Losing your partner is different to any other kind of loss,' she said, twisting her wedding band as she talked. 'Until it's ripped from you, it's impossible to realise just how entwined two lives can be. Danny's death changed every part of my life. Every time I do something, I'm not doing it with him. I eat different meals, I watch different TV, I read different books. My circle of friends changed, my financial circumstances changed, my *body* changed. Danny and I never ran together – he said he ran too much at work to do it at home – so I sort of got out of the habit. Now he's dead I run every day. Sometimes for miles and miles.'

'And what are you running from, Mrs North?' Poe said.

'Lucy,' she said. 'And that's deeper than the Grimethorpe pit, Sergeant Poe.'

'Please, call me Washington.'

She raised her eyebrows but didn't comment on his unusual first name.

'Maybe I was running *towards* something,' she said after a while.

'Like?'

She shrugged, her eyes fixed on Poe. 'An answer?'

'So are we,' he said eventually.

'But let me guess, you can't tell me what?'

'You've spoken to people before, I take it?'

'I have.'

'Poe's not like other people, Mrs North,' Bradshaw said. 'He doesn't like keeping secrets. When he can tell you something, he will.'

'You an honest man, Washington?' Lucy said.

'When it suits. And when I get to the bottom of whatever this is, if there's anything you should have been told but weren't, I will not keep quiet. That's a promise.'

'You know something? I believe you.'

'Tell me about Danny, Lucy,' Poe said.

For an hour he let her talk. She told them how she and Danny had grown up in the same Yorkshire village. How they'd been childhood sweethearts. He was the first man she'd ever been with and she was his first woman. She said that where they had lived, a once thriving pit village, employment prospects were limited. She'd supported Danny's decision to join the army and, although she hated him being on operations, she knew he was doing it for her too. She told them about nights out with the regiment and nights in with just the two of them. About how they'd planned for a family and what they would call their children. Things were good, they were happy, the future looked bright.

And then a fanatic in Afghanistan ripped a hole in the heart of Yorkshire, a hole that could never be filled. Twelve young Yorkshiremen dead, their lives snuffed out, the lives of their loved ones changed forever.

'And that's why you started the Facebook group?' Poe said.

'Excuse me?'

'The Facebook group, Justice for Tango Two-Four. You started it a few years ago.'

She smiled. 'Ah, so that's why you're here.'

'It is,' Poe said.

'It's not me you need to speak to then, Washington,' she said, 'it's my daughter, Emily.'

Chapter 71

A noise from above made them look up.

'Speak of the devil . . .' Lucy said. 'Sounds like she's finally up. She keeps Emily-time during the summer hols. Probably been talking to her friends on her computer all night.'

'According to a recent study, Mrs North, adolescents in Emily's age range typically spend nine hours a day online,' Bradshaw said.

'They're amateurs then,' she snorted. 'My Emily spends far longer than that. I really don't know when she finds time to sleep or study.'

'She doing OK at school?' Poe said.

'Fine,' Lucy said. 'She's studying post-colonialism, whatever that is.'

'It's the academic study of the human consequences of the control and exploitation of colonised people and their lands, Mrs North,' Bradshaw said.

'That sounds familiar. She'll be down for her breakfast in a second.'

Sure enough, a gangly, drowsy-looking, pyjama-clad teenager sleepwalked into the kitchen. Her red hair was twisted and tangled. Her puffy eyes were glued to her smartphone. She was tapping the screen faster than Bradshaw did. She sent something into the ether and slipped it into the pocket of her unfastened dressing gown. She yawned, rubbed her eyes and spotted the two strangers in her kitchen.

'MUM!' she shrieked. 'Why didn't you tell me we had visitors?'

'It's OK, Em,' Lucy said. 'This is Washington and Tilly. They're from the National Crime Agency.'

She quickly tied her dressing gown, pulled her hair back and fastened it. 'Honestly, Mum, you're soooo embarrassing.'

Poe held out his ID card. Bradshaw did the same. Emily's face moved from tired to stroppy.

'And I'm supposed to be impressed, am I?' she said. 'Because I can assure you' – she leaned in and read their ID cards – '*Silly* Bradshaw and Sergeant *Poo*, that I am most definitely not.'

Poe hadn't had to deal with a sulky teenager since he'd been a Cumbrian cop, but he remembered one thing: there was no reasoning with them when they were like this. Nothing impressed them, everything was stupid. Grown-ups were idiots. And, her names *were* quite creative, especially for someone who'd just woken up.

He laughed.

Bradshaw didn't.

'His name's not Poo, it's *Poe*,' she said, confused. She'd probably *never* had to deal with a sulky teenager. 'And my name's not Silly, it's *Tilly*.'

'Whatever.'

'Whatever what?'

'We're here about what happened to your dad, Emily,' Poe said gently.

'More idiots?' she snapped. 'Why don't you leave me and Mum alone?'

'Em, don't be rude,' Lucy said. 'They're here to help.'

'No, Mum, they're not. They're here to tick boxes so when the press do their annual story on us, they can say they're still in touch with the families.'

'Why were Tango Two-Four in 432s and not Warriors?' Poe said.

Her expression shifted. Became shrewd, as he had known it would. He'd be willing to bet no one had ever asked them that

278

before. And, although he knew why, Emily didn't know he knew. It was a question designed to cut out half an hour of petulance.

'The battalion was in reserve,' she answered automatically. 'They weren't expected to engage the enemy, only to take supplies to villages and outposts.'

'That's what I've been told,' Poe said. 'Look, Emily, we're not with the MoD and I don't report to them—'

'We are *supposed* to, Poe,' Bradshaw said.

'But we're not going to. And I'm looking into some things that have been happening recently. Things that seem connected to what happened in Afghanistan. Certain people are trying to shut us down.'

'They even made it so Poe will be evicted, didn't they, Poe?'

'They did. They're playing dirty now and that means we're narrowing in on something they don't want us narrowing in on. They certainly don't want me talking to you or your mum.'

'So why are you?' She looked curious.

'Because it's possible you know something that can help us. Your mum tells me she set you up with a Facebook account. Why was that?'

'Duh, you have to be thirteen to have a Facebook account,' she said.

'And you were twelve?'

'Use a calculator to work that out, did you?' she said, although Poe could tell her heart wasn't really in it. She sighed. 'Yes, I was twelve. I'd started to read about what happened. Connected with some of the kids from the other families.'

'But why did you start the group in the first place?'

Her brow furrowed. 'I don't know really,' she said. 'I suppose I must have got to the age where I wanted to know more about my dad. I thought if I started a group for the families I might find out what he was like. It's hard to ask Mum sometimes. I don't like to upset her.'

Poe nodded in appreciation. Selfish bastards was the phrase that usually sprang to mind when you thought about teenagers. In this day and age, Emily was exceptional.

'And did the families all join?'

'Eventually. Started slowly, then guys who are still with the regiment joined too. Their families as well. We now have almost one thousand members.'

'Tilly tells me it's a public group.'

'It is. If there's a whistleblower out there I wanted to make it easy for them to share stuff. Me and my friends moderate the comments but anyone can post as long as it's not offensive.'

'I understand people think your dad's section wasn't lost?'

'Mum says everyone in the army can read a map.'

Poe nodded. 'I was in the army when I was a bit younger and you're right, map reading is a core skill.'

She raised her eyebrows.

He held up his hand and laughed. 'OK, a lot younger. I was in the Black Watch.'

'Scottish infantry regiment,' she said. 'Now part of the Royal Regiment of Scotland.'

Poe was impressed. 'You know your stuff.'

'It's hard not to pick it up. A lot of the serving soldiers talk in acronyms and slang.'

'I bet. I gather some of you have questions about the suicide attack as well?'

'We do. If you hold on a sec I'll go and get the official report.'

'You have one?'

'It's Mum's really but I've made a copy.'

She disappeared, returning in less than a minute with a bound document.

Poe read it. It was the redacted version of Hannah Finch's report. There was less detail but the message was the same: for reasons unknown, Tango Two-Four had driven into a known hot area and paid the ultimate price. Conclusions weren't as sharply drawn in their report, but there were hints as to what would come out in the inquiry: a combination of user error and bad luck.

There was one easily explained discrepancy between Finch's report and the one in his hand now. In the unredacted report, the explosive used by the suicide bomber was identified as TATP; in the redacted report it was Semtex. Poe assumed that was the MoD refusing to promote homemade methods. Most people hadn't heard of TATP; everyone had heard of Semtex. It was now a generic term for explosives.

'We asked for a meeting with the report author but were told it wasn't possible,' Lucy said.

'That's unusual; what reason did they give?'

'Just that it wouldn't be possible. Something about needing to keep everything in siloes, whatever that means.'

'Means they don't want one thing being influenced by another,' Poe said. 'I suppose their thinking will have been that if WO2 Downing had met with the families it might have compromised his impartiality.' He passed the report to Bradshaw. 'Can you make a copy of this please, Tilly?'

'Yes, Poe.'

While Bradshaw used her tablet to scan the report, Poe addressed both Emily and Lucy and said, 'What else can you tell me about Danny?'

Lucy stood up. 'I'm going to have to leave you, I'm afraid. I'm due at work and I need a shower.'

Poe stood.

'No, no, please sit down,' Lucy said. 'If Em's OK talking to you, you're welcome to stay for a bit.'

'That OK, Emily?' Poe said.

'Suppose.'

When their mugs were full again and they could hear Lucy in the shower, Emily said, 'Do you want to come up to my bedroom?

I have a shelf where I keep my dad's medals and photos.'

'How about you bring them downstairs, Emily?' Poe said.

She smiled slyly. 'Don't worry, Sergeant Poe, you're not my type.'

She left the room.

'Type of what, Poe?' Bradshaw said.

Chapter 72

Danny North's medals were set in red felt and displayed in a polished mahogany box. There were four of them. Poe recognised one and that was only because he'd been awarded it as well. The medal was silver, the ribbon was purple with outer stripes of dark green. It was called the General Service Medal and was for service in the area designated by the accompanying clasp. Danny North's GSM had been awarded for service in Northern Ireland.

'When was your dad over there, Emily?' he said.

'In 2001. It was his first tour. Mum says she didn't get a full night's sleep while he was over there.'

The Troubles had largely ended with the 1998 Good Friday Agreement but there had still been sporadic outbursts of violence. The King's Royal Rifles had obviously been called in to assist the RUC. Poe's GSM was for Northern Ireland as well, although he'd been there before the Good Friday Agreement when things were a bit spicier.

'What's this medal for?' Poe pointed at one with a black, white and red ribbon.

'That's his Iraq Medal. He was there for nine months. Mum says he was different when he came back.'

'Different, how?'

'Quiet. Didn't like crowds any more. Wouldn't eat in a restaurant unless he knew where all the exits were. I think one of his friends was killed over there, someone he trained with.'

'Iraq and Afghanistan are dirty conflicts,' Poe said. 'I did two tours of Belfast and I'd take the Irish over the Iraqis any day of the week.'

'This is his Operational Service Medal Afghanistan,' she said, pointing to another one. Her eyes filled with tears but she blotted them before they could fall. Her voice wavered, 'It was awarded posthumously.'

'I'm sorry,' Poe said. And he was. Stories like Emily's were the real cost of war.

Beside him, Bradshaw sniffed. Poe didn't turn but he knew she was crying.

'The stripes on the ribbon are red, navy blue and sky blue to represent the army, navy and air force. The outer brown stripes represent the Afghan landscape.'

Which all led up to the last medal.

Unlike the others, which were circular, this one was a cross. It was backed with a laurel wreath. He didn't recognise it.

'This is actually my mum's medal,' Emily said, 'but she lets me keep it with Dad's. It's called the Elizabeth Cross and it's awarded to the next of kin of soldiers who die in combat. She got it in 2012.'

'Why the wait?' Poe said gently.

'The medal was introduced by the Queen in 2009 but it was retrospective all the way back to the Second World War. My mum had to apply for it. I remember her crying when she filled in the forms.'

'I'm sorry,' Poe said again. It seemed such a useless word.

'My dad gets taken out by a freaking ambulance packed with bombs and all Mum gets is this lousy medal. It kinda sucks.'

'It *does* suck,' he agreed. 'Tell me about your dad. Your mum must have loads of stories about him.'

Emily took them through the photographs of her father. There were about fifty – some in uniform, some in civvies – and she had a tale to tell about each one. If he wasn't alone she described who he was with and what their stories were. There was only one of him with Tango Two-Four. The twelve of them sitting on top of a 432, guns pointing skywards, all smiling. Probably feeling invincible.

'This is the last photograph of him alive,' she said. 'Of any of them.' She put the photographs down. 'Is there anything else, Sergeant Poe?'

'Tilly has a few questions about the Facebook group, if that's OK?'

'It's why you're here,' she said, wiping her eyes.

For the next hour Emily and Bradshaw talked in a language that was alien to Poe. It was all access points, file extensions and remote access. Before long he had stopped listening.

'You said you don't moderate all the comments on the group yourself, Emily?' Poe said.

Bradshaw hadn't picked up anything useful during their discussion about the Facebook page. Emily didn't think anyone had been removing comments but accepted what Bradshaw told her. She'd check with her friends, see if they'd noticed anything.

'Not any more,' she said in answer to Poe's question. 'I used to, but it's too big now. There are four of us who take it in turns. If they're unsure of anything they refer it to me.'

'So if there was anything upsetting or unusual, you'd see it?'

'I would.'

'And has there been?'

'Not really. Every now and then we get trolls but I . . . deal with them.'

Probably the same way Bradshaw dealt with trolls – by making them wish they hadn't bothered. Troll Bradshaw and you'd find yourself locked out of every computer, mobile phone and tablet you'd ever owned. And if you were stupid enough to own one of those smart houses, then your kettle would start to boil at 3 a.m. and your fridge would keep reordering eggs.

Poe didn't like the modern world. It scared him.

'There's been nothing that's worried you?' he said. 'Nothing that seemed too specific about the suicide bomb or the reasons your dad and his friends were in the wrong valley?'

'No. Most of what we get is conspiracy nutters and people sending condolences. Occasionally we get donations.'

'Donations?'

'When I started the group, I wanted a safe space for everyone to meet and talk. But pretty soon people wanted to make donations to support the families. My mum helped me open a bank account so if people wanted to donate they could.'

'How much have you got so far?'

'Not much. We haven't reached a thousand pounds yet. But people like to feel they're doing something, so that's fine. It was never about the money.'

Poe made a mental note to make a donation. It seemed the least he could do.

'One last question, Emily, and then I'll let you get on with your day,' he said. 'What do *you* think happened?'

She smiled sadly. 'You mean do I think the reason they were in the wrong valley was because my dad was on a super-secret mission?'

He nodded.

'No, Sergeant Poe,' she said. 'I don't think that. I know they weren't lost, though. Something happened out there, something the government doesn't want the families to know about.'

Poe said nothing. He thought that too.

Chapter 73

Poe had missed something. He didn't know what, but his second brain, the one that ticked over in the background while his primary brain made rash decisions, was working overtime. He recognised the signs: a nervous energy and an inability to concentrate on anything.

'You didn't mention Christopher Bierman, Poe,' Bradshaw said.

They had said goodbye to Emily North, promised to keep in touch and were soon back on the A66 heading towards Carlisle.

'I didn't. If Emily thought her dad's death had something to do with Bierman it would have been on Facebook before we'd even got in the car.'

'What if she'd brought it up?'

'She didn't.'

'But if she had?'

'I'd have changed the subject.'

'I liked Emily, Poe. She's been dealt a rotten hand but she's managed to get on with her life.'

'She has,' he said. 'I wonder what's worse, never knowing your father or knowing him only to lose him?'

He didn't hear Bradshaw's response. Saying it out loud had transported him back to his childhood and the mother he'd never known. So even as he asked the question, he knew what Emily's answer would have been: the same as his. He'd give anything, absolutely *anything*, to spend just five minutes with his mother.

Tell her he was sorry for hating her. Sorry for not trying to find her.

Just tell her he was sorry.

And in the background his second brain continued to tick over.

Poe reran his conversations with Lucy and Emily North when he got back, convinced something important had been said, or not said. He briefly considered calling Lucy but he dismissed it. Whatever his mind was searching for, he didn't think Lucy or Emily were aware of it.

Melody Lee popped her head in and asked how things were going but he could tell her priority was now the summit. He briefed her, then went back to his notes. An hour later Hannah Finch did the same. She wanted to know where they'd been.

'Just tugging on a couple of loose threads,' he said.

'And what threads might they be?'

'Just told you, loose ones.'

She glared at him and said, 'Tilly, you're the brains of this outfit – please tell me where you've been.'

'Go boil an egg,' Bradshaw said.

It was seven o'clock and Poe was tired. If he left now he could take Edgar for a long walk. The spaniel hadn't had a great day. He'd spent the morning in Lucy North's garden and the afternoon in the back of his car.

'Come on, Tilly,' he said. 'We'll pick this up again tomorrow.'

'Blimey,' she said. She was leaning forward, staring at her computer.

'What is it?'

'You know you thought there was something not quite right with that report on the suicide bomb?'

'Not just me, Emily North thought that too.'

288

'Well, I've been running it through a program of mine for the last twenty-four hours. It's just finished.'

'And?'

'It's found something.'

Poe stood up so quickly his chair toppled over. He didn't bother picking it up.

'Are you familiar with plagiarism software, Poe?'

He wasn't, but it seemed self-explanatory. 'I assume it compares documents to see if one's been copied from another.'

'Basically,' she said. 'But most software is flawed.'

'How so?'

'Plagiarists can easily elude detection by rogeting.'

'Which is?'

'It's when you substitute enough keywords in a document to fool a standard plagiarism checker.'

'What, like change explosion to blast, soldier to infantryman, that type of thing?'

'Exactly that type of thing, Poe. Do that enough times and plagiarism checkers will mark a document as original despite the bulk of it having been copied from another.'

'And your program has found a similar document?'

'Yes, Poe,' she said happily. 'You see, I tweaked a program I already had. I added string matching, stylometry and a cosine similarity measure among other things.'

Poe waited.

She sighed. 'Basically my program looks for synonyms and an author's unique writing style. I also wrote a program that allowed it to compare documents on databases that ordinary software doesn't have access to.'

'Legal?'

'Untraceable,' she said.

They fist bumped.

'Tell me what you've found, Tilly.'

She did.

And when she'd finished Poe said, 'I'm going to fucking kill him.'

Chapter 74

The report on the suicide bomb that wiped out Tango Two-Four had been cobbled together from a hotchpotch of other reports. Bradshaw's bespoke plagiarism checker found that a large chunk of the executive summary was taken from a suicide attack on a convoy of Royal Engineers in Iraq and the technical section had been lifted directly from the IRA bombing of a Protestant pub in Belfast thirty years earlier. Her software found that seventeen unrelated reports were the source material for the document Hannah Finch had given them a few days earlier. There were even parts that had been copied and pasted from a manual on how to write reports when investigating suicide bombings . . .

No wonder the report had seemed flat and lifeless. No personal touch, no expressions of outrage. It was a complete work of fiction. Poe suspected it had been written by someone in Whitehall. If he existed at all, Poe doubted that WO2 Downing had ever dug sand from the treads of his boots.

There had been some attempt at what Bradshaw called rogeting and he called using a thesaurus, but even that had tailed off towards the end, almost as if the writer had got bored. Probably arrogant enough to think no one would ever challenge it.

They were wrong about that.

Poe parked next to his quad at Shap Wells but ignored it in favour of the two-mile walk. Edgar needed a decent run and he needed time to calm down. Going at Alastor Locke head-on wouldn't work. The old spy was too canny to fold under some light intimidation. Threatening him with public exposure wouldn't work either. He would quash the story quicker than you could say 'breach of the Official Secrets Act'.

He needed to politely ask Locke for a face-to-face meeting. Present him with Bradshaw's evidence. Put him on the spot and see what happened. Probably nothing, but it was all he had.

The key would be to keep calm, though, stay in control.

He found the spymaster in his contacts list and pressed call.

It rang once.

'Locke.'

'You sneaky twat!' Poe barked. 'It wasn't that you lied to me, it was that you did it so fucking badly. Which means you thought I was either incompetent and wouldn't find out, or so powerless it wouldn't matter if I did. Either way, you've been treating me and Tilly like dickheads.'

Oh well, he thought, as Mike Tyson said, 'Everyone has a plan until they get punched in the mouth.'

'And a good evening to you too, Sergeant Poe,' Locke said. 'It appears someone has got you all hot under the collar. And by using my context clues, I augur you think that someone is me?'

'That report your lackey gave me; it's a work of pure fiction.'

'And you know this how?'

'Never mind how I bloody know,' he snapped. 'First thing tomorrow morning I'm driving down to Manchester and the two of us are sitting in a dark room until you've told me everything I need to know. No exceptions. You don't get to decide if something's privileged or too sensitive.'

'You sound awfully wound up, dear boy. Have you thought about Pilates? I take a class three times a week. Does wonders for my blood pressure.'

'Alastor, I'm warning you, don't test me on this—'

'Where are you?'

292

'What, now? I'm at home, of course. It's almost ten o'clock.'

'That's odd.'

'Odd, how?'

'Because if you were at home we'd be doing this *facie ad faciem*.'

'Say again?'

'Face-to-face, Poe,' he said. 'I'm sitting on your couch.'

Chapter 75

Poe ran the last hundred yards, Edgar sprinting beside him, yelping with excitement. He hurled open Herdwick Croft's door and marched inside. Sure enough, Alastor Locke was sitting on his sofa. Reading glasses perched on the end of his nose, a file on his lap.

'And I've helped myself to one of your excellent beers, Poe,' he said. 'I'd rather hoped to make myself a light salad while I waited but the only thing in your fridge that was green was the milk.'

'I'm trying to see how high I can grow the mould.'

'Not to worry, not to worry. And who's this fine-looking chap?'

'He's called Edgar, and if I tell him to, he'll rip your balls off.'

'An attack spaniel? Must be a breeding line of which I'm unaware.'

'What do you want, Alastor?'

'You must stop investigating what happened to Tango Two-Four.'

'Must?'

Locke nodded. 'Must.'

Poe remained silent.

Locke spread his arms. 'But it's not all about the stick today. I come bearing a carrot.'

'And is it a carrot I'll like?'

'Possibly not. But it's definitely one you need.'

Poe glanced at the file in Locke's lap. It was cream with a

red government security classification stamped on the front: TOP
SECRET – UK/US EYES ONLY.

'What's that?'

'Do you want to know what really happened to Tango Two-
Four, Poe?'

'I do.'

'And you won't accept my word that it has nothing to do with
what I asked you to investigate?'

Poe shook his head.

'And why is that?'

'Because I've looked at this case from more angles than I
thought possible, and the only thing I'm sure of is I'm not sure
of anything. You can't know what's in that file isn't connected
because we don't know what this is yet.'

'Spoken like a true detective. Very well, Poe, but I'm warning
you, this isn't a bell that can be unrung. Once you know, however
much you'd like to, legally, it isn't something you can *unknow*.'

Poe opened a beer and drank it straight from the bottle,
savoured the way it cooled his parched throat. He pressed the
bottle against his forehead and rolled it around. It had been a long
day. Locke wasn't making sense and he had a headache coming on.

'You ready to come inside, Poe?'

He didn't need to think about it. Bradshaw would have. She'd
have taken on Locke's warning about unrung bells and completed
a quick cost/benefit analysis. Maybe decline. Flynn would have
considered the ramifications too. Maybe she'd be satisfied that
the people who needed to know these things, knew these things.

Poe wasn't wired that way. For him, secrets were the pebble in
his shoe, the pea under his mattress. He *had* to know.

'I'm ready,' he said.

'OK,' Locke said. 'Would it surprise you to know that, prior
to Brexit, Britain and France were the only EU countries with
the capability to fight on all four fronts? Land, sea, air and cyber?'

That actually didn't surprise him. The Europeans talked a good game when it came to collective defence but so far they hadn't put much into it.

'What's your point?'

'My point, Sergeant Poe, is, whether you give a fig about the "special relationship" or not – and I come very much from the "no fig" end of the scale – it is beyond doubt that the capabilities of the American military is the only thing stopping the Russians from reforming the 3rd Shock Army and rolling it across their borders.'

Poe shrugged. 'What's this got to do with Tango Two-Four?'

'Everything,' he said. He handed Poe the file. 'Tango Two-Four weren't killed by a suicide bomber, Sergeant Poe, they were killed by an AGM-114 Hellfire missile. Do you understand what that means?'

Despite the beer, Poe's mouth went dry.

'It was blue-on-blue?' he whispered.

Locke nodded.

'It was indeed. The Hellfire missile was fired by an American Apache helicopter pilot. Tango Two-Four were killed by friendly fire.'

Chapter 76

'You covered up a friendly-fire incident so you wouldn't upset American sensibilities?' Poe said. 'No wonder you're desperate to keep this secret. If the truth got out there'd be public outrage.'

'I suspect you are right,' Locke said. 'If the truth got out *now*, there would be. That's not, however, why the decision was made.'

'Why then? I was a soldier. I understand the chaos of a live combat zone. Blue-on-blues are inevitable, even in this day and age. Hell, even the SAS and SBS went at each other during the Falklands, and they're the most professional soldiers in the world. There'd have been anger, yes, but it would have been tempered by the knowledge that these things do happen. By trying to contain it, all you've done is stack up problems for the future. These things get out, Alastor, they always do. It's as inevitable as death.'

Locke removed his reading glasses. Put them gently on the couch. He fixed Poe with his piercing grey eyes.

'It must be invigorating to live in your world, Poe. One painted entirely in blacks and whites. I'm sure it's what makes you such a dogged investigator—'

'I don't think—'

'My world, however, is rarely so monochromatic. It's a pastiche of greys. You say containing this incident was a mistake, I say it was a decision that undoubtedly saved the lives of British servicemen and women.'

Poe said nothing.

'You're not convinced,' Locke said.

'You haven't convinced me.'

'Well, let me paint you a picture of what happened a couple of years before the Tango Two-Four incident. Iraq this time. A pair of American A-10 'tankbusters' opened fire on a British convoy. Our tanks were flying the coalition flag, they had Union Jacks painted on their armour, and they were using the correct radio frequencies. Despite that, the Americans strafed them with shells the size of milk bottles. Thousands of them, at a rate of five hundred rounds a minute. One soldier died, several more were injured. This report,' – he gestured to the manila file – 'the Tango Two-Four report, is everything we know about what happened on that terrible day. When you read it you'll notice one thing's missing.'

'What would that be?' Poe said.

'The names of the American helicopter crew. Do you want to know what happened to them?'

'Not as much as the families of Tango Two-Four would, I suspect.'

'Nothing,' Locke said. 'Just as they did in Iraq, the Pentagon refused to identify their pilots. Even under a cast-iron guarantee of anonymity, they snubbed our request to attend the inquest. The US press didn't even report on it. It was as if it never happened.'

'I'm not seeing—'

'Do you know what relations were like between the two sets of troops on the ground after the Iraq incident?'

'Strained?' Poe said.

'The prevailing view was that any American who accidentally killed a Brit got a free pass. Our troops were on the verge of refusing to work with them. And things got heated. A troop of Royal Marines beat a Delta Force patrol to a bloody pulp. Some US Rangers beat up one of our signallers in retaliation.'

'Which reduced combat effectiveness,' Poe said.

'It did. To this date the Pentagon has refused to identify a single person involved in any friendly-fire incident. And do you know what that makes Her Majesty's Government look like?'

'Impotent?'

'Worse. And because every time we embarrass them by asking for something we know we can't have, we lose a tad more influence. The special relationship gets that little less special.'

'So you had the report fabricated?' Poe said. 'Invented a suicide bombing so the Americans didn't have to refuse another request?'

'Both sides fabricated the report. And, as distasteful as it sounds, it did allow for a safer environment for our troops to work in.'

'This WO2 Downing, the report author, does he actually exist?'

'He does,' Locke said. 'On paper at least. And that's all I'll say on the matter.'

'Is any of it true?'

Locke held his gaze and said, 'Other than the manner of their death, everything is as it is written. For reasons unknown, Tango Two-Four were in the wrong place. They'd left the green zone and had travelled into the unsafe red zone. Al-Qaeda had been operating in that area, so from the Apache pilot's point of view, they were a legitimate target.'

Poe considered what Locke had said. Finally he picked up the file and skimmed through it. 'Why are you showing me this?' He paused. 'It's so I have to stop speaking to the families, isn't it?' he said, answering his own question. 'Now I know the truth, I'll be breaching the Official Secrets Act if I keep looking into it.'

Locke shrugged. 'A mean but effective trick, I'm afraid.'

'And making me homeless by getting your pet minister to repeal that byelaw? Was that a mean but effective trick too?'

'No, that was just mean. I'm sorry, Poe, but some of my colleagues lack subtlety. It's bad form going after someone like this and, if I had known about it, I would have stopped it.'

Poe opened the file again. 'What do you think happened to

the Apache pilot, Alastor? Do you think he suffers the same way the families suffer?'

'I think we both know the answer to that, Poe.'

'Do you think he was even disciplined?'

'Disciplined?' Locke said. 'They probably gave the man a damned medal.'

Which was when Poe's second brain told him what it was he'd missed.

Chapter 77

Medals . . .

That's where the answers would be found. Medals earned, medals *not* earned. It was what Poe's second brain had been trying to tell him. What he had missed.

He got rid of Alastor Locke as soon as he could without raising suspicion. He'd tried to appear calm, a difficult thing to do when his insides were fizzing.

'Are we in agreement, Poe?' the spy had said before he left Herdwick Croft, the Tango Two-Four file secured in his briefcase. 'You will cease any and all investigations into the deaths of Tango Two-Four, you will not contact any more family members and you will not discuss the contents of that report with anyone, not even Tilly.'

He'd stared at Poe, trying to force a response out of him. 'Well?' he said.

'Yes.'

'Yes, what, Poe?'

'I won't do any of those things.'

'And I have your word?'

'You do.'

'Good man.'

As soon as he'd gone, Poe scrolled through the contacts on his phone. He found who he wanted and pressed call. While he waited for an answer he muttered, 'Sorry, Alastor, I had my fingers crossed . . .'

'Lucy North,' the voice on the other end of the phone said.

'Hi, Lucy, it's Sergeant Poe from the National Crime Agency. We were at yours this morning.'

'Oh, hi. What's wrong, have you left something here?'

'Nothing's wrong. I'd like to speak to your daughter, if I could?'

Lucy must have put her hand over the handset as when she shouted, 'Emily, phone!' it was muffled. 'She's on her way, Sergeant Poe. She's not in trouble, is she?'

'Absolutely not.'

'OK, she's here.'

'Sergeant *Poo*, what can I do for you?' Emily said. 'Don't tell me, you've changed your mind about seeing the inside of my bedroom.'

There was then a spirited exchange of ideas in Yorkshire, one that ended when Emily yelled, 'I was joking, Mother! Obviously, I was joking, he's like one hundred years old!'

Poe waited impatiently.

'Sorry about that, Sergeant Poe. Mum can be very literal sometimes.'

'Copy that,' Poe said, thinking of Bradshaw. 'I'll be quick, Emily. Earlier today you showed me the medals your dad earned. There were four of them: the General Service Medal, the Iraq medal, the Operational Service Medal Afghanistan and the Elizabeth Cross that was awarded to your mother.'

'That's right.'

'I'm just wondering why you didn't show me his Military Cross. Everyone in Tango Two-Four was posthumously awarded one for their actions in securing the freedom of Captain Jack Duncan. I thought you'd have been proud to show it off; it's the military's third-highest honour and they're not awarded that often.'

Emily didn't know that Jack Duncan had lived the last few years as Christopher Bierman and he saw no reason to tell her.

'That's right, they were, Sergeant Poe,' she said. 'Everyone involved in the rescue of Jack Duncan *was* awarded the Military Cross.'

'But not your dad?'

'He was not.'

'And why was that?'

Poe knew, but he needed Emily to confirm his suspicions.

'Because he wasn't part of the rescue. He only joined the section the day before he died. A man called Sean Gardiner, the section medic, had become indisposed. My dad was drafted in to replace him. I've searched for Sean online as I wanted to tell him it's not his fault, but I haven't been able to trace him.'

Indisposed, Poe thought. Army speak for ill, ill-disciplined or drunk.

'Your dad was the section medic?' he said. 'I wasn't aware of that.'

'He wasn't like a doctor or anything, but I think there was one soldier in every section who was given advanced first-aid training. As they were on a hearts-and-minds mission, they couldn't leave without one.'

'So Sean Gardiner was the original section medic?'

'Yes, he was Tango Two-Four's medic when they rescued Jack Duncan, not my dad.'

And another piece of the puzzle dropped into place . . .

Chapter 78

Poe called an emergency meeting for eight o'clock the following morning. They met at Herdwick Croft. He had already been out and bought a selection of pastries for him and Melody Lee and a fruit salad for Bradshaw.

'Where's the spook?' Melody Lee yawned.

'Hannah Finch isn't in the loop any more.'

'It's because she spies on us,' Bradshaw explained.

'She does?' Melody Lee said. 'Wow, who'd have thought a member of Five would do that?'

'I know, right?'

'What we doing here, Poe?' Melody Lee said.

'I know who our murderer is,' he said.

Bradshaw's mouth opened in astonishment.

Melody Lee said, 'You're shitting me?'

Poe took them through the sequence of events as he saw them. That the twelve men who had died in the suicide bombing – he saw no reason to breach the Official Secrets Act just yet – were not exactly the same twelve men who had rescued Captain Jack Duncan, aka, Christopher Bierman. That a soldier called Sean Gardiner had been replaced by Danny North the day before Tango Two-Four were killed.

When he'd finished, he said, 'Tilly, you thought someone has been,' – he referred to his notes – '"systematically and permanently removing data from all discoverable sites". That photographs and the occasional bit of text were being deleted and someone was "monitoring gossip on Tango Two-Four" on social media?'

'I did, Poe. Why?'

'Because I've been up all night looking for Sean Gardiner and there's barely a trace of him.'

'You found him?'

'I found evidence of him,' he said. 'The *Telegraph* listed all the posthumous medals awarded that year – he was one of twelve King's Royal Rifles who received the Military Cross for the rescue of Captain Jack Duncan. I cross-referenced that with the men who died in the suicide bomb. Sean Gardiner and Danny North were the only names not on both lists.'

'So, there's been a thirteenth member of Tango Two-Four out there all this time,' Melody Lee said. 'One we didn't know about.'

'No, Special Agent Lee, there's been a thirteenth *rat* out there all this time. And for some reason he's killing everyone involved with Christopher Bierman.'

'There's more,' Poe said. 'Something we should have realised and something I've only just been made aware of.'

He and Melody Lee had broken for coffee. Bradshaw had taken it personally that Sean Gardiner had managed to hide his existence from her. She was staring at her laptop, brow furrowed, fingers moving like a concert pianist. If there were traces of Gardiner online, Bradshaw would find them.

'Emily North said her father was the section medic,' he continued. 'Trained to a higher standard in first aid. He was drafted into Tango Two-Four when Sean Gardiner became "indisposed", whatever the hell that was about. I'm betting Gardiner was also trained to that higher standard. I looked it up last night and one of the things section medics are taught to do is insert saline drips.'

'Shit,' Melody Lee whistled. 'That means he'd have had no problem inserting that IV line into Bierman and pumping him full of Ritalin.'

'It also explains why there was a double knot on just one shoe. Gardiner would have had to remove it to insert the drip. When he put the shoe back on, muscle memory meant he'd have tied a double without even realising he had. I was only in the army a short while and I still tie my shoes with double knots.'

Melody Lee pulled up her trouser leg. Her pumps were also tied in double knots. 'Muscle memory for feds and cops too,' she said. 'Can't be tripping up when you're running down some scumbag.'

Poe nodded. 'I don't know why he's waited so long to go whacko, though,' he said. 'It's been, what, fifteen years?'

'That isn't as ass-crazy as you might think, Poe.'

'No?'

'It takes time to disappear. To *really* disappear. The FBI occasionally work with the US Marshals and one of their primary roles is to find people who don't want to be found. And some of these assholes have assets and skills at their disposal. You know what the most effective way of disappearing is?'

Poe shook his head.

'You do the things you'd expect. You cut up your credit cards, you stay off the internet, you stop flying anywhere. You become unbanked.'

'Remove all traces of your old life, basically?'

'That's right. But if you want to take it to the next level, you have to remove all traces of what's in here.'

She tapped her own head.

Poe frowned.

'Human brains work on cues,' she said. 'We remember things when we are given a prompt. How many times have you heard the first beats of a song and had instant recall of the lyrics?'

It was true, he thought. He might not listen to the Clash's *London Calling* for months, but as soon as the opening riff sounded he knew he'd be able to sing along to the whole album.

'Lots,' he said.

'Photos are the same. When you're trying to disappear they're your worst enemy. They hold your image in the mind of the person searching, whether that's law enforcement or family members. They can be carried from door-to-door, they can be pasted on to mailboxes, they can be put on most-wanted lists. Showing someone a photograph is effective; *describing* someone is worse than useless. If there's no image of a person's face, what that person looks like is forgotten pretty damn quick, I can tell you.'

'Tilly will find him,' he said.

'I will, Poe,' Bradshaw said. 'In the meantime, I've found something on that *other* thing you asked me to look into.'

She passed him a black and white photograph. It was a school cricket team. The Waterford School for Boys, Under 17s, 1st XI. Taken decades ago judging by their bats, pads, gloves and whites.

'What's this?'

'Have a look at the last name on the top row.'

Poe did. 'It's—'

'It is, Poe,' Bradshaw cut in, glancing at Melody Lee. 'But more importantly, look who's standing next to him.'

Poe looked again.

'Bloody hell,' he said.

Chapter 79

'I can't find Sean Gardiner,' Bradshaw said miserably.

'What?' Poe said. 'Not even a trace?'

He didn't know why he was surprised. Emily North seemed to be as computer savvy as Bradshaw and she'd not been able to find him either, despite having had more time and far more motivation.

'There's the occasional reference in national newspapers, databases he obviously couldn't access, but all his images have been erased.'

'Nothing of him out in Afghanistan? No happy snaps?'

'Nothing, Poe.'

'That's . . . surprising.'

'It ain't that surprising,' Melody Lee said. 'Your guys will get the same instructions our guys get when they're on ops – they're warned not to post photos online. Not only does it compromise operational security, the Russians can and will steal it out of the ether. Grab the pic as well as all your data. Find out who you are and where you live. Some of our guys have had pictures of their families emailed to them when they've been out in the field, which we've traced back to a Moscow psy-ops unit. They're just messing with their heads but who needs that shit going on?'

'Special Agent Melody Lee's right,' Bradshaw said. 'There are very few photographs of Tango Two-Four and those there are were posted after they'd returned to the UK.'

'We need to find him, Tilly,' Poe said. 'We're close, I can feel it.'

'If he's as computer literate as it seems, I can't imagine he's using the name Sean Gardiner any more,' Melody Lee said.

'Not a chance,' Poe agreed. 'We need a photograph. We can put it on the front of every paper, the lead on every news show. Make him the most famous man in the country. Do that and we'll have him inside twenty-four hours.'

'I'll try again, Poe,' Bradshaw said. She pushed her glasses up her nose, blew hair out of her eyes and started typing.

'I still can't find him,' Bradshaw said, 'and I've run out of databases I can legally search. I'm sorry, Poe.'

'Not your fault, Tilly. And at least it confirms the type of person we're up against.'

'Tech-savvy, ruthless, well-resourced and highly motivated,' Melody Lee said. 'Have I missed anything?'

'Knowing what you know now, will this change anything summit-wise?'

'No. This is about Christopher Bierman and whatever shit he got himself into when he was in Afghanistan. It's unrelated to the summit and I'll report that. It'll be a UK-based organisation that's behind this, which is why they waited for him to come back. It's nothing to do with the summit; that was just the thing that lured Bierman to his death, unfortunately.'

Poe agreed. 'You sticking around or you needed elsewhere?'

'My black ass will have to be at Scarness Hall from now on in,' she said with a smile. 'But pop in sometime, I hear they do an excellent afternoon tea.'

'Fair enough,' he said. They shook hands.

'Goodbye, Special Agent Melody Lee,' Bradshaw said. 'It was very interesting working with you. You have a fascinating vocabulary.'

'I sure as shit do, honey. See y'all later and, Poe, if you want my advice,' she added with a sly grin, 'I'd bite the bullet and make pals again with Hannah Finch.'

'And why would I do that?'

'Sure, she's a ballbuster, but if she was reporting on you, it was because she was under instruction.'

Poe shrugged.

'But mainly it's because she has access to the MoD's database and you don't,' she continued. 'This dude might have removed every image of himself from the internet, but I'll bet you a pound of steak fries he hasn't been able to remove it from his army record.'

Chapter 80

'I thought I was told to go boil an egg?' Hannah Finch said, the speakerphone loud in the dry, still air of Herdwick Croft.

'You were,' Poe said. 'Did you enjoy it?'

'What do you want, Poe?'

'I need a question answered.'

'Just the one?'

'Just the one.'

'Ask it,' she said, 'then piss off.'

'On a scale of one to ten, how motivated are you to solve this case?'

'Ten.' No hesitation.

'Careful, Hannah, on my scale, ten is the highest amount of motivation, not the lowest.'

'Fuck you, Poe.'

Poe didn't respond.

Bradshaw said, 'Rude.'

'What do you need?' Hannah sighed.

'Access to someone's military record.'

'Why?'

Poe told her, left out nothing.

'So you want me to break into the Army Personnel Centre? Get you a photograph of this Sean Gardiner?'

'No. I want you to make a legitimate request to the Army Personnel Centre and get me a photograph of Sean Gardiner.'

'I'll see what I can do.'

She rang off.

'What do we do now, Poe?' Bradshaw said.

'We wait, Tilly,' he said. 'We wait.'

But not for long. Hannah Finch got back to them within the hour.

'I've sent Tilly an email,' she said. 'I'm sure she'll have some bespoke facial recognition software but, I'm telling you now, Poe, it's no one I recognise and the face isn't flagged on any of our systems.'

'Damn,' he said. He'd really been hoping they had already met Sean Gardiner somewhere along the way.

Bradshaw's laptop pinged. 'Got it,' she said.

He sat down and waited for the picture to download. The internet connection at Herdwick Croft was non-existent but Bradshaw had somehow turned her smartphone into a mobile hotspot. She called it tethering, he called it a case of not needing to know. It was slower than she was used to but it brought up the picture eventually.

Poe stared at Sean Gardiner. It was a typical army picture. Head facing the camera, full colour, no smiling. Like a passport photograph.

And he didn't recognise him.

'Who the hell are you?' he said.

Bradshaw didn't waste time. Finch was right, she did have her own facial recognition software. She talked Poe through it as she entered Gardiner's picture.

'I took the best-in-class biometric artificial intelligence software and tweaked it,' she said. 'Added features like iris recognition, skin-texture analysis, made it better at coping with profile pictures, that type of thing. I also refined some of the cruder bits of coding and gave it access to more databases.'

'Uh-huh,' Poe said.

'And obviously I preferred a photometric algorithm over a geometric one.'

'Well, duh.'

'I know, right? You'd have to be a total idiot to use a geometric algorithm these days,' she said. 'Anyway, the program's running now, depending on how . . . oh, it's finished. That was quick.'

She dragged the cursor over an icon, clicked the trackpad and brought up the results. She stared at the screen and frowned.

'Well, this is all very odd,' she said.

Chapter 81

'Hannah, we have a problem,' Poe said.

'What's up, Poe?' she said. 'You need access to the Prime Minister's personal laptop now?'

'Tilly's facial recognition program, it's found Sean Gardiner.'

'Bloody hell, that was quick. Who is he? What name is he using?'

'That's just the thing – unless he has a . . . how did Tilly describe it, a "statistically unlikely doppelgänger", Sean Gardiner is an actor in New Zealand who specialises in condom adverts.'

'Come again?'

'As many times as you like, apparently. According to him they're the safest brand on the market.'

'I'm not following you, Poe. Are you saying Sean Gardiner emigrated to New Zealand to pursue an acting career? Decided it wasn't for him and moved into the murder business instead?'

'No, that's not what I'm saying at all. The man in those adverts is called David Hurford and he's still promoting safe sex. They call him the condom guy over there.'

'The condom guy? Are you fucking kidding me?'

'I doubt it's a name he chose for himself,' Poe said. 'But I've just spoken to his agent and he assures me that David has had steady work. Hasn't left Auckland this year, let alone New Zealand.'

'I assume Tilly's program hasn't made a mistake?'

'What do you think?'

'It hasn't!' Bradshaw yelled from across the room. 'Tell Hannah Finch about your theory, Poe.'

'Yes, Poe,' Finch said. 'Tell me about your theory. Tell me how someone has hacked into one of the most secure databases in the world and switched photographs. Because I assume that's what you think. And if you do, you're wrong. Not even Tilly could hack into that system. It's just not—'

'That's not what I think happened, Hannah,' Poe said, ignoring the fact that Bradshaw had hacked into an MoD-encrypted laptop during the Curator case. It had taken her two minutes.

'What then?'

'You ever heard the phrase "If it ain't broke, don't try to fix it"?' he said.

Chapter 82

Poe hadn't been to Glasgow for years. He remembered it as a city struggling to find its identity, as it went from industrial trade hub to cosmopolitan tourist destination, and it was now one of the most vibrant and dynamic cities in Europe. Judging by the way it gleamed, the transformation was almost complete. On any other day he wouldn't have minded wandering down Buchanan Street, mingling with the crowd, watching the street entertainers. Seeing if any could match the utter shamelessness of Bugger Rumble.

But that afternoon he had a different reason for visiting the city: Glasgow was where the Army Personnel Centre was located. He, Bradshaw and Finch were paying a surprise visit to Edward Pritchard, the man who had uploaded the picture of the condom guy to Sean Gardiner's military record.

They were in Finch's car – a low-end Land Rover. She pulled up on the double yellows next to the main entrance and turned off the engine.

'Ready?' she said.

'You're not allowed to park here, Hannah Finch,' Bradshaw said.

'This is a sort of "park anywhere car", Tilly.'

Poe knew the car's registration wouldn't appear on any DVLA database, or if it did it would have a red flag next to it saying, 'Piss off.'

'But—'

'It'll be fine, Tilly,' Poe said. 'Come on, let's go and see this idiot.'

Kentigern House, the Army Personnel Centre's building, was unapologetically modern; an equal measure of uninspiring and drab. The type of building the architect purposefully omitted from his CV. It was made of yellow brick and each floor was smaller than the one underneath. They were connected by sloping, brown-framed windows. It looked like a half-arsed attempt at a pyramid, one where the builders had started strongly but lost enthusiasm after the base was finished and they saw what it was going to look like.

It was almost noon and the concrete forecourt was thrumming with men and women enjoying the Glasgow sun. Some sipped from cardboard coffee cups, others ate sandwiches. All of them wore ID cards on lanyards.

Poe followed Finch into the building, correctly guessing that her ID trumped his.

'Duty manager, please,' she said to the woman at reception.

They were clearly expecting her – even in MoD buildings a visit from Five was a big deal – because the woman said, 'I'm the duty manager – Mhairi Forster. As requested, we haven't told him you're coming. He's been at his desk all morning.'

'Do you have an interview room?'

Forster nodded. 'Several.'

'I need the most secure and I need you to ensure that no one can overhear what we're discussing. Depending on what happens, Sergeant Poe may need to arrest Mr Pritchard. If that's the case, he'll request Police Scotland take him to the nearest station.'

Although the question was written all over her face, Forster was old enough and wise enough not to ask what her employee had done.

'I'll have him brought down,' she said.

Chapter 83

Poe would lead. He had the salient details to hand and had been in interview rooms all his adult life. Finch would provide supplementary information, including laying down the consequences for Pritchard if need be, and Bradshaw was there in case there was technical information neither of them understood.

Edward Pritchard looked like the type of man who'd had nosebleeds as a kid. Bespectacled and wearing a worn brown suit, he nervously scratched his armpit. He had a bony face and a blade of a nose. His eyes were weak and jumpy, his expression thin and sour. His hair was so fine Poe could count the moles on his scalp. He exuded guilt and when he saw Finch's ID card he visibly greyed.

Poe didn't think this would be a difficult interview. 'How old are you, Mr Pritchard?' he said.

'Fifty-seven.' His voice was high-pitched and brittle.

'Really? That's a stroke of luck.'

'It is? How?'

'Because, even though the pension age goes up soon, by the time you get out of prison you should be able to collect it.'

'But I haven't done—'

'Were you or were you not given a free charging cable for your phone?' Poe said. 'The accompanying paperwork explained that you'd been selected to take part in a user trial.'

'No, that's not what—'

'You plugged it into your home computer and inadvertently

uploaded two malicious bits of software.' He turned to Bradshaw. 'What were they again, Tilly?'

'Keystroke logging and remote access malware.'

'You were then contacted with what you were required to do,' Poe continued. 'The consequences of failing to comply were also made clear.'

'But . . . but how do you know all this?'

'Because, Mr Pritchard, this isn't the first time this man has forced people to do his bidding this way. You're just another sap in a long line of saps. Now, we don't know what it was he used against you, but we soon will. There's someone at your house now going through your computers – for your sake, I hope it's something embarrassing and not something illegal.'

The way Pritchard blanched, Poe knew it was the latter. Indecent images of children would be his first three guesses.

'Police Scotland will be dealing with that,' Poe continued. 'We're here for what he made you do.'

'May I have a glass of water, please?' he croaked.

'No, you may not. The man behind this is called Sean Gardiner and for years he's been actively removing his photographs from the internet. Making it harder for people to remember what he looks like. But to remove his photo from the MoD database he needed help. That's where you came in. He gave you a photograph of an actor in New Zealand and made you upload it to his army record. Am I right?'

'Almost,' Pritchard whispered. 'I provided the photograph. I'd been thinking of going to New Zealand for a holiday and when I went looking for a picture to use, the site I'd been on last had the condom advert front and centre. The quality and size of the man's picture were ideal, so I used it.'

'But all else was as I stated?'

Pritchard nodded.

'We're now at the point when you decide how much time

you're prepared to do in prison. Give me what I need and Miss Finch will ensure you're not prosecuted under the Terrorism Act. Stall us, even once, and you'll wake up in Barlinnie for at least the next quarter of a century. These are facts, not threats, Mr Pritchard. Do you believe me?'

He held Poe's eye for what seemed like an age. Finally he nodded and said, 'What do you want?'

Poe leaned in. Rooted his elbows on the desk. 'You know what we want, Mr Pritchard. We want the original photograph, the one Sean Gardiner had you remove. We need to know what he looks like.'

It took ten minutes for Mhairi Forster to locate an isolated workstation for them to use and a further five while Pritchard tried to locate the deleted photo.

'We haven't got time for this,' Poe said. 'Tilly, swap seats with him.'

'She's not authorised to access this information,' Forster said.

'Oh shut up,' Poe said.

'I beg—'

'He said "shut up",' Finch said. 'Tilly?'

'What day did you switch the photographs, Edward Pritchard?' Bradshaw said.

'Fourth of May, three years ago.'

'Ah, *Star Wars* day.'

'Eh?' Poe said.

'Found it.' She pointed at a printer in the corner of the room. 'Is that switched on?'

'Yes, it's number—'

'I know what number it is.' Bradshaw fiddled with the mouse, typed in a few commands and the printer was soon clunking.

Finch was nearest. She grabbed the photograph and stared at the image. Shook her head. 'I don't recognise him.'

She passed it to Poe. He glanced at it, not expecting to

recognise him either.

Instead he said, 'Oh shit.'

It was Cookie, Scarness Hall's chef.

Chapter 84

'I need eyes on Nicholas Anstey, aka Cookie, and I need them on him now!' Poe yelled into his mobile. He listened to the response. 'Well go and fucking get him then!'

They were tearing through the outskirts of Glasgow, Finch breaking so many traffic laws not even Bradshaw could keep up. Poe had got through to the temporary guardhouse at Scarness Hall and the officer who answered was now trying to find his boss, Detective Inspector Shelton.

It didn't take long. A burst of static filled his ear. Someone using a radio had been patched through to his phone.

'Detective Inspector Shelton.'

'Sir, this is Poe. I need eyes on Nicholas Anstey.'

'I'll send someone up.'

'No!' Poe said. 'Just get eyes on him. He's the prime suspect in the murder of Christopher Bierman and he may be armed.'

'You're sure?' Shelton said.

'I am.'

'Stay on this line. I'll get back to you.' He clicked off.

They waited in silence. Poe stared at the clock on the dashboard.

One minute. Two minutes. Three. Five. Six. Finch navigated out of the city and raced on to the M74. She dropped a gear and overtook a police car. The cop joined her in the outside lane and matched her speed. Poe waited to see blue lights in his wing mirror, but the onboard ANPR camera, the cop's automatic number plate recognition system, must have flagged the car as 'leave alone'. The traffic cop slowed and returned to the middle lane. Finch kept accelerating. The needle touched one hundred and kept moving clockwise. He hoped Bradshaw couldn't see how fast they were going. He glanced in the back. She was on her phone.

'What you got there, Tilly?'

'That video you asked for has just landed in my inbox, Poe.'

'What video?'

'Someone called Max Greene sent it. He was one of the protestors you spoke to. They were filming people going in and out of the village. I think you said they were getting used to the light for when the summit actually started.'

'Oh, that video,' he said. 'Irene finally came through, did she?'

'Max says he's been away for a few days, which is why it's so late. Do you want me to go through it?'

He shrugged. 'Not sure we need it now.'

'If I get the time I will anyway.'

Poe went back to staring at the clock on the dashboard. Another minute had passed.

Seven minutes now.

Then another. Eight.

His phone chirped. Even though he'd been willing it to ring, he still jumped.

'Poe.'

'We have eyes on Anstey,' Shelton said. 'We've put a perimeter around him.'

Poe's shoulders slumped in relief. He put his hand over the speaker. 'They've got him.' He said to Shelton, 'What's he doing?'

'Looks like he's making a big pot of soup.'

'It'll be stock,' Poe said automatically, a fractured memory of another case, one that had taken him into the orbit of a Michelin-starred chef.

'Excuse me?'

'Doesn't matter. Hold the perimeter until I get there. If you need confirmation of my operational command, check with Superintendent Nightingale.'

'Already checked, Sergeant Poe. Unless we think there's a risk to life, we'll keep our distance and await further instructions.'

Poe ended the call. Rolled his neck and arched his back as far as he could in the confines of the seat. 'It's almost over,' he said.

Finch said nothing.

'What is it?'

'Didn't you say that no new members of staff had started at Scarness Hall since they were given the nod? If that's the case, how is it Sean Gardiner has a job there?'

Poe considered that for a moment, but only for a moment. 'If it ain't broke, don't fix it,' he said again.

Finch nodded in understanding. 'He played his JANUS cable trick on someone on the venue committee.'

'That's my guess. Found out the venue before it was announced then got a job there.'

'Jesus, he's good,' she said. 'If only for my peace of mind we need this arsehole off the . . .' Her phone rang. 'Damn, it's supposed to connect to the car's speakerphone but it's playing up at the mo. Can you answer it, Poe?'

'I need to be able to answer mine.' He passed Finch's phone to Bradshaw. 'Tilly, can you see who this is? Remember to say you're not Hannah when you answer. You don't want to unwittingly hear the nuclear launch codes.'

Finch shook her head. 'You have no idea what we do, do you, Poe?'

'This is Matilda Bradshaw, not Hannah Finch,' Bradshaw said. 'I repeat, this is Matilda Bradshaw, not Hannah Finch.' She put her hand over the microphone. 'Was that OK, Poe?'

'Very clear, Tilly,' he said.

'Thank you, Poe.'

'Now, ask them what they want.'

'What do you want?'

Poe hid his smile. Bradshaw's social skills had come on remarkably but she reverted to type whenever she was in stressful situations. She listened for almost a minute then said, 'OK, Constable Adams, I'll pass the message on. Thank you for calling and I hope you have a pleasant evening.'

She passed the phone back to Poe.

'Who was that, Tilly?'

'It was the team who searched Edward Pritchard's house,' she said. 'They found nothing on his computer that he could have been blackmailed with.'

'What, nothing at all?'

'That's what they say, Poe. They're sending everything down tonight so I'll have a proper look tomorrow.'

'That's odd,' Finch said.

'It *is* odd,' Poe agreed. 'If there was nothing on his computer, why did he give everything up so easily?'

His phone rang again.

'Poe.'

'Anstey's getting ready to leave camp, Sergeant Poe,' Shelton said. 'My guys don't think they can contain him in the street and I'd rather not put unarmed officers at risk.'

'Take him,' Poe said.

Two minutes later Shelton was back. 'Target secure,' he said. 'He tried to run but we got him.'

Chapter 85

Finch sped into the village, only cutting her speed when the roads narrowed and the sharp bends reduced visibility. They were soon at the outer cordon, considerably beefed up since the last time they had been there. They were waved through, didn't even have to slow down.

They did have to stop at the guardhouse outside Scarness Hall's grounds but only long enough for the gate to be raised.

Detective Inspector Shelton met them in the car park.

'Where is he?' Poe said.

'In one of the downstairs bedrooms. It's been converted into a bad weather pressroom.'

'And he tried to run?'

'He did. Stopped as soon as he had a weapon pointed at him.'

'He's been read his rights?'

'Did it myself.'

'I want a search team here,' Poe said. 'He used a gun in a previous murder. It could still be on the grounds.'

'I'll see to it,' Shelton said.

Poe turned to Finch. 'I want a quick word before he's transported to Durranhill,' he said.

Lewis Barnes rounded the corner. He was pulling a golf carry case, the kind golf bags are stored in when they're going on a plane.

'Sir, sir!' he said. 'They've arrested Cookie!'

He looked worried. Poe remembered him saying that Anstey

326

had baked a cake every year for his birthday. Probably thought they'd been friends. There wasn't anything he could say to soften the blow so he didn't try.

'He has, Lewis. I'm just going to have a word with him now. See if we can't get it sorted out.'

Lewis nodded slowly, clearly not convinced.

'Looks like you're off golfing again?' Poe said.

'Yes, sir,' Lewis said. 'I'm taking some golf clubs up to the course, then caddying for one of the important people. He says if he beats his handicap he'll let me drive his Jaguar F-Type round the car park. I've never even been in a Jaguar, never mind driven an F-Type, sir.'

'Let's hope he has a good round then, Lewis.'

'Yes, sir. And when I get back I'll clean the bugs off that lady's car if you want.'

'See you later, Lewis.'

He didn't move, though. Just stood there looking lost and forlorn.

Nicholas Anstey, aka Sean Gardiner, was the picture of defiance. Handcuffed to the rear, he scowled and growled at the officers in the room with him. When he saw Poe he leapt to his feet.

'What the fuck's going on?' he snarled.

'Sit down, Mr Anstey,' Poe said.

Anstey glared at him, strained against his restraints.

'Sit!' Poe snapped. 'If you don't, I'll have you taken straight to Durranhill.'

He sat.

'I ain't saying anything without a solicitor, shipmate.'

'I'll talk, you lis—'

'But I will say this. You've got nothing. Fuck all. It didn't happen. Even if you knew the plan, that you stopped it from happening means nothing illegal happened.'

Poe glanced at Finch, saw she was equally perplexed. 'What plan?' he said.

'Piss off.'

'Have it your way, *Sean*,' Poe said.

A flicker of uncertainty passed over his face.

'Who the hell's Sean?' he said.

'Hannah, can you please tell Mr Gardiner what's going to happen if he keeps playing dumb?'

'Certainly, Sergeant Poe. Well, first of all I'll ask you to arrest him under the Terrorism Act. That will give us fourteen days to question him. By then you'll undoubtedly have charged him with blackmail, breaking into classified databases, obtaining pecuniary advantage by deception—'

'Ooh, that's a good one,' Poe cut in. 'I hadn't thought of that. Anything else?'

'Armed robbery and possession of a firearm.' She paused. 'Oh, and I almost forgot – you'll probably want to charge him with the murders of Christopher Bierman and Terry Holmes.'

Anstey stared at her in astonishment.

'Whoah!' he shouted, jumping to his feet again. 'Are you mad? I haven't killed anyone! Ever! And the last time I held a gun was on *Vigilant* back in 2004!'

'HMS *Vigilant*?' Finch said. 'You're claiming you were a submariner?'

'Man and boy, shipmate.'

'You weren't in the King's Royal Rifles?' Poe said. 'You didn't serve in Afghanistan in 2006?'

'Of course not,' he said. 'I left the navy in 2004 and trained as a chef. Been jobbing around the country ever since.'

'So why did you run from the police?'

He started squirming.

'I think you'd better start talking,' Poe said.

He clearly thought so too. He opened his mouth and admitted everything.

And it wasn't long before Poe realised they were still being played . . .

Chapter 86

'He reckons he was involved in some hare-brained scheme to mess about with the plumbing in one of the guest bedrooms,' Poe said to Superintendent Nightingale. She'd arrived as soon as she heard about the arrest.

'Why?' she said.

'He says they were planning to put a sump on the waste pipe.'

Nightingale's jaw dropped. 'I refer you to my previous question,' she said eventually. 'Why?'

'They wanted – and I can't actually believe I'm saying this – to steal one of the VIPs' turds. They planned to bottle it then put it behind the bar in their local. They even had a little brass plaque ready. Someone at the pub had dared them. He reckons that years ago, Princess Margaret was a guest on a submarine and the officers did the same to her toilet. Engineered the plumbing and stole one of her stools. According to Anstey, it's still in a glass jar in the officers' mess.'

'That true?'

'I heard rumours when I was in the army,' Poe said, 'but even then I thought it was a load of bollocks.'

'And the argument he was having with McDaid that you witnessed?'

'He says one of the maids found some weird porn in McDaid's room. Gossiped about it and Anstey heard. Thought he'd use it to get access to the bedrooms when they'd finally been allocated.'

'Why would McDaid have access to the VIP bedrooms?'

330

Nightingale said.

'He occasionally needs to drop off printouts of flight itineraries,' Poe said. 'Particularly when there's been a change to the schedule.'

'I'll get one of my lot to talk to him,' she said. 'If he corroborates the story, do you want to let Anstey go?'

'I haven't completely ruled him out yet,' he said. 'Can we charge him with something? Keep him safe for a bit.'

'Conspiracy to outrage public decency, maybe. I'll get one of my custody sergeants on it. They're the most creative when it comes to this type of thing.'

As Nightingale left to speak to McDaid, Finch knocked on the door and entered the room.

'He's still adamant,' she said.

'You believe him?'

'I believe he was in the navy, not the army. He showed me the *Vigilant* tattoo on his shoulder and it didn't look new. And to be honest I don't think he's bright enough to be the person we're looking for.'

Poe nodded. He thought that too. 'Can you get someone in Glasgow to re-interview Edward Pritchard?' he said. 'Find out why he showed us a photo of Anstey when we came knocking.'

'I already have a team there.'

'Good.'

'I don't understand why Gardiner did this,' she said.

'I don't either. It took us . . . what, five minutes to confirm we had the wrong man.'

'So why bother?'

Poe shrugged. It didn't make sense. Everything Gardiner had done up to now had served a purpose. So why have the cook arrested? If he were setting Anstey up as his patsy, he'd botched it big time. And someone this prepared didn't make mistakes like that.

So, if Anstey wasn't a patsy, what was he?

Poe ran through everything that had happened since Anstey's photograph had been found on the Army Personnel Centre's database. They'd recognised him. They'd taken immediate action to detain him. They'd spoken to him and they'd all but confirmed he wasn't involved. Two hours from start to finish.

So what had Gardiner gained? All he'd done was cause a kerfuffle. It didn't make sense.

But of course, it *did* make sense.

Perfect sense.

'Walk with me, Hannah,' he said.

He left the room and went back out into the car park. Looked around but, bar the gardener waist deep in the pond, it was empty.

'We're being watched,' he said casually.

It was testament to her tradecraft that she didn't spin round and look.

'By who?' She turned and smiled at him. Matched his demeanour.

'No idea.'

'You sure?'

'Only explanation,' he said. 'The cook was Gardiner's tripwire. His warning that we're closing in.'

'Which means he had to be here to see it.'

Poe nodded.

'Damn, he's good,' she said.

A group walked out of the hall's main entrance and headed towards the patio next to the walled garden. Probably taking tea in the afternoon sun.

'Keep an eye on this lot,' Poe said. 'See if you spot anyone acting odd.'

The men and women walked past them. Talbot, the summit coordinator, was with them. Poe could hear them discussing the recent burst of activity.

'Probably just a drill,' one of them said.

'Better safe than sorry,' Talbot said, glaring at Poe as he passed.

'What about him?' Poe said.

'Career civil servant,' Finch said. 'Been doing this for years. Hasn't served a day in uniform.'

Anderson, the hotel manager, walked round the corner of the hall and made his way to the gardener working in the pond.

'Him then?'

She shook her head. 'We've blown it, Poe,' she said. 'He'll have already implemented his escape plan. Someone this good doesn't have an alarm without knowing exactly what he's going to do when it goes off.'

'And without a face or a name we can't even tell the border agency who to look out for.'

'We've been beaten, Poe,' she said. 'We didn't . . . what's up with her?'

Nightingale had charged out of the main entrance and was now sprinting towards them.

'What is it, ma'am?' Poe said.

'It's Patrick McDaid,' she said breathlessly. 'We can't find him.'

Chapter 87

'You've swept the building and the grounds?' Poe said.

'We have,' Nightingale said.

'And he's not in his room?'

'No. And it looks like he left in a hurry.'

'He hasn't signed out?'

'Definitely not.'

'And he didn't just forget?'

'Unlikely,' Finch said. 'We're close to the summit now and that means there's overt and covert surveillance in place. The only way in and out is via the front gate.'

'And all the helicopters are on the ground,' Nightingale added. 'There hasn't been a flight today.'

'So Patrick McDaid kills his business partner for some reason,' he said, 'and he uses the cook as a tripwire so he knows when to run. He gathers up a few personal possessions then what . . . just disappears off the face of the earth? How's that even possible?'

He thought about how he'd try and get out of an area that had heavy surveillance. Not on foot. And not in a car. A thought occurred. At least, not in the *front* of a car . . .

'Are vehicles searched going out?' he said.

'Only on the way in,' Finch said. 'Why?'

'He was in the boot of a car.'

Finch didn't immediately respond. 'Logically, that's the only way he could have done it,' she said eventually.

'We need to know who's left the site since the cook was

arrested,' Poe said to Nightingale. 'If we're right and the cook was his warning, he'll have left as soon as he could. If we can identify the car he was in, we may be able to track him via ANPR.'

'On it,' Nightingale said. She jogged off in the direction of the gatehouse, her phone already glued to her ear.

Poe turned to Finch. The spook had paled. Her shoulders had slumped. She looked defeated.

'How did I miss this?' she said. 'I signed off on Bierman & McDaid.'

'We don't know what this—'

'Alastor was right. It *was* too soon. I should have listened to him but I wanted to prove myself. Wanted to . . .'

She faded out.

'Finished feeling sorry for yourself?' Poe said. 'I was about to say that we don't know what this is yet.'

She looked up. 'What do you mean?'

'McDaid doesn't feel right,' he said. 'The person who blagged the pop-up brothel for the night had said to Jefferson Black's man, "How's your bum for spots?" That's a colloquialism used almost exclusively by British squaddies. No one else uses it. No way would an American know to use it. McDaid being Sean Gardiner makes no sense.'

'Why has he run then?'

'I don't know.'

She ran her hands through her hair. 'What a bloody mess,' she said.

Her phone rang. She glanced at the screen.

'Marvellous,' she said. She pressed receive. 'Hello, sir.'

As Finch updated Alastor Locke, Poe thought about McDaid. Something was niggling. His own phone rang. It was Bradshaw. Probably wanting to know what was happening. He killed the call. He needed to stay on his current train of thought.

McDaid had said something to him. Possibly something

about Bierman. Was it about how they had funded their business? Possibly, he thought. His phone buzzed again. He ignored it.

Something Finch said caught the attention of his second brain. 'What did you say, Hannah?'

'I was just telling Alastor that this has all gone wrong.'

'That's not what you said, though,' he said.

'It was the gist.'

'What were the exact words you used?' Poe urged. He didn't know why but he knew it was important.

'I don't fucking know, Poe,' she snapped. 'I don't choose my language that carefully.'

'Pass me your phone,' he said, reaching for it.

'Fine,' she said.

'Alastor, word-for-word, what was the last thing Hannah said?'

'I don't know if I can remember exactly, dear boy,' Locke said. 'She's very upset. Not the best day for her, career wise.'

'Cut the shit,' Poe said. 'You didn't get to your position by not listening properly.'

'Quite right,' he said. 'She said the whole thing had exploded in her face.'

Poe's brain snapped to attention.

And this time he thought he saw the entire chessboard.

Chapter 88

'Who had access to that fabricated report on the suicide truck?' Poe said to Alastor Locke. 'The unredacted one with TATP as the explosive, not the sanitised version with Semtex that the families received.'

'Where are you going with this, dear boy?'

'I think we've missed something.'

'Put me on speakerphone, Poe,' he said.

He handed Finch her mobile. 'Alastor wants to be on speakerphone.'

Finch touched the screen. 'You're on, sir,' she said.

'Right, what's Poe talking about?'

'He asked who's seen the unredacted report.'

'Why?'

'Humour me,' Poe said.

'Very well,' Locke said. 'The report author, obviously. Few bigwigs in the MoD. Couple of senior civil servants. The Defence Secretary signed off on it and I think one of his junior ministers was involved. Couple of other cabinet members. You and Miss Bradshaw. On the British side, I believe there were twenty-seven people all told.'

'Was Christopher Bierman told?'

'Absolutely not. It had nothing to do with him. And even if it had, he had nowhere near the right security clearance to see it.'

'What about on the American side?'

'Maybe a few more as they have a more complex chain of

command, but it will have been kept to a minimum. Chairman of the Joint Chiefs. Secretary of Defense. Few others. Strictly need-to-know.'

'What about the friendly-fire helicopter crew?'

'Almost certainly,' Locke said. 'Both of them would have been brought into the loop to ensure they didn't start talking about what had really happened.'

'That it never happened?'

'Exactly. They'd have been told it was going to be alternatively explained, what the explanation was and, more importantly, why.'

Poe's phone rang. Bradshaw again. He rejected the call.

'What's this about, Poe?'

'When I first spoke to McDaid he started banging on about how he'd read his Bible from cover to cover and God could be a real sonofabitch sometimes.'

'And he was referring to what happened to the King's Royal Rifles who rescued his friend?'

'He was, sir,' Poe said. 'Said Bierman went down with a bad case of survivor's guilt.'

'Understandable.'

'What's your point, Poe?' Finch said.

'My point is this, Hannah. The exact words McDaid used when he was telling me this were, "And then an asshole suicide bomber drives an ambulance packed with TATP into them."'

Finch frowned. 'No, that's not right, Poe. He must have said Semtex.'

'No,' Poe said. 'He *should* have said Semtex as that was the only explanation available to him or Bierman. But he didn't, he said TATP. And the reason I can say this with absolute certainty is because I didn't know what TATP was. Special Agent Lee had to tell me.'

'Crikey,' Locke said. 'If Poe's right then there's only one plausible explanation.'

Poe nodded.

'He was the Apache pilot. It was Patrick McDaid who fired that Hellfire missile into Tango Two-Four.'

Chapter 89

Hannah Finch looked stunned.

'Are you telling me that the person who killed Tango Two-Four has been at Scarness Hall all this time?' she said.

'I'm absolutely certain of it,' Poe said.

'But why didn't he say anything? If he had even the slightest suspicion Bierman's murder was connected to his time in Afghanistan, surely he'd have told someone.'

It was a fair point. Accidents happened in the fog of war. They were inevitable and, while it wasn't something you'd put on the first page of your CV, there was no reason *not* to tell someone.

But he hadn't.

'What if he couldn't tell anyone?' Poe said.

'Because he wasn't allowed to?'

'No. That wouldn't explain the rest of the stuff that's been going on. Don't forget there's a looted antiquity link we haven't got to the bottom of yet. Bierman isn't the only person to have been murdered by Sean Gardiner.'

'What then?' Locke said over the phone.

'I don't know,' he said. 'But the only thing that links Bierman, McDaid, Gardiner and Holmes is Afghanistan. It's there we'll find the answers.'

Poe looked at Finch. 'We need to find Patrick McDaid before Sean Gardiner does.'

'Shit,' she said. 'You don't think McDaid's involved at all, do you? You think he's the next victim.'

'Do what you need to do up there, Hannah,' Locke said, his voice tinny but urgent.

The connection went dead. Her phone immediately rang again. She glanced at the screen.

'Unknown number,' she said. 'Hello?'

She frowned then passed the phone to Poe. 'It's Tilly.'

'Tilly, what's up?'

'Where have you been, Poe? I've been trying to call you for ages.'

'Where are you? You disappeared after we got here.'

'I'm in the media suite,' she said. 'They have fibre-optic broadband there. Why didn't you answer your phone? Did you arrest the cook? Is he Sean Gardiner?'

'No, we're still being played,' he said.

He brought her up to date.

'Gosh, you have been busy,' she said.

'We have,' Poe said. 'And we need to find Patrick McDaid before Gardiner does.'

'You think Sean Gardiner is still here?'

'I'm convinced of it.'

'I'll be quick then,' she said. 'I was actually calling because I've been through the video footage the protestors sent you and there's something that doesn't correlate with what you told me.'

'Can it wait, Tilly? I need to speak to Jo Nightingale about coordinating the search.'

'It can wait, Poe,' she said.

He paused. Bradshaw saw things that others didn't. He'd better hear what it was.

'Tell me, Tilly,' he said.

'You said that Lewis Barnes couldn't drive, didn't you?'

'I did, yes.'

'Well, he's driving on this video, Poe.'

'You must be mistaken, Tilly. He has a learning disability that disqualifies him.'

But even as he said it, he knew he was wrong.

Chapter 90

'We need to find Lewis Barnes, ma'am!' Poe yelled into his mobile. 'I saw him an hour ago; he can't have got far.'

He and Finch were sprinting to the gatehouse. Alarmed at the noise they were making – they were screaming into their phones, Poe to Nightingale, Finch to Locke – the armed cops had their weapons raised, safeties off.

Poe slowed as he approached; Heckler & Koch MP5 sub-machine guns and nervous cops were a dangerous combination.

'Barnes has been working with Sean Gardiner all this time?' Nightingale said.

'No, ma'am, Lewis Barnes *is* Sean Gardiner,' Poe panted.

'OK, you can explain later,' she said. 'Where are you?'

'The gatehouse.'

'I'll see you there.'

Poe ended the call and shouted to the nearest cop, 'Lewis Barnes, where did he go?'

DI Shelton, the detail commander, stepped out. 'What's this about, Poe? I thought it was Patrick McDaid we were looking for?'

'It was. It is. But Lewis Barnes is our priority now.'

Shelton turned to the cop beside him. 'Didn't he sign out with John Banks?'

'Yes, sir, an hour ago.'

'Who's John Banks?' Poe said.

'One of the summit staff,' Shelton said.

'John was heading into Carlisle, sir,' the cop said. 'He was dropping Lewis off at Brampton Golf Club. He had a caddying job there.'

'The golf club?' Poe said. 'You're sure?'

'Positive.'

'He must have his car stashed there,' Finch said. 'He's making a run for it. As soon as we tripped his Nick Anstey alarm he knew we were closing in.'

Poe said nothing.

'What?' Finch continued. 'You don't think so?'

'This is about revenge. For some reason, Christopher Bierman had to die, Terry Holmes had to die; no way is McDaid getting a pass.'

'But McDaid's gone to ground . . . hasn't he?'

'I think your optimism's misplaced. McDaid's missing and Barnes was dragging a case more than big enough to transport the corpse of a fully grown man.'

'Shit!' she yelled. 'Shit! Shit! Shit!'

Nightingale, panting heavily, ran up and joined them.

'I've asked for roadblocks on all major routes but you know what Cumbria's like, Poe – for every A-road, there's another fifty B-roads. We can't cover them all.'

'I think Barnes has McDaid with him,' Poe said.

'Alive?'

'No idea.'

'So, if my lot see him they could well be in a hostage situation?'

'Possibly.'

'What's he driving?'

'Tilly couldn't make out the reg on the protester's video,' Poe said. 'And as far as we knew, he *didn't* drive. He's had half an hour's head start already.'

'He could be anywhere,' Nightingale said. 'You're ahead of everyone on this, Poe; where do you think he is?'

'He had to at least pretend he was going to the golf club,' he said. 'He was dragging a big golf case; if he'd asked for a lift anywhere else it would have raised suspicions. Where he is now is anyone's guess.'

'Do we know why McDaid's so important to him?'

'Not allowed to say, ma'am. But I can tell you, in his eyes at least, Barnes does have legitimate motivation.'

'Shit!'

DI Shelton joined them. 'That was John Banks, ma'am,' he said. 'He did drop Lewis off at Brampton Golf Club. I've moved a team from the outer perimeter. They'll be there in five.'

'Thank you,' Nightingale said.

Poe looked at her.

'We taking your car or mine?'

Chapter 91

Brampton Golf Club, with views of Talkin Tarn, the Pennines and the Lake District mountains, was considered one of the jewels of Cumbria. It was three miles from Scarness Hall and outside the security perimeter. Poe navigated the narrow lanes, closely followed by Shelton in an armed response four-wheel-drive.

When they saw Talkin Tarn, the kettle-hole lake formed by a retreating glacier, Poe slowed and Shelton turned off his blue lights. The golf club was only a few hundred yards away; if Barnes was still there, there was no point spooking him.

Poe turned in to the car park. Shelton pulled up beside him.

'There's just the one exit, sir,' Poe said through his open window. 'Can you stick your car in it, make sure no one can get out?'

'Will do,' he said. 'Linda?'

Shelton stepped out and the female cop in the passenger seat shuffled across, dropped the car into reverse and backed up to block the exit.

Poe abandoned his BMW next to the putting green in front of the clubhouse. A couple of old dears hovering over a three-footer looked up in astonishment as a bunch of hairy-arsed cops ran past them.

'Now what, Poe?' Nightingale said.

'Spread out and look for him, I suppose.'

'Anything from the armed unit you sent ahead of us, DI Shelton?' Nightingale said.

'No, ma'am. I just told them to get here. That's their vehicle over there. I thought they'd have been waiting by it . . .' A squirt of noise from his radio made him stop. Shelton dipped his head, pressed the transmit button and said, 'Say again.'

A tinny voice came over the airwaves. 'We have eyes on the target, sir.'

'Where?' Shelton said.

'The sixteenth hole.'

'Is McDaid with him?'

'Yes, sir.'

'Alive?'

A pause.

Then, 'I think you'd better get down here, sir.'

Nightingale arranged for the golf course to be evacuated. Shelton's unit had turned back the golfers on the fifteenth hole and those playing the seventeenth and eighteenth were now back in the clubhouse, craning their necks to see what was happening.

An armed cop ran up, sweating under the weight of all his equipment. 'With me, ma'am,' he said, and immediately turned round.

They followed him at a brisk jog.

'The sixteenth is called "Hell Bent",' the armed cop said, blowing heavily. 'When you see what's happening up there you'll realise it's been well named.'

'You have him boxed in?' Poe said.

'We do, sir.'

'Does he know you're there?'

'We're in plain sight, sir.'

They were running parallel to the B6413, the road they'd taken to the clubhouse. Golfers and caddies were staring at them. After a hundred yards they came across the first group of golfers who had been stopped by Shelton's unit.

'I say,' one of them said.

They ran past him.

The lead cop slowed to a walk. As they neared the sixteenth hole's raised tee, another armed cop stepped out of the treeline.

'Any change?' the first armed officer said to him.

'He's still there.'

Poe didn't understand. If the armed cops could see Barnes, and there was a risk to McDaid's life, they could shoot.

'Where are they?' he said. 'I can't see them.'

'Up there, sir,' the second officer said. He pointed towards the green, which, according to a small wooden sign, was 310 yards away.

Poe strained his eyes. The green was protected at the front by a horseshoe bunker and at the back by thick woodland.

'What am I looking at?' he said. 'The green's empty.'

'Not the green, sir. The oak tree to the right of it.'

Poe adjusted his line of sight and saw what he was pointing at.

And immediately understood why they hadn't been able to shoot Lewis Barnes.

Why no one could.

Chapter 92

'There's a hostage negotiator on standby for the summit,' Nightingale said. 'The assistant chief says we're not to do anything until he arrives.'

'Waste of time,' Poe said. 'Barnes has been planning this for years. No way does he get talked out of it.'

'Doesn't matter. We're a command and control service and I've been given a lawful instruction. We *will* wait for the hostage negotiator.'

'Can I have a word, Poe?' Finch said.

She stepped away. Poe followed her.

'You think this is the wrong call?' she said quietly.

'You know everything I know, Hannah. What makes you think he'll give up now?'

'And the hostage negotiator's not going to help?'

'In my experience they're little more than accredited scapegoats. Only called when the police are out of operational solutions and the incident commander wants someone outside their immediate chain of command to shoulder part of the blame.'

'He's going to kill McDaid, isn't he?'

Poe nodded.

'Think you can talk him out of it?' she said.

'No. I don't think anyone can. I think Patrick McDaid's a dead man.'

'Want to give it a go?'

'So I can be *your* scapegoat?'

'Because I want McDaid alive, Poe. We've had our differences, and I fucked up with that ceramic rat, but you're the best chance he has. And you already have a rapport with Lewis.'

'He was acting, Hannah. That special educational needs thing was a charade. A mask, one that gave him unrestricted access to all parts of Scarness Hall. Allowed him to ingratiate himself with the people he needed to. He's single-minded and he's calculating. He's been on a mission for at least three years and McDaid is probably the final part of it. If he wants to kill him, he's going to kill him. No one will talk him out of it.'

Finch stared at him. Eventually she said, 'Want to give it a go?'

Poe didn't hesitate. 'Too bloody right I do.'

Finch raised her phone to her ear. 'You get that, sir?' She put her hand over the microphone. 'Sorry, Poe, Alastor was listening in. Saves me going through it all again.' She removed her hand and listened for a short while, nodding once. 'I'll tell her now, sir.'

Finch ended her call and joined Nightingale, who was talking to DI Shelton. Poe joined them.

'Detective Superintendent Nightingale,' Finch said, 'I've spoken to my director and he agrees with my field assessment: Patrick McDaid has information that is potentially damaging to this country. I'm therefore assuming control under the grounds of national security. Your chief constable is being told now. When your hostage negotiator arrives, please hold him at the clubhouse.'

Nightingale didn't hesitate. 'OK,' she said. 'As I said just now, I'm part of a command and control structure. I hereby acknowledge transfer of command to the Security Service. DI Shelton?'

'Yes, ma'am?'

'Hannah Finch has control now. Please pass this on to your units.'

'Ma'am.' Shelton leaned into his radio and began issuing instructions.

'What do you need from us?' Nightingale said.

'I need a radio set to the same frequency as your armed cops.'

Nightingale got her one. 'Anything else?'

'Hold the perimeter. The armed unit will keep their weapons trained on him but they will only fire with my express permission.'

Nightingale nodded at the nearest officer. He relayed the instructions.

'And, as we don't have time to get Poe mic'd up, I'm going to need a mobile phone.'

Nightingale handed Finch her own mobile, an iPhone. Finch fiddled with it, then passed it across.

'Say something,' she said to Poe, pressing her own phone against her ear.

'This isn't going to work.' He heard his voice on Finch's phone.

'Perfect. I've called my phone from yours so the two now have a live connection. Both are on speakerphone so we'll be able to hear each other.'

He tucked the phone into his top pocket. 'Say something to me,' he said.

'This *is* going to work.'

The voice coming from his pocket was tinny but clear.

'If you think it's getting out of hand, don't hesitate,' Finch said. 'Say the word and I'll give the order to shoot.'

'But let's hope it doesn't come to that,' Nightingale said.

'Ready?' Finch said.

'As I'll ever be,' Poe said.

Finch pressed her radio's transmit button. 'I'm sending someone down to talk to Lewis Barnes. Please stay calm everyone; I don't want any accidents.'

She took her finger off the button and looked at him. Held his gaze.

'Good luck, Poe,' she said.

Poe nodded, then stepped off the sixteenth tee. With his arms held out like da Vinci's *Vitruvian Man*, he began walking towards the most ruthless man he'd ever met.

Alone.

Chapter 93

Like holes on all championship-length golf courses, the first part of the sixteenth was obstacle free. If you could only hit the ball a hundred yards from the tee, the greenkeeper wasn't going to bother putting a bunker in for you. Poe passed the wooded area on the right and the thick rough on the left, then stepped on to the landscaped part of the fairway. His arms were beginning to ache. He had held them out since he'd stepped off the tee. But Barnes could see him now. Lowering them wasn't an option.

After two hundred yards he reached the landing zone, the area of the fairway that attracted the majority of tee shots. It was lush and mowed short but scarred with the divots of the players who had wanted backspin on their second shot.

He kept walking.

Lewis Barnes watched and waited.

When he was fifty yards away Poe stopped, lifted up his shirt and did a 360-degree turn so Barnes could see he had nothing hidden.

'Can I approach, Lewis?' he called out.

'You want the bugs scraped off your windscreen again, Mr Poe?' Barnes shouted back. No goofy grin this time. His expression was cold and flat.

And calm.

'Just want to talk.'

'You'll need to stand in the bunker.'

'Fair enough.' He'd expected as much. Hard to rush someone when you're standing in soft sand.

The crescent-shaped bunker protecting the front of the green was long, thin and deep.

Poe stepped into it. Felt his feet sink into the sand.

'Can I come to your end?' he said.

Barnes paused. Then said, 'You can, but I want to see your feet.'

Poe edged round to his right. When he got to within ten yards of Barnes, as close as he dared, he sat on the grass and dangled his legs in the bunker.

'I'm on a live audio feed, Lewis,' he said. 'I'm going to describe what I can see, if that's OK?'

'There's nothing left to hide now, Mr Poe,' Barnes said.

Poe studied the scene in front of him, describing it for Finch and Nightingale as he did. He'd never seen anything like it. It looked like one of Hieronymus Bosch's depictions of hell.

Next to the green was an ancient oak tree, bulky and mute in the still summer air. Old enough to have been an acorn in the nineteenth century, its bark looked like the cracked earth found in parched riverbeds. Great boughs, strapping and powerful and dappled with pale-green lichen, jutted from its trunk like deformed limbs. Poe could see two names and a declaration of love carved into the gnarly oak. He wondered if they were still together. Possibly not if one of them had seen fit to bring a knife on a date.

Beneath the oak, great ropes of thick, interlaced roots protruded from the earth. Acorns littered the ground like pebbles on a beach.

And it was underneath the branches, among the acorns and roots and the dappled shadows, that Lewis Barnes had parked a golf cart.

A golf cart that had turned the ancient oak into a hanging tree.

Barnes was in the driver's seat. Other than a beanie-type woollen hat, presumably there to keep the sweat from his eyes, he was wearing the clothes Poe had seen him in earlier.

He was calm and in control and oblivious to the plight of the man above him . . .

. . . who was standing on the roof of the golf cart.

Patrick McDaid's hands were tied behind his back and a barbed-wire noose was pulled tight around his neck. The wire was secured to a sturdy branch above the cart. It was taut. Despite McDaid standing on his tiptoes, Poe could see that the wire was digging into the cartilage around his windpipe. Some of the barbs had pierced his skin. Blood flowed freely. He had an egg-sized lump on his forehead and one of his eyes was swollen shut.

The cart was on a natural slope but Barnes had his foot on the brake. The moment he removed it, the cart would roll forwards and McDaid would hang. It was why Barnes had wanted Poe in the bunker. His only chance of saving McDaid was rushing Barnes and getting his own foot on the brake before the cart moved.

And that was no chance at all.

'That's a double-wire Nice knot around his neck, Mr Poe,' Barnes said. 'Do you know what that is?'

Poe didn't, but he could guess. 'Something that can't be undone?'

'Close. It's an irreversible sliding knot. If Mr McDaid steps off the roof of the golf cart his body weight will tighten it. And yes, you're right, it can't be undone. Not without some stepladders and a pair of wire cutters.'

Poe mentally reviewed everything in front of him. Tried to see if Barnes had made a mistake, anything that might give him an edge. Didn't matter how small.

If he had, Poe couldn't see it.

Barnes had improvised the most effective dead man's switch he'd ever seen. Had ever *heard* of. Breathtakingly simple, absolutely foolproof. This was why the armed cops hadn't been able to take a shot. The second Barnes's foot came off the brake, Patrick McDaid died.

Poe looked up and revised his thinking. The living gallows hadn't been improvised at all – it had been meticulously prepared. The barbed wire hadn't been hastily fixed to the branch above the cart; it had been professionally secured with two-inch galvanised staples. They were embedded deep in the wood and Poe couldn't see any hammer marks. They had been put in with a mechanical staple gun. He suspected the wire had then been wrapped around the branch until it was needed. The oak was in full leaf and the chances of it being discovered were practically zero. And even if it had been, Poe doubted this would be the only one Barnes had set up in advance.

'Should I call you Lewis Barnes or Sean Gardiner?' he said.

'Have you heard of the Ship of Theseus, Mr Poe?'

'I don't think so.'

'It's a thought experiment. A ship captained by Theseus is kept in a museum. Over the years some of the wood begins to rot so it's replaced. After a century all the original wood has been replaced. The question is this: is it still the Ship of Theseus or is it something else?'

Poe didn't answer.

'Sean Gardiner no longer exists,' he continued. 'I'm Lewis Barnes now.'

'I can call you Sean Connery, if you prefer. That was you wearing the mask in the bank heist?'

Barnes paused again. Seemed to be making a decision.

'At your shervishe,' he said in a bad Scottish accent.

Poe looked at McDaid.

The American was terrified. His eyes were bulging. His

sweat-drenched face was beetroot-red as the noose trapped blood above the neckline. If he passed out, he died, and Poe reckoned he knew that. He was taking small, rasping breaths. Trying to breathe without moving.

'Looks like you have everything under control then, Lewis,' Poe said. 'The armed cops can't shoot you and I can't rush you. You want to talk?'

'We can talk,' Barnes said.

'We know about the bank heist and we know the reason for the ceramic rats. We know there's a link with looted antiquities and that Christopher Bierman – or Captain Jack Duncan as he was known then – was involved. You were one of the soldiers who rescued Bierman and we know you weren't with Tango Two-Four when they went to the wrong valley two days later.'

'What else?'

'We know Mr McDaid was the Apache pilot who killed Tango Two-Four in that awful friendly-fire incident and we know our government said it was a suicide bombing, believing it would save British lives in the long run.'

'You have been busy,' Barnes said. 'Is there anything you don't know?'

'Motivation,' Poe said. 'We know you're motivated, we just don't know why. Not really.'

Barnes said nothing for several moments. When he did speak, Poe got the feeling he was back in Afghanistan.

'I was a soldier,' he said, his eyes on something only he could see. 'I've polished my boots until they gleamed and I've cleaned my rifle until it shone. I've shot SA80s, GPMGs and RARDEN cannons. I've dropped rounds down mortar tubes and I've thrown grenades. I've tabbed until the blisters on my feet bled and I've carried more weight on my back than a Blackpool donkey.'

'And let me guess, you've never seen the busload of nurses from Guildford that were invited to all your parties either?'

Barnes blinked, came out of whatever trance he was in. 'You served too?'

'Black Watch. Before your time. And I lost mates, too. Not as many as you and in nowhere near as tragic circumstances, but you know what I didn't do?'

'Enlighten me.'

'I didn't go on a murderous rampage. I didn't torture anyone and I didn't ruin lives. In short, I didn't disgrace my friends by becoming a self-absorbed arsehole.'

'You stayed loyal to them?'

'I did.'

'I didn't,' Barnes said.

'What, just because you weren't killed with the rest of your section?' Poe said. 'War's like that, Lewis. Careful people get killed and careless people survive. The whole thing's a fucking lottery. You drew the winning ticket, get over it.'

Barnes ignored him. 'You were right about me disgracing my friends, Mr Poe.'

'I was?'

'You just have the timeline wrong.'

'Tell me what happened then, Lewis,' Poe said. 'Tell me why these people had to die.'

Barnes paused. Again. There was something going on that Poe couldn't quite put his finger on. He seemed distracted, as if he wasn't fully concentrating.

'What I'm about to tell you is a game with many players,' he said. 'Some had cameos, others had starring roles. There's intrigue and there's betrayal, but at the end of the day it all boiled down to one thing.'

'And what's that, Lewis?'

'An oliphant.'

Chapter 94

'An oliphant?' Poe said. 'What the bloody hell's an oliphant?'

'An oliphant's an intricately carved hunting horn made from an elephant's tusk, Mr Poe,' Barnes said. 'Very old.'

'Valuable?'

'I'm told they fetch a decent price at auction if they're still in good condition, but the oliphant in question was Egyptian and that made it *very* valuable. According to Captain Jack it might have been unique.'

Poe took a moment.

'I think you'd better start at the beginning, Lewis,' he said. 'Why don't you tell me what happened?'

Barnes took on that faraway look again. 'You already know most of it,' he said.

'Tell me anyway.'

'Tango Two-Four were out on a security patrol,' he said. 'We'd done almost a hundred of them by then. They were exciting at first, you know? Chance of some action, maybe put our training into practice. But like anything, it got old fast. The heat was fucking outrageous and because it was a live op, the 432 was fully crewed. Even when I was on training cadres back in the UK, I'd never been in the back of a 432 when it was fully crewed. Ten of us in cheap seats, armed and in full body armour, the driver and the section commander on the hatches. Can you imagine that, Mr Poe? The heat of the desert, a packed and enclosed armoured vehicle?'

'Hot?'

'Almost unbearable. And we'd done this every day for months. On the day we came across Captain Jack we were snapping at the slightest provocation. So when we came under fire, the section commander leaned down and asked if we wanted to get out and have a go at them. We jumped at the chance. Weren't supposed to, of course. But we knew we outgunned them and we wanted to strut our stuff. Show them what happens when you shoot at British soldiers.'

'I've read up on it,' Poe said. 'The firefight was supposed to be short and one-sided?'

'We had a turret-mounted gimpy and they didn't,' Barnes said. 'Pretty much all you need.'

Poe didn't doubt it. The general-purpose machine gun, the GPMG or 'gimpy', was belt-fed and fired 850 rounds a minute. It was one of the most devastating machine guns in the world, and a game changer if all the enemy had were worn AK47s and unreliable pistols.

'Anyway,' Barnes continued, 'we cleared the compound and processed the men who'd chosen to give up rather than die.'

'And that's when you found Christopher Bierman, sorry, Jack Duncan?'

'He was chained to a bedframe. Poor fucker was starved and dehydrated. I was the section medic and I put a litre of saline in him before we moved him. His veins sucked it up like a condemned man having his last cigarette.'

'You called it in?'

'Not straight away,' Barnes said. 'And we're getting to the crux of the matter now. You see, this al-Qaeda cell weren't kidnappers, and their resistance under fire showed they weren't really fighters either. They were only holding Captain Jack until the cell that was going to livestream his beheading were ready.'

'So if they weren't fighters or kidnappers, what were they?'

'Part of AQ's antiquity network,' Barnes said. 'Their job was to tax what the locals unearthed, or lend them the mechanical tools to dig for more antiquities. They never held much at any one time as the demand was so high.'

'But they had this oliphant?'

'They did. And they'd been bragging about it to Captain Jack.'

'Who, because of his interest in antiques, knew how much it was worth.'

'Exactly,' Barnes said. 'So before we called it in, we made a pact. We would take the oliphant and hide it on the 432. When we got back to camp we'd stash it in his kit so it followed him back to the UK. He would sell it, then we'd split the proceeds. He was to get twenty per cent and the twelve of us would share eighty. Seemed fair.'

'What did it look like?'

'Do you know something? I didn't actually see it until much later. And it looked kind of ordinary actually.'

Poe filed 'see it until much later' in his mental filing cabinet.

Barnes cocked his head again. Paused before he continued.

'Anyway, we did exactly as we'd planned. We waited for Captain Jack to be evacuated and, after the investigators cleared us, the guys who hadn't gone back on the helicopter with him made their way to camp with the oliphant. The section commander went straight to the officers' mess and said he had some kit of Captain Jack's he needed to return. He was given a pass to get into Camp Leatherneck. He attached a five-dollar sticker to the oliphant so it looked like it came from the local market, then wrapped it in some of his T-shirts. Stuffed it into the bottom of his MFO box.'

Poe wanted to ask how Bierman had known to go to Terry Holmes but he didn't want to interrupt Barnes. He hoped to get a more detailed account later.

'What happened next?'

Barnes's shoulders slumped. Emotion showed on his face for the first time.

'Two things, Mr Poe. The first was that Captain Jack asked to see Ken, the section commander. Said he wanted to thank him before he was shipped back to the UK. So Ken went to see him in the field hospital. Spoke to him alone.'

'And it wasn't to thank him?'

'It was not. Captain Jack told him about a cache of antiquities that the al-Qaeda unit had shown him on a map. More bragging, I suppose. Said that with the unit dead or captured it was there for the taking. Enough to make everyone rich. He thought the oliphant was part of a pair and the other one might be with this cache. If we had both they would triple in value. Proposed a fifty/fifty split this time.'

A feeling of dread crept down Poe's spine. He asked the question he already knew the answer to.

'And this cache of looted antiquities was in the valley you weren't supposed to be in?'

Barnes nodded. 'You've skipped to the last page. Yes, it was. Ten miles from where we were supposed to be but it shouldn't have been too dangerous. It was technically a red zone but we had the biggest teeth in that part of Afghanistan. Even if we had bumped into another al-Qaeda outfit we had the firepower to deal with it.'

'Tango Two-Four went out two days after the rescue?'

'They did. We had a compulsory rest day because we'd come under fire but the section went to the valley the next time they drove out of camp.'

'But you weren't with them?' Poe said.

Barnes's shoulders slumped even more. His eyes glistened.

'I was not,' he said, his voice breaking. 'I'd been having problems. Alcohol mainly, but I was also taking pills. The day after the firefight it came to a head. I got wasted. Benzos washed down with warm lager. Woke up in a ditch covered in puke and drenched in piss. The section commander said he wasn't putting up with it any more. Told me I had to dry out. Reported me to the platoon sergeant and I ended up on a charge. Someone called Danny North replaced me as the section medic. Poor bastard. He was supposed to be going on leave the next week for the birth of his daughter.'

'And when they went to recover these antiquities they were killed in that awful friendly-fire accident,' Poe said.

'It's a workhorse, the 432, but it's old and no match for modern missiles. Especially the Hellfire that bastard on the roof fired at them. The boys didn't stand a chance.'

'But these things happen, Lewis,' Poe said. 'Blue-on-blue, friendly fire, whatever you want to call it, in the extreme pressure of a combat zone they do happen.'

Barnes glared at the roof of the golf cart. He eased his foot off the brake a touch and the cart rolled forward six inches. It wasn't far.

But it was enough.

McDaid's feet scrabbled for purchase. He didn't find any. With his toes barely touching the metal roof, he slowly started to spin. His face turned purple. White foam flew out of his mouth as he tried to suck air through his constricted windpipe.

'Your call, Poe,' Hannah Finch said through the speakerphone.

Poe reached for the iPhone. He wasn't prepared to watch Barnes murder McDaid in cold blood. Not in front of him. Barnes saw what he was doing. He selected reverse and backed up. McDaid's feet scrabbled to find something solid to stand on again. His breathing eased slightly.

Poe left the iPhone where it was.

'We don't practise summary executions in this country,' he said, 'but do that again and I'm giving the order to shoot.'

Barnes ignored him. He thumped the roof.

'You, you Yank prick, tell Mr Poe all about this friendly-fire incident.'

Chapter 95

While he was being hanged, McDaid had ended up with his back to Poe. It was a while before he could shuffle around.

'No accident,' he croaked when he eventually faced him.

'What do you mean "no accident"?' Poe said. 'I've read the official report. It was a classic blue-on-blue. They were in the wrong area and the vehicle had an outdated identification system. I know you meant to fire that Hellfire, but you didn't know it was Brits you were killing.'

McDaid said nothing.

Barnes thumped the roof again, hard enough for McDaid's feet to bounce in the air.

'On purpose,' McDaid rasped.

The noose was making it hard to hear him properly. Poe asked him to repeat what he'd just said.

'No accident. Shot them on purpose.'

'On purpose, Mr Poe,' Barnes said, spitting out the words like a bad mint. 'I suspected as much, obviously. Thought it just a bit too convenient. Bierman tells us about the hidden antiquities after he gets back to camp. Why not tell us on the day we rescued him? We could have gone straight there. But no, he waited two days. I thought then, and I know now, that Captain Jack had changed his mind. Decided he wasn't happy with just twenty per cent, not when he could have fifty.'

'Fifty? Why not one hundred . . .' He didn't finish; the answer was obvious. 'Fifty for him, fifty for McDaid?'

'Exactly. This way he got to keep a bigger chunk. He and this murdering bastard used the proceeds to start up their fucking helicopter company.'

'But . . . how?' Poe said. 'How the hell could McDaid know where Tango Two-Four would be? He'd need to have flight plans to follow. He couldn't have just gone looking for them.'

'You've got it back to front,' Barnes said. 'It was Patrick McDaid who told Captain Jack when and where his Apache would be patrolling. Captain Jack then told Tango Two-Four's section commander that was where the cache of looted antiquities was located. My friends went to McDaid, not the other way around.'

'And because it was a red zone, he could legitimately fire on them without his co-pilot getting suspicious.'

'More or less word for word what Captain Jack told me.'

'You getting this, Hannah?' Poe said into the phone in his top pocket.

'We're getting it, Poe,' she said, her voice small and tinny.

'OK, for now I'll take you at your word: Tango Two-Four's friendly-fire accident was anything but. And I'll go along with you thinking you had a legitimate grievance against Christopher Bierman and Patrick McDaid. My question is this: why did you wait so long?'

Barnes stared straight ahead and said, 'You've served. You'll know what the Glasshouse is?'

'Colchester?' Poe said. 'Yeah, I know it.'

The Military Correctional Training Centre in Colchester was the establishment that provided corrective training to servicemen and women sentenced to periods of detention. The MoD claimed it wasn't a prison but they weren't fooling anyone. Known by squaddies as the 'Glasshouse', they had two categories of detainees: those who would be soldiering on after sentence and those who would be discharged.

'How'd you end up there?' Poe said.

'The problems I'd been having in Afghanistan got worse after my friends died. Much worse. I drank more and started self-medicating with a cocktail of drugs. Pretty soon the pills weren't enough and I began using heroin.'

'You went to the Glasshouse for drug use?'

'No,' he said. 'I went to the Glasshouse for assaulting the three MPs who came to arrest me for drug use. I broke the elbow of one, the nose of another and ruptured the eardrum of the third. I got twelve months.'

'And with the drug use you wouldn't have been allowed to soldier on.'

'I was discharged.'

'OK, that accounts for a year or two. It doesn't explain the huge gap, though.'

'Two reasons,' Barnes said. 'I came out clean but I was still a psychological mess. It took me a long time to get my head straight.'

'The other reason?'

'It wasn't practical. Captain Jack moved to the States when I was in the Glasshouse, and with my drug conviction I couldn't get an ESTA.'

The Electronic System for Travel Authorization was how the US assessed who can and can't enter their country. With convictions for drugs and violence, Barnes would have had to be interviewed by a consular officer to get a visa. Poe reckoned he wouldn't have wanted that kind of attention.

'You had to wait for him to come to you?' he said.

Barnes nodded. 'There were things I needed to do while I waited anyway,' he said.

'Things like the murder of Terry Holmes?'

'Things like that,' he agreed.

'How did you find him?'

'Captain Jack had said the oliphant was unique. I knew it would eventually hit the open market. The buyer wouldn't be able to help themselves. They'd want to show it off. I knew it would resurface somewhere.'

'And it did?'

'It did. I assume you know about the main weapon in my armoury?'

'The JANUS cable?'

'Yes. You won't believe how stupid people can be if they think they're getting something for free. By targeting key people I was able to reverse engineer the route the oliphant took. From where it is now to where it landed in the UK. Traced it all the way back to Southampton and Terry Holmes, a stolen antiquity dealer masquerading as a pawnshop owner.'

'How did Bierman know about Terry Holmes?'

'It turns out the al-Qaeda unit that held him were proud of what they did and, as Captain Jack was going to be beheaded, they were happy to show him their contacts. He remembered the name Terry Holmes and sought him out when he got back to the UK.'

'Bierman told you this?'

'After some . . . physical prompting.'

'OK, so you find the oliphant and, as harsh as it is, given he was only a bit player in all this, you murder Terry Holmes—'

'Bit player?' Barnes snorted. 'You don't know everything then.'

Poe ignored him. He didn't have time to get into that right now. Not while McDaid was fighting for his life on the golf cart's roof.

'Using the JANUS cable you get advance notice that Scarness Hall will be awarded the summit contract,' he said. 'You become Lewis Barnes and get a part-time job there. You then ensure that Bierman & McDaid are awarded the summit's executive transport contract.'

'I did.'

'And you set up Nick Anstey so you knew when we were closing in?'

'If you arrested Cookie, the end game had started.'

'How did you stop Edward Pritchard showing us your photograph when we arrested him? Why did he show us Nick Anstey's?'

'The guy from the Army Personnel Centre?'

'I'm told there's nothing on his computer that would have forced his hand.'

'There was, though,' Barnes said. 'Indecent images of children. Lots of them, all on the cloud. I temporarily removed his access to them. Told him if I had his continuing cooperation it would all go away. Also said he'd get twenty-five grand if he did what I asked. The moment Cookie was arrested I sent a link to the images to Police Scotland. They'll have everything this time tomorrow. Don't worry, Pritchard isn't walking away from what he's been doing on the internet.'

Poe grunted in satisfaction. 'How did you tempt Bierman out of Scarness Hall?' he said. 'And why didn't he recognise you?'

'I was wearing a helmet and had camouflage cream all over my face the last time he saw me. I knew he wouldn't remember me. Not after all this time had passed. And how do you think I got him to come to Carlisle with me?'

'No idea,' Poe said.

'I used his greed. Found a picture of a Chinese jade statue. Said it was at my gran's house in the village. Asked if he would look at it for me. You should have seen his eyes light up. Knew with my supposed learning disability he could rip me off. I gave him an address in the village and met him outside. Whacked him on the head and stuffed him in the boot of my car. Drove him to the brothel you found him in. Had a little chat.'

'You injected him with Ritalin so you could keep him awake?'
'I needed information and his life was forfeit.'
'And Mr McDaid? Is his life forfeit?'

Chapter 96

'We're at the end now, Mr Poe,' Barnes said. 'Time for me and Mr McDaid to die. If you don't want to get shot in the crossfire, I suggest you step back and let it happen.'

Poe's mobile rang, confusing him for a moment.

'May I?' he said. 'This is my personal phone, not the one in my top pocket. Don't do anything.'

'Be my guest. I'll wait.'

It was an unrecognised number.

'Poe,' he said.

'It's Hannah,' Finch whispered. 'I've borrowed a phone, which is why you don't recognise the number. Don't say anything, just listen. Nod if you understand.'

Poe nodded. It wasn't a difficult instruction.

'You need to end this now,' she said. 'Certain people are following your conversation and they're getting nervous about what they're hearing. McDaid murdering twelve British soldiers in cold blood is a nightmare for both the Americans and us. I'm being told that both men dying wouldn't be a bad result. Operational command of the armed police is no longer a field decision. The new advice is, because of the cramped nature of the driver's space, if Barnes is shot in the head there's a high chance his foot will stay on the brake. If they have a shot they've been instructed to take it.'

'They wouldn't,' Poe said.

'There's a spirited and frank exchange of views going on right now,' she said. 'Superintendent Nightingale has told her units to ignore what they're being told and to wait for your command but, at the end of the day, they've been given a direct order. They might not feel they have a choice.'

Poe checked his surroundings. He could see the armed cops from the first unit. Didn't know if there were others out there now. He stood up and got out of the bunker. Began walking towards the golf cart.

'What you doing, Mr Poe?' Barnes said.

'Saving your life,' he said.

Chapter 97

'I said, what are you doing?' Barnes said.

'I need you to trust me,' Poe said.

'And why should I do that?'

'Because you need to trust someone and I'm the only person here.'

Barnes said nothing.

Poe covered the final ten feet. When he was standing next to him he leaned in. Tried to shield as much of Barnes as he could.

'This needs to end, Lewis,' he whispered. 'What happened in Afghanistan was a terrible thing but there is no way the government will let the truth out.'

Still Barnes said nothing.

'You're an ex-soldier, I'm an ex-soldier,' Poe said. 'The only position the armed cops have a bead on you is from behind me. The tree is protecting your left flank and the back of the golf cart is protecting your rear. I've put myself between you and the most likely line of fire so our fates are combined right now but they *can* move position. There might be others I can't see. You need to put the handbrake on and step out of the golf cart and you need to do it now.'

'And what next?'

'I'll arrest you.'

'And what about him?' He tilted his head to the roof.

'I'll arrest him too.'

'Will he be tried?'

'I don't know, Lewis. The establishment will undoubtedly try to make it go away quietly. Any evidence you give will be challenged and any confession you got from McDaid will be ruled inadmissible.'

'Inadmissible?'

'He has a barbed-wire noose around his neck. Even if it goes to trial, no judge will allow it to be heard. And if you've collected evidence it'll have a D-notice slapped on it quicker than you can say frogspawn. The press won't be allowed to report it.'

'It's hopeless then?'

'People will know,' Poe said. 'It may never enter the public domain but the right people will know. That's enough. It *has* to be enough.'

Barnes appeared to consider this. Eventually he chuckled.

'You're right, Mr Poe,' he said, 'the press don't publish this type of original source material any more. But that doesn't matter, not in the age of WikiLeaks, of Edward Snowden, of citizen journalism.'

Poe frowned. His phone rang again.

This time it was Special Agent Melody Lee. He pressed receive.

'Poe,' she said, 'you ain't gonna believe the shit I'm seeing.'

Which was when he noticed a light blinking in the tree. He could see it now that he was up close to Barnes. He looked up and saw another.

'Oh, I think I will,' he said.

Chapter 98

'My country's let me down once, Mr Poe,' Barnes said. 'Do you think I wouldn't have contingencies for when they tried to again?'

Poe said nothing. Just stared at the cameras in the oak tree. They were unobtrusive and professionally mounted on brackets, their green lights blinking softly. As well as being a gallows with an unbeatable dead man's switch, it seemed Barnes had turned the oak tree into a recording studio. Poe stared into one of the cameras and knew he was being seen all over the world.

'Do you like them, Mr Poe?' Barnes said. 'They've been live-streaming since the moment I arrived. One to a dedicated website hosted by a server in Switzerland, the other direct to social media. McDaid's confession, our chat, it's out there now. The government can't suppress this; it's already viral.'

Barnes was right. It had been the reason for Melody Lee's call. Thousands of people were watching. He didn't need to be Bradshaw to know that by tomorrow it would be hundreds of thousands.

He lowered his head and said, 'This is being livestreamed, Hannah. If they shoot him, the whole world sees it.'

'I'm on it,' came the tinny reply.

'What's next, Lewis?' he said. 'You're in charge and the world's watching.'

'There's nothing more dishonourable than a dishonourable soldier, Mr Poe,' he said. 'We shouldn't have helped Captain Jack steal that oliphant. Whatever happens next, the families will have to live with the fact that the boys would be alive now if they hadn't tried to engineer an easy payday. But what Captain Jack did, what Patrick McDaid did, was beyond the pale. Soldiers don't do that to each other. Never.'

'They'll be vilified, Lewis,' Poe said.

'As they deserve to be.'

'But you know something? Public opinion's fickle. Right now it'll be on your side. The public might hear that you've murdered people but that's in the abstract; they haven't *seen* you murder anyone. But the moment you take your foot off that brake you lose. If you dangle McDaid from a barbed-wire noose do you know what will happen?'

'Justice?'

'No. People will be horrified, Lewis. And that horror will then turn to sympathy. They'll turn you into the monster and McDaid into the victim.'

For the first time Barnes looked uncertain.

'Some sins can never be washed clean,' he said. 'He has to die.'

'But if he hangs, Lewis, *that's* the story. That's the lead on the news tomorrow, that's the section people will gravitate to on the inevitable Wikipedia page. The only way to win is if you put the handbrake on and step out of the golf cart. You have to let him live.'

Barnes tilted his head. Seemed distracted again.

'Lewis, I need an answer,' Poe urged.

'One moment, please,' he said. 'Let me think.'

Poe watched him. He was far away again.

'You're sure?' Barnes said.

'About what?'

Barnes didn't answer.

'Lewis, am I sure about what?'

Barnes frowned. 'OK, we'll do it your way, Mr Poe,' he said, reaching up and pulling off his beanie hat. His head started to steam. He pulled the handbrake and, using his arms as leverage, shunted across the driver's seat.

As soon as he was out of the golf cart, Poe said, 'On your stomach, Lewis. Hands behind your head, fingers interlocked. Let's not have any accidents, not when we're doing so well.'

Poe heard footsteps. He turned and saw cops running towards him.

It was over.

Chapter 99

Two days later, London

Not quite over . . .

Poe had one more job to do. And this time he needed Bradshaw.

She had used Google Maps to find the building they wanted: a three-storey Georgian townhouse on Dover Street in Mayfair. Like the rest of the houses on the street, it had been built with pale limestone. It was symmetrical and balanced, like it had been designed using Excel.

The door was 10 Downing Street black. A polished brass plate engraved with the name of the business was screwed to the stone beside it. There was no description of what the nature of the business might be. Poe suspected that, if you had to ask, you weren't their type of customer.

He pressed the doorbell. He didn't hear anything but he doubted it was broken. Establishments such as this were understated but efficient. He looked up and saw a discreet camera above the door. He held his ID card up to the lens.

'I owned houses here once,' Poe said while they waited.

'Really?' Bradshaw said.

'Had a hotel on Park Lane too.'

'Wow! You never told me. Were they part of your dad's property estate?'

'No, he had to pay me rent.'

'But why on earth would you make your dad . . .' She trailed off. 'You're talking about a game of Monopoly, aren't you, Poe?'

He grinned.

'Doofus,' she said.

The door opened. A man wearing purple livery and a top hat stood aside and let them in. He gestured towards a fussy-looking man in a three-piece suit.

'Welcome to Alcock & Sons, Sergeant Poe,' the man said. 'I must say we're all intrigued as to why our little bank might have come to the attention of the National Crime Agency.'

'And you are?' Poe said.

'Bates,' he said. 'I'm a senior partner here.'

'You have a first name, Mr Bates?'

'Of course. But while I'm in this building I'm just Bates. It's a bank tradition.'

'Mr Bates it is.'

'Just Bates, no Mr.'

Poe felt like throwing a 'Master' in front of his name just to see what he'd do. He resisted. The world of private banking was alien to him but he doubted they would be shy about lodging an official complaint.

'Bates it is then,' he said. 'This is my colleague, Tilly. You may call her Tilly.'

Bates frowned, unsure if Poe was being sarcastic. He was.

'You said you don't know why we're here, Bates?'

'Only that you want to have a look around. We have risk assessments occasionally, of course. We have to as part of our insurance arrangements but private companies, never official bodies, conduct them. Has there been a credible threat against the bank?'

Poe ignored the question. 'Can we have a look around, please?'

'Of course,' Bates said. 'As you may have guessed, we're standing in the lobby.'

It was unlike any bank lobby Poe had ever been in. For a

start they were the only ones in it. There were no tellers, no cashiers, no one walking around with a clipboard. There were no cash machines. No pedestals with deposit slips and pens on chains.

It looked more like a museum. Or one of those gentlemen's clubs where they only serve mutton and jam roly-poly.

The walls were wood panelled; polished black and white marble tiles made the floor look like a chessboard. A chandelier hung from a high, pale yellow ceiling bordered by intricate white coving. There was no designated waiting area; instead there were half a dozen burgundy leather wingback armchairs. It was a lobby that oozed money. No, Poe thought. That wasn't quite right. It was a lobby that oozed *old* money.

Professionally lit oil paintings hung from regular gaps in the wood panelling. Poe studied them. He stopped at the only one he recognised. A John Constable. It was a study of an English landscape, of a way of life that no longer existed. A hay cart, leafy trees and a clouded sky. A rural idyll for which parts of the establishment still yearned.

'That an original?' Poe said. He doubted Alcock & Sons would have anything as tacky as a copy in their lobby but he wanted to be sure.

'A minor work,' Bates said.

'Expensive?'

'What do you know about private banking, Sergeant Poe?'

'Only what I read on the way here.'

Bates removed something from his inside pocket and handed it to Poe. It was a chequebook. Poe flicked through it. The cheques were printed on cream faux-parchment and the font was Germanic. It looked like it should have been under a display cabinet. Poe handed it back.

'You pay for something with a cheque drawn from a bank like ours, Sergeant Poe, and you're not just making a transaction, you're making a statement.'

'About?'

'About who you are,' Bates said. 'It says, this is a person who prefers a more traditional approach to intergenerational wealth management. The type of person who prefers speaking to a human when it comes to their money. Our bankers know everything about a client's circumstances and they advise them accordingly. They'll sit down with them over tea and homemade shortbread, discuss their plans for future investments, and offer bespoke solutions to whatever they need.'

'What's a cheque?' Bradshaw said.

Poe snorted.

'It's like private health insurance then?' he said. 'You can get everything you need via the NHS, but if you want to feel special you go private.'

'We call it going back to the future,' Bates said. 'A traditional approach to the modern world.'

'Why the art then?' Poe said. 'Wouldn't your clients prefer you invested their money instead of spending it on luxury items?'

'Our clients expect to be treated with the utmost respect in all that they do. It is no different at their bank. You say to have a John Constable hanging in our lobby is extravagant; I say it is expected. A painting such as that says Alcock & Sons is a serious bank that understands tradition. It says we will be discreet and we can be relied upon.'

'What about that piece over there?' Poe said, pointing towards a free-standing glass cabinet. Without waiting to be asked, he walked towards it.

'Ah,' Bates said. 'The pride of our collection.'

'What is it?'

'It's an oliphant. A very rare one.'

'An oliphant?' Poe said.

'A hunting horn carved from the tusk of an elephant. There

are a few of these about but this is the only Egyptian one known to have survived the Fatimid Caliphate. It's over a thousand years old and it is a most delightful addition to our collection.'

Poe bent down and studied the hunting horn.

It was cream with nicotine-coloured stains, like the teeth of a heavy smoker. Other than the mouthpiece and two indented bands for the straps, it was entirely covered in decorative work. There were animals Poe recognised and ones he didn't. Men with bows and spears hunted them. Everything was intertwined with vines. It was a stunning piece of a culture's heritage and had no place in a stuffy bank in a snooty part of London.

'Ivory was used as a hunting horn because it produces a low-pitched sound,' Bates said.

'How much did you pay for it?' Poe said without turning. He couldn't tear his eyes away.

'You must understand items such as this don't come on the market very often. I'm afraid the bank paid almost four hundred and thirty thousand pounds.'

Poe nodded. More confirmation.

'But worth it,' Bates said, misinterpreting his nod.

'Do you know its provenance, Bates?'

'Why?' he said warily.

Poe spread his arms and gestured all around. 'Reputation is everything with you guys, isn't it?'

'It's an important part of who we are, yes.'

'And your clients expect discretion?'

'I've already said that they do.'

'That's a shame then.'

'What is?' Bates said. 'What is this about, Poe?'

'Alcock & Sons don't do social media, do they, Bates?'

'Certainly not. We work exclusively on referrals.'

'Majority of your clients won't be on social media either, I expect.'

'I imagine they have more important things to be getting on with.' He theatrically checked his watch. 'As do I, as it happens. Now, I've given you more time than I'd scheduled, but I really must be getting on. I have a very busy day ahead of me.'

'You have no idea how right you are,' Poe said.

'I beg your pardon?'

'Do you watch the news?'

'Of course.'

'So you'll have seen that incident in Cumbria a couple of days ago? The one on the golf course?'

'Only what they showed on the ten o'clock news. It looked awful. What has that got to do with Alcock & Sons?'

'Your bank's about to become famous, *Mr* Bates,' Poe said. 'Very famous.'

Poe told him why.

And when he had finished he had to help Bates into one of the burgundy leather armchairs.

Chapter 100

'Objects like that can't possibly be traced over millennia,' Bates moaned. 'You think everything in the British Museum was acquired legitimately, or do you think some items might have started their journey with a less than stellar provenance?'

'Legally acquiring antiquities, particularly ones that have transferred from one generation to the next, is incredibly complex,' Poe said. 'I understand that. But you're a respectable bank, not a shady backstreet dealer – you had a responsibility to do extensive due diligence, a responsibility you either ignored or spectacularly messed up. Either way, you're screwed.'

Bates put his head in his hands and groaned. 'Just how bad is it?'

'Tilly?'

There was an ornate incidental table beside the armchair in which Bates was slumped. Bradshaw kneeled beside it and opened her laptop.

'I can't share the bank's wi-fi password, I'm afraid,' Bates said. 'Against policy.'

'That's OK, Bates,' Bradshaw said. 'I logged on when we were waiting outside.'

'What Tilly's about to show you is an edited version of the incident. It only contains the parts that are directly relevant to the oliphant in your display case.'

Bradshaw pressed play. Lewis Barnes and Patrick McDaid appeared on the laptop screen. After a while, Poe himself appeared.

Bates gasped. 'You were there?'

Poe said nothing.

As Bates watched the rest of the video, Poe watched him. By the time it had ended his jaw had hardened and Poe knew he was already thinking about how he might spin it. Probably best to nip that in the bud now. He had things to do that needed Bates's cooperation.

'How many times has the full video been viewed, Tilly?' Poe said.

'Over a million times now, Poe.'

Bates grimaced. 'Surely not. It's only been two days.'

'And how many times has it been downloaded?' Poe said.

'We don't have the numbers yet, but, given the file size, statistically between seven and eight per cent of viewers will have downloaded it, to either view offline or upload it to their own sites and blogs.'

'Earlier, I said Alcock & Sons was about to become famous,' Poe said. 'I misspoke. I ought to have said you're already famous. Or should that be infamous?'

'It's infamous, Poe.'

'Thanks, Tilly, I always get those two words confused.'

'How do you know that this man was talking about this oliphant, though?' Bates said. 'You heard me say there are many of them.'

'Actually, what I heard you say is that this is the only surviving piece from the Fatimid Caliphate.'

'Well, yes, that's what it was sold to us as. But, as you know, the world of antiquities is full of chancers and scoundrels. There could be a dozen, no, two dozen fake Fatimid Caliphate oliphants out there. There's no way you can be certain he's referring to this particular piece.'

Poe nodded.

'Unfortunately for Alcock & Sons, Bates, Lewis Barnes had

contingencies for this rather predictable defence. Tilly, can you show Bates the new video, the one that was uploaded last night?'

Bradshaw selected a different video file.

The sixteenth green of Brampton Golf Club disappeared.

And the lobby of Alcock & Sons appeared, the very lobby they were standing in now.

Chapter 101

'You say you work on referrals, Bates?' Poe said. 'Well, Lewis Barnes is a resourceful man. At some point, he managed to get one of those referrals. As you can see, while he waited to be seen, he spent time wandering around your lobby. Unfortunately for you, he did this while wearing a hidden camera. If Tilly turns up the sound,' – he waited while she did – 'you can hear his commentary.'

'So, this is it then,' Lewis Barnes said, his voice creaking with emotion. 'This is what they died for. I've tracked it through each stage of its journey – from Captain Jack's compound to Terry Holmes's pawnshop, from the black market to the auction house. And finally to where I am now: a private bank in Mayfair. Irrefutable evidence of each stage of the oliphant's journey can be downloaded from the new media pack on the website.'

Bates's jaw was ticking uncontrollably. He looked as though he was going into shock. 'But he's in prison,' he croaked. 'How could this have been posted last night?'

'He's still in police custody, actually,' Poe said. 'But Tilly tells me it's easy enough to set up a scheduling calendar. Once that's done, you don't need to do anything else. Your content gets posted automatically at the time of your choosing.'

'I'll need to call an emergency board meeting,' Bates said. 'And there's a PR firm we occasionally recommend to clients who have . . . required their services. I'd better call them too. Warn them we might need them. There's always something that can be done to lessen the impact.'

Poe rolled his eyes.

'I don't think you quite understand what's about to happen, Bates,' he said. 'Not only are you about to be vilified by the press, the UK and US governments will need a scapegoat and the only option they have is to come down hard on the people involved in the smuggling trade, and that includes end users like you. They'll be so desperate to change the narrative that they'll throw you under the bus.'

'People will see through that.'

'You think? You're in the fickle court of public opinion now and their evidence threshold is nowhere near as high as the Crown Prosecution Service's.'

'There'll be a prosecution?' he gasped.

'My colleagues in the transnational organised crime unit will be here later today. And, as the trade in looted Afghani antiquities is inextricably linked to the funding of terrorism, the security services are involved as well.'

Bates said nothing.

'If I were you, I'd spend the rest of today preparing for their visit,' Poe continued. 'And please listen to this advice, Bates: you need to admit everything, share any evidence you have. Publicly state you were in the wrong and do this before the government does. Say that you intend to cooperate and mean it. That's how your bank survives this. Your board may advise otherwise but I'm telling you, the moment you try your London tricks is the moment you lose.'

Bates came to a decision. His cheeks regained some colour. He straightened his tie and stood, ramrod straight like a sergeant major.

'I will not hide the bank from this,' he said. 'Our strength has always been our reputation and the only way we'll regain it is by doing as you suggest. That starts now. What do you need?'

Chapter 102

'You have CCTV in the lobby,' Poe said.

'We do,' Bates said. 'Our clients don't like to think they're being watched but it's an insurance requirement unfortunately.'

'I want to see the footage. Tilly here will navigate your system if you don't know your way around it.'

'Follow me,' he said.

Like staff-only parts in all grand buildings, the security suite was plain and functional. A desk that could have come from any office supply company took up half the room. A bank of monitors covered most of the wall. They were all switched off.

'I'm not sure how this works, to be honest,' Bates said. He pressed a few buttons on a keyboard and jiggled a mouse. Nothing happened.

'Tilly,' Poe said. 'Show Bates how to operate his own security system please.'

Bradshaw pulled up the ergonomic chair and reached for a small black box. She pressed a button and the monitors flickered into life. Four of them showed the now empty lobby, the rest were of the bank. Some rooms were empty; others had people working in them. One of the monitors showed a boardroom with a huge portrait overlooking the long table.

'Mr Alcock?' Poe said.

'Indeed,' Bates confirmed.

'Is the CCTV room staffed?'

'The head of compliance is responsible for on-site security and he has a tablet that's paired to the CCTV system. This means he doesn't have to stay in here all day. Everything goes to remote monitoring at night. The system is permanently recording, I understand, but only when there's movement.'

'It's a motion-detection camera system, Bates,' Bradshaw said, already in the guts of the system. 'The surveillance DVR starts recording when it detects pixel changes in the images it's receiving from the cameras.'

Poe and Bates looked at her blankly.

'I really don't know why I bother,' she muttered.

'You have the timestamp of the recording Lewis Barnes made, Tilly?' Poe said.

'I do.'

'How long to—'

'Here it is, Poe,' she said. 'I'll send it to the big monitor in the middle.'

Bradshaw split the screen to show images from the cameras in the lobby. She pressed play. The first person they saw was the liveried man who had let them in.

He entered the lobby and opened the front door. Lewis Barnes stepped through. He was wearing a suit and carrying an expensive briefcase. Instead of the goofy grin Poe was used to, he exuded a confidence only people who know their instructions will be followed to the letter command. The man in purple's bearing stiffened.

Lewis spoke to him for a moment, checked his watch and took a seat. The liveried man left the lobby. As soon as he was out of sight, Lewis stood. To anyone who didn't know otherwise, Lewis spent the next five minutes studying the exhibits in the bank's lobby.

'Is that him?' Bates said.

'That's him,' Poe confirmed.

Bates opened an online visitor log. 'He called himself Warren Bright,' he said. 'He was early.'

'Intentionally so, I imagine,' Poe said. 'He wanted some time to himself.'

'He was extremely well credentialled. Said he was considering us for part of his portfolio. Provided references and an introduction from one of our clients. We had no reason not to take him seriously.'

'We think he was using a buttonhole camera,' Poe said. 'That's why the footage is a bit shaky.'

'He's not speaking, though,' Bates said. 'The video you've just shown me had commentary.'

'It was added later,' Bradshaw said. 'Easy to do.'

'That's that then,' Bates said. 'It seems our oliphant *is* his oliphant.'

Poe stared at the screen. Something didn't add up.

'What's the matter?' Bradshaw said.

'Nothing,' he said. He arched his back and rolled his shoulders. 'Look, I'm starving. Any chance you can rustle up some of that homemade shortbread you mentioned earlier, Bates?'

'I'm sure that's possible.'

'And maybe a cup of coffee? We haven't had breakfast yet.'

'I'll get it now.'

'And you'd better take Tilly with you. She knows how I like my coffee and she'll want to see what fruit teas you have.'

'I'm OK, Poe.'

He didn't answer. Eventually Bradshaw turned. He winked and dipped his head towards the door.

'On second thoughts, Bates, I will go with you,' she said. 'I need to check vegan butter was used in the shortbread.'

As soon as the door had shut behind them, Poe took Bradshaw's seat. He'd watched her navigate the system and it looked fairly intuitive. He hovered the cursor over the fast-forward button and kept clicking. For five minutes he watched bank employees speed about their business, like a really dull episode of *The Benny Hill Show*.

He found what he was looking for almost a week after Barnes had entered the lobby of Alcock & Sons. He pressed pause.

He leaned in and studied the image on the screen.

'Oh, you've got to be kidding me,' he said.

Poe's phone rang an hour later. He had a mouthful of sausage and bacon but answered anyway.

Bradshaw, tucking into a bowl of granola with soya milk, looked up quizzically.

'Ma'am?' he said.

'I really don't understand how you know these things, Poe,' Nightingale said.

'You found them?'

'Exactly where you said they'd be.'

'Damn,' he said. He'd really hoped he was wrong.

'What does it mean, Poe?' Nightingale said.

'It means I've got to have a very difficult conversation with someone.'

Chapter 103

Poe knocked on the door.

Lucy North answered immediately.

'Sergeant Poe,' she said. 'What a surprise, we were talking about you yesterday.'

'You were?'

'In a good way, of course. We watched the video of Patrick McDaid's confession again last night. I'm so glad you were able to save Sean. That poor man has been through enough.'

'It's why I'm here. I wanted to bring you and Emily up to speed.'

'Come in then.'

Poe followed her down the hall and into the kitchen.

'Emily!'

'What?'

'Sergeant Poe's here to see us.' She turned and said, 'I can't give you long, I'm afraid. Although it's the summer holidays, Emily's school is having a careers' day and I'm needed at work.'

'Shouldn't take too long,' he said.

She poured him a coffee from a steaming filter machine.

'Thanks,' he said. 'It was an early start.'

Emily North slouched into the room. Her eyes were still half shut and her hair looked as though it had just received a charge of static electricity. Without looking at Poe, she pulled it back into a ponytail. She slumped into the seat opposite him.

'Silly Bradshaw not with you, Sergeant Poo?' she said.

'Emily, behave,' Lucy said.

'Day off,' Poe said. He sipped his coffee, then eased himself back in the chair. 'And I'm not here in any official capacity.'

'Oh?' Lucy said.

'I just wanted to let you know what's happening. Given the agencies involved now, it's possible that keeping the families informed might not be seen as high priority. I thought, because Emily has that Facebook group, I could tell you what I know and you could tell everyone else?'

'That OK, Em?'

She nodded enthusiastically. 'I'll do it this morning.'

'You're going to careers' day this morning, young lady. You can do it this afternoon.'

Emily scowled. Poe suspected it wasn't the first discussion they'd had about careers' day.

'The first thing is that the Americans are playing ball this time,' he said. 'No choice really, considering how damning McDaid's confession was. They have agreed this matter can be dealt with by the UK.'

'What's that mean, Sergeant Poe?' Lucy said.

'It means they won't demand McDaid's repatriation to the US. He'll stand trial here and, given the evidence that Sean Gardiner – or as I knew him, Lewis Barnes – gathered, he'll have to plead guilty.'

'Won't it be inadmissible?'

'The barbed-wire noose confession will be, but I've seen the rest of the evidence – we're gathering more every day – and it's compelling.'

'Good,' Lucy said.

'I still wish Sean had hanged him, though,' Emily said.

'The second thing is that the National Crime Agency's trans-national organised crime team are heading an international task force to dismantle the smuggling network that Captain Jack

Duncan put the oliphant in. I'm told that the first round of arrests will be made soon. The rest will follow.'

'You can't know that,' Lucy said. 'There'll be some who wriggle out of it to start again somewhere new.'

Poe shook his head. 'Not this time,' he said. 'Because of the links to Tango Two-Four, MI5 will soon be treating this as a matter of national security. It'll be one of their top priorities.'

'How can you be so sure?'

'Because I've seen an old cricket photograph.'

Lucy and Emily both frowned. Poe didn't elaborate.

Instead he said, 'Yesterday, Alcock & Sons turned over the oliphant to the British Museum so it can be returned to its country of origin.'

'Which is where?'

'We think Egypt.'

'The bank will claim it on their insurance,' Emily said. 'They won't end up out of pocket.'

'They've agreed not to,' Poe said. 'This is about damage limitation for them now. They've also agreed to make a donation to the families of Tango Two-Four. I understand that today an amount equal to what they paid for the oliphant will be deposited into the bank account you have set up to receive donations.'

Lucy and Emily exchanged glances.

'What?' Poe said. 'What don't I know?'

Emily smiled. 'Since that video went viral, Sergeant Poe, we've had so many donations I can't even count. People from all over the world have been sending us money. We have a meeting soon to decide what to do with it. The Royal British Legion has agreed to manage it for us but we need to form a committee. Mum's agreed to chair it.'

'Blimey,' he only just managed to say. He had been expecting something like this.

'What's going to happen to Sean?' Lucy said. 'He must have

been suffering from post-traumatic stress disorder for him to do all those horrible things.'

'Undoubtedly,' Poe said. 'I haven't spoken to him since his arrest but I'll keep a weather eye on him. Make sure he's being advised well.'

'But . . . why would you?'

'Like I said the last time I was here, I was a soldier too. I can understand, if not condone, what he did. He'll go to prison for a long time, but hopefully he'll get out while he still has some life left in him.'

Poe checked his notebook. Made sure he'd covered everything.

'I think that's it,' he said. 'If you ever need to know what's going on, if you think you're being stonewalled, give me a call. Crimes such as this are like wounds – the more light you can shed on them, the quicker they heal.'

Lucy North stood. She took his cup to the sink. When she turned her eyes were glistening.

'Thank you, Sergeant Poe,' she said. 'If you hadn't been involved I doubt we'd have had such a positive result.'

After Emily had sloped off to careers' day, Lucy finished the last of her coffee. When she had drained her mug, she stood and shook his hand.

'I suppose I'd better go to work,' she said.

'Not yet,' Poe said.

'Oh?'

'I think we need to have a little chat, don't you?'

She held his gaze and nodded.

'Yes, I think we do.'

Chapter 104

'Two things have been bothering me about this case,' Poe said. 'Shall I tell you what they are?'

Lucy North eyed him shrewdly. 'I doubt I'll be able to stop you,' she said.

He offered her a humourless smile.

'The first is that Lewis Barnes was an infantryman,' he said. 'Now, I've had his entrance test scores checked and, while he was intelligent, he wasn't off-the-charts intelligent. And he specialised as a medic, which admittedly is a useful transferable skill when it comes to keeping someone awake while you interrogate them, not so much when it comes to writing the complex viruses that were on those JANUS cables. And not so useful when it comes to setting up websites and Swiss servers to livestream devastating confessions.'

Lucy said nothing. Took a sip from the bottle of water she'd opened, her eyes fixed on his.

'Details like this keep me awake at night, you see?' he said. 'I tell the people I work with that perfection is the enemy of good. That no case is ever fully solved, that there are always unanswered questions. But I rarely take my own advice and this really bothered me.'

He reached for the other bottle of water on the table. 'May I?' he said.

'It's for you.'

'So I checked whether he'd completed a computer course

while he was at the Glasshouse. Part of his transition to civilian life.'

'And had he?'

'He had actually. But it was the type of course that I could do with going on. A "here's the keyboard, here's the mouse" type of course. It certainly wasn't a course that would churn out another Tilly Bradshaw.'

He looked at her, smiled. 'You never actually told me what you do for a living, did you, Lucy?'

'I don't think I did, Sergeant Poe.'

Poe waited.

'I assume you already know,' she continued. 'I run a cyber security company.'

Poe nodded. 'And I assume you employ the type of person who *would* be able to write the complex viruses we found on those JANUS cables?'

Lucy shrugged but didn't answer.

He knew he was threading a needle. If he went in too hard she'd shut down. Tilly might get her in the end but he wasn't sure that was what he wanted yet.

'Anyway, the second thing that bothered me,' he said, 'was the way Lewis was acting while we talked. Now, I realise it was a high-pressure situation, the culmination of years of planning and he couldn't afford for anything to go wrong, but . . .'

'But what?'

'But he seemed distracted, like he was listening to music that only he could hear. At first I thought he was being cautious. Thinking about everything he said, knowing it was being live-streamed to the world.'

'I've watched it too,' Lucy said. 'I mean, who hasn't? It's the highest-trending video of the year. And I agree, Sean *did* look distracted. But as you say, he definitely has PTSD. I bet he was distracted most of the time.'

Poe nodded and took a swig of water. Took his time screwing the bottle top back on when he'd drained it. Gave it a twist to make sure it was tight. Lucy watched him.

'This is the part where you start talking,' he said. 'And don't think you're in a position to hold back, because you're not.'

'I don't know why you think I would tell you anything,' she said.

Poe didn't immediately answer.

'Because you made a mistake,' he said eventually. 'Only the one and so far I'm the only person who's noticed it.'

Chapter 105

'If you hadn't uploaded the Alcock & Sons video, we'd have been none the wiser. How Lewis Barnes became so technologically proficient would have been chalked down to being one of those things.'

'You think the video in the bank's lobby had something to do with me?'

'Think? Yes,' he said. 'Prove? No.'

'I'm not following you.'

'Simple, really. When I went to Alcock & Sons I had them over a barrel. So much so they were more than happy to let me watch – and download – their CCTV footage.'

'You saw Sean shooting the video?'

Poe shook his head. 'I saw Sean shooting *a* video. But the one he shot was not the one that was uploaded to his website.'

'But . . .' She trailed off as she realised anything she said might be incriminating.

'The video that was uploaded to the website looked like the one that Lewis shot,' he said. 'It was taken from the right angle and from the right height. Almost identical actually.'

'But you don't think it was?'

'I don't.'

'You seem sure.'

'The oliphant is behind a glass display case,' Poe said. 'And the thing about glass, one of its defining characteristics really, is that it's reflective.'

For the first time she looked worried. Poe knew that before the video was uploaded she'd have been through it frame by frame, making sure there was nothing incriminating in it. But here he was anyway.

'And what did it reflect, Sergeant Poe?' she said, her voice tight and anxious.

'It reflected a flash of light, Lucy. Not a flash from the phone shooting the video, more like the flash when you're in a room and someone a few yards away takes a photograph.'

'So what?'

'Lewis was alone in the lobby when he shot his video. There was no one to flash a camera.'

Lucy opened her bottle and took a long drink. Poe knew she was thinking. Wondering how much he knew, how much he'd told people.

'So I kept going through the bank's CCTV,' Poe continued, 'searching for the person who did shoot the video.'

'Did you now?'

'And lo and behold, a week later a group of women came in. Looked like they were on an organised visit. And one of those women videoed the oliphant, didn't even need to conceal what she was doing as they were obviously there to view the lobby's art. And while this woman was videoing the oliphant, a flash went off. One of her friends had snapped a pic of a nearby Constable.'

'And?'

'And the woman videoing the oliphant was you, Lucy.'

'Well fancy that,' she said.

Chapter 106

'Of course,' Poe said, 'when there's a second person involved, someone who knows about computers and websites and writing viruses, Lewis doesn't need the technical skills I couldn't explain him having. He provided the operational expertise, this second person provided technical support. The scalpel to his hammer.'

'I think you've been working too hard, Sergeant Poe,' Lucy said. 'You need to get a Netflix account, maybe chill for a couple of weeks.'

'I wish people would stop saying that,' Poe said. 'I don't know what Netflix is and I've never "chilled" in my life. No, what I do is obsess about things, Lucy. And when I realised Lewis had had help, I went back and reviewed the golf-course video. And I became convinced of something: Lewis wasn't distracted because of his PTSD, nor was he checking his language before it went out to the world.'

'He wasn't?'

'He wasn't. He was pausing because he was listening to someone.'

Lucy held his gaze, a wry smile playing across her lips.

'But how could that be?' he continued. 'I was standing right next to him and I couldn't hear anything. It didn't make sense. Until I remembered that Lewis had been wearing a stupid beanie hat. It's twenty-five degrees and he's wearing a woollen hat. I had thought it was to keep the sweat out of his eyes but now I know different. Do you know what he did when he gave himself up, Lucy?'

She shook her head.

'He removed his hat and shunted across the front seats of the golf cart.'

'I think I saw that on the video,' she said.

'Completely innocuous ...' Poe said. 'Unless, of course, removing his hat was just misdirection. That what he was really doing was removing something from his ear. And instead of shunting across the seats, he was actually wedging that same thing between the two cushions. Something he didn't want us to find when we searched him.'

'Seriously, you're in more need of Netflix than any person I know.'

'You want to know what I did next?'

She shrugged.

'I called someone I trust and asked her to search the golf cart. No one had thought to do it yet. No immediate need to. Do you know what my colleague found wedged between the two front seats?'

'Bubble gum?'

'A Bluetooth earbud. And do you know what she found hidden in the lining of the roof?'

'That crinkly paper they use for golf ball wrappers?'

'A smartphone.'

'And where are these devices now?'

'Safe,' he said.

'Safe? What does that mean?'

'We'll get to that,' he said. 'Anyway, here's what I initially thought had happened. Lewis wanted to take revenge for what had happened to Tango Two-Four but he couldn't do it on his own. He needed someone good at computers and he couldn't just ask anyone. He'd have to trust them and, as they'd be going up against all sorts in this mission – pilots who weren't going to admit anything, an organised gang of antiquity traffickers, even his own government – they'd need to be as motivated as him. And where better to look than the families of Tango Two-Four? Surely there'd be someone in that pool of desperate people who'd be able to help him.'

'And you think he recruited me as his partner?' she said.

'No, Lucy. I said that's what I initially thought. You see, at the end, when I was telling him that if he livestreamed Patrick McDaid's hanging he'd lose all public support, he paused then said, "You're sure?" I assumed he was asking me – I even answered him. But I now know he was seeking permission. It wasn't Lewis Barnes who decided to let Patrick McDaid live, it was the person he was working with.'

'What are you saying?'

'I'm saying I got it back to front. I don't think Lewis Barnes recruited you, Lucy – I think you recruited him.'

Chapter 107

'This is your one chance to tell me what happened, Lucy,' Poe said. 'It won't happen again. If you refuse, or leave something out, I'm arresting you. I don't care how well you think you've covered your tracks, Tilly will uncover them. You'll spend twenty years in prison and Emily will have to deal with losing a mother as well as a father.'

'You wouldn't,' she said, her eyes suddenly wet.

'It's my job. Why wouldn't I?'

'Because you know what happened! What happened to all the others.'

'The end justifies the means?'

'Yes!'

'The law doesn't work that way, Lucy.'

'The law's wrong then!'

And Poe was reminded that, despite everything she'd been a part of, she was still a grieving widow, she was still a mother trying to raise her daughter on her own.

'I agree,' he said softly.

They settled into an uneasy silence.

Poe broke it.

'Tell me what happened,' he said. 'I'll decide what to do when I know everything.'

'Are you recording me?' she said after several moments.

'No.'

'You recorded Sean.'

'I told him I was.'

She said nothing for almost a minute.

'I need to make a phone call then,' she said.

'A solicitor?' Poe said. 'We're not there yet.'

'Not a solicitor, Sergeant Poe, I'm calling James.'

'And he is?'

'You'll see,' she said. 'And while we're waiting for him I'll tell you all about a monkey called Bertrand and a cat called Raton . . .'

James, it turned out, was one of Lucy's employees. He was middle-aged and looked like an unrepentant sex tourist. He entered the kitchen and, without saying a word, opened a metal briefcase.

'James is one of my specialists,' Lucy said.

'Your phone please, sir,' he said.

Poe handed over his mobile without a word. James slipped it into a Faraday pouch, a smaller version of the one MI5 had used in Manchester. He zipped it up, then removed a gadget from his briefcase. It was about the same size and shape as one of those giant Fruit Pastilles tubes Poe could only ever buy at Christmas.

'This is an RF wireless signal detector wand,' he continued. 'I'm going to check you're not sending out a signal.'

'Go ahead,' Poe said, standing up and holding out his arms.

James ran the wand carefully over his front and back, not unlike being checked by airport security.

'He's clean,' he said.

'Thank you, James,' Lucy said.

'Sean Gardiner left the Glasshouse a broken man,' Lucy said after James had left. 'He'd gone in dependent on drugs and alcohol, and all prison did was delay what he wanted to do.'

'Which was?'

'Die,' she said.

'He'd planned to kill himself?'

'Drink himself to death, actually, but it amounts to the same thing.'

'You know this how?'

'He wrote to me,' she said. 'It was a few years after he'd been released. He wanted to apologise for Danny having to take his place on that patrol.'

She sipped her water. Cleared her throat. 'But I wasn't having that,' she continued. 'My husband, Emily's dad, was dead because of him. A badly spelled letter didn't absolve him.'

'What did you do?'

'I tracked him down to a bedsit in south London. I was ready to give him a piece of my mind but the moment I saw him it was clear there was nothing I could say that he hadn't been thinking for years.'

'Then what?'

'I bought him breakfast. Made him eat something solid. And it was while we were eating that he told me what had happened. What had *really* happened. That Tango Two-Four had helped Captain Jack Duncan steal the oliphant and he was convinced they'd been killed so he could keep it for himself.'

'That must have been awful to hear.'

'Devastating,' Lucy said. 'And I became angry.'

'Understandable.'

'And over breakfast we made a vow. We didn't know how, but the people involved had to pay for what they'd done. We didn't know how Christopher Bierman, that was the name he was using by then, had arranged for Tango Two-Four to be blown up by the suicide bomber – because that was what we still thought – but we knew he'd somehow found a way. It was the only thing that made sense. If we could get him back to the UK, Sean would make him talk.'

Poe thought back to the horrific way Christopher Bierman's life had ended. Decided he wasn't going to lose any sleep over it. He said nothing.

'So we started planning. The first thing we had to do was get Sean clean. He was desperate to help but knew he wasn't "battle fit", as he called it. I anonymously funded a private rehabilitation place for him near the Cairngorms. He spent six weeks drinking water and having treatment for his PTSD.'

'It worked,' Poe said. It wasn't a question.

'It helps when you have the right motivation.'

'What then?'

'We needed a black float.'

'Black float?' Poe said.

'I could have funded this myself but I didn't want to expose the business. People rely on me for their mortgages and weekly shopping. This was a private venture and it had to be funded privately. We needed a way to coerce people into donating money. Luckily, I'd just been reading an industry magazine article about these programmable mobile-phone cables—'

'The JANUS cables?'

'Yes. I bought some from a supplier in the States and, without knowing why, my guys reverse engineered it. Sean and I posted them in nice packaging to the people we'd selected. Said they'd won a free trial. Didn't work all the time, of course. A lot of these cables would have just been used to charge phones, or put away as spares. But enough of our targets used them to connect their phones to their computers. As soon as they did, we were able to hack into their accounts.'

'And some of those people had secrets?' Poe said. 'Secrets they'd pay to keep quiet?'

She nodded. 'When we had enough money we went on to the next stage: tracking down the oliphant and everyone involved in the supply chain.'

'How long did that take?'

'Two years. These people are naturally secretive, but, because I have contacts abroad I could call on, and because their business relies on moving black-market goods to the open market, there's always a way in.'

'And you found it?'

'Terry Holmes,' she said. 'He was Captain Jack's UK contact.'

'And for that he had to die?'

'What do you know about him?'

'A fair bit,' Poe said. 'We've spoken to his daughter. He doted on her. He was a bit of a lad. Dabbled in fencing stolen goods but otherwise he seemed harmless. When I was speaking to Lewis, sorry Sean, at the golf course, he hinted there were things I didn't know about him. Was he right?'

Lucy smiled, but not nicely.

'He was. Terry Holmes wasn't the loveable scamp everyone thought he was, Sergeant Poe,' she said. 'He was the network's point man in the UK. He dealt directly with al-Qaeda and more latterly ISIS. He was encouraged to actively seek out non-network goods, antiquities that hadn't entered the country via their smuggling routes.'

Which explained why Terry Holmes had surreptitiously filmed Bierman in his pawnshop – when he was dealing with someone from outside his network he'd have needed to do due diligence. Bierman had probably had to hire the safety deposit box while Holmes did his checks.

'Terry Holmes knew full well that the money he paid for the looted antiquities funded their atrocities because he was dealing with them directly,' Lucy continued. 'Some of these atrocities were perpetrated against British soldiers. He was a legitimate target. Sean insisted.'

Poe considered this. Decided he wouldn't tell Susan Holmes. If it got out then it got out, but he wasn't telling her that her dad had been in bed with al-Qaeda and ISIS. No one needed that on their conscience.

'Sean recruited him for the bank heist. Told him he was there to assess the value of anything that was found.'

'And he agreed?'

'He was a very greedy man. Sean told him he could have first refusal on anything they stole if he helped.'

'But he was only there to be killed in front of the safety deposit box?'

'Sean wanted to make a statement.'

'He certainly achieved that,' Poe said.

'We'd also stumbled upon a problem. The organisation involved in the supply of looted antiquities was too big, too powerful for us to tackle on our own. And most of them lived abroad anyway. Sean couldn't travel because of his drug offences and I couldn't leave Emily.'

'Which was why you left the ceramic rat with Terry Holmes,' Poe said.

'We knew we'd need to involve the police at some point and Sean said that if we connected the death of Terry Holmes to the future death of Christopher Bierman, they'd have no choice but to investigate. And who knew what they'd uncover. What *you'd* uncover, as it turned out.'

'You used the JANUS cable on a member of the venues committee to ensure you knew who'd be hosting the trade summit?'

Lucy nodded. 'And another to ensure Bierman & McDaid were awarded the executive transport contract.'

'Sean gets a job at Scarness Hall a couple of months before it's announced so it doesn't attract suspicion. Makes his preparations to abduct Captain Jack.'

McDaid too, Poe thought. They didn't yet know of his guilt but they still needed something from him. He'd spin back round to that later.

'He then gets Bierman out of the grounds by pretending he has an antique for him to look at,' Poe continued. 'Sean reckoned Bierman wouldn't be able to resist taking advantage of someone with a learning disability. Which was why Bierman didn't tell anyone where he was going. If an accusation was made that he'd ripped off Lewis he could simply deny the whole thing had happened.'

'Exactly,' Lucy said.

'So Sean arranges to meet him in the village. He overpowers him and takes him to a brothel he knows is empty. Has an "enhanced" chat and finds out the suicide bombing was nothing of the sort – Patrick McDaid had staged a friendly-fire incident. You adapt your plan to punish McDaid as well, while at the same time ensuring the public find out what really happened to Tango Two-Four.'

'That's it,' she said. 'And because we knew the government would have to double down on their lie, we bypassed everyone and used the tools of Emily's generation.'

'You told the world.'

'And at the same time, the evidence we'd collected was emailed to every major newspaper in Europe and the US and uploaded to our website. You know everything else.'

She went to the fridge and brought back two more bottles of water.

'Why did you have to shoot the video in Alcock & Sons' lobby? What was wrong with Sean's? If he'd uploaded his video to your website, this would never have unravelled. It would have gone down like you intended.'

'The Bluetooth connection failed,' she said.

Poe said, 'Unlucky.'

She shrugged.

'And the Facebook page you set up for Emily?' he said. 'How did that fit in?'

'It didn't. Emily genuinely wanted to know more about her dad. It was a bit of a nuisance actually. I had to spend hours monitoring the damned thing. We couldn't risk a photograph of Sean being uploaded. It was handy in the end, though – as Emily said, the donations coming in have been extraordinary.'

Poe nodded but didn't respond.

'What's going to happen now, Sergeant Poe?' she said, opening her water. 'Am I leaving here in handcuffs?'

'You are,' he said. 'Stand up.'

'But . . . why?' she asked. 'I've told you everything.'

'Have you?'

'I have.'

'You haven't,' he said. 'You haven't told me why the livestreaming of Patrick McDaid's confession started a full fourteen minutes after Lewis had strung him up.'

'I don't know why,' she said quietly.

'I think you do,' Poe said. 'Hannah Finch, my MI5 contact and all-round pain in the arse, has done some digging and Bierman & McDaid's bank accounts now have no money in them. I'm guessing one of the things Lewis extracted from Christopher Bierman in that brothel was his bank passwords. As well as killing him, you planned to strip him of his assets. And probably because he and McDaid didn't really trust each other – I mean, how could they after what they'd done together? – their accounts required two passwords. I think Lewis spent those fourteen minutes getting McDaid's passwords and relaying them to you. While the livestreaming was going on, and with both passwords, you were stripping their business accounts.'

'If that *has* happened,' she said carefully, 'it would all be put in the pot that the British Legion is going to manage for us. It will be doing some good.'

'Can it be traced back to Bierman & McDaid?'

'I'd imagine it has been broken down and donated to the fund in small amounts by people who have no idea they'd been so generous.'

'And perhaps there's a slush fund somewhere?' Poe said. 'One for Lewis Barnes. Might go towards some legal help? Perhaps something for when he gets out of prison.'

'Perhaps,' she said.

Poe took a moment. 'Good,' he said eventually.

'That's it?'

'I need some assurances and they are non-negotiable. First, there's a woman you targeted when you breached the safety deposit box company. She worked in the CCTV control room. She was planning to leave her abusive husband and you used it against her. She's only just got out of prison for what you forced her to do. You'll do whatever you need to do to set her up with a new identity, a new job and a big lump sum.'

Lucy nodded. 'I expect she'll have a run of good luck very soon, Sergeant Poe. Anything else?'

Poe planted his elbows on the table.

'Yes,' he said. 'This stops now.'

Lucy scowled, put her finger to her mouth and chewed on a hangnail. 'As long as everyone does their job and catches—'

He banged his fist on the table. Ignored her startled jump. 'No,' he growled. 'This. Stops. Now. You're good but you're not that good. If I find out this is still going on I'll unleash Tilly. Believe me when I say this – you do not want her in your life. You will lose.'

He paused.

'And so will Emily,' he added.

Lucy shrank back in her chair, stared at her now empty bottle of water for several moments. Poe saw a tear creep out of the corner of her eye. She wiped it away and sniffed.

'Let us handle it, Lucy,' Poe said, softer this time. 'You've given us everything we need and we'll have MI5's resources to call on soon. If I need your help, I will ask for it.'

'You promise?'

'I do,' he said. 'This smuggling network doesn't know what's about to fucking hit it.'

Chapter 108

One of the peculiarities of living like he did was that, even in the searing heat, Poe had to light his wood-burning stove if he wanted hot water. But it was a surprise when he crested the hill and saw smoke rising lazily from his chimney.

The list of people he knew well enough to let themselves in and build a fire was not long. Bradshaw, who didn't know how to light a fire anyway, was back in Hampshire working on SCAS's new case – a killer the press had dubbed Spring-heeled Jack. He had just collected Edgar from Victoria, and Nightingale, Hannah Finch and Melody Lee were all being debriefed in Manchester. He'd ignored the request to join them.

He had nowhere near enough time to go through his list of enemies, but he didn't need to. Whoever was waiting for him in Herdwick Croft had lit a fire and the only reason to do that was so he'd have advance warning they were there.

Poe approached Herdwick Croft with more curiosity than caution. As soon as the quad came to a halt, Edgar was off, barking and scratching at the door. The spaniel loved it when people visited; they brought him treats.

Poe was still fifty yards away when the door opened and a tall, lean man bent down and fondled Edgar's ears.

Alastor Locke.

Perfect.

'You here to arrest me?' Poe said.

Locke smiled.

'I should, you know,' he said. 'If you'd left the family alone none of this would have happened. This has been humiliating for the country. The Prime Minister's fuming, the head of my service has had her ear chewed. Far better if you'd let nature take its course, old chap.'

'Let the armed police shoot Lewis, you mean,' Poe said. 'Leave Patrick McDaid hanging, literally.'

'That would have been a clean solution,' Locke admitted. 'We would have refuted the confession and suppressed the evidence.'

'It was being broadcast around the world. And the evidence had already been released.'

'Yes, but we didn't know that then. So, although your name is mud with some people, there is also a begrudging acceptance that you inadvertently stopped a bad situation from becoming a disaster. By placing yourself in the line of sight you stopped this country making a mistake from which it would take fifty years to recover.'

Poe said nothing.

'Listen, dear boy,' he said, 'I started your wood-burning stove so I wouldn't alarm you, but apart from that I haven't touched a thing. I did entertain the idea of making myself a cup of tea but you don't seem to have a kettle.'

'You're thirsty?'

'It's been a long week and it is rather hot.'

'Something stronger then?'

'A nice port perhaps?' he said, the corners of his eyes creasing as he suppressed a smile.

'I have beer or water.'

'Beer it is then.'

Poe opened two bottles of Spun Gold and poured them into pint glasses. He handed one to Locke and sat down.

'Excellent,' Locke said after taking a healthy drink.

'You didn't answer my question,' Poe said.

'And which question was that?'

'About whether you're going to arrest me.'

'Like I said, I should.'

'But you won't.'

'And why's that?'

'Because I know your name. Your real name.'

Locke stared at him. 'You really do work with a remarkable woman. She's wasted working for the NCA.'

'But she's happy, Alastor. There's never going to be a Tilly-shaped hole for a Tilly-shaped peg to slot into, but I suspect SCAS is pretty close. If she wants to move on, I won't dissuade her, but I wouldn't bet on it.'

'Oh?'

'She doesn't like secrets. She thinks they're the same as lying. And when she has to lie she—'

'Gives you a spastic colon?'

'Exactly,' Poe said. 'But the other thing about Tilly, and one of the things I love her for, is that she has the strongest sense of loyalty of anyone I've ever met. So, when I said that it might be worth knowing who it is we're working with, she took it seriously.'

'Sorry to be the bearer of bad news, Sergeant Poe, but our opposing security services already know my real name. I get a birthday card from the Russian attaché every year. Nice bottle of vodka, too. If you think exposing my name is a threat, I can assure you, it isn't.'

'Whatever else I am, Alastor, I'm a realist,' Poe said. 'I know we need people like you and Hannah, and I know you probably need anonymity to do your job. I have no intention of exposing you.'

'Yet you don't think I'll have you arrested?' Locke said, smiling.

'There's more chance of the Black and White Minstrels reforming.'

'You'd better explain.'

'You see, one of the things Tilly found when she was profiling you was an old school photograph of yours.'

Poe pulled a folded sheet of glossy paper from his inside pocket. He passed it to Locke. 'A cricket photograph actually,' he continued.

Locke slipped on a pair of reading glasses and studied it. 'Good grief,' he said. 'I haven't seen this for years. The Under 17s 1st XI. I was a decent opening bat and I could turn my hand to off spin if the captain thought the pitch might offer turn.'

'And who's the boy standing next to you? The one wearing the wicketkeeper's gloves?'

Locke glanced to his left. 'Ah,' he said.

'Indeed,' Poe said. 'Standing next to you is none other than the current Secretary of State for Housing, Communities and Local Government. The same man who repealed the byelaw that Tilly based my entire eviction defence on.'

Locke said nothing.

'It was you who got that byelaw repealed,' Poe said. 'Not some over-enthusiastic spook.'

Locke held up his hands. 'You have got me,' he said.

'But why?'

'You had to be warned off, Poe,' he said. 'You were getting too close to an unpalatable truth. The threat of losing your home was supposed to bring you to heel.'

'Bite him, Edgar,' Poe said.

The spaniel didn't even bother opening his eyes. Just thumped his tail on the floor a couple of times, then started snoring again.

'Scary,' Locke said.

'He's had a long day.'

'It seems I misjudged you.'

Poe stared at him.

'Don't lie to me,' he said. 'You knew exactly what you were

doing. You knew how I'd react. That I'd dig in. You actually said as much when we met in Manchester. It was why you had approved my working on the case to begin with. By warning me not to get involved with the families of Tango Two-Four, you *invited* me to get involved with the families of Tango Two-Four. You knew it was there that I'd find the answers.'

Locke drained his pint.

'May I have another?'

'Help yourself,' Poe said.

Locke did. He stood and looked out of the window as he poured his drink.

'You are like running water, Poe,' he said. 'If someone blocks you, you go around them. Or over them. You can't be stopped and you can't be managed. Your young DI, Stephanie Flynn, comes close apparently, but she's the exception, not the rule.'

'You wanted this exposed?'

Locke walked back over and sat down. He put his drink on the table and stared at Poe with those piercing grey eyes.

'You're bloody right I did,' he said.

Chapter 109

'This wasn't just about leaking a friendly-fire incident, though,' Poe said. 'If it were, you'd have found a much easier way of doing it. Used some of that . . . what do you call it, tradecraft?'

Locke took a sip of his drink.

'This is the cat's pyjamas,' he said. 'I must get Mrs Locke to order some. She prefers me to drink port but I find there's only so much of the damned stuff I can take. Anyway, I digress. Do you know what the term "playing behind the conductor's beat" means, Sergeant Poe?'

'I think you already know the answer to that.'

'One of Mrs Locke's great passions is the patronage of second-rate, sometimes third-rate, orchestras. And sometimes, when the country can't conjure up a crisis for me to manage, I get dragged along to a Bach or a Brahms recital. Now, when a top-rate orchestra performs, it sometimes looks as though they are playing behind the conductor's beat. There's a slight delay between the music and the baton's downbeat. To the uninitiated, it can seem that the orchestra isn't paying attention or, worse, it does not have the skills to keep up. The truth is rather different. A really good orchestra open their sound *after* the downbeat. There's only a fraction of a delay but it allows them to prepare the type of sound the conductor is hoping to achieve. So rather than following the beat rigidly, they *interpret* it.'

'I take it there's a point to this?'

'The orchestras Mrs Locke seems to like don't understand the concept of playing behind the conductor's beat. And the result is that the recital is wooden. The beat isn't right. It has a bad beat.'

Poe considered this. 'You knew that Bierman and McDaid had conspired to kill Tango Two-Four?'

Locke shook his head. 'Nothing so . . . definite,' he said. 'But the whole thing had a bad beat to it. This country has the finest fighting men and women in the world. They are the best trained and they are the best led. It is impossible for a British infantry section to get so badly lost. And if they weren't lost, then they wanted to be where they were. That had never been explained. Not by anyone. Also, I didn't like the way Jack Duncan fled the country so quickly. I met the man once and, if he had survivor's guilt, I'm a Frenchman.'

He paused. Took another drink. Wiped his lips.

'So yes, I set you loose,' he continued. 'Gave you help when I could and a psychological prod when I couldn't.'

'I was your cat's paw?' Poe said, thinking about Lucy's story about Bertrand and Raton.

'If you like.'

'Weren't you scared about upsetting the Americans?'

'Do you know something, Poe?' he said. 'Those of us who have been in the game long enough remember the Cold War as the good old days. Our enemy was ruthless, dangerous and cunning, but at least we knew who they were. Our relationship with America is . . . complex. And, while it's true we do not wish to spoil that relationship, there are other, more forward-thinking people who believe we are in danger of becoming a vassal state. Their view is that we should pare back our reliance on the United States and build deeper alliances with our oldest friends and our nearest neighbours.'

'Are you one of those forward-thinking people, Alastor?'

'Do you really want guns sold in ASDA, Sergeant Poe?' he

said. 'The privatisation of the NHS? Chicken washed in chlorine? Because that's what their lobbyists are already pushing for.'

'That's a yes then.'

'The "special relationship" has always been a load of balderdash anyway,' Locke said. 'Churchill invented it as a PR device to whip up support for American involvement in the war.'

'It's time to reset our agenda?' Poe said.

'That is a succinct way of putting it, Sergeant Poe. And yes, this country needs a bit of realignment now. *Especially* now. Which brings us neatly to your price.'

'My price?' Poe said.

'There must be something you want.'

'This smuggling ring gets shut down. I don't care how it's done but I want every end user embarrassed in the newspapers. I want the middlemen and the gang members in jail. I want you to lead on this and report to me weekly.'

'Done,' Locke said. He removed a small notebook from his pocket and wrote something down. 'It falls under our terrorism purview anyway. Anything else?'

'It seems Terry Holmes was more complicit than we first thought,' he said. 'If you can let his daughter down gently, please do. She's just as much a victim in this as anyone.'

'I'll do it myself.'

Poe looked around Herdwick Croft. At the ancient granite walls, at the cracks of light that peeked through the tiny gaps in the stonework.

At his home.

'I'm not ready to leave here,' he said. 'Not yet.'

'Already done,' Locke said. 'It turns out that the Secretary of State for Housing, Communities and Local Government had asked the local authority to repeal the wrong byelaw. In fact, I'm assured it will never be repealed and you will never be forcibly evicted from this wonderful fell.'

'Good,' Poe said, some of the recent tension immediately leaving his neck and shoulders.

Locke stood. He offered his hand. Poe ignored it.

'I haven't finished,' he said.

'Don't kill the golden goose, Poe,' Locke said, but he took his seat again.

'I'm going to ask you for a favour now, Alastor,' Poe said. 'You're not going to ask why I need it, and you're not going to say that it can't be done. Your response will be: "Yes, Sergeant Poe, I'll get on to this immediately."'

'And what favour is this?' Locke said. 'I am limited in my powers.'

'Nine months before I was born, my mother attended a diplomatic party at the British Embassy in Washington, DC,' he said. 'I have a list of the Americans who attended, but I need to know who else was there. Staff, guests, caterers, everyone.'

The man who had raped his mother all those years ago, his biological father, had bought himself decades' worth of pain. Poe intended to make sure he was paid in full.

'What's this about, dear boy?'

Poe wagged his finger. 'What did I say your response was to be?'

Locke stood again. This time Poe didn't stop him. He offered his hand and Poe took it. They shook, briefly.

'Yes, Sergeant Poe,' Locke said. 'I'll get on to this immediately.' And with that, he left.

Chapter 110

Poe fed Edgar and put a potato in the oven. He'd bought some good cheese earlier. With all the drama and tension of the last few days his stomach was craving something simple.

While he waited he did some simple stretching exercises. Tried to work out a fortnight's worth of kinks and strains. He was feeling flat, the way he always did after a big case had finished. Edgar watched him, bemused. Eventually he barked.

'Want to go out?'

Edgar got off the sofa and padded across to the door.

'OK,' Poe said. 'We can spare half an hour.'

Which was when his mobile rang.

Poe looked at the screen.

It was Steph Flynn. A stab of panic hit him hard in the stomach. He pressed receive. 'Boss. Is everything all right? Is the baby OK?'

'The baby's fine, Poe.'

'What's up? Where are you?'

'The office.'

'The *SCAS* office?'

'Of course, the SCAS office. What other office would I be in?'

'I . . . I don't understand.'

'I had a long chat with Director van Zyl last week. Long story short, I've agreed to come back. Part-time, initially. Zoe's taking some time off to look after the baby. She's been wanting to anyway.'

Poe didn't say anything.

'But the reason I'm calling now, Poe,' – and he could tell she was smiling – 'is that we have a problem . . .'

She told him what it was.

And, after a while, he smiled too.

Author's Note

Well, here we are again. Another Poe novel in the bag, and one that almost didn't exist. I've had this idea knocking around my empty skull for a few years now. But first came *The Puppet Show*, the plotline of which was originally earmarked for the third in the DI Avison Fluke series. Those of you who have read my first series might be able to transpose the characters in the first Poe book to the established characters in *Born in a Burial Gown* and *Body Breaker*. I then thought I might write it as the sequel to *The Puppet Show*. Having two successive books with historical motivations might seem a bit lazy, though, so I cobbled together *Black Summer*, a book that sprang from nothing more than wanting to set an impossible puzzle for Poe and Tilly to solve. I wanted to write what is now *Dead Ground* as the third Poe book, but, as it was for a new contract, I gave my editor, the supremely awesome Krystyna Green, three potential plotlines. The first was about a magician. Krystyna said absolutely not. Magicians were only one step below clowns and deserved everything they got. The second was my early thoughts on *Dead Ground*, but it was a bit too much of a thriller then, and Krystyna rightly rejected that as well. The third was what turned out to be *The Curator*, to which she gave the thumbs up.

But the plot for *Dead Ground* wouldn't go away. Whichever book I was working on, it was there in my mind, like background music. But it was still too action-focused, and that was a problem. Then I remembered I had the seeds of a plot for a safety deposit box heist in which, instead of valuables being stolen, someone was killed and a ceramic rat left at the scene. I did some author gymnastics. Moved things around. Lost bits. Added bits. And so *Dead Ground* came into the world. Was it exactly as I'd imagined? Of course not. But none of my books end up the way I intend them to.

It's still my favourite of the series, though.

A word on the King's Royal Rifles. They don't exist as a regiment now, but they used to. The King's Royal Rifle Corps was raised in the American colonies in 1756 as an infantry regiment. They were subsequently numbered the 60th Regiment of Foot and served with distinction throughout the British Empire for two hundred years. In 1958, along with the Oxfordshire & Buckinghamshire Light Infantry and the Rifle Brigade, the regiment formed the Green Jackets Brigade, eventually being amalgamated into the Royal Green Jackets (my drill sergeant was RGJ). As a result of the Future Army Structure review in 2004, the Royal Green Jackets amalgamated with all the other light infantry regiments to form a single large regiment called The Rifles. So, almost 275 years after being raised, the King's Royal Rifles Corps is now the 2nd Battalion, The Rifles.

Something weird now. Some of you may know this, but I'm sure others won't (I know I didn't). When the judge in a civil matter issues a **judgment**, because it's being used in a legal context, the correct spelling is without the 'e' after the 'g'. I, of course, didn't know that and typed out judgement. Luckily, in Howard, I have an extremely competent copyeditor.

That said, the British legal system isn't quirky, it's f*****g weird . . .

A word of warning (or is this consumer advice?). I invented the name 'JANUS cable', but I didn't invent the sneaky b*****ds. They are out there now, so be careful. Purposefully leaving them in hotel rooms and not claiming them is one of the main ways criminals get them into circulation. If they remain unclaimed, hotels sometimes keep them as spares. An unsuspecting guest might check in and, after realising they've forgotten their charging cable, will ask reception if they have one they can borrow . . .

But they're everywhere now. My advice is never use a charging cable that isn't your own. If you forget one when you're away, bite the bullet and buy one from a reputable shop. Never ever borrow one.

You might end up as a sap in a novel . . .

Acknowledgements

Right, let's get this bit over with. The acknowledgements. To make it easier this year, I've split it into two categories. First up, those who deserve a mention because of their hard work, diligence or the help they provided when this novel was being written, edited or marketed.

And then there are those who *don't* deserve it but who have once again managed to guilt me into getting their name in the back of a book.

The Deserving:

My editor, Krystyna Green, for championing Poe and Tilly from day one and for her expertise in developing the series into where it is now. And thank you for letting me push boundaries occasionally. It's a true partnership and one I hope lasts for many more years.

And while we're on the top team, I know Krystyna's effortless efficiency is entirely down to Sarah Murphy. Thanks for keeping us both right, Sarah, and thanks for blowing off your mates so you could attend that Dagger's reception . . .

My agent and friend, David Headley, for taking a chance on an unknown author in 2016, and for shaping my career ever since. It's been a hell of a ride so far, David – long may it continue. If only you had better taste in music . . .

Martin Fletcher, for moulding each novel, keeping them

consistent and for whittling down all the excessive crap I tend to write in the first couple of drafts. Also for providing those valuable moments of procrastination as we discuss music and cricket. And for some reason whether Wimbledon Common actually exists. I'm from the north, what do I know? Wimbledon Common is where the Wombles came from, how the hell am I supposed to know it's a real place . . . And just to be clear when I asked if Paddington's Peru really existed as well, I *was* joking . . .

My copyeditor, Howard Watson, always gets a nod. Howard not only corrects my appalling grammar, he provides the consistency across all the novels, including the Fluke series. He also does the fact checking, and that's not an easy job the way my mind wanders. Some of the bloopers he's found would fill a book. He is the man who, after the book had been through at least ten people in the industry, noticed that, in *The Puppet Show*, according to the timeline I had originally set up, Poe would have joined the police when he was eleven years old . . .

Sean Garrehy, the incredibly talented dude who designs my covers, has my eternal gratitude. I may need three goes each time I write your surname, Sean, but that's probably on me, not you. I'm not sure I'd want to be inside your head when you're interpreting what's on the inside of mine, but f**k me, these covers are extraordinary, and one of the reasons the series has been so successful. But don't get too cocky, mate – at some point I may just do what I've threatened and write that book about the inside of a ping-pong ball.

Of all the people who deserve a massive thank you, just for having an astonishing amount of patience, it's publishing's number one desk editor, Rebecca Sheppard. I have consistently asked her to change things right up to the wire, sometimes just minutes before a book goes to print. The colour of the napkin in *Black Summer* and Poe's kettle in *The Curator* immediately spring to mind, but I'm sure you have thousands of examples if anyone wants them. Cheers, Rebecca – having you marshalling everyone involved in the book's production gives me more peace of mind than you'll ever know. And thank you for explaining the difference between a hanging hyphen and a random typesetting error. That it was the former when I had accused it of being the latter is not a lesson I'll ever forget.

Beth Wright and Brionee Fenlon used to get lumped together for some reason. Probably because I still don't really understand the difference between publicity and marketing. Maybe it's time I made more of an effort.

Here goes:

Beth, cheers for teeing up all the awesome events I try and fail to wriggle out of. The newspaper and magazine reviewers you're able to get advance copies in front of never ceases to amaze. Thanks for the beer chats and curries, but maybe *not* thanks for sending Joanne that video of the little boy telling the monkey to f**k off at the safari park. It was funny the first time she made me watch it, maybe not so much the 900th . . .

For making sure the books have more exposure than is decent, I say a big thank you, Brionee. I don't pretend to understand the reports you send me. Tilly would, but I'm definitely Poe-like in this regard. It's OK, though, I just ask David if it's good and he always nods and says, 'Yes'. And thank you for being a proper northerner.

That was too much effort, quite frankly. Consider yourselves lumped back together next time.

A huge thanks to Roger Lytollis, Joanne Craven and Joan Deitch for their sterling proofreading efforts. If there are still typos in the book, it's their fault, not mine.

And finally, from the editorial side of things, last but certainly not least, Hannah Wann. I kind of get the impression that behind all the frantic flapping that happens when someone as chaotic as me has a book coming out, you're the one holding it all together. Making sure what needs to happen, happens. If the editorial team were a jigsaw, you'd be a corner piece. And not just blue sky either. You'd be the bit with the swan's leg on, or something. You can put that on a T-shirt if you want, but I want commission.

And now a handful of non-editorial acknowledgements.

The lads – and it *was* all lads back then – of 21 Engineer Regiment Workshop REME get a nod of thanks. Not so much a tight crew as a happy gathering of pissheads, but you *were* the inspiration behind this story. And we had some fun, didn't we? Now, p**s off and buy a copy . . .

Andy Atkinson gets thanked again for helping me understand how the JANUS cable would work. I'm not sure I enjoy our chats, Andy – they scare me too much.

For the first time, my good friend Crawford Bunney (yes, that *is* his real name . . .) has been promoted to the deserving list for daring me to use the phrase 'bugger, rumbled' in this book. I told him to p**s off back to where his sort are tolerated, obviously, but when it came to naming the part-time tramp, full-time street performer, that silly phrase popped into my head and Bugger Rumble was born. I think he'll occasionally crop up as the series progresses, as he was a fun character to write.

A quick word of thanks to my beta reader, Angie Morrison. So here it is: thanks.

All those booksellers out there – you're awesome, you know that, don't you? I'll list the ones I know personally, and this year I hope to get to a lot more of your shops. I would have done so in 2020, but, you know, there was a bug going round . . . So, a huge double thumbs up to Lucy at Bookends, Catherine at the New Bookshop, Fiona at Waterstones Durham, the gang at Hills, Elaine and Will at Sam Read Bookseller, Richard at Heffers, Ali and the gang at Waterstones Carlisle and everyone at Goldsboro.

And finally, a massive thumbs up to all the bloggers and

readers out there. A book isn't a real book until someone's read it, and if it weren't for you guys, I would still be that weirdo who drank too much and giggled all day. Instead of being the weirdo who drinks too much, giggles all day and occasionally writes something . . .

And so to . . .

The Undeserving:

Stuart Wilson.
That's it for this year, I'm afraid. Sorry, mate.

Anyway, I'm finishing here as I'm busy – Poe and Tilly are crossing swords with a dude called the Botanist, and at the moment he's winning . . .

Mike
April 2020
(Yes, that's how far ahead these books are written.)

New in 2022!

Keep reading for a sneak peek at the next gripping Washington Poe story,

The Botanist . . .

Chapter 1

Iriomote Island, Japan

There were bastard trees and there were wait-awhile trees and there was a building that didn't exist.

The bastard trees had masses of six-inch thorns protecting their trunks. Touch one of those and you'd learn a sharp lesson. The wait-awhile trees were less stabby, but equally annoying. Their thin, hook-tipped vines dangled from branches, catching, entangling and immobilising the unwary.

But it was the building, not the flesh-piercing thorns, that held everyone's attention. It was squat and grey and had been reclaimed by nature. Thick roots had prised apart stonework and collapsed one of the walls. Guano from the fruit bats roosting in the tree canopy had painted the roof white.

The group stared in astonishment.

'What is it?' Dora, a woman in her early twenties, asked. She was halfway through her gap year. In six months she would do what her father wanted and take a job in the City, then marry her portfolio manager fiancé and knock out a brood of zestless children.

'I'm not sure,' their guide replied. He was called Andrew Trescothic and he had trained in the black art of jungle navigation with the British Army in Belize. 'Probably left over from the war. There are supposed to be some Operation Ketsu-Go buildings on the island somewhere.'

'Ketsu-Go?'

'The suicidal defensive strategy designed after the Emperor realised he could no longer win. Called for the entire Japanese population to resist an invasion under the banner "The Glorious Death of One Hundred Million". He thought if the Americans were facing catastrophic casualties it might undermine their will to fight for an unconditional surrender. Maybe opt for an armistice instead, one that didn't involve occupation of the Japanese mainland. Part of the strategy was to build inland fortifications to store fuel and ammunition. This building's not accessible for fuel, so I suspect it was used as an ammo dump. The allies emptied them after Japan's surrender, but most of the buildings were left intact.'

'Wow,' Dora said. 'So nobody's seen this since the war?'

'It's possible.'

It wasn't. Trescothic was a no-frills kind of guide and he had been leading groups across the jungle island for five years now. He knew where all the Operation Ketsu-Go fortifications were, and he made sure each group 'discovered' one on every trip. After they had taken their photographs and had a poke around, he would leave it a year or so. In an environment as harsh as this it wasn't long before the building looked as though it hadn't been touched in decades. He figured it was a harmless deception and it certainly increased the size of his tips when they got back to base camp.

'Can we go in?' Dora asked.

Trescothic shrugged.

'Don't see why not,' he said.

'Cool!'

'But watch for snakes.'

All that remained of the wooden door were rusty hinges. Dora and most of the others entered cautiously.

The last one, a man wearing an unacceptable hat, turned and said, 'Aren't you coming, Andrew?'

He shook his head.

'Maybe later.' Andrew knew what was in there. A boxy room and a large underground storage area. Japanese signs on the walls and animal scat on the floor. Same as all the others. He reckoned they'd be inside for fifteen minutes or so. Five upstairs, five in the underground storage room and five more for happy snaps. Plenty of time to get a brew on.

He hadn't even had time to pop in a teabag when he heard Dora scream. He sighed. They'd probably stumbled across a dead animal. It had happened in a different building a couple of years earlier. A group discovered the decomposed body of an Iriomote cat, a subspecies of leopard only found on the island. It had fallen through a hole in the roof and trapped itself. Poor thing had starved to death.

Trescothic got to his feet and entered the old fortification. He could hear the group. They were in the underground storage area. He jogged down the stairs but was met by Dora running back up.

'I think I'm going to be sick,' she said.

He sighed again. These city slickers really needed to toughen up. The same thought crossed his mind at least once a trip. These modern-day explorers weren't as robust as the squaddies he had trained with all those years ago. The slightest thing upset them. A dead animal, a mean comment on Twitter, a dodgy statue . . .

He fixed his face into the stern, no-nonsense ex-soldier the group expected him to be, and entered the storage area.

Thirty seconds later he was back outside, panting heavily, scrambling for the satellite phone in his rucksack.

It wasn't a dead animal that had caused Dora to scream.

This was something else entirely.

Something monstrous.

At the same time as Trescothic was on his satellite phone, a nondescript man wearing unremarkable clothes stepped out of a plain white van in a car park on an industrial estate on the outskirts of Glasgow. He walked into Banner Chemical Supplies and approached the counter.

'I'd like two hundred litres of acetone, please,' he said to the man wearing a polo shirt bearing the company insignia – a stylised B, underscored with a test tube.

'You got photo ID?' the man said. 'Acetone is a category three precursor chemical as it can be used to make explosives. Company policy is we take IDs.'

The nondescript man produced a driver's licence bearing an instantly forgettable name. The man behind the counter entered the details into his computer. After the acetone had been paid for, he said, 'You parked outside?'

'I am.'

'The guys will bring it out for you. Help you load it.'

'Thank you.'

'Oh, one last thing. I need to put down something in the "reason for purchase" field on the computer.'

'I have a vermin problem,' the nondescript man said.